For I delight in the law of God, in my inner being, but I see in my members another law waging war against the law of my mind and making me captive to the law of sin that dwells in my members.—The Apostle Paul (Rom. 7:22-23)

WAGING WAR

A Christian's Cognitive Behavioral Therapy Workbook

Heather M. Freeman

WAGING WAR

A Christian's Cognitive Behavioral Therapy Workbook

Heather M. Freeman

Christian Publishing House
Cambridge, Ohio
#WagingWarBook

Christian Publishing House
Professional Conservative Christian Publishing of the Good News!

WAGING WAR: A Christian's Cognitive Behavioral Therapy Workbook

ISBN-10: 1-945757-42-6

ISBN-13: 978-1-945757-42-6

Table of Contents

To my God, my Creator, and my Savior.

I cannot do anything in my life but through you.

To all those hungry for a better life, knowing that the life you have been living is not how it was meant to be. I pray that through this journey you can be free.

FOREWORD Letter to the Reader

My Dear Friend,

I know in starting this workbook, you are wondering if your trials and struggles are known by any other or if you are alone, facing this on your own. Let me reassure you that you are known by the one true God and so is your struggle. Don't think for a second that He doesn't know or feel your pain. It is a similar struggle others face every day. It is the same struggle I have been blessed to help hundreds of teens and their families face through the years. When I was assisting families in my work, it was in a setting where I was not allowed to share with them all aspects of this battle they were attempting to wage regarding their thoughts and urges. I was teaching them what I could, which was very effective and helpful, but not as impactful or changing as it could have been if I had been free to teach with the hope and love of Jesus Christ. The topic that was often difficult to discuss and teach on was when I had resident's tell me that they believed they were damaged goods or were broken somehow. I had to explain as much of the truth as I could without sharing all of it, which as we know is never as effective or meaningful. Let's get on the same page before you proceed; you believe you are broken and damaged. Well, the truth is, you are, but not in the way, you think. See you think you are broken and damaged goods but what you mean is that something in your brain isn't quite right or your emotions are off keel. Like a car that has a faulty part, you think that when you were made someone made a mistake. You think that you have something in your body that is not functioning the way it is supposed to be like your issues have a biological basis that if we could just find the right medications or the right surgery and you would be all better. I tell you the truth that you are damaged but not physically in your body as though you were a faulty product. You are broken in the same way that I and every other being on this planet is. We are all broken; we were born that way. There is nothing biological that will fix this damage; it is in our soul that we find the damage and the damage is from the sin that was brought into our world a long time ago.

(1) We are all imperfect beings living in an imperfect world, and this brokenness is compounded by the fact that God's Word says we are mentally bent and lean toward doing bad. You talk about the urges you have that you just cannot seem to stop like the urge to hurt others, to curse, to argue, to be disobedient to your authority figures. This is what God's Word is referring to when it says that we are mentally bent toward doing bad. We read, "When the LORD saw that the wickedness of man on the earth was great and that the whole bent of his thinking was never anything but evil, the LORD regretted that he had ever made man on the

earth." (Gen. 6:5, AT) (2) We have a wicked spirit creature, Satan the Devil, who is misleading the entire world of humankind. We read, "Be sober-minded; be watchful. Your adversary the devil prowls around like a roaring lion, seeking someone to devour." (1 Pet. 5:8, ESV) It is his effort to encourage the urges you have by planting further thoughts of them in your mind and to offer temptation that would seem so great that you feel urged to give in. (3) We also live in a world that encourages and readily provides the things we desire that we know to be wrong catering to our urges to do wrong and furthermore offering excuses for when we give in so that we continue to give in. We read, "For all that is in the world—the desires of the flesh and the desires of the eyes and pride in possessions, is not from the Father but is from the world. And the world is passing away along with its desires, but whoever does the will of God abides forever." (1 John 2:16-17) (4) We are unable to understand our inner person, which the Bible informs us is wicked: "The heart is deceitful above all things and desperately sick; who can understand it?" The apostle Paul tells us, "just as sin came into the world through one man, and death through sin, and so death spread to all men because all sinned." Suffice it so say, you cannot change the world that you were born into, the devil that will tempt you, nor can you change the fact that a part of you has urges and desires for wrongdoing, the parts of you that you will never fully understand, but there is one part of you that you can control that will have an effect on all the other things, you.–Jeremiah 17:9; Romans 5:12.

Essentially, as sad as it is to say, we do create our own stresses, and as shown in point number (1) above, it is a result of our imperfect selves and our imperfect world that we experience stress. This stress is compounded by the temptations and challenges at times placed upon us by Satan, our enemy who wants to cause us harm, point number (2). This is all further compounded by the fact that we live in a world, point number (3), that will offer us anything we want to fulfill our desires and readily offers excuses when our conscious confronts us for our wrongdoing or silences our conscious to the point we no longer see it as wrong. We read, "But each person is tempted when he is lured and enticed by his own desire. Then desire, when it has conceived gives birth to sin, and sin, when it is fully grown, brings forth death." (Jam. 1:14-15, ESV) Only by an active faith in Christ, and a true understanding of our imperfection, can we hope to function in an imperfect world, defeat Satan, gain control over our imperfect flesh, allow God to read our heart and help us **not** to fall victim to our own desires of the eyes.

It does not take long for us to realize that we live in an imperfect world, imperfect in the extreme! For example, we think of the severe poverty and crime that exists in the richest country in the world, the United States. We are aware of the drugs and drug dealers on every street corner, the gunfire in the middle of the night, the liquor store on every corner, the one parent or no parent families. We think of the roach or rat infested, run down buildings of slumlords. Almost all of us need not think of these things, as we have lived these things. This sounds utterly dreadful, and they are from the richest country in the world. If we spoke of third-world countries, it would boggle the mind how a supposed humane society would allow such things. Yes, we are imperfect and live in an imperfect world. This is no excuse for the above wrong conduct, but like an alcoholic, if we cannot identify and own the problem, recovery is impossible.

One may wonder how such a wealthy country such as the United States could allow such environments to exist. Before we end this publication, we will find the answer that may surprise some and offend others. However, in short for now, it is not the United States fault, it is primarily our fault and to a degree, our family and our communities. Of course, we do not deny that as we grow from infanthood into adulthood, we are affected by society: teachers, friends, neighbors, coworkers, news media, and entertainment. Yes, those around us influence us. Some would have us shift all the responsibility over onto society. A kind of 'he made me do it,' he being society. Our environment can be a contributing factor, but never **a cause**. In other words, Johnny grew up in the ghetto slums of Chicago, Illinois; his father was a drug dealer and a gangster, his mother was a prostitute to support her drug addiction, and his five older brothers got into gangs and sold drugs. All of this may very well contribute to Johnny becoming the next gang member and selling drugs. Nevertheless, this home environment will not **cause** it, making it inevitable.

(1) If we have some personality disorders, bad habits, and so on, it becomes easier, or so we think, to say, 'it is societies fault,' it's my childhood,' 'life has kicked me in the teeth,' 'it's my parent's fault.'

(2) 'I am very concerned about my problems, which no one seems to understand, and appreciate.'

(3) 'My problems are a part of who I am; I simply have to live with them.' I have tried for years to change, and it is useless.'

The answer to our problems does not lie entirely within others, society, or our childhood. If we the reader, cannot come to grips with this truth, there will be no progress. The answer to our problems is staring back at us each morning as we look in the mirror, getting ready for our day. Yes, we are the solution to our problem, and it is all about us taking an active approach in us. We need to take in knowledge and gain understanding so that when life or ourselves comes after us, we can stand our ground.

Dealing with Destructive Self-Defeating Thoughts

Prayer as Rational Self-Talk

Self-talk is what we tell ourselves in our thoughts. In fact, it is the words we tell ourselves about people, self, experiences, life, in general, God, the future, the past, the present. It is all the words that we say to ourselves all the time. Actually, if we regularly cultivate and entertain slights against us or the deeper personal affronts, it can lead to destructive depression, mood slumps, our self-worth plummeting, our body feeling sluggish, our will to accomplish even the tiniest of things is not to be realized, and our actions defeat us.

Intense negative thinking will always lead to at least a minor depressive episode or simple, painful emotion. Our thoughts based on a good mood will be entirely different from those based on our being upset. Negative thoughts that flood our mind are the actual contributors of our self-defeating emotions. These very thoughts are what keep us sluggish and contribute to our feeling frustrated, angry, or worthless. Therefore, this thinking is the key to your relief.

Every time we feel down about something, we need to attempt to locate the corresponding negative thought we had that led to this feeling down. It is these thoughts that have created our feelings of frustration, anger, or low self-worth. By learning to offset them and replace them with rational thoughts, we can actually change our mood. Remember the thoughts that move through our mind, with no effort; this is the easiest course to follow. It is so subconscious that they even go unnoticed.

The centerpiece of it all is the mind. Our moods, behaviors and body responses result from the way we view things. It is a proven fact that we cannot experience any event in any way, shape, or form unless we have processed it with our mind first. No event can depress us; it is our perception of that event that will depress us. If we are only sad over an event, our thoughts will be rational, but if we are depressed wrathful, or anxious about an event, our thinking will be bent and irrational, distorted and utterly wrong.

It may be difficult for each of us to wrap our mind around it, but we are superb at telling ourselves outright lies and half-truths, repeatedly throughout each day. In fact, some of us are so good at it that it has become our reality and led to annoyance, stress, irritation, anger, even depression, and anxiety. This section should be a beginning in helping us to start identifying these lies and half-truths.

Lies about Self

- ☐ I am dumb
- ☐ I am unattractive
- ☐ No one really likes me
- ☐ I have no talent
- ☐ I am miserable
- ☐ This always happens to me
- ☐ This is the story of my life
- ☐ Life is never going to change
- ☐ I am so lonely
- ☐ I am no good

Lies about Others

- ☐ He always makes dumb comments
- ☐ He is always saying things like that
- ☐ No one really likes him
- ☐ He has no respect
- ☐ He makes me miserable
- ☐ He always making me unhappy
- ☐ Why does he always do that
- ☐ He is never going to change
- ☐ He should ...
- ☐ He is no good

DEGRADING SELF

1. Self-degrading:

I am so stupid

I never get anything right.

Everything I do seem to fail. Even when I do all I can to make someone love me; they just end up rejecting me.

6

2. Situation Degrading:

Life is the same every day; I do not even know why I bother getting up!

Life just kicks me in the face every day—it stinks!

3. Future Degrading:

I am never going to make it in life; I do not know why I even try. It is a waste of time!

DEGRADING OTHERS

1. Degrading Others:

He is always saying rude things

He never goes a day without insulting me

Everything word out of his mouth seems to be meant for me. Even when I do all I can to make things right, he just keeps hurting my feelings.

2. Situation Degrading:

He treats me the same every day; I do not even know why I bother trying to remain friends!

He makes life miserable for me–He is not worth my efforts!

3. Future Degrading:

I am never going forgive him again; I do not know why I even try. It is a waste of time!

I will never talk with him again. Forgiveness, what is that!

I will avoid him like everyone else that mistreats me. Forgiveness? Never!

We must appreciate that our thoughts can deceive all of us, contributing to our belief that the negative mood, which has been created, because of our thinking, is a reality, when it is not. If we have established a negative way of thinking, an irrational way of thinking, our mind will simply accept it as truth. Within a moment, we can alter our mood, and it is not even likely we notice it taking place. These negative feelings seem as though they are the real thing, which only reinforces to the deceptive thinking.

If we are under mental distress, and we find ourselves having anger issues or mild depression and are unhappy much of the time, we need to be in prayer for Holy Spirit. However, we need to act on behalf of our prayers as well. It is likely that we can combine our spiritual pursuits with some self-help cognitive therapy. If things have become more involved, we may want to speak with the elder or pastor. However, if we are moderately depressed, where things feel unbearable because we are having feelings of despair, we need to get some professional help from a Christian counselor. Our recommendation of a placed to find an excellent Christian counselor is found in the footnote below.[1]

Romans 15:13 Updated American Standard Version (UASV)

13 Now may the God of hope fill you with all joy and peace in believing, so that you will abound in hope by the power of the Holy Spirit.

Dr. David Burns wrote, "feelings are not facts!" Our own thinking can easily trick us. Regardless of what deception our depressed brain tells us, we will accept it as total truth. In fact, it does not take but a partial second to establish these irrational thoughts with ourselves. Therefore, in many cases, we are unlikely to notice it even happening. These negative thoughts feel so right and give credibility to the lie.

Self-Defeating Thoughts

While many are well aware that self-defeating thoughts and behavior(s) are harmful to themselves, they also know that resisting and overcoming them is another story. Self-defeating thoughts and behaviors can become deeply rooted over the years and can be extremely resistant to efforts to change them. Trying to curb such thinking can be exhausting and even painful, spiraling into depression in and of itself.

Humans being in the state of imperfection should not expect perfection in this endeavor. Our genetic heritage, inherent weaknesses, and experiences make it impossible for us to avoid all self-defeating thoughts and behaviors. Therefore, lovingly, we do not demand perfection of ourselves, nor should we of others.

However, this consideration on our part does not absolve us of our responsibility to <u>control</u> our thinking and thus our feelings that lead to moods and behaviors. Behavioral scientists say that self-defeating thoughts, like good ones, are learned and developed over time. If that is correct, then self-defeating thoughts can just as surely be **un**learned! Of course, ridding ourselves of self-defeating thoughts that may have dominated our lives for years will be difficult. We should not underestimate the struggle ahead of us. There will certainly be setbacks and failures. However, rest assured, things usually get easier with time.

---

[1] www.aacc.net/

The more we work at it, the more our new behavior will become a part of us. How?

Life: Common everyday events, both positive and negative

Thoughts: Your thinking interprets each of these events throughout the day

Mood: It is developed not by the day's events; no, it is developed by our perception of those events, by our thinking.

Every bad feeling that we have is a direct result of our bent thinking. If one finds themselves embedded in day-in-and-day-out of negative thinking, there is most certainly going to be an outburst of anger, or some mild depressive episode follow. We will not be so bold as to use the word "cause," but instead, we will say *contribute*. Thus, we will find that those continual negative thoughts will contribute to emotional spiral until it arrives at the bottom floor of a depressive episode.

Breaking Away From Bent Thinking

1. Identify and own our bent thinking. We have to self-analyze our days. We must slow down and identify what thinking error we are having and write it down. This is called mental journaling. If we are careful and wisely analyze, we can keep track of the thinking stimulus that sets off our feelings, followed by our actions. In our prayerful conversations with God, we can identify the thinking error, and internally discuss the irrational thought with God. Why is it irrational thinking? What would be the rational thought?

2. Replace the bent (irrational) thinking with rational thinking. We start self-branding ourselves: "I am no good," "I am lazy." Or we self-brand others: "he is always saying things like ..." He is rude." We should immediately stop and start to reason rationally with ourselves. "No I am not no good, this is doing nothing but making me feel worse, I am a good person who makes mistakes like everyone else." Or, "Well, he isn't always saying bad things, and we all slip in what we say at times." Positive self-talk should be done at length, keeping it honest, and aloud if possible.

3. Keep Records. Each day we need to write down the episodes of negative self-abuse, bent thinking that we go through, as well as the forms. In addition, the time spent in rationalizing with the negative thoughts. At the end of the day, summarize it in a short paragraph. We should see a decrease almost immediately in our first week.

4. Let others know. Keep our friends and family in the loop of what we are attempting to do. Periodically ask them if they notice a change in attitude and mood. Explain to them that it is best if they are honest with us. Also, prepare mentally for a possible negative feedback. Simply use the feedback as an instrument and know that more work is needed.

5. The most important key is to be practical and balanced. It took many years to achieve our way of thinking; it is not going to change overnight. In addition, if we put 50% into the putting on a new person, we will get 50% out of it. If we put 100% in, we will get 100% out of it. We should notice a small difference in a week, but we should see tremendous changes in about a four months period, some maybe six months to a year.

6. Pray to God. We need to bring God into the picture, for him, nothing is impossible.--Psalm 55:22; Luke 18:27

Read the list below of Twelve Distorted Thoughts. These were developed with the idea of focusing on the culprit that is guilty of the distortion (self), and what it is (thinking). As we work our way through this book or any self-help book, we should have the Twelve Distorted Thoughts in front of us (mentally, i.e., memorized).

Twelve Distorted Thoughts

1. SELF-ABSOLUTE (THINKING)

With this frame of mind, there is no middle ground. One who has a setback in life and sees it as nothing more than a life-ending result. To receive one bad mark on a work evaluation is the same as receiving all bad marks.

2. SELF-SWEEPING (THINKING)

If a bad event happens to us, we say: "This is the story of my life." We see our life as a never-ending series of negative events. For us, one bad event might as well be a thousand because we blow it up in our mind.

3. SELF-BRANDED (THINKING)

We own every negative event that happens in our life as being our fault. We carry the weight of the world on our shoulders. If something positive happens, it is a freak accident, because nothing good happens to us.

4. SELF-CLASSIFYING (THINKING)

As these negative events unfold on us, we own those that are not even ours; we begin to classify ourselves as "losers," "total failures," "disappointments," "let downs." It is to the point that we even begin to question why we were even born.

5. SELF-RATIONALIZING (THINKING)

We perceive life in a negative manner, even though, much of our lives may be just fine. We refuse to acknowledge the good in our lives or the possibility of it becoming good.

6. SELF-PROPHECY (THINKING)

We see everything as ending negatively, so we end up fulfilling our own negative thinking. An adverse event happens to us, and we have already mapped out in our mind the dreadful course, followed by a tragic ending. John calls to say he **cannot** make the dinner date tonight. At once, Lisa is offering reasons as to why he has broken off the date: 'he doesn't like me;' 'he has found someone else' and on and on.

7. SELF-PSYCHIC (THINKING)

We regularly have a feeling that someone is thinking badly of us or talking badly about us without any evidence. We assume that bad things just always happen to us.

8. SELF-AMPLIFYING (THINKING)

Small negative things, events that happen to each of us every day, are amplified (to become more marked or intense) to unrealistic measures by our overactive thinking. Maybe they spill something on their shirt, are rejected from a potential date, or lose their favorite pair of shoes, so they will think, "This always happens to me!"

9. SELF-FOCUS (THINKING)

We focus in on the negative details, seeing nothing else. We refuse to see the bright side of any situation. If one attempts to point to some positive aspect of anything, we negate them and their audacity even to consider such a thing.

10. SELF-PROJECTING (THINKING)

Jim should have done this. Jane should have said this. Mark should not have done that. This is simply projecting us on everyone else.

11. SELF-LABELING (THINKING)

I am no good! I am not a good mother. I am a poor student. I am stupid.

12 SELF-PERSONALIZING (THINKING)

With no evidence, we make ourselves the scapegoat because we will always blame ourselves for everything. Lisa thinks, 'If only I were a better wife!' Lisa, as a verbally abused wife, thinks, 'it's my fault; I must be doing something wrong.' On the other hand, Lisa may scream at her husband habitually, so much so that he loses his self-esteem, "I can never do anything right.'

Dealing with Our Imperfections

Mental distress is not a part of healthy living. The important aspect is that it can be overcome by learning some simple methods that will elevate our moods. The techniques of having rational self-talk with God and identifying our irrational thinking will reduce the symptoms of a variety of mental distresses (frustration, anger, jealousy, anxiety, etc.). The idea of how we think is how we feel has been in psychology books for over one hundred years. However, it has been in God's Word, many Bible books, for about 2,000 – 3,000 years. God's Word and cognitive therapy can help us control the symptoms that lead to mental distress and help us to recreate an entirely new personality. Paul calls it putting on the new person and removing the old person.

1. Swift Improvement of Thinking Errors: For those suffering from a milder form of mental distresses such as depression or anxiety, control of thinking and the new personality can be achieved in as little as three to six months, depending on the level of effort placed into oneself.

2. The Ability to Fully Grasp: In the end, by way of deep study in God's Word, we will fully grasp exactly why our moods alter and have at our disposal, numerous principles to apply in controlling these mood swings. We will understand the difference between bent-thinking and rational thinking and be able to recognize the level of our mood.

3. Control Not Removal: Our irrational thinking is a part of the person that is imperfect; it can only be controlled, not cured. However, there will be new life-skills that we will learn to cut off and control the distorted thinking and emotion before they consume us.

4. New Person: This new person can be maintained, but we have always to be aware of the symptoms, events, and situations that can contribute to a setback.

First, one needs to recognize that ALL of their moods are brought on by our internal self-talk. This is based on the way one looks at something: perceptions, mental attitudes, and beliefs. The way we feel at this very moment is based on the self-talk that is going on between our ears.

Second, when one is distressed mentally, such as mild depressed frustration, anger, jealousy, or anxiety; really any negative mood, their thoughts are dominating the mood. We perceive not only ourselves but also the entire world in such a way that it regulates our moods. Moreover, we will buy into this false reality. If we have hit a low, we will move into the stage, believing that 'this is who I am, and it has and will always been this way.' As we reflect on the past, only those bad moments will surface. In addition, we will project this bad past as an ongoing reality for our future, creating a feeling of hopelessness.

Third, we must realize that this thinking that creates our moods are really a gross distortion of reality; this is why we are so affected by them. Although they appear valid at present, we will find that they are irrational and just downright wrong. Our mind is like a transmission in a car, where our thinking is a result of mental slippage and not an accurate perception. As we progress in rational thinking, and we begin to master methods that will help us identify this mental slippage, we will start to remove that way of thinking, and we will begin to feel better for longer periods of time until it is the norm.

Fourth, we will begin to use the Scriptures in an entirely new way. It is paramount that we take note of how the Scriptures offer us far more than the mere surface knowledge that we have grown accustomed to, and see that by our having an accurate, deep understanding, with the application, we can begin to alter our old person into an entirely different person. It is highly recommended that the reader considers three other publications by this author as well.

Acknowledgements

When I was very young, I use to play in the rain believing that there was never an impossible situation or a person who could not be saved by God. I was carefree and believed that I could be anything I wanted to be as long as I had God with me. There is no one that God cannot save, and it is this belief that has pushed me all of my life. There were many times when I wanted to give up and for a time had lost sight of the power of God, but my husband, my soulmate, would never let me. He sacrificed and pushed me always to reach the full potential God had put in my heart and soul. I would not be here if it were not for God and the love that my husband shows our daughter and me every day. You are amazing, and through your love, I see a glimpse of God I would never have if it were not for you. Thank you for challenging me, loving me, and encouraging me every step of the way. Thank you to my dad. You taught me to love no matter what and to never judge a book by its cover; to have the courage to see behind the obvious into a person's life and have compassion. You once told me I was your inspiration. That will stay with me all the days of my life. Thank you to my mom for you taught me never to stifle my voice, no matter what the world may tell me. Finally, thank you to my kids. Over time, I have had some of the best patients I could ever ask for. You have taught me that first and foremost God made us to be amazingly resilient and the stories and trust that you have all shown me is a gift I can never repay. Your journeys have changed my life, and I am better for having been allowed to share a brief moment with you. Thank you.

Introduction

I have worked with at-risk youth for close to seven years, and every time I meet with a new resident at the residential treatment center (RTC) where I work, I am overcome by their statements that they are just not good enough. I facilitated a group therapy session today in which a 12-year-old male patient expressed that if we have on average 40,000 thoughts per day as I was teaching them, then he has had 10 years of using those 40,000 thoughts on self-degradation leading him to the belief that not only is "everybody stupid but so am I so what is the point." He went on to ask his peers and me why we should even try when it doesn't matter in the end. He daily struggled to have controlled behavior, actively seeking ways to cause trouble for those in positions of authority over him. He was often met by what would be perceived in our world as a normal reaction of anger and frustration with the goal to punish him to make him listen to directives. His 40,000 thoughts per day had worked themselves into beliefs and therefore perspectives that had become shackles around him which now have such a strong hold on him that he is restrained from reaching the potential and purpose woven into his soul at his creation. Until he recognizes these chains, breaks them, and finds a way to stay free of them, he will never live a fulfilled life.

What many fail to realize is that you cannot tackle this sickness from the outside. Surgery has to be performed, and unlike the medical field, this surgery is most difficult because it is surgery on the part of the body no one can see and no one but God understands; surgery on the soul. Cognitive Behavior Therapy (CBT) is an attempt at facilitating that surgery, and it is very effective; one of the most scientifically backed treatment paradigms available right now, but it is surgery without the surgeon. It's like brain surgery with an orthopedic surgeon. If I'm having surgery, I want the surgeon that knows the most about the part I'm having treated, and in this case, that would be God. Before CBT was even a thought, the Bible wrote about the idea that in order to control ones' actions and emotions one must first control their thoughts hence, this workbook is a combination of the biblical teachings and the techniques that are empirically based in CBT.

If you are struggling with controlling addictions, emotional instability, impulsive acts you later regret, interpersonal problems, or simply feel like life is not how it is supposed to be; then this workbook is for you. In this book are all of the techniques I educated my patients on regarding CBT and the principles I was restrained from teaching in a secular environment. When you work through this book, it's me and you working together to take you from life as you know it to searching for God and the freedom and purpose He created in you.

Set The Mood Music:

Derik Minor- Change the World Ft. Hollyn

Section I The Foundations

According to the National Association of Cognitive-Behavioral Therapists, CBT is based on the idea that our thoughts cause our feelings and behaviors, not external things, like people, situations, and events. The benefit of this fact is that we can change the way we think in order to feel or act better, even if the situation does not change.

Fix your thoughts on what is true and honorable and right. Think about things that are pure and lovely and admirable. Think about things that are excellent and worthy of praise. Philippians 4:8

Building your knowledge of Cognitive Behavioral Therapy (CBT) and what God said through scripture thousands of years ago will unlock the shackles on your mind and bring you freedom to your life.

Chapter I What is Cognitive Behavioral Therapy

A Quick Look:

- What are Automatic Thoughts?

- External and Internal Stimulus.

- The basis of CBT: Events, persons, places, or things are not what affect how we feel. It is our perception of these things, i.e., our environment that contributes to how we feel. Something happens in our life, which enters our mind and influences our thinking, which then affects how we feel and act. Therefore, if we are going to control how we feel, think and act, we must control our environment to the best of our abilities. In addition, we must control our perception of the events in our life.

- CBT only addresses part of the picture.

- Those in the Bible came from horrible environments and pasts, were still chosen to have their stories, and words included and used to teach millions of people how to overcome their situations. It is in the Bible that the foundational thoughts of CBT were born long before Aaron Beck developed it.

Supplementary Assignments:

- Take a moment and tell your story. What are your current thoughts on change, your situation and life, and what has your journey been so far?

- Be 100% honest with your therapist or support person and let them know where you are in regards to wanting change to take place in your life or if you don't want anything to change. This will better help them to help you.

- If you don't want change, then take a moment before proceeding and explain the things you love most in your life. Process why the things that your loved ones have identified to you as problems, are things you want to continue doing. Discuss this with your support person or therapist before proceeding.

Aaron T. Beck developed cognitive Behavioral Therapy in the 1960s after doing research on the psychoanalytic therapy approach. He found out that sitting on a couch facing a wall talking to Dr. Freud was not working. This motivated him to go back to the drawing board to figure out how he could help people in better ways. He came up with this idea that people with unstable moods have these repetitive spontaneous thoughts that are automatic. Therefore he coined these thoughts, creatively enough, *"automatic thoughts."* I know what you're thinking; this is groundbreaking, right? According to Beck Institute, he believed these 'automatic thoughts' surround three topics, the world, the future, and ones' self. When a person is living in this world, they see and hear a lot about their environment through their five senses, seeing, tasting, touching, hearing, smelling, and feeling.

> If you were not craving Chocolate and Cheetos before, you are now!

Take you for example, in this very moment, sitting there wherever you are. There is background noise, and you are sitting on something, maybe hard or soft. You may be hungry and craving chocolate or Cheetos. These are examples of stimulus in your environment that may be happening, but it is not the whole story. You may have had a fight with your mom or dad today, had a bad day in class, or got a bad grade on an exam. All of these are internal stimuli that are going on while you're reading this page. Your brain has this amazing capability of doing so many things at once, and part of that is thinking. We can be focusing on a task, but not even be thinking about it, and have our mind be in 10 million other places in the span of five minutes. It's difficult to track all of that, isn't it? Now stop thinking of what you're going to eat when you finish this chapter, and get your head in the game and <u>remember; to change and control your emotions and actions, you must first master control over your thoughts.</u>

External vs. Internal Stimulus

All that multi-tasking leaves you with not only *external stimulus (what is going around you)* but also *internal stimulus (what has been going on in your mind or body)*. The external one is easy to identify. Are you cold, hot, hungry, uncomfortable, tired, or not feeling well? They are physical, but the tough ones are the internal ones. This is when things get a little more difficult to put your finger on. *Internal stimulus or what is going on in your mind or body*. For example, your external stimulus last night may have been your parents fighting in the living room, thinking you were asleep or doing homework not able to hear them. That was your environment, but your internal stimuli are the feelings and thoughts that have continued since last night that you still experience and may experience for a long period of time. Things that happen to us and around us leave impressions. It is like when you push your finger into silly putty. It leaves a dent that takes a long time to spring back up. That is how our world makes impressions upon us. The harder and deeper you push, the longer it takes to spring back up. The deeper your environment impacts you, the longer it will remain to impact your thoughts and your feelings.

Therefore, CBT says that because none of us have 100% control of our environment, the only thing that we can control is ourselves. This is awesome...talk about freedom, right? Unfortunately, not all of us are blessed to be born into families with safe and healthy parents. Not all of us are born into families where love is communicated and expressed in healthy and Godly ways. Some of us are born into environments where we get impacted deeper and deeper with either being made to feel unsafe, being harmed, and hearing words of hate and anger. For some, our environment is not just a one-time momentary stressor, but a daily and repetitive nightmare that we fear we will never escape. In those situations, what do you do when the childhood song, "sticks and stones can break my bones but words can never hurt me" does not make us feel better, and words really do hurt when we hear them day after day, year after year? I have taught CBT for a long time in a place where it was all I could teach; I was restricted from sharing where the foundations of CBT really came from before it was called Cognitive Behavioral Therapy.

Teens, young adults, and kiddos would tell me their stories of situations that made me want to reach out, yank them from their environment, and state that they never have to experience that again, but the reality is we cannot always change the environment. The hardest part was that some of those whom I got the privilege to meet had been in it for so long that it became their normal, and they had grown to be so comfortable with it that anything different felt weird. Sure they didn't like the consequences they had to face as a result of their choices, but after a while, it had become normal to live in their dysfunction. Believe it or not, some of my patients didn't want to try to see change, and they actively sabotaged or ruined every effort of others or even their own effort, on purpose.

This is the other safety measure of our brains. Not only can we do a number of tasks at once, but also our brain protects us by adapting to the environment around us. Things that would normally shock us and cause us to panic the first time we experience them, have now become our normal and we are so used to having to deal with them, that we don't even recognize them to be a problem. This protective component in your mind has shielded you from experiencing shock every day, but it has also, in turn, dulled your ability to feel and experience emotions or empathy which is necessary to drive us to want change. You become used to it, so why then should you change? Does CBT still work then; simply to say, change your thoughts to change your outcome, or is there another element, which we are missing?

CBT and the Bible

CBT is amazingly effective at treating a number of issues. Research tells us that it is one of the most scientifically backed interventions for change that is available, and it is widely accepted by most insurances nationwide, for this reason. CBT tells us that we need only think of our situation differently, and everything else will change and be better, but I fear this only addresses a minor aspect of a bigger picture. If life is only about imagining our world to be lilies and roses, then a person could be in the midst of the evilest acts and come out unscathed. But we know that to be false. No matter how positive a spin a person puts on their situation, sometimes the actions of another, or the situation we are dealt, is never going to look okay or be bearable. How then do we cope or go on with life and not become absorbed by the evil?

If simply having a positive perspective is not enough then what is? To understand what the missing component to CBT is, you must first understand what came before CBT. The Bible is one of the oldest known compilations of letters and books ever written, and it is estimated by many sources to be more than three thousand years old. In Scripture, you find the same foundations that currently create the basis of CBT. The idea of controlling one's mind to control their actions and perspectives is found in many books of the Bible, such as the scriptures featured below.

Apostle Paul

Philippians 4:4-9 Updated American Standard Version (UASV)

Do Not Be Anxious Over Anything

[4] Rejoice in the Lord always; again I will say, Rejoice. [5] Let your gentleness be made known to all men. The Lord is at hand.[2] [6] In nothing be anxious; but in everything by prayer and supplication with thanksgiving let your requests be made known to God. [7] And the peace of God, which surpasses all understanding, will guard your hearts and your minds[3] in Christ Jesus.

---

[2] Or "The Lord *is* near."

[3] Or "your mental powers; your thoughts."

⁸ Finally, brothers, whatever is true, whatever is honorable, whatever is just, whatever is pure, whatever is lovely, whatever is of good report; if there be any virtue, and if there be any praise, think on⁴ these things. ⁹ The things you have learned and received and heard and seen in me, practice these things, and the God of peace will be with you.

4:4. Again Paul returns to the key theme of this letter: joy. He calls believers to **rejoice** at all times and repeats the call for emphasis. This includes the bad times as well as the good (compare Jas. 1:2–5). Christians should be known as joyful people. Such joy resides not in circumstances or positive attitudes toward life. Joy reigns in the heart only when Christ is Lord of life. Joy is always **in the Lord**.

4:5. A practical way to have joy is by exhibiting **gentleness** to all. This lets the church and world see that you belong to the Lord. The Greek word *epieikēs* means "yielding, gentle, kind." It includes the ability to go beyond the letter of the law in treating others, to provide something beside strict justice. It does not insist on personal rights or privileges. Christ embodied such gentleness in his dealing with all people (2 Cor. 10:1; compare 1 Tim. 3:3; Titus 3:2; Jas. 3:17; 1 Pet. 2:18). Why should we surrender personal rights for others? **The Lord is near.** In both time and space, God is available to us. He is not far removed in heaven but present in our hearts to hear and relate to us. His nearness also means he knows us and what we are. In time, God is near, for he is coming again. Then we will receive our rewards for living like Christ rather than like the world.

4:6. Joy replaces anxiety in life, so Paul advises the Philippians not to be **anxious about anything**. The cure for anxiety? Prayer! Worry and anxiety come from focusing on your circumstances such as imprisonment or persecution which Paul and the Philippians faced. Anxiety or worry doesn't accomplish anything, but prayer does (Jas. 5:16). Jesus warned against worry which demonstrates a lack of trust in God (Matt. 6:25–34).

4:7. The peace of God comes from prayer involving both asking God for earthly needs and thanking God for his presence and provision. The expression appears only here in the New Testament. God's peace reflects the divine character, which lives in serenity, totally separate from all anxiety and worry. Such peace is like a squad of Roman soldiers standing guard and protecting you from worry and fret. Such peace is not a dream of the human mind. The human mind cannot even comprehend this kind of peace, wholeness, and quiet confidence. Such peace protects the two organs of worry—**heart** and **mind that** produce feelings and thoughts. Such protection is real, available in Christ Jesus. Those who do

---

⁴ Or "dwell on these things; *ponder these things*"

not trust and commit their life to Christ have no hope for peace.

4:8. Continuing his strong imperative style, Paul suggested what should occupy our minds rather than anxiety and worry. Paul understood the influence of one's thoughts on one's life. Right thinking is the first step toward righteous living. What is right thinking? It is thinking devoted to life's higher goods and virtues. Thus Paul picked up a practice from secular writers of his day and listed a catalog of virtues that should occupy the mind. Such virtues are not limited to the Christian community but are recognized even by pagan cultures.

True is that which corresponds to reality. Anxiety comes when false ideas and unreal circumstances occupy the mind instead of truth. Ultimately, thinking on the truth is thinking on Jesus, who is the truth (John 14:6; Eph. 4:21). **Noble** refers to lofty, majestic, awesome things, things that lift the mind above the world's dirt and scandal. **Right** refers to that which is fair to all parties involved, that which fulfills all obligations and debts. Thinking right thoughts steers one away from quarrels and dissensions to think of the needs and rights of the other party. **Pure** casts its net of meaning over all of life from sexual acts to noble thoughts to moral and ritual readiness for worship. Thinking on the pure leads one away from sin and shame and toward God and worship. **Lovely** is a rare word referring to things that attract, please, and win other people's admiration and affection. Such thoughts bring people together in peace rather than separating them in fighting and feuding. **Admirable** is something worthy of praise or approval, that which deserves a good reputation. Pondering ways to protect one's moral and spiritual image in the community leads away from worries about circumstances and possessions that project a different image to the community and which thinking cannot change.

The catalog of virtues Paul sums up in two words: **excellent** and **praiseworthy**. The first encompasses what is best in every area of life, the philosophical good for which every person should strive. Here it is especially the ethical best a person can achieve. The second term refers to that which deserves human praise. The catalog of virtues thus reflects the best life a person can live and the best reputation a person can thereby achieve in the community.

Finally, in this verse, Paul gets to his point: think on these things. That, joined with prayer will relieve all anxieties and lead one to praise God and live life the way he desires.

4:9. Is such noble thinking possible. Paul says, "Yes, it is. Look at my example." This is not braggadocio or pride. It is the state every Christian should live in, a state of being an example for all who observe you. The example includes Paul's teaching, the tradition he received from the apostles and passed on, his reputation for Christian living, and the Christian lifestyle they saw him practice. If they obey Paul, God will bless them with his peace (see v. 7; John 14:27; 16:33).[5]

1. What is the key to having Joy in hardship according to Paul's suggestion?

_____

2. What will happen if you pray to God for your needs and thank Him for what He has done?

_____
_____
_____
_____
_____

3. Fix your thoughts on what things and what will you get in return?

_____
_____
_____
_____
_____

4. If Paul was in prison awaiting sentencing, possibly facing news that he would be killed, why did he focus so much in this Scripture on where to fix your thoughts, when these could have been his dying words?

_____
_____
_____
_____
_____
_____
_____

This verse may seem like just a good suggestion or maybe you are thinking that it was easy for the author to state, but the Apostle Paul wrote this. To understand how powerful these words were and still are, you need to know what battles he was fighting when he wrote them. He

---

[5] Max Anders, *Galatians-Colossians*, vol. 8, Holman New Testament Commentary (Nashville, TN: Broadman & Holman Publishers, 1999), 261–263.

wrote these words in a letter to a church he had started in a city called Philippi. This was a very large city at the time, picture a smaller version of Rome, and from the best guess of theologians, Paul was writing from a place he was often found; in prison.

Paul started off holding to his Jewish beliefs and was so offended by the claim that Jesus Christ was the Messiah, God in human form sent to save the world from sin, that he started doing the bidding of the Jewish leaders; hunting down early Christians who made these claims to imprison them. He tortured them for information and often times would murder them. He was traveling on the road to a city called Damascus where he had been given information that the disciples were staying. His plan was to capture them, return them to the Jewish leaders in Jerusalem, and then likely to execute them.

The disciples were a group of men who had followed Christ while he was here on Earth and had begun spreading the word to the world that Christ was risen from the dead after saving the world from their sins. Paul was struck suddenly by blindness and had to be taken to a nearby inn to stay as no one understood what had happened. He had written in the book of Acts that he had a vision of Christ asking why Paul was persecuting Him and His followers. During the time he was blinded he was told of a man who would come to him and heal him of his blindness in the name of Christ. He waited, and soon everything that he had envisioned occurred. Paul was never the same. His name was Simon when he was the killer of Christians, but he was named Paul when he was made a new creation having been saved and changed by Christ.

Why am I telling you about this? Because so often we have the thought that the writers in the Bible are like the "churchy people" we see in our community. They are people who seem like they have it all together. We assume they came from families where Mom and Dad were still married, no one was ever hit, and they went to church every Sunday. God knows that not very many of us come from homes that are perfect. I don't know if 'perfect' even exists because I've never seen it. Therefore, he gave us Paul, a man who was a murderer. A man who tortured the very people Christ loved. But yet do you know who wrote the majority of the New Testament in the Bible—Paul. The man who use to hunt down and murder Christians later became one, and then was regularly beaten, whipped, tortured, and imprisoned because he started teaching about Christ's love. This is who is writing about focusing on being thankful to God. A man who was beaten and sent to jail so many times that he probably started to feel more comfortable there than in most other places. When you read that passage and these next few, understand he was writing them when he was bleeding, starving, suffering, cold, uncertain as to how much longer he would even live and understand how powerful it is to be feeling that way physically, but to allow your mind to think on things of thankfulness and love.

2 Corinthians 12:7-10 Updated American Standard Version (UASV)

7 Because of the surpassing greatness of the revelations, for this reason, to keep me from exalting myself, there was given me a thorn in the flesh, a messenger of Satan to torment me, to keep me from exalting myself! **8** Three times I implored the Lord about this, that it would depart from me. **9** And he said to me, "My grace is sufficient for you, for my power is made perfect in weakness." Most gladly, therefore, I will rather boast about my weaknesses, so that the power of Christ may dwell in me. **10** Therefore I take delight in weaknesses, in insults, in times of need, in persecutions and difficulties for the sake of Christ, for whenever I am weak, then I am strong.

12:7. Paul was tempted to become **conceited** in light of his **surpassingly great revelations**. To keep that from happening, God sent him **a thorn in** his **flesh**. This expression is similar to the Old Testament terminology, "thorn in the side" in the Septuagint, where it was a metaphorical description of trouble inflicted by God. It is difficult to know precisely what the apostle had in mind. He also called it **a messenger of Satan** that brought him **torment**, but said nothing else. Endless suggestions have been made, but three proposals are feasible: (1) Paul had a physical ailment, perhaps an eye disease (cf. Gal. 4:15) or a speech impediment; (2) Paul spoke of continuing opponents in the churches; (3) Paul pointed to some troubling demonic activity, perhaps some severe temptation.

12:8-9a. Despite this uncertainty, Paul's main idea is clear. He asked God **three times** to remove this thorn from his life, but God told him that divine **grace was sufficient for** him. The tense of the expression **he said** may also be translated as "he has said," indicating that Paul saw God's statement as more than simply directed toward his situation. God wanted Paul to find comfort and security in the **grace** he had received in Christ—the same thing God desires for all believers.

In fact, in this particular case, God's denial of Paul's request turned out to be to Paul's greater good because it was to God's greater glory. God told Paul that divine **power is made perfect in weakness.** Throughout the Scripture God delights in displaying his power in situations where human strength is weak (1 Sam. 14:6-15). When God's people are weak, then God's strength becomes evident.

12:9b. As a result, Paul determined that he would **boast all the**

more gladly about his **weaknesses.** He quit complaining, **so that Christ's power** might **rest on** him. The terminology translated "rest" (*episkenoo*) may be translated as "to tabernacle" or "pitch a tent." It is likely that Paul drew upon Old Testament imagery of the glory of God coming upon the tabernacle (Exod. 40:34–38). If so, he learned that taking delight in his thorn actually brought the blessings of God upon his life.

12:10. From this understanding of his weakness, Paul concluded that he would **delight in weaknesses** rather than abhor them. **Insults, hardships, persecutions,** and **difficulties** were causes for joy because in these times of weakness, Paul was **strong** in the power of God.[6]

Process with your support person what he means in this scripture. Look specifically at the following sections: *I begged the Lord to take it away, but each time he said my power works best in your weakness.* Write below what this means to you and how it applies to your struggles.

1. What are the current struggles in your life that you beg could be taken away?

   _____

   _____

   _____

   _____

   _____

   _____

   _____

   _____

2. What does Paul mean when he says the Lord replied, "My power works best in your weakness"?

   _____

   _____

   _____

   _____

   _____

   _____

   _____

   _____

   _____

---

[6] Richard L. Pratt Jr, *I & II Corinthians*, vol. 7, Holman New Testament Commentary (Nashville, TN: Broadman & Holman Publishers, 2000), 427–428.

Paul says,

Romans 12:2 Updated American Standard Version (UASV)

² And do not be conformed to this world, but be transformed by the renewing of your mind, so that you may prove what the will of God is, that which is good and acceptable⁷ and perfect.

12:2a. The person who has truly sacrificed himself or herself to God will be distinguished by one overriding characteristic that informs the rest of life. That characteristic is the unwillingness to be conformed to **the pattern of this world**. Or, as J. B. Phillips put it in his widely-known translation of this verse, "Don't let the world ... squeeze you into its mold." Paul gives the offensive key to this defensive posture—but first a closer look at that which the believer is committed to avoiding.

The NIV rendering of *aion* by **world** is not quite as telling as its primary translation, "age." The NIV's **pattern** is not in the Greek text. It is an expansion of the verb *suschematizo*, to conform to. Literally, the verse says: "Do not be conformed to this age." "Age" carries with it a sense of the beliefs, the philosophies, the methodologies, and the strategies of the fallen world in which we live. It is not just the world and its people in their fallen state. It is the worldviews and practices that derive from the fallen state that define the age in which humans live at any time in history.

Paul elsewhere calls this age "evil" (Gal. 1:4), and says that "the god of this age has blinded the minds of unbelievers" to the gospel (2 Cor. 4:4). This age has wise men, scholars, and philosophers who believe that their answers to life are to be preferred over God's (1 Cor. 1:20), but whose wisdom will lead them to nothing (1 Cor. 2:6). Paul warns believers against being deceived into measuring true wisdom by "the standards of this age," and suggests instead that believers become "fools" with regard to this age so that they might become truly wise (1 Cor. 3:18). This age (world) is a dangerous place: "We know ... that the whole world is under the control of the evil one" (1 John 5:19).

If we do not allow ourselves to be conformed (present passive imperative of *suschematizo*), then we will not be one with (*sun*) the schemes (*schema*) of the age in which we live. While the same word for schemes is not used in the Greek text (*schema*), the same sense is implied by Paul's words in 2 Corinthians 2:11 and Ephesians 6:11 where he makes reference to Satan's schemes and strategies against believers. If Satan is the god of this world (and he is), and if the whole world lies in his power

---

⁷ Or *well-pleasing*

(and it does), then the believer must resist the pressure to conform morally, intellectually, and emotionally—and ultimately behaviorally—to Satan's schemes for life. We are not to act like the "wise" of this age—those who follow their own satanically-inspired will and practices rather than God's.

And what offensive measure keeps the believer from being conformed to this present evil age? The consistent and deliberate **renewing** of the mind. To make new (Paul here uses the noun, renewal, *anakainosis*, instead of the verb *anakainoo*, to make new) is a combination of "new" (*kainos*) and "again" (*ana*). Paul uses the verb form in 2 Corinthians 4:16 where he says "we are being renewed day by day," and in Colossians 3:10 where he says that the new self "is being renewed in knowledge in the image of its Creator."

Both of these uses of the verb shed light on his use of the noun here, especially the Colossians reference where he highlights a renewal of knowledge "in" (*kata*, according to) the image of God. In other words, believers are coming out of Satan's domain where lies and depravity are the language and currency and depraved minds (Rom. 1:28) are the norm. Therefore, our minds must be renewed in knowledge according to the image of God, not the age in which Satan rules.

The ongoing, repetitive nature of the renewal is drawn from the present passive imperative of *metamorphoo*, to change form. It is from this Greek word that our "metamorphosis" derives—"a transformation; a marked change in appearance, character, condition, or function" (*American Heritage Dictionary*). The English definition describes perfectly the "metamorphosis" which took place before the disciples' eyes as Jesus was transfigured (*metamorphoo*) before them: "His face shone like the sun, and his clothes became as white as the light" (Matt. 17:2), "whiter than anyone in the world could bleach them" (Mark 9:3).

These dramatic images are a picture of how different the believer is to become as, day after day, he or she is being transformed by the renewing of the mind. Instead of being *conformed* to the present evil age, believers are to be *trans*formed into the image of God insofar as knowledge and behavior are concerned. Paul has already stated that it is God's ultimate goal for believers "to be conformed to the likeness of [God's] Son" (Rom. 8:29). But in this verse, the "conformation" is of a different sort than the "conformation" to the world that we are warned against in our present verse. We are warned against being shaped into (*suschematizo*) the patterns and schemes of the world, system in which we live.

On the other hand, Paul says that we are being "made like" Christ.

Here the word conformed is *summorphos*, made up of *sum* (with) and *morphe* (shape or form). The former word for conformed has to do with exterior structures and designs, things which are changeable, not permanent. The latter word, suggesting how we are being conformed to Christ, has to do with being made like something else in essence or in form, something that is durable and not just an exterior structure. W. E. Vine clarifies, saying "*Suschematizo* could not be used of inward transformation" (Vine, p. 122).

12:2b. But how exactly is the renewing to take place? What is to "fuel" the metamorphosis that takes place in the believer's life? Transformation ("conformation" to the image of Christ) happens when the renewed mind begins **to test and approve what God's will is—his good, pleasing and perfect will**. It is the will of God—his standards, his desires, his motives, his values, his practices—which gradually pull the monarch butterfly of the believer out of the world's cocoon into which he or she has been squeezed. It is a knowledge and practice of the will of God that leads to spiritual growth and maturity in the Christian's life.

Ultimately, the will of God is all that matters, as Martin Luther King, Jr., so eloquently said, "Like anybody else, I would like to live a long life. Longevity has its place. But I'm not concerned about that now. I just want to do God's will" (Ward, p. 282).

Test and approve in the NIV is actually one word, *dokimazo*, which means to test and (by implication or extension) to approve. Both words can be subsumed under the idea of "prove," as rendered by the NASB—"that you may prove what the will of God is." The idea here is that the renewed mind can discover and put into action—thereby proving or demonstrating—the will of God. His will is **good, pleasing and perfect**, and in doing his will, the believer demonstrates sacrificial living.

That is, when a person chooses to sacrifice the preferences of the flesh (the normal human disposition), and chooses to do the will of God instead, the life of sacrifice is seen. It is as the seventh-century Spanish archbishop and scholar Isidore of Seville said: "The whole science of the saints consists in finding out and following the will of God" (Ward, p. 45). And is one whose safety was threatened on many occasions said, "The centre of God's will is our only safety" (Betsie ten Boom, sister of Corrie ten Boom, in Ward, p. 239).

This concludes Paul's introductory exhortation following eleven chapters of doctrinal foundation. It would not be off the mark to say that all of Romans 1–11 could be summarized under the rubric of "the mercy of God." Starting with the initial chapters when the utter sinfulness of humans is revealed, it quickly becomes obvious that mercy is all that can save the human race. By the time we get to the end of chapter 11, Paul declares that God's grand purpose is to have mercy on all (the elect) without exception. Therefore, when Paul says in Romans 12:1, "in view of God's mercy," he is saying, "in view of Romans 1–11"; "in view of your sin, God's salvation, your sanctification, and God's sovereignty, it really is a spiritually reasonable thing for you to sacrifice yourself for him." That is Paul's conclusion to Romans 1–11 and his introduction to Romans 12–16.

If the first eleven chapters of Romans demonstrate God's mercy, the next four chapters are how believers respond to God's mercy by demonstrating sacrificial living. In the rest of chapter 12, sacrifice is expressed and evidenced in the body of Christ and in personal relationships. In chapter 13, sacrifice is seen as believers submit to civil authorities and to the dual commands to love God and neighbor. And finally, in chapters 14 and 15, sacrifice is seen as believers give up their personal preferences in the church so as not to cause a weaker Christian to stumble and sin.

To return to the point made in the introduction to this chapter, the contents of the next four chapters contain much practical advice for Christian living. But to disconnect these chapters from Romans 1–11 is to disconnect them from their power source, for the motivation to sacrifice in the Christian life is the mercy of God.[8]

There is so much being said in this one verse. First, let me outline for you that Paul is warning us about what all Christians must be concerned with, "do not be conformed to this world, but be transformed by the renewing of your mind." (Rom. 12:2) We notice that Paul started verse 2 with "**do not** be conformed to **this world**." The "do not" implies that some of the Christians in Rome may have been struggling with letting their former lifestyle go, or that Paul was warning all Christians in Rome to watch out for the influence of the world that Jesus said we were to be no part of, namely, no part of wicked humankind. (John 17:14) In addition, Paul exhorted the Christians in the city of Corinth, to be "those making use of the world as those not using it to the full." In other words, we do not involve ourselves in the wicked human society fully. The other phrase in Romans 12:2, "this world" is referring to immoral and violent speech, conduct and attitudes that are so common among unbelievers. For the Christians in Rome at about 56 C.E., "the world" involved the values and morals, customs, manners, and lifestyles that characterized the Roman world.

---

[8] Kenneth Boa and William Kruidenier, *Romans*, vol. 6, Holman New Testament Commentary (Nashville, TN: Broadman & Holman Publishers, 2000), 364–367.

It is so easy to feel pressured to do what those around us are doing. It is all the rage for girls to wear short skirts and shorts because the world says that you are not popular if all the boys don't want you. It is easy to give in when someone asks you to go to a party and to drink what they are all drinking because you don't want to look like the lame loser not having fun. You don't think Rome had parties. Rome was known for being the lewdest, or mostcrude of all people. They sold slaves for more than just housework at the Colosseum. They forced the gladiators to be more than just fighters because the wealthy women thought they were physically attractive. Romans were decadent, or immoral in every way. Paul knew this better than anyone did because, though he was Jewish, he was also a Roman citizen.

Don't think for a second these people didn't know how hard it was to go against the crowd. Nero was Caesar of Rome, and he would burn Christians at the stake for proclaiming their faith. They knew the consequences of going against the crowd better than most. Paul was trying to encourage the church to remain strong when their strength was failing and they were starting to give in to what those around them thought were best.

1. What are the customs of our society that you have seen regarding sex, our thoughts, popularity, how to 'feel good' or to be better?

_____

_____
_____
_____
_____
_____
_____

2. How does God transform our minds and what will happen when He does? Hint: 'Transform' refers to the changing of one's being to a completely new being and it is very clear that this change comes from inside, not outside.

_____

_____
_____
_____
_____
_____
_____

3. What does the scripture mean when it says "Then you will know what God wants you to do". What does this show us?

_____

_____

_____

_____

_____

_____

_____

_____

_____

4. Do you have someone like Paul who will encourage you to go against the crowds when the peer pressure is on? If so, who is it?

_____

_____

_____

_____

_____

_____

_____

_____

_____

_____

Colossians 3:2 says, "Let heaven fill our thoughts. Do not think only about things down here on earth".

1. What does it mean to "let heaven fill our thoughts"?

_____

_____

_____

_____

_____

_____

_____

_____

_____

_____

_____

Listen to Skillet's song "Monster"

Hint: Remember, Paul faced life and death every day.

Jesus said,

Mark 7:20-23 Updated American Standard Version (UASV)

[20] And he was saying, "That which comes out of a man is what defiles him. [21] For from inside, out of the heart of men, come injurious reasonings, sexual immorality,[9] thefts, murders, [22] acts of adultery, greed, acts of wickedness, deceit, sensuality,[10] an envious eye, slander, pride, and foolishness. [23] All these wicked things come from within and defile a man."

7:20–23. Jesus showed how the observance of external rules does not correct the "nature" of the heart. The heart is the core for motivation, deliberation, and intention. He gave a list of behaviors and characteristics that come from the heart.

Evil thoughts is the spring from which all the other "bad" attitudes and activities arise. Jesus was making it clear that doing the right things does not mean that a person is "right" on the inside. No amount of hand washing can change the selfish nature of the heart or make it clean. There is only one way. His name is Jesus. By trusting in him for our salvation, we can be changed from the inside out.[11]

Jesus is the only person in this world who has ever been without sin, perfect in the eyes of the Father. We do not know much about the life of Jesus before He started His ministry, but we do know the story of his birth. We know how his parents Mary and Joseph came to know of his coming into the world. In the Gospel of Mathew, we hear of the coming of Jesus from Joseph's perspective, that he was considering breaking his engagement off with Mary quietly so as to not bring disgrace to her publicly. However, he fell asleep before doing so and he was visited by

---

[9] **Sexual Immorality**: (Heb. *zanah*; Gr. *porneia*) A general term for immoral sexual acts of any kind: such as adultery, prostitution, sexual relations between people not married to each other, homosexuality, and bestiality.–Num. 25:1; Deut. 22:21; Matt. 5:32; 1 Cor. 5:1.

[10] **Sensuality, Debauchery, Promiscuity, Licentiousness, Lewdness**: (Gr. *aselgeia*) This is behavior that is completely lacking in moral restraint, indulgence in sensual pleasure, driven by aggressive and selfish desires, unchecked by morality, especially in sexual matters.–Mark 7:22; Rom. 13:13; 2 Cor. 12:21; Gal. 5:19; Eph. 4:19; 1 Pet. 4:3; 2 Pet. 2:2, 7, 18; Jude 4+.

[11] Rodney L. Cooper, *Mark*, vol. 2, Holman New Testament Commentary (Nashville, TN: Broadman & Holman Publishers, 2000), 119.

an angel who told him not to be afraid of marrying Mary, reassuring him that the child she carried was not from any man but was conceived by the Holy Spirit to fulfill Scripture and save the world from its' sins. After this, Joseph listened to the angel and brought Mary home to be his bride.

Sometimes because of our obedience to God, we are called to do things that will bring us danger, pain, judgment and criticism. The hardest tasks in life are not laid before the feet of the bravest of people. Certainly, Joseph and Mary had many things that weighed heavy on their mind. Only Joseph and Mary knew of the tremendous secret that Jesus was the Son of God. Gabriel tells Mary, who is but a teenager that she will give birth to a baby. The angel said, "Do not be afraid, Mary, for you have found favor with God. And behold, you will conceive in your womb and bear a son, and you shall call his name Jesus." But Mary said to the angel, "How is this to be since I know no man?"[12] And the angel answered and said to her, "The Holy Spirit will come upon you, and the power of the Most High will overshadow you; and for that reason the one who is born will be called holy, the Son of God."–Luke 1:26-56.

Matthew 1:18 BDC: Mary was a descendant of Adam and an imperfect sinner. Therefore, how could Jesus, Mary's firstborn be perfect and free from sin in his physical body? The apostle Paul tells us at Galatians 4:4 that the Father "sent forth his Son, born of a woman." How did the laws of heredity work with this union of perfection (the life of the Son) with imperfection (the ovum or egg cell in Mary's womb)?

How was the life of the Son transferred from heaven to earth to be united, in the fertilization of an ovum or egg cell in Mary's womb? How could Jesus, as the actual son of Mary, a genuine descendant of forefathers Abraham, Isaac, Jacob, Judah, and King David and legitimate heir retain the same identity that he had in heaven? (Gen. 22:15-18; 26:24; 28:10-14; 49:10; 2 Sam 7:8, 11-16; Lu 3:23-34) The Scriptures reveal that the Holy Spirit caused the conception, namely, the fertilization of an egg cell by the transferal of the life of the Son from heaven to Mary's womb. The Holy Spirit would have canceled out any imperfection in Mary's ovum, producing a pattern of genes that was perfect from the conception. Matthew tells us that Mary "was found to be with child by the Holy Spirit." (1:18) Luke tells us that the angel said to Mary, "The Holy Spirit will come upon you, and the power of the Most High will overshadow you; and for that reason the one who is born will be called holy, the Son of God." (Lu 1:35) In other words, the Holy Spirit fertilized Mary's egg by the life of the Son. At the same time, the Holy Spirit formed what we might call a defensive wall that protected the Son in

---

[12] Meaning, *I am not having sexual relations with a man*

36

Mary's womb so that no imperfection could affect the developing embryo, from conception up unto the time of the birth.

Joseph feared than Mary had been with another man. However, he feared even more for Mary's life, as she would have been stoned to death for cheating on her fiancé.[13] After the angel's visit to Joseph in a dream, his fear was relieved, as now he knew Mary had not been with another. Joseph did not tell anyone and took Mary home with him, a public action that served, in effect, as a marriage ceremony, giving notice that Joseph and Mary are now officially married, everyone considering Joseph to be the biological son of Joseph. Jesus grew up very poor. The Scriptures show that Jesus had four brothers: James, Joseph, Simon, Judas, and at least two sisters. He came from a working class family. Joseph raised Jesus as his own, and he teaches Jesus to be a carpenter. In fact, Jesus is referred to as "the carpenter's son." In addition, people said, "This is the carpenter." The life of Joseph's family is built around the worship of the Father at the synagogue in Nazareth, and especially regular trips to the temple in Jerusalem.

The life of young Jesus was definitely no life of ease, He and His parents struggled financially (Matt. 13:55; Lu 2:4; compare Lu 2:24 with Le 12:8), lived under the oppressive Roman government, as well as the Jewish leaders of Palestine. Moreover, Mary alone had to raise all of those children, with the oldest Son Jesus bearing much responsibility at an early age. Why? The death of Joseph's is not explicitly mentioned in the Scriptures. However, most Bible scholars agree that he died when Jesus was young, shortly after Jesus visited Jerusalem when he was twelve years old. Think about that, the Son of God was not given to a rich family, He was not spared living under an oppressive government, and He was not freed from the pain and difficult times of His human father dying when He was young or any of the hundreds of difficulties He faced in His young life. What we do know is that both Mary and Joseph obeyed the word of God and Jesus from a very early age made every decision based on the Scriptures. Generally speaking, when we obey the Word of God, we can avoid many of the pitfalls in life. We too live in a world where we have to make big and small decisions every day; life changes bring uncertainty and fear of the unknown.

Many young teen females have found themselves pregnant, unmarried, and now the weight of the world has just doubled for them. However, God has given us a guidebook, the Bible, to get through these difficult times. While it cannot help us to ship over the difficulties of

---

[13] In Bible times being engaged was viewed the same as being married. If either party cheated, the punishment would be the same as if they had been married.

imperfect human life, it can help us avoid much and strengthen us to cope with the rest. No person in the Scriptures lived a charmed life, be it Enoch, Noah, Abraham, Rebekah, Rachel, Moses, King, Ruth, David, Mary, Joseph, Jesus, or the apostle Paul, Peter, James, or John. In fact, many of these major Bible characters suffered many hardships far worse than we will ever know. However, they all had one thing in common, that is, they walked with God. What does it mean to walk with God? It means that we follow the life-course outlined by God's Word. Yes, the Word of God, the Bible is the standard by which we can measure our walk with God. On this, the author of Hebrews wrote, "For the word of God is living and active and sharper than any two-edged sword, and piercing as far as the division of soul and spirit, of both joints and marrow, and able to judge the thoughts and intentions of the heart." (Heb. 4:12) We have already learned that all humans are born mentally bent toward evil, in addition, we cannot fully understand our inner person, and our natural desire is to do wrong. However, we are also born with a conscience that will guide us toward good and if it has been defiled by the world up to this point, have no fear. The Word of God can retrain the conscience, where it will again help us to make the right decisions, even in the heat of difficulty, tragedy, and heartbreak.

"It is the thought-life that defiles you. For from within you, out of a person's heart, comes evil thoughts..." Why does it start in your thoughts? If you have ever done something you knew to be wrong, then you know that it started in your mind. You tested it out maybe by dropping statements to your friends about it subtly before you did it to see what their reaction was. Like when you had sex for the first time. I guarantee you thought about it first. Maybe you were curious on how to do it or were introduced first by watching pornography. You may have had abuse in your past that introduced you to it way before you would have chosen. Either way, it has remained in your thinking, which now consumes you. People often say they did not think when they did something but, at some point or another, you thought about that type of act or specifically this one before you did it.

There is a song by Mercy Me called *Slow Fade*. It talks about how getting to the point where our relationships are falling apart is a slow fade. We find ourselves in detention centers or jail; we are addicted to drugs, alcohol, or pornography. We did not just wake up and choose this life, but it happened with seemingly small choices that added up over time to deliver us to this point in our life. What does that mean? It means this downfall started before you were even aware that it started. This verse says that it comes "from within you, out of a person's heart". This means that our behavior on the outside came from within. It came when a seed was planted a long time ago in your mind and because of your continued thoughts along the same lines, your continued behavior, and your continued association with those that water that seed, the thought took root and grew .

The second part of Jesus' statement is, it is these sins, which separate us from God. Do you ever feel like you have a part of you that you wish you could be rid of? Like no matter how hard you try, you continue to struggle with being selfish. You find yourself in the toughest life situations wishing you could use that drug or go back to it after having been sober. It is almost as if there is a part of you that you are fighting; as you know this is not how you want to be, but you cannot seem to get away from this part of yourself that is somewhere within. Jesus talks about how our evil nature is inside us. This is what this workbook is all about. This is why Jesus came. He came because a long time ago, his Father created a man and a woman. The Father used to walk with them, talk with them, and laugh with them. He prepared everything for them, so they never had to wish for anything. Life was exactly as he had created it for them: painless, easy, carefree, and loved.

Then came temptation, then came our fall and after that moment God could no longer walk with us. In came disease, hunger, pain and work, old age and death. God had to find a way to get back to us because he did not make us for life like this. He made us to be able to go for walks with Him; to be able to look Him in the face, hug him, and never to want for anything. He made us to be with Him but now we are separate from him because of what we allowed to enter, the Enemy. He wanted us with him so much that he sent his only Son to die for us so that his Son would take the fall for all we had let in and we could be one with him again. When Jesus said that these things separate us from him, it is because when we sin we are choosing to be with the Enemy instead of with Christ. It is like picking teams. When you act like the Enemy you start to look more and more like the Enemy which is opposite of God, and we are choosing things that separate us from being able to be near to Him.

1. If you are to see real, lasting, genuine change it has to come from where?

_____

_____
_____
_____
_____
_____
_____
_____

2. Why does God want us to act in ways that He says are right? Is it to restrict us from the fun things in life?

_____

_____

_____

_____

_____

_____

3. Why does Christ say that these behaviors separate us from God and what is Jesus' goal, what does He want most?

_____

_____

_____

_____

_____

_____

4. Where do the urges to do what is wrong come from? (We will expand on this question more in later chapters)

_____

_____

_____

_____

_____

_____

_____

5. Where do we fight the battle for control over our mind and therefore our behaviors?

_____

_____

_____

_____

_____

_____

_____

2 I will give heed to the blameless way.
  When will you come to me?
I will walk in the integrity of my heart
  within my house;
3 I will not set before my eyes
  anything that is worthless.
I hate the work of those who fall away;
  it will not cling to me.
4 A perverse heart shall depart from me;
  I will not know evil.

5 Whoever slanders his neighbor in secret
  I will destroy.
Anyone of haughty eyes and of arrogant heart
  I will not endure.

6 My eyes shall be upon the faithful of the land,
  that they may dwell with me;
the one walking in blamelessness
  shall minister to me.

7 He who practices deceit
  shall not dwell in my house;
He who speaks lies
  shall continue before my eyes.

101:2. I will be careful (i.e., "be attentive to," "give diligence to") **to lead a blameless life**. David purposed to pursue a life of personal holiness. A blameless life is one that is faithful and obedient, one to which no blatant sin can be charged. He asked God, **When will you come to me?** Here is a desperate prayer that God would strengthen his resolve to pursue the path of personal integrity. His pursuit of holiness should begin in the privacy of his own house, where he lived, in his own private world. God's truth must be fully integrated into every area of his life.

101:3a. David understood the close connection between his eyes and his heart. Whatever is worthless before one's eyes can produce wickedness within one's heart. The eyes are the gateway to the heart. Through the eyes, temptation enters the heart. If David was to remain blameless in his heart (v. 2), his eyes must remain singular and pure.

101:3b. To the contrary, those who fall into sin are **faithless men** who fail to remain steadfast to God's Word. David pledges to be pure and faithful. He refuses to allow the unfaithfulness of others to pull him down.

101:4. The godly believer shuns evil in every form. **Men of perverse heart** are those who are inwardly crooked, the very opposite of the blameless. David would have **nothing to do with** such evil men lest he be corrupted by their sin. He determined to repudiate everything that was **evil** and, therefore, potentially destructive to his soul. David refused to allow any practice of sin to enter and remain in his life.

101:5. David knew the potential negative influence others could have upon him. Whenever someone comes and **slanders his neighbor** in secret, he would reject that person and refuse this sin. The slander is seen as coming from one with **haughty eyes** and **proud heart**. Neither would David allow prideful people to have close access to the inner circle of his life. If he did, they would influence him for evil.

101:6. David purposed to look for faithful people with whom to surround himself in his administration. David must work in partnership with people of moral integrity who were faithful to God and his Word. David would look for those who were **blameless** in their personal lives to serve him. The word **minister** is used often in the Old Testament of the priests and Levites who functioned in the tabernacle (Deut. 10:8; Num. 3:6). But it can also be used of court officials who assisted the king in his daily functions (cp. Exod. 24:13; 2 Sam. 13:17–18).

101:7. Conversely, David declared that no one who practiced **deceit** would **dwell in my house**. This refusal involved repudiating evil in many forms, including disloyalty, unfaithfulness, hypocrisy, disguising one's intentions, spreading lies, and gossip. Tolerating any of these sins would create friction in David's court. Such factious people would not serve with him, no matter how gifted, talented, or popular they were. The one who practices deceit also speaks falsely, eventually, against David. Such an evil person would not stand in his presence. He would be relieved of his duties and removed from office.[14]

You have just read from King David. King David ruled in Jerusalem some 3,080 years ago, and Jesus Christ came from his lineage. King David started off a shepherd. He would eventually go on to fight the giant Goliath with a slingshot and a few rocks to win a war. He would become a best friend to the prince of Jerusalem and would marry the princess of Jerusalem. He was forced into hiding after King Saul got jealous of his success. King Saul would plot to murder him and search for him when he

---

[14] Anders, Max; Lawson, Steven. Holman Old Testament Commentary - Psalms 76-150 (Kindle Locations 3636-3659). B&H Publishing. Kindle Edition.

was in hiding, sending assassins to try to murder him. David would eventually become the King of Israel despite Saul's best attempts to prevent this. David sounds like the golden boy right? Not quite. David made mistakes; he would go out one day and see from his balcony a woman bathing on her rooftop. That woman was named Bathsheba, and he lusted after her so much that he sought her out, and then would take her to his bed despite his knowledge that she was married to a man named Uriah, one of his soldiers. King David fell in love with Bathsheba, and she became pregnant as a result of their choices. To hide this, David had Uriah brought home to be with his wife and then he sent Uriah to the front lines of the war knowing he would be killed.

We have God's golden boy here who now has slept with a married woman, gets that married woman pregnant, and goes on to murder her husband after bringing him home to be intimate with his wife to cover the fact that the child Bathsheba was carrying was his and not her husbands. David later begs forgiveness for his sins and has to face the consequences of his actions. He feels guilt, not shame, and he does the following things, which lead to his ability to rebuild relationships and lead his people, even though he made such a major mistake.

1.   He recognizes what he did was wrong and he accepts that it was wrong without making excuses.

2.   He has empathy and recognizes the impact of his actions on others.

3.   He apologizes for what he has done, he does not simply say he is sorry, but he says the following: *Create in me a clean heart, O God. renew a right spirit within me. Wash me clean from my guilt. Purify me from my sin. Restore to me again the joy of your salvation, and make me willing to obey you.* (Psa. 51:1)

4.   He then starts to make amends by making changes and not continuing to live in sin.

Because of the above responses to his mistakes, David is known in history still as the man after God's own heart.

Sometimes we have good intentions; sometimes we truly want to be better. Is that you? You see the way you lose your temper, the way you argue with your family, the way you treat your siblings. You know you don't want to be like that, but you cannot seem to help it. It just seems to come out of you no matter how hard you try. Look at David's first line, *"I will be careful to live a blameless life—when will you come to my aid?"*. He has these high aspirations to live a life of integrity and to always do the right thing, but he begs for assistance, *when will you come to my aid.*

He is asking God to help him with these things. 'This is how I want to live God,' he says, 'will you help me do it.' David was the golden child, but he recognized how hard it was to do the right thing and he made mistakes, big ones. He was still forgiven, and even though he made major mistakes, he was able to fight from making them again. How did he do this? He asked for God's help to live in the way God wanted him to, and not act in the way he knew was wrong.

1. What type of life did David want to live?

_____
_____
_____
_____
_____
_____

2. What type of behaviors did David struggle against?

_____
_____
_____
_____
_____
_____

3. Did he think it would be easy and how did he seek help?

_____
_____
_____
_____
_____
_____

4. Was he always successful in following these principles in his life?

_____
_____
_____
_____
_____
_____

5. How did he react when he made mistakes? Did God abandon him? What were the four steps David went through to rebuild what he had damaged by his wrongdoing?

_____

_____

_____

_____

_____

_____

_____

_____

1 Peter 1:13-14 Updated American standard Version (UASV)

[13] Therefore, gird the loins of your mind,[15] and being sober-minded,[16] set your hope fully on the grace that will be brought to you at the revelation of Jesus Christ. [14] As children of obedience,[17] do not be conformed according to the desires you formerly had in your ignorance,

---

1:13. This verse sets the time line boundaries for our behavior. The first word, **therefore**, points back to the preceding discussion that focused on our salvation hope. We entered into that hope when we committed ourselves in faith to the death and resurrection of Jesus Christ. The last words in this verse, **when Jesus Christ is revealed**, point ahead to an undisclosed day in the future when Jesus Christ will come to earth the second time. Christians must not forget the first chapter of our salvation or ignore its final chapter. The first affects the second. The second affects the first. From the outset believers are to live each day for that great final day.

How do we do this? First, **prepare your minds for action.** In the first century, people who wanted to walk or run quickly faced a problem. Before they could quicken their pace, they had to gather up their loose flowing robes with a belt so they would not trip and fall flat on their face as they set off for their destination. Translating that into daily living, Peter said, "Pull your thoughts together. Don't let anything hinder your mind as you put it to work for God." In other words, have a disciplined mind.

---

[15] I.e., *prepare your minds for action (mental perception)*

[16] **Sober Minded:** (Gr. *nepho*) This denotes being sound in mind, to be in control of one's thought processes and thus not be in danger of irrational thinking, 'to be sober-minded, to be well composed in mind.'–1 Thessalonians 5:6, 8; 2 Timothy 4:5; 1 Peter 1:13; 4:7; 5:8

[17] I.e., *obedient children*

Be self-controlled expresses the same idea. A loose paraphrase might be, "Stay on your toes spiritually." Be realistic about what you face in your life as a Christian. Be alert and ready in your whole spiritual and mental attitude, because it is so easy to slide, especially when you are suffering. In those moments it is very difficult to "pull your thoughts together," and to "be realistic" about your circumstances. The tendency of our mind is to scream exaggerations and denials. The inclination is to lean away from spiritual concerns.

That will be our fate unless we **set** [our] **hope fully on the grace to be given** [us] **when Jesus Christ is revealed.** The main emphasis is on putting one's hope completely in the final demonstration of the grace of God in Jesus Christ. At this moment, we enjoy only the beginning of that grace. What we have experienced of grace up to this point in our lives does not begin to compare with the grace that will be ours at the second coming of Christ. We must have the long view in mind, or the short run will kill us. Peter is really issuing a command: "Keep looking toward your final salvation, which will be fully experienced when Christ returns. You have been saved, you are being saved, and you will be saved, so don't get off course." Our future hope is not simply a theological doctrine with little or no practical application. It is, in fact, an ethical hope. It has behavioral consequences. If we really believe in the second coming of Christ, this belief must make a difference in the way we live.

1:14. The difference in the way we live is described by Peter's words, **as obedient children.** Obedience does not produce a believer in Jesus Christ, but true belief will always produce obedience in a believer in Jesus Christ. Part of this obedience is our nonconformity to evil desires. The verb *conformed* means "to be fashioned into something." The word describes the practice of adopting for oneself a pattern or mold of life that is changeable and unstable.

The emphasis of verse 14 helps us see that this conformity does not begin with outward actions, as much as it begins with our attitude, our mind-set, our character. Peter is referring to a conformity of thought and purpose. What God requires in us is a total change of purpose. Our outward life will change only as it is a natural outworking of an inner change. Conformity is a lack of obedience that adopts the attitudes, mind-sets, and purposes of the culture of which we are a part. Conformity belongs to the time of ignorance when we did not know Christ and so lived like the world.

One of the prevailing attitudes of our culture is, "I don't want any problems, any pain. I do not deserve to experience difficulties or trauma in any measure." As believers, we are not to adopt that mind-set. We are to conform to the example of Christ, the Suffering Servant.[18]

This is the last verse of the chapter. Peter, the disciple who wrote this verse was also the disciple who denied Christ three times while Christ was being arrested and beaten. Peter was a fisherman by trade and he was with Christ from the beginning of his ministry, all the way to his execution. He says a great deal in just four lines. First that we are to exercise self-control which means we will want to do things, have different feelings, and urges to certain acts, but we are to have control over our actions, despite how we may feel. This is what separates us from animals. We are by biology animals, but we have awareness that animals do not have. We know the difference between right and wrong. We have ethics, morals, and values, something animals do not have. We have compassion and empathy. We are to act with control of ourselves, meaning you will be at war with our physical and emotional selves, fighting for control of our minds so we can control our actions.

We are *His children*. Jesus Christ is the King of Kings, the Lord of all. He is the alpha and the omega, the one and only God, the Creator of all things, and we are His children. This means that no matter what you do, no matter who you are, or where you are at, you are royalty and part of a kingdom that will never fall. You are important and valued. Now that you are aware of the difference between right and wrong, you no longer have the excuse of 'I didn't know' to fall back on. Now, doing wrong or right is a choice you knowingly make, therefore you can and must be held accountable for your choice. Choose wisely.

1.   What does it mean to have self-control? How does this apply to you?

_____

_____

_____

_____

_____

_____

2. What does Peter mean the special blessing at Christ's return?

_____

_____

_____

_____

_____

---

[18] David Walls and Max Anders, *I & II Peter, I, II & III John, Jude*, vol. 11, Holman New Testament Commentary (Nashville, TN: Broadman & Holman Publishers, 1999), 11–12.

3. How much does God value you? Is your value or what you are worth, determined by what you do or is it something else? What determines your worth?

_____

_____

_____

_____

_____

_____

> *We love because He first loved us.– 1 John 4:19.*

It is important for you to know as we close that each member of the disciples, those that walked with Christ before his crucifixion, were all killed for sharing the story of Jesus. They all wrote letters encouraging us to live following the principles of God and to love one another. Yet they each met their end at the hands of another. Paul was beheaded in Rome after having been held captive in prison. Peter was crucified upside down because he stated he was not worthy to die in the same way Christ died. Andrew was told to deny his faith in Christianity or be tortured and then crucified. He refused, and he was tortured and then hung on the cross by ropes so that his death would take longer. He preached love and forgiveness to those that passed by as he was hanging. James was beheaded but, his accuser was so moved by his courage that he became a believer and was executed next to him. John was banished to the island of Patmos and died there of old age. Philip was tortured and crucified. Bartholomew was tortured, and some historians say he was crucified, but others say he was skinned alive and then beheaded. Thomas was killed with a spear. James was stoned to death. Simon was crucified. Judas killed himself after betraying Christ.

Why did I tell you this? It is easy for us to respond to others' statements by saying, "easy for you to say," and think that the person speaking to you does not have the knowledge or authority to offer advice. You need to know what these men regularly went through in order to understand the gravity of their words. Life or death, being beaten, being tortured, facing the uncertainty of where they would sleep and what they would eat was a daily experience; some of you know what this is like. It was in the midst of this that they spoke words like, *We love because He first loved us.–1 John 4:19.*

Further Thoughts

Chapter II Tools

Proverbs 4:20-24 Updated American Standard Version (UASV)

20 My son, be attentive to my words;
    incline your ear to my sayings.
21 Let them not escape from your sight;
    keep them in the midst of your heart.
22 For they are life to those who find them,
    and healing to all their flesh.
23 Keep your heart with all vigilance,
    for from it flow the springs of life.
24 Put away from you crooked speech,
    and put devious talk far from you.

4:20–24 In contrast to the previous instruction in 4:10–19, which spoke of two paths to choose from, this instruction admonishes the youth to walk a single path. Keep focused straight ahead. Do not turn to the right or to the left where temptation always lurks.

The instruction of the parent will bring wellness: **for they are life to those who find them, and health to a man's whole body** (v. 22). The health mentioned here (מַרְפֵּא, marpēʾ) includes mental, moral, and physical well-being. The son is called upon to give his undivided attention to his father's instruction.

The instruction begins first by affirming that wholeness comes about through keeping the instructions learned from the wise in one's **heart** (i.e., mind). The prudent person will listen and heed moral teaching. The wise person will **guard** his or her **heart** (i.e., mind) with all vigilance; **for it is the wellspring of life** (v. 23). Second, the sage exhorts the student with the following piece of advice: be careful about **your mouth**, that is, the way you speak (v. 24). **Keep corrupt talk far from your lips** (v. 24) is a rebuke of duplicity of speech. We might say, "Do not talk out of both sides of your mouth." The sages have much to say about the power of words. In Proverbs, the mouth and the heart (i.e., the mind) are the most important organs. One's speech reflects the inner character.[19]

---

[19] Dave Bland, *Proverbs, Ecclesiastes & Song of Songs*, The College Press NIV Commentary (Joplin, MO: College Press Pub. Co., 2002), 80.

A Quick Look:

- S.M.A.R.T Goals
- Change: Yes or No?
  - Stages of Change
- Self-Fulfilling Prophecy
- Preemptive Strike
- Insight-Take a deep breath, we are diving deep.
- Coping Skills
  - Universal Coping Skills

Supplemental Assignments:

- Process what your coping skills have been up until this point.

- Before you are asked to create some goals, think about the things you want to get out of your life, and the feedback others have given you regarding the things that will hold you back from achieving your goals.

- Suggest Song: Not for Sale (feat. Kefia Rollerson) Bizzzy-Surrender

Life is best described in my mind as an ocean. There are so many places you can go; the options are limitless. This can be a freeing fact, or it can be a dangerous one. Life has its' storms that will toss you against the rocks and leave you out to dry, but it also has its' warm sandy beaches that will let you relax and basque in the sun. If you go on a voyage and don't have a destination, it is easy to get lost and find yourself in places that you would rather have never gone. If you stay in those places too long, it can leave you shipwrecked, but if you know your course and stay on track then you can have a better chance of getting to your sandy beach, even if there is a sudden storm. However, if you don't have an anchor, then you will easily be tossed by the waves. When you do get off track, and we all do, if you know where you are supposed to be, and you have the crew to help you get there, then you can easily adjust course. Let's take a moment to decipher what this means to you.

1. What do the waves that toss you on the rocks represent? Process what the waves have been in your life. (*Hint: think about the things that have occurred that have been out of your control that have brought you strife or struggle.*)

_____

_____
_____
_____
_____
_____

2. What does the ship-wreck represent in your life? (Hint: Think about the things in your life that have occurred that have caused you strife or struggle as a result of your choices.)

_____
_____
_____
_____
_____
_____
_____
_____

3. What type of places have you gone that have caused you to lose your course and become ship-wrecked?

_____
_____
_____
_____
_____
_____
_____

4. Who is your crew? Are they a crew that will help you get back on course or do they steer you to trouble?

_____
_____
_____
_____
_____
_____
_____

5. What anchors you in your life, what holds you steady when the waves of life start to rise and become difficult? (Hint: These are your core beliefs or values that are unchanging in the face of struggle.)

_____
_____
_____
_____
_____

S.M.A.R.T goals

Mapping your Destination

> **SMART Goals**
>
> S-Specific
>
> M- Measurable
>
> A-Attainable
>
> R-Realistic

Proverbs 4:24-27 says to *avoid all perverse talk; stay far from corrupt speech. Look straight ahead, and fix your eyes on what lies before you. Mark out a straight path for your feet; then stick to the path and stay safe. Don't get sidetracked; keep your feet from following evil.*

Originally seen in the November 1981 issue of Management Review by George T. Doran, S.M.A.R.T goals is a mnemonic for setting objectives in corporations but can be transferred for use in your personal life. It is as follows: specific, measurable, attainable, realistic, and timed. Goals need to give you a map to outline progress toward an objective, as well as offer a way to ensure you are on course. Otherwise, it is easy to deviate and suddenly find yourself far away from your destination. Do you know what the objective is in your life? Do you know what you want out of your life, or better yet, do you know what you don't want? Making goals does not mean you have to have the next twenty years of your life mapped out. The purpose of setting goals is to allow you to know the general direction you want to go and to help you understand the individual steps it will take to make your hope a reality.

Sometimes it is easier to start with identifying what you don't want. It does not mean that what you wanted to do when you were ten years old is going to be your future necessarily. God has a way of revealing His plans to us over time, but it does mean that if you have a goal in mind, it will allow you to be motivated so that if you do change your mind, you are already making progress toward it. Sometimes, especially when you are young, you think you want something until you try it and see what it will really be like. Then suddenly you change your mind. It's a hard balance in having a goal and staying on course, but still riding the waves a little bit and having some freedom

Original Version: *"I want to stop feeling angry."*

Reworked Version: *"I want to learn how to express my anger in a healthy way by using different techniques to remain calm so that I can discuss what is upsetting me openly and work to resolve, or solve the issue."*

to be open to new ideas. Make your goals specific but not so specific that you miss out on things you never thought about before. So let's look at some steps to making S.M.A.R.T goals.

The first part of the mnemonic is Specific. This part of making a goal means you need to have details. When I was working in a residential treatment center (RTC), many of my patients would tell me, "Mrs. Heather, I'm here because of my anger. My goal is not to be angry." You may be laughing right now because of how silly this sounds, but many of my kiddos thought this was a great goal. The first step to making this a S.M.A.R.T goal is to recognize that it is impossible. This goal is neither realistic nor attainable. It is not possible to never feel an emotion. On average, people experience some level of anger at least three times a day. Feeling anger is not the problem. What we choose to do with our anger is.

The specific part of this goal would be identifying that the emotion is not the problem, the behavior is, and identifying what we do when angry that we want to change. We would process this and discuss that when they get angry they self-harm, isolate, bottle it up and think about it over and over, or they become aggressive destroying property or hurting others. It was these things that caused the problems, so now our goal is not to change their emotions, but to look at ways we can change what they do with the emotion. We would then identify what behaviors would be better. Each individual is different, but overall, most people wanted to be able to talk about what was making them angry in a calm manner and, be able to work to better address and resolve the problem. We became much more specific. We started with, '*I want to stop getting angry,*' and worked through it to the point that we created this goal instead; '*I want to learn how to express my anger in a healthy way by using different techniques to remain calm so that I can discuss what is upsetting me openly and work to solve the issue*'.

The goal is not done, though; we haven't made it measurable yet. It is difficult to measure things such as '*learn different techniques,*' but if we were to say that we want to learn how to use CBT and the Four Pillars and list specifically what we will do each day to work on this, then we have something measurable. So we would add to our goal by saying, "*...by using Cognitive Behavioral Therapy and the Four Pillars, working with my therapist or support person every therapy session, complete all of my therapy assignments to practice these techniques, fill out a Four Pillars worksheet three times a day and process my anger or other feelings, and document daily what has made me angry and how I handled the situation using CBT and the Four Pillars.*"

We need to ask ourselves if our goal is something that we can actually do; is it attainable. We also need to look at the techniques we have identified. Will doing a Four Pillars worksheet every day, working in your Waging War Workbook, and going to therapy, help you achieve your goal. The answer for this goal is yes; these are all realistic and appropriate ways of achieving our goal. Finally, we must give ourselves a time limit. We must state that we want to have made considerable changes and have reached our goal by the end of a certain time period. This does not mean that we will no longer continue to work on our goal to maintain our changed behaviors, but that we will have succeeded in altering our previous behaviors and replacing them with the goal behaviors.

In the end, our goal has gone from *"I want to stop feeling anger,"* to, *"I want to learn how to express my anger in a healthy way by doing the following: taking a few minutes to process my feelings if needed and later return to the situation and talk about my emotions openly and calmly, work with the other person to come up with a solution or to come to a conclusion for our conflict. (This is the goal behavior.) I will learn how to do this by practicing Cognitive Behavioral Therapy every day, using the Four Pillars worksheets to process my emotions three times a day, and will process what is written with a support person. I will attend family therapy where I will practice with my support person and family, talking openly about my emotions in session and I will have completed all of my therapy assignments prior to individual therapy, and readily work with my therapist checking in on my progress weekly. I will write down every time I get angry in a daily journal at breakfast, lunch, and dinner to display my efforts to change my behavior. I will check in with my accountability partner who is Jim-Bob every day at 4:00pm after school. I want to see a change in my behavior having gone at least thirty days not showing my previous behaviors of verbal or physical aggression. (This is how measurable the goal is.) The goal is realistic, attainable, and it is timed.*

Let's take a moment to work on your goal. A lot of times, many people have multiple goals. You need to decide what aspect of your life this goal is going to address. Work with your support person to identify your S.M.A.R.T goals.

1. What do you like about the lives of others around you? What do you not like? Explore what aspect of your life you want to change.

_____

_____

_____

_____

_____

_____

2. What is the long-term goal for you? (Remember: Specific but nothing too specific. You don't need to know all of the details for twenty years from now.)

_____

_____

_____

_____

_____

_____

3. What are the short term goals (near future) that you can work toward that will keep you on track to achieve the long term goals from step 2?

_____

_____

_____

_____

_____

_____

4. Who is going to help you stay on track? Identify some support people to help you remember your goals and stay away from things that will cause you to deviate from the plan you have set. What are the risky places that can lead to ship-wreck in your life regarding this goal?

_____

_____

_____

_____

_____

_____

5. What are the things you will do to achieve your goal, the steps that will take you to the objective?

_____

_____

_____

_____

_____

_____

_____

_____

_____

List your S.M.A.R.T. goal here. Ask yourself: is it Specific, Measurable, Attainable, Realistic, and Timed?

_____

_____

_____

_____

_____

_____

_____

_____

_____

_____

_____

_____

_____

_____

_____

_____

Do You Want Change?

Thought: *"I can be good for a while, but it never lasts so why try anymore"*

Lie: *"I was born damaged and it is my brokenness that makes me bad. Being good means I have to put on a mask to hide what is underneath. The mask always falls off so why even try."*

Before we go any further in this workbook, there is something I need to apologize for. I assumed we were on the same page. Pun intended. I assumed that you wanted to change things in your life. After identifying the things that have been happening in your life, either in your environment in the current moment, or what happened in the past, I assumed there were things that you saw that you did not like. Before we go on, I need to ask you what your thoughts are on this. Where I work, I see a lot of teens from a lot of different backgrounds, and they didn't all come with the same perspective in mind regarding changing their lives for the better.

Some of my patients, when we first met, would tell me not to waste my time; nothing was going to change so we might as well not even try. A common statement that I often heard residents make was, "I can be good for a while, but it never lasts so why try anymore." This always bothered me because being good is a very vague term, one which I have no idea the meaning. The term good is a state of being not a choice. There is a major difference. A person being good or bad makes me think of food. If food is bad, you throw it in the garbage because it will make you sick if you eat it. If food is good, then it is something that is either very delicious in taste or something that will provide your body with nutrition. To state that a person is either good or bad is like saying they are damaged or not.

By saying 'I can be' it is as if you're saying you have to act. Underneath the obvious words, what is sounds like you are really saying is, "I can fake being put-together for a period of time but then my mask comes off, and it all falls apart." This means you not only believe you are not good, meaning you believe you are damaged or broken, but you also believe that your actions and behaviors are not an outcome of choice but determined by how you were born. This would show that you believe you have to fake being good, meaning that eventually, the world is going to find out just how broken you really are.

If these beliefs are yours, then your lie has already defeated you. Once milk in my fridge goes bad, I can't do anything with it. I have no choice but to throw it away. The first evidence I can offer to you that will prove that people are neither good or bad is this; if that statement were true, then there would be no reason for this workbook. If a person is born bad and the only option was to simply give up because you cannot make something that is bad become good again, then there would be no point in offering a workbook to change the unchangeable. I don't know if you have noticed, but this is just the second chapter of this workbook leaving several more. I don't spend the rest of the workbook talking about how hopeless it is when people go bad. Therefore, it is obvious that people are not either good or bad, we are all born as imperfect beings, and our promise is this, we are all going to screw up somewhere along the lines. I have made mistakes in my life, and so has everyone else on this planet. You and me, we are in the same boat. Our mistakes may look different, but they are no worse or better than any other is.

When I had residents come to my office saying, "what's the point," I would always tell them they had two options. Continue to believe that they are born with something wrong with them, and they are damaged goods with no hope of ever having a better life or recognize that this is a lie, and start changing what you can control; your choices.

Truth: You were perfectly made. Your choices do not mean you are bad, just that you have made bad choices.

If you are sitting there asking yourself what is the point, then I want you to know that my arms are wrapped around your shoulders right now praising God that this workbook has made it into your hands because, brother or sister, I'm praying that God will use this book to set you free from this lie. Your choices do not determine who you are. Your choices are broken yes but, they are the result of your fears and insecurities, not you as a creation. You were not made broken, you were made perfect, but this world and some of its' brokenness have impacted your heart, leaving impressions on you that are still trying to bounce back.

I know you want things to be different. You look at your life, and you know this is not how it is meant to be. You and your mom are not supposed to be saying that you hate one another. Sneaking out in the middle of the night to go spend time at that party may be fun at the moment but, deep inside when you're alone, you know how it makes you feel. The rumors that get started because of where you were last weekend; the way you feel when you look at yourself in the mirror. If proud, loved, ecstatic, on fire, feeling exhilarated about life, is not how you feel, then my friend, something is wrong. Life is meant to be awesome, and you were created for such a purpose that is beyond your wildest dreams. Hold on tight because we are about to break you out of the prison you have been in for far too long. To jailbreak you, though, I need to give you some tools to remove the shackles you have voluntarily put around your mind.

First, let's identify what part of the change you are at. Before we do that I want to explain how "treatment" goes. For this workbook to be effective, you need three things: willingness, knowledge, and insight. Before we go on to the knowledge, which you will get, before we describe the act of having insight, we need first to find out if you are willing. You may have been dragging your feet all the way to where you are now, dreading opening up this book. You may have had someone buy it for you and strongly suggest you use it. You may have begrudgingly agreed. Either way, we need to assess where you are at in the process of change. To make change happen a person must first take an inventory of where they are at in their life, their job, their relationships, their legal situation if that applies, and decide if they are happy with how things are going so far. The primary areas I want you to look at are listed below, and if they don't apply to you then don't stress about it, just move on. If it does apply to you, then take a minute and ask yourself honestly if you are completely happy with how things are in that area. If there is anything that you do not like, no matter how trivial, or small, then the answer is "no," and there is no middle ground; it is either yes or no.

1. Are you 100% happy with all aspects of your relationships with your family? If not, what would you like to change?

_____

_____

_____

_____

_____

_____

_____

2. Are you 100% happy with your romantic relationships thus far? If not, what would you like to change?

_____

_____

_____

_____

_____

_____

_____

3. Are you 100% happy with your school situation, in the classroom, your grades, social interactions there? If not, what would you like to change?

_____

_____

_____

_____

_____

_____

4. Do you have a legal situation? If so, is this something you would want to change? Describe below.

_____

_____

_____

_____

_____

_____

5. Finally, are you happy with your reputation? What is your reputation currently and what would you like it to be? Remember: reputation builds your legacy.

_____
_____
_____
_____
_____
_____
_____

6. What do you believe is the right way to live and treat others around you?

_____
_____
_____
_____
_____
_____
_____
_____
_____
_____

7. Do your actions stand as proof of your beliefs as listed in question 6? If not, what do your actions say about your beliefs?

_____
_____
_____
_____
_____
_____
_____
_____
_____

Change: Where are you at?

I don't like how things are right now, but I don't know what I want instead • I want to change and I know what I want life to be like, I just don't know how to make it happen. • I want change, I know what I want, and I know what I need to do to make it happen. • I am actively working to achieve the change I want.

What stage of change are you in? <u>Stage One</u>: I don't like how things are right now, but I don't know what I want instead and I'm afraid of

62

trying for change. <u>Stage Two</u>: I don't like how life is, and I know what I would like life to be like instead. I just don't know how to get there. <u>Stage Three</u>: I don't like how life is, I know what I want instead, and I do know what I need to do to make it change. I'm just not doing it consistently yet. <u>Stage Four</u>: I don't like how life is right now. I do know what I want instead and I am actively doing the steps it takes to make change happen and I am maintaining change. Sometimes people are afraid of change because they are afraid of failing. Because of their fear of failing, they decide to either not try at all or to sabotage any hope they had in the first place. The first is referred to as ***self-fulfilling prophecy*** and the last is called a ***pre-emptive strike***.

The self-fulfilling prophecy is when a person believes they know for a fact that they are going to fail, or that something is going to happen, usually for the worse, and they give up. A self-fulfilling prophecy, believe it or not, is totally logical. If you know for a fact that you are not going to win the race, then just stop running right or just go ahead and sit down on the track and take a rest. When a person believes for a fact that they are going to fail, then there is no doubt, so it makes sense to save their effort, their energy, and their pride and just go ahead and give up. This one is all about saving face. You don't want to try and have everyone see you try and then fail.

If I go golfing, I know that I'm really bad at it, so I'm always nervous that when I go up to the golf ball and get ready to swing that I'm going to swing and miss the ball. What is better; refuse to swing at any of the holes and have 100% chance of losing and never get any better or, have 50% chance of winning and a 100% chance of improving if I try. Sure I may make myself look like the nube that I am, but at the end, I can choose to have tried and improved, even though I still lost.

The only way that this type of logic is, in fact, logical is if you could really know the future, which you cannot. My weatherman, though he is very good, can only predict the weather, but sometimes when he calls for snow, it rains instead. No matter how many signs point to the inevitability in your mind that you are going to fail and go back to your old behaviors, or that you mom is going to leave you like your father did, or that you are going to fail the test anyways, you still will never know for sure. This is your fear talking because these are the things you are afraid of. It may seem at the moment like the smart thing to do, give up before you lose so you can say "I didn't lose, I just didn't try." In the end, you lost anyways. You are afraid of losing, so you guarantee that future by giving up. That doesn't get you closer to your goal my friend, that gets you further from it. What is the worst that will happen? You will try and mess up, but in the end, you can say you tried and you can have learned something in the process that could make your next attempt successful.

Something I challenge you to do in this workbook is put aside your fear, your pride, and your insecurity. Those things will cause you to be okay with giving up, but I don't want you to give up. I want you to try and try and try again because you never know when that attempt will be the success. You may think you are not good enough and know that you are going to screw it all up, but I ask you...why? Those thoughts hold you back, and I beg you, don't let those fears cheat you of the future you were created for. Try, try, try and never give up no matter how grim the future may look. Some of the hardest times in life, the times you want to give up, are what you have to go through to get you to where you are supposed to be. You would not be here if you had given up when you were being faced with hardship. You never know, maybe what you are persevering through is what will get you to the other side, but if you give up, you will never know. Is fifty percent chance of incredible worth fighting for compared to one-hundred percent chance of guaranteed disappointment?

Preemptive Strike

A preemptive strike is a military term that refers to an event in which one person strikes before the other has a chance to. In battle, it would be like if the U.S is thinking that Russia is going to bomb us, so we bomb them first. Obviously, if we do this, then we could start a war, not to mention the number of lives that would be lost. In a relationship, the same type of fallout would occur. Let's say that you believe your girlfriend is going to cheat on you, so you go and cheat on her before she has the chance to. You believe your boyfriend is going to leave you, so you leave him first. You believe your father is going to give up on you, so you give up on him and refuse to give him a chance.

This type of behavior occurs as the result of a great deal of faulty thinking and self-talk based on fear and insecurity which fuels the beliefs to be so strong. Stepping outside of the situation, you can see that this is silly. It is a response that causes what you fear to be reality. You literally make it happen because of your fear. Are you banging your head against the wall yet at how crazy this is because I cannot tell you how many times I have seen people act with a pre-emptive strike and even tell me about it, justifying what they did. After they got done telling me this elaborate story as to why they acted this way, I would repeat it back to them, and then they would be banging their own head against the wall. (Figuratively of course.) So let's take a moment to process. Grab a cup of tea or coffee and let's explore.

8. What have you learned about a Self-Fulfilling Prophecy?

_____
_____
_____
_____
_____
_____
_____
_____

9. In what ways have, you acted on a Self-Fulfilling Prophecy?

_____
_____
_____
_____
_____

10. What was the outcome?

_____
_____
_____
_____
_____
_____

11. What could have happened had you not acted on a Self-Fulfilling Prophecy?

_____
_____
_____
_____

12. What have you learned about a Preemptive Strike?

_____
_____
_____
_____
_____
_____

13. In what ways have, you acted with a preemptive strike?

_____
_____
_____
_____
_____
_____

14. What was the outcome?

_____
_____
_____
_____
_____
_____

15. What could have happened had you not acted with a preemptive strike?

_____
_____
_____
_____
_____

Insight

In the activity above, you spent time to discuss what your environment was like and you processed how that has impacted you thus far. You have processed this hopefully with your support person and your support person no doubt has encouraged you to gain in your level of what we call insight. What the heck is that you ask? _Insight simply means that you have been able to look inside yourself, beyond the surface level and have a new understanding as to why you feel the way you do or why you have reacted to a situation the way you did._ An example of levels of insight would be as follows:

You go to talk to your mom one night about some things that were happening at school with your friends that bothered you and your mom hurriedly says as she is juggling your flailing little sister that she cannot talk right now, can she check in with you later. Later comes, but Mom never does. You get angry and later that night when she asks you if you got your homework done. You angrily spout out, "yes". She corrects you for your attitude and a lovely fight ensues.

So what really happened here?

Level 1: I was angry.

I got angry because Mom takes the time to ask about my stupid homework, but doesn't care about what I want to talk about. She just cares about stupid crap and doesn't really care about me.

Level 2: Let's get deeper people!

Anger is what we call a 'secondary' emotion meaning it is an emotion that we feel in response to first feeling another emotion, the 'primary' emotion. Therefore, anger was the secondary emotion that I felt in response to first feeling forgotten, unimportant and that my mom doesn't understand me.

Level 3: Oh how low can you go...how low can you go...

I know that Mom loves me and does care about me, I was just coming at a bad time, and she got caught up and distracted. She may have forgotten to check in with me later about our conversation, but that does not mean she forgot about me. I guess it just really bothered me because my mom and I haven't had much time together just the two of us since my little sister was born.

Level 4: Oh man...now we're getting somewhere.

Now you start to process how you miss your mom and really just want more time together. You and your support person begin to process ways you can comfortably share this with your mom to improve your interactions in the future as well as ways to communicate at the moment before the fiasco fight takes place.

This is the goal, but it takes effort and a great deal of trust in your support person to process to a deeper level than the surface. The reason insight is so important is that you cannot solve anything in this workbook without it. I cannot stress to you enough that unless you are willing at some point or another to take an honest look into your heart and mind to understand more than just the behaviors, you will never see real change. You will see superficial, short-term change but nothing lasting. Real change is from the inside-out, not the outside-in. People try to act right or get it together, but it never will be until you get to the source. If you think of change like this, maybe it will help.

Imagine this picturesque scene at a beach. Now picture that as you are laying out your beach towel getting ready to head into the waves. You expectantly dip your toes in the water ready to feel relaxed and soothed, but instead, you feel sticky. Oil is mixed with the water, and as you look up and out to sea, you can see that it is covering the once pristine beach with it destructive ooze. They bring in crews for days and clean up the surface of the oil but no matter how much they fight, they come back to the beach, and it is covered again and again, day after day. People start to look around for a ship that wrecked and is leaking, but no one can find the source.

Finally, someone suggests getting divers to go down deeper and deeper below the surface to see if there is a source below. As they get deeper and deeper into the water they find a leak in an oil pipeline. They bring out a crew and dive deep to repair the damage. This time they clean the surface of the sea and even though there is still occasionally residue that finds its' way to shore, the oil starts to disappear and over time the beach returns to its' once pristine scene where thousands of people now come to enjoy the waves and soak up the sun.

Insight

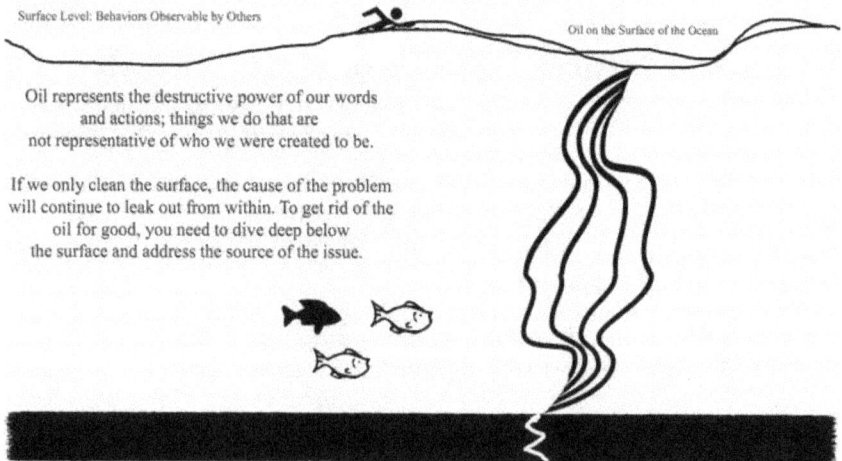

Surface Level: Behaviors Observable by Others

Oil on the Surface of the Ocean

Oil represents the destructive power of our words and actions; things we do that are not representative of who we were created to be.

If we only clean the surface, the cause of the problem will continue to leak out from within. To get rid of the oil for good, you need to dive deep below the surface and address the source of the issue.

16. What does the oil represent? Apply this to you.

_____

_____

_____

_____

_____

17. What is the ocean representing?

_____

_____

_____

_____

_____

18. The act of having insight is represented by what?

_____

_____

_____

_____

19. Why did it not work when the crews cleaned the surface before they had found the sunken ship?

_____

_____

_____

_____

_____

_____

20. Apply this analogy to yourself? How is the idea of real changing being an inside-out approach displayed in this analogy?

_____

_____

_____

_____

_____

_____

_____

Coping Skills

Supplementary Reading: Job 1:13-22, Job 2:11-13; 2 Corinthians 12:7-10

Have you ever heard the word "cope" before? The word means to handle effectively, something that is difficult and in the origination of the word through history; it is referenced in battle, as in to meet in battle. Battle is a very dangerous and traumatizing place, and for the word cope to be referenced in that situation sheds some light as to its' importance. In our situation you will hear it used as a verb, to cope with something difficult, and also as, a coping skill. A coping skill can really be anything on the planet. You have used a lot of coping skills already and maybe didn't know you were using them. Let us go down the list: drugs, alcohol, food, and prescription medications are used as coping skills in our society quiet often. So is coffee, the television, social media, when your mom calls your aunt, when you walk away from your sister, and when you go hide in your bedroom and close the door turning your Ipod up as loud as the earbuds will allow. Those are all used as coping skills. Shocked yet? Well, like many things in our society, some things may be used as a coping skill but that does not mean they are in fact an effective coping skill. Drugs are extremely effective at distracting a person from their problems. If they were not effective then millions of people would not be using them world-wide. However they are not effective coping skills.

An effective coping skill has two purposes; first to allow you to be distracted and remove yourself from the stressor and second to allow you to return to the problem for resolution after you have thought through the situation calmly. The first part is easy; all of the examples of common so-called coping skills meet the first requirement, but the second weeds out almost all of them. Running on a treadmill or working out at the gym are considered effective coping skills, but they can only be an effective coping skill if they allow you to calmly and rationally return to the stressor in your mind or physically, to resolve the issue. Not all coping skills are created equally either. For example, I love hot cocoa. If you ask anyone in my family, if I have my John Wayne coffee mug and it is full of hot cocoa, then I have had a very emotional or stressful day, and I need some quiet time with my cocoa mug. If the little hotel "do not disturb" signs could be hung on a person, then that is mine. It means I need some

> *An effective coping skill has two purposes; first to allow you to be distracted and remove yourself from the stressor and second to allow you to return to the problem for resolution after you have thought through the situation calmly.*

space; I am coping right now! This is a coping skill for me because it first gives me some space, is comforting to me, and it allows me to calmly and rationally think about what is bothering me so that I can work myself through it using the Four Pillars. Then, in my mind or in person, I return to the situation that bothered me to find resolution or alter my perception of it. However, this is not a coping skill I can do in the midst of the stressor.

If my job is working in a restaurant and I just had a particularly difficult customer, do you think my boss is going to let me go in the midst of Sunday rush to have my "hot cocoa break"? I don't think so. So in the midst of that trigger, so I don't lose my job for responding how I want to at the moment, I have to employ some "hold me over" kind of coping skills that I refer to as Universal Coping Skills. **Universal coping skills** are coping skills as defined above, but the difference is that these do not require you to leave the situation or to use anything. Here are some examples: meditation, visualization, deep breathing, repeating positive statements in your mind.

The Bible is an amazing place to teach you how to cope with difficult situations, and in some of the situations the individuals found themselves in, it was like being in the midst of battle. For example in the book of Job he loses his entire family, all of his livestock which would represent his money and his farm. He goes on to lose his health. I mean the man is sitting here with his children dead, his house caved in, and he loses his livelihood, and his response is to say (Job 1:21 NLT) *I came naked from my mother's womb, and I will be stripped of everything when I die. The Lord gave me everything I had, and the Lord has taken it away. Praise the name of the Lord!* In the midst of tragedy he gives praise to God, and then he mourns with his three friends. Praise in the original meaning in Greek and Hebrew means to celebrate, to have thanksgiving, to adore God and worship Him and revere Him.

Later in the Bible, you read about a man named Paul. Paul's story is that he is in and out of prison for preaching to people that Jesus loves them. Paul was often beaten, starved, and the target of much criticism by many of those around him. In the midst of great danger to his life, not to mention his spirit, he praises God saying he is happy about his struggles because when he is weak then God has the opportunity to be strong for him and use Paul's struggle to show others how God can provide and work miracles in hopeless situations; such a powerful statement. Study the scriptures from the beginning of the chapter with your support person and process them. There is no better example of seeking God in the midst of tragedy than this. It is in these moments that, what psychologist like to call CBT, is used to find a different perspective on the situation than what is expected in our society and labeled as normal.

Let's take a break, talk to your support person, and identify some coping skills before we continue.

1. What are Universal Coping Skills?

_____

_____

_____

2. What is the difference in effective and ineffective coping skills?

_____

_____

_____

_____

_____

3. Identify 5 of the ineffective coping skills you use to use.

_____

_____

_____

4. Identify 5 effective coping skills you can or have been using.

_____

_____

_____

_____

_____

5. Identify 10 Universal Coping skills.

_____

_____

_____

_____

_____

_____

_____

_____

_____

Further Thoughts

Chapter III The Four Pillars

Ephesians 1: 18-23 Updated American Standard Version (UASV)

[18] having the eyes of your heart enlightened, that you may know what is the hope to which he has called you, what are the riches of the glory of his inheritance in the holy ones, [19] and what the surpassing greatness of his power is toward us believers. It is according to the working of the strength of his might [20] which he brought about in Christ, when he raised him from the dead and seated him at his right hand in the heavenly places, [21] far above all rule and authority and power and dominion, and every name that is named, not only in this age but also in the one to come. [22] And he put all things in subjection under his feet, and gave him as head over all things to the congregation,[20] [23] which is his body, the fullness of him who fills up all things in all.

1:18–23. Specifically, Paul prays that we might comprehend:

- our hope

- our riches

- God's power

Our **hope** is built on the promises which are ours in Christ. We need to know our spiritual future is based on the promises of God and find strength and courage in that hope to live in the present. To understand and embrace that hope in present living requires spiritual progress.

Paul also wants us to know our future **riches.** It is tempting to focus on our present need and poverty. Instead Paul challenges us to focus on what God has promised. These riches may refer to our present spiritual riches in Christ in being freed from sin and made ready for fellowship with God. They may also refer to our heavenly possession of the riches and glories of God. It's likely both aspects are meant. Such riches are part of our **inheritance.**

Finally, Paul prays that we might be enlightened to comprehend the magnitude of God's **power** which he exercised in bringing us our salvation. The power God demonstrated in raising Christ from the dead and placing him above all creation is the same power he is exercising toward us to bring about the blessings which he has promised us. Such power guarantees we will receive the hope and riches. That power is also available to us to make the hope and riches the focus of present life so

---

[20] Gr *ekklesia* ("assembly")

that we live God's way and not the world's, seeking God's inheritance and not the world's.[21]

A Quick Look:

- Four Pillars of Cognitive Behavioral Therapy, a tool to understand stressors and interactions that are the total of several separate interactions making one major struggle in a person's life.

- Four Pillars: Self Talk, Faulty Beliefs, Perception, Behaviors, and Outcomes that reinforce the cycle.

- Faulty Beliefs come from *fear and insecurity, assumptions, and justification.* They are lies we say to ourselves to protect ourselves from the truth which can often be scary.

Supplemental Assignments:

- Keep a thoughts journal. One of the best ways to understand how your thoughts lead to your feelings and behaviors is to capture a glimpse of what your 40,000 daily thoughts look like. Do you think on things that are encouraging, or do you think on things that are defeating? Take one week and document in a journal what your thoughts were, at least ten thoughts, before or after every meal for seven days.

The Four Pillars

A Cognitive-Behavioral Tool

Do you remember how in the introduction I discussed with you that some stressors are from our *external* environment (happening around us right now) and some stressors are *internal* (they had happened around us and have left impressions on us)? This tool is one that will help you understand how both of those stressors over time have brought struggle to your life in various forms. In order to do that, you have to use everything I have taught you up until this point to be able to use this tool effectively. Most importantly, this tool requires you to have insight, so if you are still struggling with that, I encourage you to go back to Chapter 1 and review the worksheets. If you feel like you are getting pretty good at having insight, then let's get started. *The four pillars are Self Talk, Faulty Beliefs, Perceptions, and our Behaviors, followed by an opportunity to process how the outcomes led to the self-talk becoming stronger.*

---

[21] Max Anders, *Galatians-Colossians*, vol. 8, Holman New Testament Commentary (Nashville, TN: Broadman & Holman Publishers, 1999), 94.

Before you can use this tool in its' entirety, you need to understand that this is a cycle, which means that one pillar builds into the next one, and the behaviors, and our environments' reactions to our behaviors reinforce, or strengthen our self-talk. If you are to change any part of this cycle, you have to start at the base, the self-talk, because from that comes everything else and your beliefs are reinforced by the outcomes of your behaviors and choices. Your behavior is the only thing that is seen by others, not your thoughts or beliefs, but your thoughts and beliefs control your behaviors. Self-talk is the place to start making a change, and our thinking occurs in our minds. On average, an individual has 40,000 thoughts per day. What is found in those 40,000 thoughts will control everything else you do in your life; how you feel and how you act. Do you know how you use those thoughts? Do you use them to build yourself up and your situation? Alternatively, do you use them to break yourself and your situation down? We all struggle with doubts and with fears. Nevertheless, how much of your 40,000 daily thoughts do you devote to your doubts, fears, and insecurities?

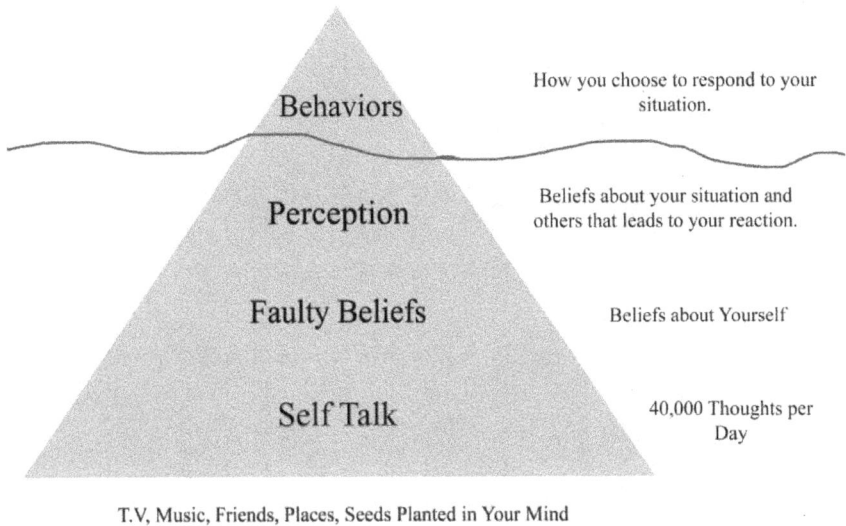

Behaviors	How you choose to respond to your situation.
Perception	Beliefs about your situation and others that leads to your reaction.
Faulty Beliefs	Beliefs about Yourself
Self Talk	40,000 Thoughts per Day

T.V, Music, Friends, Places, Seeds Planted in Your Mind

Think of it this way; imagine that there are two sides to you, one side that is selfish seeking only to get whatever you can out of those around you in the easiest way possible, and the other side of you that seeks to love and genuinely care for those around you. Both have equal opportunity to have power over you, but if you fix your thoughts on things that are only serving to yourself and you disregard the needs of others, which side of you are you feeding? It is a simple fact that the more something is fed, the stronger it will become, so that when it comes down to battle for who will control you, the selfish side of you versus the selfless side, the one that you fed most will win.

Obviously, if I were to ask you what your self-talk is on any given day, I don't expect you to list all 40,000, even if you were able to. Although I would be interested to see if you were able to; that would be phenomenal. No, I want you to think about a specific topic that has been a problem for a long time in your life. Think of a struggle that you have had for a long period of time such as the problems you have at school, the struggles you have with your mom or dad, the lack of relationship with any authority figure, or that you feel you have no one. Identify your topic and then we will go from there.

What is your topic or problem behavior?

_____

What is your self-talk in regards to that problem or topic?

_____
_____
_____
_____
_____
_____

How often do you have self- talk like this? Give me a percentage out of 100%.

_____

You did a great job. Push yourself and make sure you are being honest. It is easy to cheat yourself and not share what your deepest, scariest thoughts are. Trust me, there is no judgement. No one is going to look over your shoulder and freak out. We have all had had terrible thoughts about ourselves or others at one point or another. It is a struggle we all have to go through. You are not alone in this. I promise.

Faulty beliefs are the outcome of what you invested your thoughts in. If you have a jar, and you categorize your thoughts into each jar, faulty beliefs would be the jars that you put your individual thoughts into. It is the belief that those thoughts build. Over time you build a habit of thinking; like dirt roads that become interstates. At first, that thought is going solo, having been the original one either introduced by someone who said something to you, or any number of introductions. That first thought is the trailblazer, but over time as you have more and more, that path goes from a dirt path in your mind to an eight-lane highway where thoughts just zoom by, building and solidifying that belief. This is a tough section in the Four Pillars because now you have to think about the beliefs you hold regarding yourself and the environment as a result of your thoughts, and then I ask you to challenge them. This may sound easy, but if you believe something to be true, how do you separate what you believe to be true from the real truth?

What are your faulty beliefs or the lies you buy into?

_____

_____

_____

_____

_____

_____

Now we take it one step further. The way we believe about ourselves impacts how we see our situation. This is when we discuss what our perception is. Our perception is the way we view the world around us. Elton John did a song about wearing rose colored glasses and how his glasses shade the world. If you think of your perception as the glasses or filter, the color of your glasses will shade your view just like a filter will determine how you interpret the things around you. This is exactly how perception works, like a filter deciding what you will focus in on and what you will be blinded to. If faulty beliefs are your beliefs about yourself and your actions, then perception is your overall viewpoint about others, the world, and your situation.

What is your perception of the topic you chose to look at?

_____

_____

_____

_____

_____

_____

_____

This brings us to the final pillar; Behaviors. This is the easiest of all the pillars because it is surface level and requires no insight, just list what you do. Think specifically about the topic that you have identified to discuss. The final step in the four pillars is about knowing how the outcome of your behaviors reinforce, or make your self-talk and faulty beliefs even stronger. Discuss this in the questions below and then compare what you have completed, to the example below.

What are your behaviors regarding the topic you chose?

_____
_____
_____
_____
_____
_____
_____
_____

What was the outcome of those choices?

_____
_____
_____
_____
_____
_____
_____

How did the outcome reinforce, or prove to you what you had thought to be truth?

_____
_____
_____
_____
_____
_____
_____

Questions you have for support person?

_____
_____
_____
_____
_____
_____
_____
_____
_____

Example of Four Pillars in Use

Topic: Having sex with numerous partners not caring about where when or who.

Self-Talk: I've got the reputation already so why not. That's all I'm good for anyway. No guy is ever going to care about me really. Not even my parents care about me or who I am so why would anyone else. This world operates on what you can provide and what you have to do to get ahead. The only way he will love me is if I give him what he wants. Everyone will laugh at me anyways if I don't. I'm not a prude like those goody-two-shoes. It's just about having fun. It's not that big of a deal. Everyone is doing it so it must not be that bad.

Faulty Beliefs: I need the acceptance of others to feel okay with myself. I have nothing good about me except the value others place on me. If the world says it is okay to do, then it must be.

Perception: The world will judge you by what you can offer it, and if you are not able to offer much then you are not worth much. Your worth is determined by others thoughts of you so you have to make them believe you are worth a lot by acting and proving you can do what others cannot or will not do. No one really cares in the end.

Behaviors: You will be in constant competition with all of your peers, primarily female peers because you weigh your worth on physical attractiveness and capabilities. Those that have gifts that you don't have are competitors, so you will always look at others in a comparing manner. You will offer your body to others to win over their allegiance to you and be hurt and feel rejected and not good enough when they leave. Behaviors: Promiscuity (sex with multiple partners), gossip, bully, defy authority figures, no respect for myself or others.

Outcome: You will never feel fulfilled and feel exhausted because you cannot do everything since we all have our own talents, but you want them all, so you will feel worthless and never good enough. You will be abandoned by all of those whom you have had physical unions with because they will sense your insecurity and your drive to be better will never allow you just to relax and enjoy being yourself. This will cause a great deal of drama with superficial relationships that will leave you feeling like there is something wrong with you. This will only fuel your beliefs that you are not lovable and not good enough leading to a continuation of these behaviors if you do not challenge these lies with the truth.

Disclaimer: I'm sure many of you can identify with this, but the good news is...it is all based on lies, and none of it is true. You are worthy, you are good enough, and you are made perfectly so you don't have to win anyone over. One who loved you before you were even a thought made you; He loved you knowing what would become of your life and what all of your choices would be. He knew it all and still spread His arms on the cross for you.

One thing that may help you is to understand what I mean when I refer to faulty beliefs. I mean the lies you believe about yourself and your world. Faulty beliefs also known as thinking errors or lies. I don't care what you call them; just know that they are typically based on one or all of these three things: our fears and insecurities, assumptions, or justification. It is one or a combination of these three things that typically drives our behavior and so often backfires in our face. It is what drives us to do the illogical, even though at the moment it sounded like the best thing to do. Have you ever had that moment? That moment when you thought that what you were doing was going to cause a certain outcome, but it did the exact opposite of what you wanted. I did a group therapy session on this very thing in fact. I asked the kids to recognize those moments when they use their behaviors to communicate instead of their words, and it backfired. Confusing right, well that is typically what people think when others use their actions to express something instead of using their words. It leaves people confused.

Examples of this would be when you had a really bad day at school, so you come home and are really mopey. You go to your room and blare your scream-o music and sulk throughout the house dropping hints with your behavior that you had a bad day, hoping someone will notice and ask you what happened. When no one asks you about it, you get upset thinking that it just proves what you knew, no one cares. Then your feelings are hurt. That makes you angry, so you go into the kitchen with a bit more force behind your steps, and when your mom asks how your day was you get angry at her and say with a slight tinge of sarcasm, "It was fine, nice of you to finally ask." Your mom picks up on the attitude and calls you out for it. This creates the beginning of an argument where both of you will end having hurt feelings. Any of this sound familiar? The problem with trying to communicate by dropping hints is that no one knows what your hints mean, and instead of just talking about it everyone makes assumptions and acts on their assumptions, including you.

Being on the outside of that scenario, it is easy to see how the argument arises and how to prevent it, but we have all been in a situation similar to that. Imagine how many arguments would be cleared up if people would do more communicating instead of just talking. There is a major difference. We talk, talk, talk all day long but rarely do we actually communicate meaningful information. That would be too scary right? Fear has a good habit of making us think that if we talk about what is real, people will reject us and we don't ever say what we really want to. There are a lot of faulty beliefs that come from fear and insecurity, assumption, or justification. My favorites are *jumping to conclusion, that doesn't apply to me, emotional reasoning, personalization, labeling, should or must, mental filter, over-generalizing, magnification, and all or nothing.*

Jumping to conclusions has two parts; first, it is mind-reading and the second is telling the future. There are a lot of times when we think we know what another person is thinking, so we react to what we assume they are thinking instead of just asking to be sure. In other cases, we think we know the future, like when you said you were going to mess up and everything would be ruined; yeah you were being a fortune-teller in that one because you didn't really know if you would mess up. You assumed you would, and therefore you did. You can't know unless you try and who knows, sometimes our mistakes end up being the best thing that happened to us. God has a way of making the direst of situations into our best life story. People make movies of those moments because they leave us in awe of how such a hopeless situation could be made to bring so much life and joy to people. I don't know what walk of life you may be coming from, but I do know this; you were meant for amazing things. The junk you're dealing with right now may seem like you are drowning, but hold tight because this may just be the moment you are grateful for later. Once you reach the other side, you may look back and thank God you went through it because you wouldn't have the knowledge, the people, the love, or the closeness to God that you have now if you hadn't experienced that struggle.

List how you have jumped to conclusions by fortune telling or mind reading in the past and describe how the situation would have been different if you had challenged this belief?

_____

_____

_____

_____

_____

That doesn't apply to me is a faulty belief that describes entitlement. Entitlement is when we believe we deserve things and shouldn't have to work to earn them; things like freedom, trust, privacy, and respect. A lot of times what fuels this faulty belief is the thought that because of what you have experienced, how you have been taught, or what you have gone through, permits you to act or do things that you know is wrong. This type of thought keeps a victim a victim and will prevent a victim from becoming a survivor. Wondering what I mean by that statement? Let me explain myself before you smack me.

A victim becomes a survivor by accepting what happened to them to make them a victim at one point but becomes a survivor by deciding not to allow what happened to define them. A Survivor decides instead to allow it to make them stronger and drive them to even more fully pursue God's purpose in their life. A victim remains a victim when they let what happened to them hold them hostage to the incident for years. I'll apologize for this example ahead of time, but it is the hardest example that I have seen in my experience. Because I was sexually abused, I have the right to touch or do to whomever, whatever I want. Because I was hit, I can hit. Because you cursed at me, I can curse whoever I want. Because they stole from me, I can steal from you. Not only does the victim never become a survivor, but the victim ends up becoming the villain. This is probably one of the hardest faulty beliefs to overcome because you think you have the right to act in a certain way and refuse to recognize, until now hopefully, that you are creating a situation in which you remain the victim, if not becoming the perpetrator.

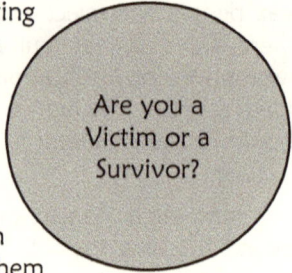

List how you have operated on this faulty belief in the past and describe how the situation would have been different if you had challenged this belief?

_____
_____
_____
_____
_____
_____

Emotional reasoning is when you believe that how you feel about a situation is the reality of the situation regardless of reason or logic. Here is an example, because I feel like I made a fool of myself, then I am a fool, or because I feel like the situation is hopeless then it must be. If you struggled with depression, suicidal ideations, or self-harm, then you likely struggle with this faulty belief regularly. It is a belief that will quickly spiral out of control because at its' base is your emotional state controlling your thoughts and your perceptions. We all have experienced the tide of our emotions. If your reaction to a situation is based on your emotional state, then it will be difficult to predict how you will respond to any given scenario since we all have ups and downs. This faulty belief only highlights those emotional ups and downs and will make them more severe.

84

List how you have operated on this faulty belief in the past and describe how the situation would have been different if you had challenged this belief?

_____

_____

_____

_____

_____

Personalization is another lie that has two different directions in which it can go; blaming others or blaming yourself. This is a faulty belief that you employ to keep either yourself from having to accept accountability for your actions or to prevent others from having to accept accountability. In one hand you either refuse to face the fact that you made a mistake, or you want to take the blame for another's actions to save others from having to face their mistakes. You either will be walked all over or you will be the one walking all over others. In either case, this will cause a lot of problems in your relationships and ultimately prevent you from going to God. It is when we recognize our mistakes that we can truly appreciate the sacrifice of Christ when he died for us. If we take the blame for another then we prevent them from accepting and learning from their own mistake. Eventually, this will lead to resentment and an unequal relationship with one person taking all the blame and the other being perfect, which is not reality or truth.

List how you have operated on this faulty belief in the past and describe how the situation would have been different if you had challenged this belief?

_____

_____

_____

_____

_____

Labeling is an easy one; you simply assign a label to yourself such as "I am _____". You fill in the blank with whatever it is that you regularly call yourself. What is bad about this one? Do you live in a box? Can one word define you? I don't know about you but, one word cannot define me. The God of the universe made you and considers you His most precious creation for which He is most proud. Do you really think that one word can define us? You cannot be summed up by saying you are stupid or whatever else it is you say in that blank space. By assigning a label to yourself, you put yourself in a box and limit yourself from achieving all the other things God has planned for you. You prevent hope from entering the situation much like saying, "I'm damaged", or, "I'm bad".

List how you have operated on this faulty belief in the past and describe how the situation would have been different if you had challenged this belief?

_____

_____

_____

_____

_____

_____

Should or Must to me is one that can plague a person when they have made a mistake. If you have had thoughts that surround saying, "I should have done better," or, "If I only had done that instead; I should have known better," then you have struggled with this faulty belief. This is a huge tool of faulty thinking that will keep you trapped in a cycle of shame. This is where I introduce to you that there is a difference between shame and guilt. Shame and guilt is often an area where we will find ourselves under attack not only of our own assaults making us feel less worthy, but also attacks from the enemy. Bottom-line, you are human and you are going to make mistakes. We are inherently born with the struggle of free-will which means we will make mistakes by choosing the wrong path from time to time, we must accept that as a fact. However we can still strive to be better and to learn from our mistakes; to aspire to be something more than we are. Shame will tell you that you are the problem, whereas guilt will tell you that what you did was the problem. There is a huge difference. These are four steps to overcome mistakes we have made and prevent our guilt from becoming shame.

1. What needs to be changed in our lives that are causing the problem, or the mistakes we are making?

2. Have empathy for those whom you have wronged with the mistakes and choices you have made and listen so you can validate the pain you may have caused .

3. Apologize for the mistakes you have made, genuinely striving never to make the same mistake twice.

4. Start making a plan to change and be willing to let them hold you accountable to keep you on the right track toward maintaining change.

Healthy Relationship	V.S.	Unhealthy Relationship
Give & Take		Give or Take
Both Members Benefit Mutually		Only One Memeber Benefits

Shame is a Me, Me, Me perspective in which you make a mistake, feel bad for the mistake and then make statements of shame, beating yourself up. You call yourself names and maybe even self-harm, forcing those that you have hurt to put aside their own pain from what you have done and feel the urge to comfort you because of the things you do or say to yourself. Eventually, they will resent you for this and become exhausted having nothing left to give. Let me give you an example of what this looks like. You get angry because your mom is telling you that you will be grounded if you go to the party. This argument escalates into a fight in which you get physically aggressive with her. You punch her in the face, and in seeing how hurt she is as a result of your actions, you break down and start calling yourself names and you go to your room and self-harm or make suicidal statements.

Maybe you even start to do things to sabotage your future because you keep repeating how bad you are since you punched your mom. Your mom loves you and hates to see you breaking down so badly, so she ignores the fact that you have just broken her nose, maybe for the first time or maybe the tenth, and she comes beside you and tells you how much she loves you and cares for you, begging you to stop beating yourself up. You were the one in the wrong, the person who was hurt is now comforting the person who did the hurting. Over time, as this cycle repeats and repeats and repeats, mom gets tired of comforting the one who continues to hurt her and becomes calloused to the self-harm and suicidal statements. You start to get angry at mom saying she does not love you and doesn't care about you. Mom doubts herself and doesn't know what the right way to act is and becomes exhausted. You both end up being on the losing end, and the relationship is damaged.

List how you have operated on this faulty belief in the past and describe how the situation would have been different if you had challenged this belief instead?

_____
_____
_____
_____
_____
_____

Process how this example applies to your life and what you have learned from it.

_____
_____
_____
_____
_____
_____
_____
_____
_____
_____
_____
_____
_____
_____
_____
_____
_____

Mental Filter is a faulty belief in which you choose only to see what will prove your statement, but you refuse to see anything else. An example would be if I say, "I don't like what you did, but I will always love you," and you only hear, "I don't like you". It is taking words out of the sentence that you want to hear to prove your case and solidify what you have already assumed to be true, yet it is not what is said. If you are struggling with this, maybe the best thing you can do is wait until you can come to a point where you can actually hear what is being said, or see what is really going on and not take things out of context.

List how you have operated on this faulty belief in the past and describe how the situation would have been different if you had challenged this belief?

_____

_____

_____

_____

_____

Over generalizing would be when you take a single incident and over-generalize to say that it applies to all situations. For example, I am blonde so if I were to be rude to you and you were to respond by saying that every blonde you ever meet will act the same way I did. I doubt you would ever do that because that example sounds ridiculous right? This example sounds a little less ridiculous. "The last time I tried to talk to you about this you were busy; you're always busy." Hint: when you see always or never, it is likely a statement in which you are over-generalizing.

List how you have operated on this faulty belief in the past and describe how the situation would have been different if you had challenged this belief instead?

_____

_____

_____

_____

_____

Magnification and Minimization are two opposites. Magnification is when you take something that is really small into make a huge situation. The old saying, turn a mole-hill into a mountain is an example of this. The other side of it is minimization, when something that really is a big deal, being turned into nothing. "Oh I just tried to get them fired, it was their fault, they stole my parking spot, it is not a big deal, they totally deserved it."

List how you have operated on this faulty belief in the past and describe how the situation would have been different if you had challenged this belief instead?

_____

_____

_____

_____

_____

_____

Finally, we come to All or Nothing. All or nothing is all about extremes. It is when we say that we either get everything that we want, or nothing at all. If I don't get an A on this assignment, then I may as well fail the class. Get the idea? This is seeing the situation as if there are only extremes and refusing to see the progress in effort or small wins, even if it is not the big win.

List how you have operated on this faulty belief in the past and describe how the situation would have been different if you had challenged this belief instead?

_____

_____

_____

_____

_____

_____

Process Questions:

1. What are the Four Pillars and what do they mean?

    _____

    _____

    _____

    _____

    _____

    _____

2. What is required of the individual using the Four Pillars if the tool is to be successful?

    _____

3. What are the three things Faulty Beliefs are always based on?

    _____ & _____

    _____

    _____

4. What are your top 5 Faulty Beliefs and what fuels these beliefs, be it past experiences, situations, or statements?

_____

_____

_____

_____

_____

_____

_____

_____

_____

_____

_____

Do some practice four pillars on the major problems in your life.

Four Pillars Assignment on this Chapter's Topic

Self-Talk (40,000 individual thoughts summarized)

_____

_____

_____

_____

_____

_____

_____

_____

Faulty Beliefs (Beliefs about yourself and your situation as a result of your thoughts.)

_____

_____

_____

_____

_____

_____

_____

_____

Perception (The faulty beliefs about your environment as a result of your faulty beliefs about yourself and your environments)

_____

_____
_____
_____
_____
_____

Behaviors (What you choose to do)

_____

_____
_____
_____
_____
_____

Finally, identify the outcome and how it reinforces the self-talk.

_____

_____
_____
_____
_____

Four Pillars Assignment on this Chapter's Topic

Self-Talk (40,000 individual thoughts summarized)

_____

_____
_____
_____
_____
_____

Faulty Beliefs (Beliefs about yourself and your situation as a result of your thoughts.)

_____

_____
_____
_____
_____
_____

Perception (The faulty beliefs about your environment as a result of your faulty beliefs about yourself and your environments)

_____
_____
_____
_____
_____
_____

Behaviors (What you choose to do)

_____
_____
_____
_____
_____
_____

Finally, identify the outcome and how it reinforces the self-talk.

_____
_____
_____
_____
_____
_____
_____
_____
_____
_____

Further Thoughts

_____
_____
_____
_____
_____
_____
_____
_____

Section II Preparing for War

Mathew 13:19 Updated American Standard Version (UASV)

¹⁹ When anyone hears the word of the kingdom and does not understand it, the wicked one comes and snatches away what has been sown in his heart. This is the one on whom seed was sown alongside the road.

In order to know how to fight for control over your mind, you must first understand how you lost control and who you are fighting, in an effort to get it back. This battle is about more than just "happy" thoughts.

Let us talk Truth vs. Deceit.

13:18–19. These verses connect Jesus' explanation of the parable of the sower and the soils (13:18–23) with the disciples' privilege as hearers of the truth. Jesus was saying to them. "Because you have responded to what you have already seen with eyes, ears, and hearts of faith and humble obedience, I will show you even more. You have proven faithful with little, so I will trust you with much."

Jesus identified the **seed** as **the message about the kingdom**—its arrival in Jesus and the way to participate in this kingdom. The "message about the kingdom" is probably identical to the "good news of the kingdom" in 4:23; 9:35. 24:14.

The soils were the issue. Throughout the parable's explanation, Jesus compared the four kinds of soil with various kinds of people who had been exposed to his teaching. The first soil, that "along the path" (13:4), was packed and hardened by traffic. It represented the person who **does not understand** the word he had heard. The person represented by the hardened soil is one who chooses not to understand rather than a person who wants to understand but cannot. Such a person may actually understand Jesus' teaching in a literal sense but refuse to accept its truth. The biblical concept of "understanding" goes beyond the idea of mental comprehension. It sometimes includes volitional acceptance. In 21:45, the chief priests and Pharisees knew the meaning of Jesus' parable concerning them, but they refused to accept its truth.

The person who refuses to accept the word of God will fall victim to the **evil one** (Satan, represented by the birds in 13:4), who **comes and snatches away what was sown in his heart**. If given even the slightest opportunity, Satan and his evil forces—archenemies of the kingdom of God—are able to remove or distort the truth, thus making that person even less likely to accept the truth in the future. This is one manifestation of the principle Jesus taught in 12:30: "He who is not with me is against me." To refuse to accept his word is to move away from him. There can be no objective neutrality.

Many people who were exposed to the words and works of the Messiah (especially the religious leaders) fell into this category. They rejected him without any second thoughts.[22]

Set The Mood Music:

Skillet - Invincible

[22] Stuart K. Weber, *Matthew*, vol. 1, Holman New Testament Commentary (Nashville, TN: Broadman & Holman Publishers, 2000), 195–196.

Chapter IV Where Do You Stand?

Haggai 1:5-6 Updated American Standard Version (UASV)

[5] Now therefore, thus says Jehovah of armies,[23] '**Set your heart on your ways**. [6] You have sown much, and harvested little. You have sown much seed, but you harvest little. You eat, but it is not to satisfaction. You drink, but you do not drink your fill. You put on clothing, but no one gets warm. The one who hires himself out puts his wages in a bag full of holes.'"

Here "set your heart on your ways" means to think carefully about and meditate on your ways, that is, how things are going for you. God was telling them and by extension us, to stop and think about what they were doing and to think about how they were affected by not doing what was right.

1:5. The phrase give careful thought (literally, "set your heart") is a favorite expression of Haggai (1:5, 7; 2:15, 18 [twice]). Here and in verse 7, he asked the people to think about the direction of their lives (**ways**). Not building the temple was not the problem; it was merely an external symptom. The problem was much deeper—an uncommitted life. Haggai's prophecy is often used to encourage giving, particularly to building programs. Admittedly, when observing a church building in disrepair, it is easy to question the commitment of the church members. However, the problem is not the building; it is the heart. The principles that Haggai set forth reach far beyond a building program. They extend to God's work and spiritual things generally. How important are the things of God to us? What are our priorities?[24]

A Quick Look:

Are you lost or found?

Heaven Parties

The Prodigal Son

What is real love? Love is action and is a choice, not just an emotion.

---

[23] **Jehovah of armies**: (Heb. *jhvh tsaba*) literally means an army of soldiers, or military forces (Gen. 21:22; Deut. 20:9). It can also be used figuratively, "the sun and the moon and the stars, all the armies of heaven." (Deut. 4:19) In the plural form, it is also used of the Israelites forces as well. (Ex. 6:26; 7:4; Num. 33:1; Psa. 44:9) However, the "armies" in the expression "Jehovah of armies" is a reference to the angelic forces primarily, if not exclusively.

[24] Miller, Stephen B.; Anders, Max. Holman Old Testament Commenatry - Nahum-Malachi (Holman Old Testament Commentary) (p. 120). B&H Publishing. Kindle Edition.

Supplemental Assignments:

Define love in your life and write down all the ways you see the word used and what the definition seems to be every time you hear or see it.

Read the book *Jesus Freaks* to get a look at the act of love.

Read the Bible's definition of love in 1 Corinthians 13:4-8.

What has been your experience in the past that makes you feel unworthy?

What has been your experience with church or Christians that may have pushed you from God? Process this with your therapist or support person.

Read Luke Chapter 15

Set The Mood Music:

NF- Oh Lord

Lost or Found

Earlier in this workbook, you took an inventory on how happy you were in various aspects of your life and were encouraged to ask yourself if you are ready to change. I want to revisit that question. I want to ask you where you are in your life? In order to get to the meat of that question, I am going to ask a few questions to help you understand all aspects of this question. Where are you physically? Are you in a treatment center, a hospital, living with a biological parent, a step-parent or adoptive parent, a grandparent, foster family? Are you in a Juvenile Detention Center? Are you homeless right now or have you run away? This will determine part of the perspective from which you are coming.

Depending on where you are physically and what your life experience has been thus far, you naturally have thoughts on religion and faith; possibly a very strong opinion of the two. I don't want you to confuse my perspective. Religion and faith are two very different things in my point of view. Religion is a set of rules or hoops you have to jump through in order to be acceptable to God, whereas faith is the knowledge that we will never be good enough, and we choose to believe in the sacrifice that was made for us, to allow us to come to God anyways. I'm talking about faith in this workbook, not religion, because I don't believe in a religion, but I am a woman of faith. You may have done things in this life or have had things done to you that make you feel damaged, not good enough, ugly, or broken; too broken for God. Look at your perspective for a moment and ask yourself, do you believe that this whole 'Christian thing' is right or wrong for you and honestly ask yourself why.

Life is a spectrum of every extreme; young to old, new to used, novice to experienced, naive to cultured, fresh to boring, new to established, broken to fixed. Where are you in that spectrum? Are you broken waiting to be restored? Are you torn and ready to be mended? Are you hurt and still angry? Are you a survivor or a victim? Are you lost or are you saved? So much hinges on your answer. If you are still lost, then you are open to attack; as if you have been walking on a battlefield without armor, not realizing that a war was waging around you. If you are saved, then you are armored and protected from a great deal of the attacks made against you.

Have you read about all these "Jesus Freaks" and thought we are all just a bunch of crazies? I don't blame you, we kind of are a bunch of crazies, but the question is, are you still lost or have you decided to join us in our craziness? You would be surprised at how complicated people make this question. "Well, if you're asking if I believe in God, of course I do." No, that is not what I am asking. I am asking if you have been saved or are you still lost? Being saved means you have gone to the Savior, Jesus Christ, and have accepted His sacrifice in order to save you. I want to draw special attention to my wording; not ask the Savior to save you, but to accept His sacrifice to save you. He already gave it all to save you; He is simply waiting on you to recognize it, and most importantly to accept it.

Take a moment, before you jump on the "God isn't real because if He was, He wouldn't have allowed _____to happen to me," bit and listen for a second. Imagine if you were a father or a mother and consider this: you create this world full of life and love and create these beings to look like you so you can talk to them and spoil them by providing everything for them. You just want friendship with them and to delight in them. You love them like they are your children. You watched every moment as you were creating them and you took great care in making each and every one unique for a specific purpose. You orchestrated the sun rises to bring them joy. They smile, and it lights up your whole world. They hurt, and you feel like your heart is being ripped out because when they hurt, you hurt. Then in the Garden of Eden that you created for them, they betray you by listening to your enemy instead of trusting in your rules meant to protect them. They do the one thing that would cause you to be separated from them. Now you are apart from these beings you created, those beings you love so dearly, and you long to be with them again. You just want all of the lies to go away, the betrayal, the pain to have never happened, but you cannot undo what was done.

After years of trying to find ways to overcome this and come back together, you decide to act in a wild, crazy, and unexpected way. You realize that the only way to allow you to be brought back together is for a sacrifice to be made. You decide to give away a part of you made present in your son, to go live amongst those who betrayed you, even though they follow your enemy. You send your son and allow the Enemy to do what he will so that you and those you created and love can be together again. You watch as your son is loved and welcomed, and then you watch, already having known what would happen, as those you are sacrificing for betraying your son just like they had betrayed you. They beat, torture, and murder your son in the most brutal of ways. Yet you and the son still love the very people that are causing you both so much pain. Why? Because you understand that these people that are harming you are lost. As the Son said in the midst of his murder, "Father, forgive these people because they don't know what they're doing."

If you are like me, I look at this and I think of my little girl, and I immediately feel broken at the thought of losing her. I cannot imagine if anyone were to hurt her because I fear I would harbor so much anger. Yet when I read this, I see pain at the loss, but love in the sacrifice. The Father knew when he sent Jesus that He would die. He knew that we would betray him. Remember, He was sending his Son to save us. How could allowing us to kill him save us, you may ask. This is the twist in the plot; His Son was sinless which means he never broke the rules. He lived a life that was perfect. Do you know what I mean when I ask if you are "saved"? What the Son saved us from was our punishment for the betrayal against God.

We betrayed our Creator, or our Father by choosing to follow the Enemy and listen to Satan instead in the Garden of Eden. You know as a kid when you break the rules there are consequences. All of our thoughts and our actions have an outcome, and if we are left on our own, those ugly thoughts and ugly actions start to add up to the point where by the end of our life, we cannot even remember what all we did. The Son took our punishment of death so that we would never have to face the consequences for our choices. He took the fall for us.

When you put it that way, being saved is really not rocket science. If you go to jail for stealing something and there is someone there saying,

"Hey man, I got this. Take off those handcuffs, put them on my wrists and I'll do the time for you," are you going to deny them? That is what Jesus did. Christ came to us and told us that He was going to die so we wouldn't have to, and all we would have to do is take the shackles off of our own wrists and place them on his, and we would be free to go back to our Father. Doesn't that sound like an easy, "Heck yes," response?

The best part of the story is that not only is our Father a loving and sacrificing one, but He is an awesome Father and He not only sacrificed His Son, but He defeated his Enemy when His Son came out of the grave three days later. His Son died but conquered death and still lives, because nothing could separate the Father from His Son. Now when our Father looks at us, the blame is gone. Our betrayal is gone, and all He sees is us before all the ugly touched us, before we ever made one mistake. When He looks at those who are saved, they are blameless, white as snow, pure and perfect and He loves them so very much. Nothing can separate you from your Father anymore. Have you accepted this gift, this sacrifice? Have you given Him your shackles so you can be free of your mistakes and lies?

The Son tells us that the Father loves us so much that if He had 100 sheep and one of them got lost, he would leave the ninety-nine others just to search for that one lost sheep. He loves you so much that ninety-nine is not enough. He has to have rescued all of us and to know that all of are safe and secure from the Enemy. If one of us is not, He is up all night searching for them. God loves us so much, that while we are still choosing to listen to his Enemy, He is looking for ways to convince us to come to Him.

I would suggest to you that there are two different types of love; our love that is based on condition meaning it has to be earned, and the love of God that is unconditional, meaning we could never earn it, but it is freely given. No matter what you do, He will never stop wanting you or loving you. He may not like what you do or the choices you make, but His love for you will never stop. The best part of His love is that it is unconditional which means you don't have to, 'get your life together,' to come to Him because he meets you right in the middle of the mess. You don't have to worry about cleaning it up. When you let Him come into your life, you will be amazed at how the mess suddenly starts to look a little different and over time, you look around, and it's all gone.

Now that you hopefully understand how much love He has for you, you can tell me, what side are you on? Are you still lost or are you found? Have you decided to continue living with the Enemy or have you chosen to return to your Father and Creator? If you have chosen to join my camp, I want you to know that I am overjoyed to have another brother or sister in Christ. We may never meet here in this world, but we will know one another in heaven someday, and I am saving a hug just for you!

There are parties in Heaven!— Wait, What?

In heaven, the moment you said "Jesus Christ is the Savior of my soul," and you let Him enter your heart, there was a party for you. Jesus told us in Luke 15:7 that the Heavens will rejoice when just one person turns from the Enemy and accepts the gift of Jesus Christ. There are only five things that make the angels party by-the-way: When God said "Let there be light" (Job 38:7), when Jesus Christ was born (Luke 2:13-14), when a person comes to Jesus (Luke 15:7, 10), when we all join them in heaven, and there is no more separation between us and God (Rev. 5:11-12), and finally when the Enemy is defeated (Rev. 19:6-7). They are literally going to cry out in happiness and joy over you coming back to the Father. Do you know how God will respond when you make the choice to return to Him?

So he returned home to his father. And while he was still a long distance away, his father saw him coming. Filled with love and compassion, he ran to his son, embraced him, and kissed him. His son said to him, "Father, I have sinned against both heaven and you, and I am no longer worthy of being called your son." But his father said to the servants, "Quick! Bring the finest robe in the house and put it on him. Get a ring for his finger, and sandals for his feet. And kill the calf we have been fattening for the pen. We must celebrate with a feast, for this son of mine was dead and has now returned to life. He was lost, but now he is found." Luke 15: 20-24. When you come home to your Father, this is what He will say to you, and He is anxiously waiting to hug you and say, "Welcome Home my son or daughter. I have missed you so very much, and I love you more than words can say."

And while he was still a long distance away, his Father saw him coming. Filled with love and compassion, the Father ran to his son, embraced him, and kissed him.

I cannot wait to hear your story. I hope you write to me and share how God has welcomed you home. You are my brother or sister in the Father, and my heart leaps to know that you have found your way home. You have been out in the cold for far too long. This topic is the most important of all in this book because if you do not first understand where you are, then you will never know where you want to go. You need to understand that, even though you may doubt or not believe in Him, He believes in and loves you above all else. I understand that this may be difficult to grasp, especially if you have come from places in life where you didn't have a father figure; where you were treated like an object that could be shoved to the side or pushed away, but to Him, you are His everything, and He is pinning and begging for you to love Him back.

Process Questions:

What type of love is God's love?

_____

_____

_____

How did you become separated from the Father?

_____

_____

_____

_____

_____

Does God respond to a broken relationship the same way our world says we should, by giving up on it? If not, how does he respond?

_____

_____

_____

_____

In a war, there are two sides. What are the two sides to this war?

_____

_____

_____

When does heaven party?

_____

_____

_____

_____

How does the Father welcome those who had been lost?

_____

_____
_____
_____
_____
_____

If we are saved, what does the Father see when He looks at us?

_____

_____
_____
_____
_____
_____

Are you lost or have you been Found?

_____

_____
_____
_____

Four Pillars Assignment on this Chapter's Topic

Self-Talk (40,000 individual thoughts summarized)

_____

_____
_____
_____
_____
_____

Faulty Beliefs (Beliefs about yourself and your situation as a result of your thoughts.)

_____

_____
_____
_____
_____

Perception (The faulty beliefs about your environment as a result of your faulty beliefs about yourself and your environments)

_____
_____
_____
_____
_____
_____

Behaviors (What you choose to do)

_____
_____
_____
_____
_____
_____

Finally, identify the outcome and how it reinforces the self-talk.

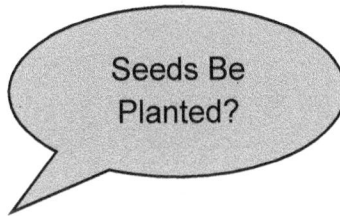

_____
_____
_____
_____
_____
_____

Seeds Be Planted?

1.) Who/What planted the seeds that led to your self-talk?

_____
_____
_____
_____
_____
_____

2.) How did you allow them to take root in your mind?

_____

_____

_____

_____

_____

_____

_____

3.) Are the seeds that were planted seeds of fruit bearing trees, which will bring you good life and sustain you or are they seeds of weeds, which will rob you and kill good things in your life?

_____

_____

_____

_____

_____

_____

Further Thoughts

_____

_____

_____

_____

_____

_____

_____

_____

_____

_____

_____

_____

_____

_____

_____

_____

_____

_____

Chapter V The Big Picture – A War for Your Soul

Isaiah 14:12-15 Updated American Standard Version (UASV)

12 "How you are fallen from heaven,
   O shining one,[*] son of dawn!
How you have been cut down to the earth,
   you who have conquered the nations!
13 You said in your heart,
   'I will ascend to heaven;
I will raise my throne
   above the stars of God;
I will sit on the mount of assembly
   in the far reaches of the north;
14 I will ascend above the heights of the clouds;
   I will make myself like the Most High.'

[*] The Hebrew (hê·lēl) means "the shining one." The Greek (ho he·o·spho'ros) means "morning star," "day star." In the Latin Vulgate (lu'ci·fer) it means, "Light bearer," but is rendered lucifer in the Jerome's Latin Vulgate. the King James Version renders Isaiah 14:12: "How art thou fallen from heaven, O Lucifer, son of the morning!"

Is this "lucifer" the Lucifer, that is, another name the Bible uses for Satan? No, it is not. It is commonly thought to be the case and many Christians refer to Satan as Lucifer.

The Hebrew word translated "Lucifer" in the Latin Vulgate means "shining one." The Greek Septuagint version of the Old Testament "bringer of dawn" and is rendered "morning star" and "day star." It is Jerome's Latin Vulgate version from about 400 years after Jesus that has "Lucifer," which means, "light bearer." This is how the name came to be in various translations including the King James Version.

Well, if "the shining one" ("Lucifer") is not Satan, who is it? It is found above in the prophetic book of Isaiah, where the prophet commanded the Israelites to "take up this taunt against the king of Babylon." This proverbial saying or taunt is directed at the Babylonian dynasty, not Satan. On this Max Anders and Trent Butler write, "This is not the fall of Satan, but the fall of a proud human being who tried to usurp divine authority and divine worship."[25] The King of Babylon was

---

[25] Anders, Max; Butler, Trent. Holman Old Testament Commentary - Isaiah (p. 103). B&H Publishing. Kindle Edition.

referred to as "the Shining one" after his fall from being a world power. (Isaiah 14:3) The haughty king wanted to elevate himself above the throne of God in Jerusalem and all neighboring nations. The taunt mockingly goes, "I [the King of Babylon] will raise my throne [the Babylonian dynasty] above the stars of God [the kings of the royal line of David]. Even though Lucifer is not a reference to Satan, the haughty pride of the Babylonian rulers certainly reflected the attitude of Satan the Devil. (2 Cor. 4:4) Beginning with Adam and Eve, Satan began to lust after power and certainly sought to set himself above the rulership of God, seeking worship for himself.

Ezekiel 28:13, 15-17 Updated American Standard Version (UASV)

13 You were in Eden, the garden of God;
 every precious stone was your covering,
sardius, topaz, and diamond,
 beryl, onyx, and jasper,
sapphire, emerald, and carbuncle;
 and crafted in gold were your settings
 and your mountings.
On the day that you were created
 they were prepared.
15 You were blameless in your ways
 from the day you were created,
 till unrighteousness was found in you.
16 In the abundance of your trade
 you were filled with violence in your midst, and you sinned;
so I cast you as a profane thing from the mountain of God,
 and I destroyed you, O guardian cherub,
 from the midst of the stones of fire.
17 Your heart was proud because of your beauty;
 you corrupted your wisdom for the sake of your splendor.
I cast you to the ground;
 I exposed you before kings,
 that they may look upon you.

Before the sin of Adam and Eve, it was in the spirit heavens that a sin and rebellion took place. Satan the Devil sought the worship that God was receiving from the angelic world and now humans. (Gen 3:1-6, 15; John 8:44; Rev. 12:7-12) Here again, the words of the prophet Ezekiel 28:12-19 are directed at another human, the "king of Tyre." Yet, it does very much parallel the course taken by Satan, the spirit son of God, who was the first to sin. There is little doubt that when Satan was first created that he was blameless until he started entertaining unrighteous thoughts until he gave way to sin. Just as the king of Tyre was removed from the mountain of God, that is Jerusalem; Satan would be removed from the presence of God for making himself a god. The king of Tyre was referred to as a guardian cherub, and Satan could have been a cherub, which is a high-ranking angel. It says in figurative language yet again that the king of Tyre was "in Eden, the garden of God." Certainly, Satan was literally in the Garden of Eden using a serpent as his mouthpiece to talk with Eve. This all definitely points to the Bible's accounts of Satan the Devil, who became haughty, used the serpent in Eden to deceive her, and is called "the god of this world." (1 Tim. 3:6; Gen. 3:1-5, 14, 15; Rev. 12:9; 2 Cor. 4:4) The best view of these verses in Ezekiel 28 is the church fathers, who understood "the background of the lament an account of the fall of Satan not given in Scripture but alluded to elsewhere, especially in Isa 14:12–17. Ezekiel would have been relying on his listeners/readers' familiarity with such an account, and they would have understood the comparison between the fall of Satan and the fall of the king of Tyre."[26]

Quick Look:

How the war started between God and Satan.

Why does Satan still fight a war he knows he already lost?

God's hope for you vs. Satan's hope for you.

Supplemental Assignments:

Read *Interview with the Devil: What Satan Would Say (If he ever told the truth)*, by Russell Wight

A great novel that displays the battle is *The Veritas Conflict*, by Shaunti Feldhahn.

To gain insight into how Satan and his demons actively work to corrupt you, even in your prayers, read C.S. Lewis' *Screwtape Letters*.

Good vs. Evil

Set The Mood Music:

Je'kob This Side of the Sky

---

[26] Lamar Eugene Cooper, *Ezekiel*, vol. 17, The New American Commentary (Nashville: Broadman & Holman Publishers, 1994), 265.

This war started a long time before the battles you face occurred. It started before our world of humankind outside of the Garden of Eden began when the Enemy first decided to go to the 'dark side.' Before I go into that story, let me first ask you, do you believe in good? Moreover, if you believe in good, do you then believe in the presence of evil? In our world, we love to glorify and talk about the evil, but the moment we start to talk about the good, people get upset that we brought up religion. We have movies about the evil deeds that occur in our world and even have a show called Lucifer that is based on Satan if the Enemy could be seen. We make the Enemy look like the sexy, bad-boy and God the prude who really isn't as good as He is said to be. We make them both look human, but they are not at all. If you believe in God but don't recognize the presence of the Enemy, or Satan, the devil, or whatever you want to call him, then you are missing out on the whole story. You will never really be able to understand the sacrifice of Christ or the war that you are in; regardless of if, you want to be if you do not recognize that there are evil forces at work.

> How has the Devil been depicted in our society? -The Sexy Bad Boy.

The Enemy, known by several names, began as an angelic son of God with another name that we have not been given in the Bible but is referred to as the descriptive name Satan ("resister") the Devil ("slanderer") in the Scriptures. He is a spirit person, and we read of him appearing in heaven in the presence of God. (Job chaps 1, 2; Re 12:9) He spent an untold amount of time with a righteous, perfect start; then, he deviated into sin, and great humiliation brought about by loss of status, reputation, or self-esteem. This angel started to believe in his own beauty; that he was better than God was, so he led Adam and Eve to believe they could walk on their own, not needing God, and the missed other angels to believe the same thing, and together they led a rebellion against God and His angels. This rebellion was quickly stopped, and this rebellious angelic son began to be known by his other descriptive names: murderer, liar, fallen, devil, Satan.

He lost the war with God. The question I always use to wonder is if he knows he already lost and will be completely conquered in the end, banished from all creation, then why does he keep fighting? Then it hit me; when you sneak out or rebel against your guardian's rules or society's rules, you know you will be caught. Maybe not right in that moment, but you know that eventually you will be caught in the end; so you decide to do as much as you can before you are caught and face punishment. That is what seems to be the logic of the Enemy. He knows he already lost against God. Out of all beings in creation, he knows from firsthand experience the power of God; remember he was allowed in His presence and was close to Him. He saw the power of God on a daily basis. He knows he has already lost. Therefore, like the spiteful being that he is, now his goal is to get back at God.

If he is going to go down, he is going to take as much down with him as he can; that is us. We are greatly loved as a part of His creation. I explained how loved we are in the chapter above. Anyone knows that the way to harm someone the most is not to harm him or her directly, but to harm those he or she loves. The Enemy wants to harm God in every way he can. Since he cannot harm Him directly, he will harm those He loves most, us. Every time one is lost to the Enemy or does something that the Enemy had wanted them to do to separate us further and further from God, it is the Enemy getting one more jab in.

The war is not over who will win, God or Satan, but the war now is over how many of us will choose to be saved by God or will choose to live by the Enemy's will. Free will is what lets us choose where our allegiance lies. God does not want to force us to love Him. Would you want to force people to love you or do you want them to choose to love you? We always want those we love to choose to love us over others. God is not worried about Satan against Him; He already won that battle, and Satan knows it. He is concerned about Satan being against us. He loves us and wants to protect us from the Enemy, but he cannot protect us unless we choose to follow Him. When we have, all heard about the gift of Jesus Christ and have had a chance to choose which camp we will belong to, God or the Enemy, then it will be finished, and Christ will return to send the Enemy out of all creation forever. Then, we will be stuck with the choice we have made. For those of us who have chosen to be protected by God, it will be awesome, but for those who have chosen the losing team, it will not be good.

> If he is going to go down, he is going to take as much down with him as he can.

Why are we talking about this? I know, you probably thought this was going to be different, but this is so important because, in a war where you have to choose sides, you need to know what and whom you are choosing. I just spent the last chapter describing the sacrifices God has made in an effort to bring you back to Him. Now I am going to describe to you the efforts our Enemy will go to separate us from God. The Enemy wants war for us. All of the things God wants in our lives, Satan wants the opposite, and he will use everything and anything to hurt you. Do you think the past life experiences were by accident? I'm not saying Satan has power over our choices, no we will always have free-will, but I am suggesting that he has the power to encourage, to degrade, and to mentally break you down to the point where you will choose to do things you never thought possible. Then he will use the shame over those actions to hold you hostage to your choices so that you never want to go to God because you don't feel worthy.

He is the prince of deceit, lies, pain, and brokenness. We are God's creation, and when something is made to be in the image of God, he wants to see it appear more like him, damaged and glorying their brokenness. This is a tough moment. When I started my work at a residential treatment center, I assumed that when individuals had been broken and abused in every way, that they would be so happy to be shown the way to change. I quickly learned that this was not the case. Sometimes when we are so broken and have been for so long, we become accustomed to our brokenness. It becomes what is comfortable and our normal, to the point where we don't even think of it as wrong anymore. After so long of living in mud, you don't realize that you have been dirty this long. After a time, the dirt seems to look clean, and you just move it around to get it out of your way without even realizing it is staining you, sinking into you, to the point where it all looks just fine. Your response to the hurt you have experienced or even committed is, "it is what it is."

Sometimes this contentment with evil is the strongest tool the Enemy has against you. You know what you are doing is wrong, but you continue to live in the mud because you look around and decide it is just too hard to worry about cleaning it all up. It is just the norm that you have been dealing with for this long, so you might as well continue. You may be afraid of anything different because you don't even know what it would be like to live a healthy life. This has been your life for so long that any other thing seems like it's fake. "That's not real-life, you don't know what real life looks like, you should see what I have seen," you may say. In all of my sessions, the hardest cases I ever came across were when individuals had reached a point in their life where they had been abused, taught that very wrong things were okay to do and were encouraged and taught to do them to other people. They didn't want to change this because it was what they were used to. Some even thought they were born for it.

Sometimes you get so used to the dysfunction of the environment from which you came, even when you hated it and knew it hurt you, you want to replicate and create it when you have changed situations because anything different feels weird and you don't know how to handle it. You understand how to respond to anger because it was your norm. You know what to do with being beaten physically or verbally, or both because that was your everyday. That was easy to deal with because you practiced it daily. Your situation may have changed, and instead of anger and wrath people meet you with love and understanding, and you don't know what to do with that. You see their love and compassion as a weakness to be exploited and used because where you come from, that makes people easy prey. People who speak with love and compassion are weak and can be easily manipulated and used for your gain in the world you may come from. This leads you to respond in a handful of ways; manipulate their love and compassion or try to sabotage it because it is so foreign to you that you don't know how to handle it. You would rather have them hit you or yell at you because that is an action you know how to respond to.

Satan is lies, God is Love.

The Enemy wants you to get so used to lies, pain, and torment that love, grace, and freedom are no longer things you seek, but things you run away from because those things are of God and he wants you as far away from God as he can get you. If the Enemy is hate, then the Bible tells us in 1 John 4:8 that God is love. Love is defined as this; *Love is patient and kind. Love is not jealous or boastful or rude. Love does not demand its' own way. Love is not irritable, and it keeps no record of when it has been wronged. It is never glad about injustice but rejoices whenever the truth wins out. Love never gives up, never loses faith, is always hopeful, and endures through every circumstance.* (1 Cor. 13:4-7, NLT) This is what God wants for you.

The Enemy wants this for you. He lost the war against God so now his war is against us, to bring as many of us down with him as he can, and if you continue to live in the mud, you are letting him win. Russel Wight writes in his book *Interview with the Devil*, describing what the Enemy wants for you.

Human, I hate you. I despise you, just as I despise the God who created you in His image and formed you in your mother's womb. I want your life on earth to be miserable and your eternity to be spent in a lake of fires. I want to fill your days and nights with temptation and sin so you can mock and oppose God, just like me. I want you to give in to the desires of your flesh—to serve me rather than Him. You see, by doing so, you will grieve and hurt God. I really am the roaring lion, and I wish nothing more than to devour you, to shoot fiery darts at you, to convince you that the Word of God cannot be trusted. I want you to believe that God is not love, that Christ is not your advocate, and that the Holy Spirit cannot keep you safely in His care. I want you to doubt everything God has said and everything He has done. (Wight 2012)

You must decide where you stand and whose side you will choose. Do you choose to side with the Enemy who wants to destroy you, or will you choose to side with the Father who loves you and was willing to send his only son to die in your place so you can come back to Him?

Process Questions:

Whose side are you on and why?

_____

_____

_____

_____

_____

What is this war over?

_____

_____

_____

_____

Why does the Enemy keep fighting if he knows he lost?

_____

_____

_____

What does the Enemy want for you?

_____

_____

_____

_____

_____

_____

What does sin do to God, and to us?

_____

_____

_____

_____
_____
_____
_____

Do you seek out, or cause dysfunction, in your environment because anything different, even though you long for it, is uncomfortable? If so, then process why.

_____
_____
_____
_____
_____
_____
_____

Four Pillars Assignment on this Chapter's Topic

Self-Talk (40,000 individual thoughts summarized)

_____
_____
_____
_____
_____
_____

Faulty Beliefs (Beliefs about yourself and your situation as a result of your thoughts.)

_____
_____
_____
_____
_____
_____

Perception (The faulty beliefs about your environment as a result of your faulty beliefs about yourself and your environments)

_____
_____
_____
_____
_____

Behaviors (What you choose to do)

_____

_____
_____
_____
_____
_____

Finally, identify the outcome and how it reinforces the self-talk.

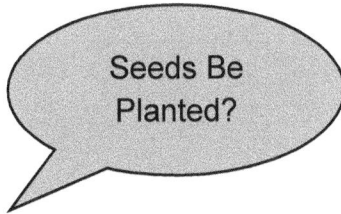

_____

_____
_____
_____
_____
_____

Seeds Be Planted?

1.) Who/What planted the seeds that led to your self-talk?

_____

_____
_____
_____
_____
_____

2.) How did you allow them to take root in your mind?

_____

_____
_____
_____
_____
_____

3.) Are the seeds that were planted seeds of fruit bearing trees which will bring you good life and sustain you or are they seeds of weeds which will rob you and kill good things in your life?

_____

_____
_____
_____
_____

Further Thoughts

_____

_____
_____
_____
_____
_____
_____
_____
_____
_____
_____
_____
_____
_____
_____
_____
_____
_____
_____
_____
_____
_____
_____
_____
_____

Chapter VI The Battlefield: Where We Go to War

Ephesians 6:12 Updated American Standard Version (UASV)

[12] For our wrestling[27] is not against flesh and blood, but against the rulers, against the powers, against the world-rulers of this darkness, against the wicked spirit forces in the heavenly places.

6:12. The reason this spiritual armor is needed is that **our struggle is not against flesh and blood.** The picture of warfare here implies that we do not face a physical army. We face a spiritual army. Therefore our weapons must be spiritual. **Against the rulers, against the authorities, against the powers of this dark world and against the spiritual forces of evil in the heavenly realms** seems to suggest a hierarchy of evil spirit-beings who do the bidding of Satan in opposing the will of God on earth.[28]

Ephesians 2:1-3 Updated American Standard Version (UASV)

[2] And you being dead in the trespasses[29] and your sins, [2] in which you formerly walked according to the age of this world, according to the ruler of the authority of the air, the spirit now working in the sons of disobedience. [3] Among whom also we all formerly lived in the desires of our flesh, doing the desires of the flesh and of the thoughts, and were by nature children of wrath, even as the rest.

2:1. In chapter 1, Paul enumerates God's spiritual blessings for us and then prays that we might be able to comprehend them. One of those spiritual blessings was forgiveness of sins and redemption by Christ. In chapter 2, Paul explains that great truth more specifically: we were spiritually **dead**, separated and alienated from God, because of our **transgressions and sins.** Later in the chapter, he talks about the

---

[27] Or struggle

[28] Max Anders, *Galatians-Colossians*, vol. 8, Holman New Testament Commentary (Nashville, TN: Broadman & Holman Publishers, 1999), 190.

[29] **Trespass:** (Gr. *paraptōma*) This is a sin that can come in the way of some desire (lusting), some thinking (entertaining a wrongdoing) or some action (carrying out one's desires or thoughts that he or she has been entertaining) that is beyond or overstepping God's righteous standards, as set out in the Scriptures. It is falling or making a false step as opposed to standing or walking upright in harmony with the righteous requirements of God.–Matt. 6:14; Mark 11:25; Rom. 4:25; 5:15-20; 11:11; 2 Cor. 5:19; Gal. 6:1; Eph. 1:7; 2:1, 5; Col 2:13.

consequences of this spiritual death, but for now he just establishes it as fact.

2:2. Paul describes the way we lived while we were in this spiritually alienated condition. We **followed the ways of this world**. That is, we lived according to the non-Christian value system. This value system is created and energized by Satan (**the ruler of the kingdom of the air**). This does not mean that non-Christians realize that their values are created and energized by Satan. In fact, most would probably deny it. Nevertheless, Satan, in his craftiness, places the things in front of us that we, in our sinful condition, find attractive, and, therefore, pursue as though they were our ideas. The **spirit who is now at work in those who are disobedient** is probably not the *ruler* **of the kingdom of the air** as the niv translation suggests but rather an impersonal atmosphere created and energized by the ruler. Satan's kingdom encourages us to have ungodly values, attitudes, and actions, much the same way a spirit of enthusiasm at a ball game might encourage us to embrace the attitudes and actions of a sports fan. We cheer, yell, jump up and down, and otherwise act in ways that we would not if we were not under the influence of the spirit of enthusiasm. Under the spirit of Satan's kingdom we act in disobedient ways we would not normally follow.

2:3. Specifically, our Satanically energized value system motivated us to gratify illicit desires. As a result, we were **objects of wrath**, meaning God's wrath, just like all other non-Christians.

The wrath of God comes on us in this life in two ways. At times we receive the natural cause-effect consequences of violating God's principles. Galatians 6:7 tells us that we reap what we sow. For example, if we are sexually immoral, we may contract a sexually transmitted disease. If we are violent or angry, we may receive the hatred and resistance of those around us. At other times God may bring his wrath on us specifically, in direct divine judgment. Such instances would be difficult to prove, but examples of such temporal judgment can be found in the Bible (Rom. 1:18–27; Acts 5:5; 1 Cor. 11:30).

In addition to the wrath of God coming on non-Christians in this life, the wrath of God will certainly come on them after death. Hebrews 9:27 says, "Just as man is destined to die once, and after that to face judgment." For the non-Christian, this is a terrifying thing. Second Peter 3:7 reads, "The present heavens and earth are reserved for fire, being kept for the day of judgment and destruction of ungodly men." Ephesians 2:1–3 presents a hopeless picture for the non-Christian.[30]

---

[30] Max Anders, *Galatians-Colossians*, vol. 8, Holman New Testament Commentary (Nashville, TN: Broadman & Holman Publishers, 1999), 110–111.

A Quick Look:

This battle is not one you can see.

Lies, deceit, and manipulation don't survive for very long out in the open.

Your environment does not control you. Your thoughts about your environment, or your perspective, does.

We digest our environment through our senses which all goes through our mind. Therefore the Enemy attacks our mind because, through it, everything else is controlled.

Supplemental Assignments:

Think of the ways the Enemy attacks you and write down how you are attacked and what your insecurities are.

The Battle Grounds

Have you ever seen a demon or an angel? Have you ever seen the devil? In horror movies often times the monster is an ugly evil-looking creature, or if it is a person, then they are usually masked or have paint to hide their facial features. Michael, Freddie, even the Joker in the Dark Knight, become more ominous and intimidating because you cannot quite see their faces. In war, we use darkness as a cover so that we can hide our attack. We have to wear special night-vision or thermal imaging goggles to be able to see the enemy in the dark because with our eyes alone we cannot see the attack. Darkness allows other soldiers to hide and because we cannot see them, they have the advantage to attack us when we least expect it. This is the same principle for the enemies of the unseen world. You cannot see them; therefore, they can attack you at will, especially when you don't believe they are there in the first place. This leaves you even more open to attack.

Lies and deceit don't survive out in the open where everyone is aware of them. They are much more effective when they are allowed to hide and when they have made everyone believe that they are not real at all. When no one knows or believes you are there, this gives you more freedom to roam about wherever you want. It also means that if people don't believe you are real or know about you, then no one has their defenses up and you can attack them at will. Think about how we talk about Satan in our society. Do we discuss his efforts out in the open or do people laugh and think it is a joke?

This war is not waged in a reality that you can see with your eyes, but you can feel it in your soul and your heart. Just like your actions do not come simply from outside of you but what you do and how you feel is a result of what is within you. This is the external (outside) and internal (inside) stimulus that I was referring to in the first chapter. Your environment is outside of you, but how often has what happened in your environment left a lasting impression internally on your mind? This is not something that a doctor can do surgery on; it is not physical. No one can see your soul, your character, your personality, or your emotions, but you can feel it, often times more strongly than any physical stimulus in this world. If our emotions, our souls, and our character are all inanimate concepts or non-physical things, then don't you think that the attacks and defenses of them will also be non-physical?

You cannot see what you are fighting against, but you can feel it. You may be so used to it that you do not pay attention to it, but it is there. It is like a heavyweight that your arms get used to carrying. All of a sudden, someone takes the weight away, you realize how heavy it had gotten, and suddenly you feel so light. This war is a war in your mind, and the prize is the control of your mind so that eventually the Enemy can have your soul. How do you guard your mind? Do you? How are you attacked in your mind? Can you think of times when you felt so dark that it was consuming you? Moments when you started down a train of thought that took you to places you have never thought you would end up. It is only after you have left that place, that you have any hope. This is just one way to describe what it is like being under attack. We can be attacked in many ways.

We talked about Job earlier in this book. He was attacked in physical ways, with the Enemy killing his wife, his children, and taking his home and his livelihood, his farm. He became essentially alone and homeless within a couple of hours. Then the attack took place in his body, causing physical illness and pain, as well as in his mind through doubts and asking why. I'm not suggesting that everything bad in your life was an attack, but I am suggesting to you that some of the things in your life that have occurred, have been in an effort of the Enemy to separate you from God, likely by using your reaction to your things in your environment.

We all live in the same world although the experiences of that world are very different amongst us all. However, our choices are not controlled by our surroundings or by others; they are only controlled by us. So what controls us? Our minds control us. It is from our mind that everything else comes. Our thoughts create a pathway for our actions and emotions to follow. We can experience a situation that would seemingly, be terrible by all definitions of it, and in our reactions and thoughts can make it something better than you could have ever imagined. A funeral being a celebration for the life that individual lived. The death of a child being what brings a husband and wife closer together as they go together to God to grieve, trusting in His love and safe-keeping of their baby, instead of breaking them apart from blame and anger. The survivor of the Holocaust forgiving her torturers because she understands that they are lost, and finding freedom herself for not holding on to grudges and bitterness. This is the difference between continuing to be a victim and becoming a survivor.

People all around the world find themselves in situations that are unspeakable, and yet the way in which they respond to the situations is different in every single person, and it is in our mind that our response is controlled. This world is influenced by the Enemy. Earth is where he was thrown when he was banished out of heaven, and here is where we reside, so we are in here with him. He can use anything for his purposes, and if we allow circumstances of this world to lead us to display things of his character, such as bitterness, aggressiveness, hostility, lies, abuse, which is opposite of what God is, then we are allowing him to control and influence us. He will seek to control and influence your thoughts because it is subtle, and it will happen when you do not realize it. If you see someone approach you with a weapon and appear to hurt you, you will put up your defenses or seek help, but if you don't realize or see the attack coming, then you are defenseless and often alone. You are easier to attack like that, so this battle is subtle, slow, and enduring; it will not be a one-time event but a daily effort of the Enemy seeking to control your entire life.

The good news is that practice makes perfect and you can get really good at protecting yourself. The enemy's efforts will likely be lessened when their attacks are not working. This means that over time, as you build up your defenses and are shielded by the Holy Spirit living in your heart, the enemy will focus efforts where they are more effective. If you are not listening and actively winning the battles for your heart, they will retreat and put more of their efforts where they find success. This can be good news if you are finding that you are successful in the battle over your mind, but if you are struggling and you allow them to win, then this can be devastating. Remember, you don't have to fight with your own abilities; you can call on Christ, and

> When you are successful in fighting the Enemy, He will focus his efforts on those who allow him control.

His Holy Spirit will protect you and fight on your behalf.[31]

Your environment does not control you, your thoughts do. The Enemy cannot make you do something, but he can and will influence you, and will focus on the source of your behaviors and emotions; your thoughts. If you looked to the example of Job when he was under attack, you will see that he was surrounded by three of his friends who shared similar beliefs as he did. At times, they would suggest to him that he had acted in ways to deserve what had happened to him, which was difficult, but they were there for him during his grieving process. Job was a leader in his community for being a good man, which is why the Enemy chose to attack him. If he had been successful in his attack of Job, he would have been able to influence many others because of Job's leadership role in the community. This is often the effort of the Enemy and his forces. Don't forget, Satan is not alone in this. Remember he led the rebellion in heaven, which means others had to have followed him. He knows very well the power of a strong leader. In war, if you attack and can bring down the leader, then others will usually follow the leader, even to their defeat. So take heart, if you are under attack, sometimes this can mean that the Enemy is losing his control of you and is fighting hard to regain the control he once had. On the other hand, you could be a strong leader who is leading others away from him, and he seeks to stop your efforts. At the end of the day, his goal is to take as many of us down as possible. Sometimes that means he will attack you because if he can get you, then it means he may have the chance to get to more. He may attack a father, leading the father to sin against his wife or family, which brings pain and anger to the family, which is a way for the Enemy to have access to the father's children and wife. If he had not attacked the father, he never would have been able to plant the seed of anger and bitterness in the father's wife and children. Our actions have major impacts on those around us. The thoughts we communicate is a seed we plant in others' minds, and it has the power to take root in their thoughts, causing there to be thoughts either of hope or of despair. The Enemy hopes that you will be one who will do his work for him and plant despair and pain in the minds of others.

---

[31] **CPH NOTE:** How does the Holy Spirit fight on your behalf? The Bible is the inspired, inerrant, authoritative Word of God that men penned as Holy Spirit moved them along. It is by our having a correct understand of God's word, the Bible, and applying it correctly in our lives. We walk with God by walking by way of His Word. Therefore, we must have a biblical mindset, a Christlike mindset, if the Holy Spirit is going to be active in our life.

FURTHER READING: How Are We to Understand the Indwelling of the Holy Spirit?
https://christianpublishinghouse.co/2016/10/05/how-are-we-to-understand-the-indwelling-of-the-holy-spirit/

Process Questions:

How does society portray Satan?

_____
_____
_____
_____
_____
_____

What do you believe about Satan?

_____
_____
_____
_____
_____
_____

What controls your actions and your emotions?

_____
_____
_____
_____
_____

What does the enemy attack us?

_____
_____
_____
_____
_____

Why is the Enemy and the battle unseen?

_____
_____
_____
_____
_____

Do you exercise control over your thoughts? Explain how.

_____

_____

_____

_____

_____

_____

_____

Do you spread seeds of hope or of despair? How.

_____

_____

_____

_____

_____

_____

_____

Are you a leader, guiding people to do the right thing, and bringing others to God? Are you a leader, guiding others away from the things of God? Are you a follower? How does this affect the type of attacks you will receive by the Enemy?

_____

_____

_____

_____

_____

_____

_____

_____

_____

_____

_____

_____

_____

_____

_____

_____

_____

Four Pillars Assignment on this Chapter's Topic

Self-Talk (40,000 individual thoughts summarized)

_____

_____

_____

_____

_____

_____

_____

_____

_____

Faulty Beliefs (Beliefs about yourself and your situation as a result of your thoughts.)

_____

_____

_____

_____

_____

_____

_____

_____

Perception (The faulty beliefs about your environment as a result of your faulty beliefs about yourself and your environments)

_____

_____

_____

_____

_____

_____

Behaviors (What you choose to do)

_____

_____

_____

_____

_____

_____

Finally, identify the outcome and how it reinforces the self-talk.

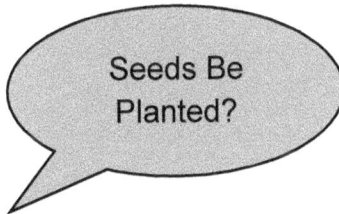

_____
_____
_____
_____
_____
_____
_____
_____

Seeds Be Planted?

1.) Who/What planted the seeds that led to your self-talk?

_____
_____
_____
_____
_____
_____
_____

2.) How did you allow them to take root in your mind?

_____
_____
_____
_____
_____
_____
_____
_____

3.) Are the seeds that were planted seeds of fruit bearing trees which will bring you good life and sustain you or are they seeds of weeds which will rob you and kill good things in your life?

_____
_____
_____
_____
_____
_____
_____
_____
_____
_____

Further Thoughts

_____
_____
_____
_____
_____
_____
_____
_____
_____
_____
_____
_____
_____
_____
_____
_____
_____
_____
_____
_____
_____
_____
_____

Chapter VII Who is in Your Company?

1 Corinthians 15:33-34 Updated American Standard Version (UASV)

³³ Do not be deceived: "Bad company corrupts good morals." ³⁴ Become sober-minded³² in a righteous way, and do not go on sinning;³³ for some have no knowledge of God. I am speaking to move you to shame.

15:33–34. Paul closed this portion of his discussion with a stern warning. He worried that those who denied the resurrection of the dead would corrupt sincere Corinthian believers. He reminded them of a well-known proverb from the Greek poet Menander: **Bad company corrupts good character**. The Corinthian believers associated with people who scoffed at the notion of a future resurrection, and Paul wanted them to break off these associations. These associates probably advocated Greek philosophy, not only denying the resurrection, but also influencing some Corinthians to pursue worldly wisdom.

Thus, Paul called the Corinthians to **come back to** their **senses**, to start thinking clearly about the resurrection by adopting the view he had elaborated in the preceding verses. This was no small matter. To deny the resurrection was to sin and rebel against God. Those who denied the future resurrection of believers were **sinning** and **ignorant of God**. They did not understand the basic things of the gospel revealed in Christ.

Paul was also concerned that associating with such unchristian thinkers would corrupt not only the Corinthians' doctrine but their behavior as well. In fact, it seems evident throughout this epistle that the sectarian thinking of the Corinthians, probably based in Greek thinking, became the basis for all sorts of sins, including: divisions, immorality, lawsuits, mistreatment of one another at the Lord's Supper, and abuse of spiritual gifts. Yet, the Corinthians continued to associate with these ignorant sinners. For this reason, Paul remarked that he gave these

---

³² **Sober Minded:** (Gr. *nepho*) This denotes being sound in mind, to be in control of one's thought processes and thus not be in danger of irrational thinking, 'to be sober-minded, to be well composed in mind.'–1 Thessalonians 5:6, 8; 2 Timothy 4:5; 1 Peter 1:13; 4:7; 5:8.

³³ The Greek literally reads, "not be you sinning" (ἁμαρτάνετε, present active imperative). The UASV and ESV correctly renders this "do not go on sinning," as the present tense often carries with it a durative or progressive sense. The Greek here brings out that there is a difference between committing a sin and willfully living in sin.

instructions **to** their **shame.** They should have been ashamed of accepting these false teachers and their ways.[34]

Job 2:11 Updated American Standard Version (UASV)

[11] Now when Job's **three friends** heard of all this evil that had come upon him, they came each from his own place, Eliphaz the Temanite, Bildad the Shuhite, and Zophar the Naamathite. They made an appointment together **to come to show him sympathy and comfort him.**

2:11. But next came the greatest assault Satan would hurl at Job—the counsel that came from his friends. What the devil spoke through Job's wife, he would speak even more convincingly through his three friends. Satan's lies can be spoken through another person, even from the lips of another believer (Matt. 16:22–23). So, having **heard about all the troubles that had come upon** Job, his **three friends** set out from their homes from various regions around Uz to support Job in his pain. His three friends **met together by agreement to go and sympathize with him,** all with the aim of bringing **comfort** to Job.[35]

Proverbs 18:24 Updated American Standard Version (UASV)

[24] A man of many friends will be broken in pieces,
   but there is a friend who sticks closer than a brother.

18:24. The first line of this verse is difficult to translate, but a literal rendering is "a man of friends [is] to be shattered or broken in pieces." In other words, a person who has chosen a wide circle of friends indiscriminately will eventually get in trouble, and his many acquaintances will do nothing to rescue him. But in the second line the writer uses a more intimate word for **friend**—literally, one who loves. It is better to have one true friend than a dozen disloyal companions.[36]

Proverbs 13:20 Updated American Standard Version (UASV)

[20] He who walks with wise men will be wise,
   but the companion of fools will suffer harm.

---

[34] Richard L. Pratt Jr, *I & II Corinthians*, vol. 7, Holman New Testament Commentary (Nashville, TN: Broadman & Holman Publishers, 2000), 267.

[35] Anders, Max; Lawson, Steven. Holman Old Testament Commentary Volume 10 - Job (Kindle Locations 885-889). B&H Publishing. Kindle Edition.

[36] Anders, Max. Holman Old Testament Commentary - Proverbs (p. 175). B&H Publishing. Kindle Edition.

> **13:20.** We must choose our friends wisely because their influence on us is powerful. The person who habitually **walks with the wise** will become more **wise**, but the person who associates with **fools** will grow like them and share the trouble that comes their way. Proverbs speaks frequently about the crucial influence of others (1:10-11; 2:12; 4:14-17; 16:29; 22:24-25; 23:20-21; 28:7).[37]

Proverbs 27:5-6 Updated American Standard Version (UASV)

⁵ Better a rebuke that is open
   than a love that is concealed.
⁶ Faithful are the wounds of a friend;
   abundant are the kisses of an enemy.

> **27:5–6** A true friend gives time and attention (v. 5) but is not always flattering (v. 6). In addition to a common catchword, both verses concern the nature of genuine friendship. Verse 5 especially points to the need for communication and interaction among people; few things are worse than being ignored, and the studied avoidance of honest contact destroys any relationship.
>
> Verse 6 is somewhat different. Whereas v. 5 concerns stifled or hidden emotions, v. 6 contrasts genuine and phony expressions of friendship. One must distinguish between salutary rebukes that spring from honest love and hollow displays of affection where no true love exists. The two verses together advise that in any relationship, an open exchange of honest and caring communication is essential.[38]

A Quick Look:

How do you determine who your friends really are?

What does the Bible define friendship as and what are the biblical examples of friendship?

Boundaries

Reputation

Peer Pressure

---

[37] Anders, Max. Holman Old Testament Commentary - Proverbs (pp. 174-175). B&H Publishing. Kindle Edition.

[38] Duane A. Garrett, *Proverbs, Ecclesiastes, Song of Songs*, vol. 14, The New American Commentary (Nashville: Broadman & Holman Publishers, 1993), 216–217.

Supplemental Assignments:

Friendship between David and Jonathan 1 Samuel 18:1-4, 1 Samuel 20:14-17

David's mourning of Jonathan's death 2 Samuel 1:17-27

2 Samuel 13:1-6 A friend leads another to rape.

Who Has Your Back?

God must think that the idea of a friend is important because you find it mentioned in the Bible in the Old and New Testament more than 107 times. Listed above are just a few examples of what the Bible has to say about friendship. If you break the word down to the meaning back in the time it was written, you would see words like this, one who loves, companion, comrade, or neighbor. Friendship can be used casually in our time such as when you hear someone at school talking about the two-thousand friends they have on Facebook. But I ask you, is that friendship? What does friendship mean to you? I have a lot of associations in my life, but I have a select group of individuals that I live this life walking next to. I consider them my friends, but when I think of them, there are levels to our friendship. This is a normal part of how people get along with one another. Friendship is a powerful thing and can be more influential on you than even your family. I don't know your situation, but I do know the power of association, and it is not something to be taken lightly.

I'm not suggesting that if you disagree with someone's choices, that you cannot speak to them or interact with them, but I am suggesting that the amount of time and the circumstance of your interactions should be different, lest you be associated with their activities and run the risk of being influenced and desensitized to their choices and lifestyle.

Who you choose to associate with, call them friends or not, will have a major impact on how you are viewed by your peers. This will determine the type of people that you will attract in your life. Your friends influence on you will alter the way you react to the world around you. This is often referred to as peer pressure, which you can deny all you want, but we both know it is real and can be very strong and hard to fight at times. I want to discuss the influence your friends have on you. In school there are cliques. You know what I mean, groups of people that seem to be into the same things. When I was going to high school, you had the jocks, the pot-heads, the party group, the nerds, and the 'E-mo' or goth kids. Within all of these groups, it was split up, but you could walk through our courtyard and know who was associated with whom just by looking at who they hung around with most. People would assume that if you hung out with the pot-head group that you smoked pot. People assumed that if you hung out with the partiers that you went to parties. You know how this works. You don't hang out with those who do drugs unless you are at least comfortable or okay with that behavior and lifestyle on some level.

My reputation, or the history and report of my behaviors among my peers, would determine the type of people that would want to spend time with me. Let me paint this clearly. If I spend a lot of time with those who are known in the school as doing drugs, having sex, and sneaking out and getting into trouble, then I am going to be lumped into these behaviors, even if I'm not actively participating. Let me be clear. Even if I am going to these parties but I'm not sleeping around, doing drugs or getting drunk, and generally just hanging about, the perception of others will still be that I'm okay with these behaviors and will eventually be doing them. If this is the perception of my peers, or this is what they see of me and what my choices show them is my list of right and wrongs, then do you think that the kids in my school who value their education, their futures, and their families are going to want to hang out with me? This is *reputation* folks, and this is how reputation works. Our reputation is created by a combination of what our choices in friends are and what our behaviors tell people about what we believe. Wrong or right, this is how social consequences occur. If you want to know a person's character, you don't need to look any further than their choice in friends, or so they say.

When I tell you I hang out with the group of kids known to be involved in parties, getting drunk and high, sleeping around, and skipping school what do you think I do? You assume I do the same thing right, or at least that I am in their circles when they are doing them. I may not have a drink in my hand or a blunt in my mouth, but if I am there with them when they are doing these things, then the assumption is that I am okay with it or at least accepting of it. People that disagree with those choices will not spend time with those that do things like that. I'm not suggesting that if you disagree with someone's choices, that you cannot speak to them or interact with them, but I am suggesting that the amount of time and the circumstance of your interactions should be different, lest you be associated with their activities and run the risk of being influenced and desensitized to their choices and lifestyle.

Why is this so important? Because it will decide who wants to spend time with you. In order to change your social circles, you have to alter the impression others have of you and show them that you do not accept those behaviors any longer. Again, I stress to you, this does not mean that you have to cut-off all communication with others that hold different beliefs, but simply that you limit the type and the circumstance of your interactions. Therapists refer to this as having <u>boundaries.</u> This is where your choices also come into play. Who our friends are is our choice, who our family is, is not.

You may come from a family that does things that you know to be wrong. You may now be living with others that are not your family because your family could not keep you due to their choices. What your family does is their individual choice; you are not destined to be like them if you do not want to be. If you are blessed to come from a family with values and beliefs that you want to keep for yourself, then you are at an advantage. Most of the time, those we associate most with is our family. It is just how it goes; they are the people we live with. When they hold beliefs that we feel are wrong, it is difficult not to fall in with what they do, which would mean having friends that uphold the values you want in your life would be even more important. Your choice is the strongest factor in determining your reputation and the impression others will have of you. Your choice of friends is probably one of the most important choices you will ever make in life. It can at times determine the roads you will travel and the direction your life will take.

A person who encourages you, allows you, or doesn't challenge you, when you cut, curse, disrespect your mom, sneak out of your house, cut class and so on, is someone who is allowing you to do things you both know to be wrong. This is where peer pressure comes in. Maybe they are putting the pressure on you, or you are the one putting pressure on them, but either way we encourage others by our choices and what we allow to happen around us. We cannot control the actions of others and sometimes we cannot control our environment, but we can control how much time we spend in an environment. You have the choice to remain in a friendship that is causing you to be influenced to make choices you know to be wrong. You have the choice to remain in a place that is causing you to be pressured or around things that you know to be wrong.

Friends can plant an idea in our mind, just by talking to us or glorifying things they do. They encourage us to act in different ways, and they can be the invitation to behaviors you never imagined you would be a part of. So-called friends can make you, or they can break you. If you want to continue doing drugs, then continue to have friends that do and think it is okay. If you want to continue to fight with your mom, then

137

continue to hang out with friends that call her lame and stupid. If you want to be mean to your little sister and have her be afraid of you, then hang out with friends who do the same to their siblings and who make fun of her. If you want to do things differently, then hang out with a true friend who will help you do things differently.

A true friend will "sharpen" you and help make you better, encouraging you to live a better life by challenging you to reach your goals. They will represent the character and hold character traits and values that you want to uphold. Your friend is an extension of you, and they reflect part of who you are. An old saying is that you learn a lot about a man by looking at the company he keeps. Those you choose to have as your confidant will reflect back to you, your values and beliefs. Look around you, do the people around you reflect the type of person you want to be?

A true friend will stab you in the face; an untrue friend will tell you what you're doing is okay because it is the easier thing to do. Proverbs 27:5-6 *Better is open rebuke than hidden love. Wounds from a friend can be trusted, but an enemy multiplies kisses.* This verse means that it is better to have someone tell you to your face that what you are doing is wrong and risk making you angry or hurting your feeling by saying it than to have someone lie to you to make you feel better about what you did. One makes you feel better at the moment but allows you to do things you will later regret, the other risks your moment of wrath to encourage you not to make a mistake. You tell me, which friend actually puts your true well-being first?

Process Questions:

What is your reputation thus far? In other words, what have you taught people through your choice in friends and in your choice of behavior, to expect from you?

_____
_____
_____
_____
_____
_____
_____
_____
_____
_____
_____

What do you want your reputation to be?

_____
_____
_____
_____
_____
_____

Do your friends challenge you to act better, or do they condone or accept what you do when you know it is wrong?

_____
_____
_____
_____
_____
_____

Do your friends represent the person you want to be?

_____
_____
_____
_____
_____
_____

Identify who your friends are that encourage or allow your unhealthy behavior? (Be specific, list names.)

_____
_____
_____
_____
_____
_____

What is a true friend and compare them to an untrue friend?

_____
_____
_____
_____
_____
_____
_____

Identify people in your life that would challenge you or a place where you could find "true friends".

_____
_____
_____
_____
_____
_____

What does the saying "A true friend will stab you in the face" mean?

_____
_____
_____
_____
_____
_____

Describe the power of friends?

_____
_____
_____
_____
_____
_____

What is peer pressure and how does it impact you?

_____
_____
_____
_____
_____

What do I mean when I describe boundaries?

_____
_____
_____
_____
_____
_____

Do your current friends plant seeds of fruit bearing trees or weeds? List who plans what type of seed.

_____

_____

_____

_____

_____

_____

_____

_____

Four Pillars Assignment on this Chapter's Topic

Self-Talk (40,000 individual thoughts summarized)

_____

_____

_____

_____

_____

_____

_____

Faulty Beliefs (Beliefs about yourself and your situation as a result of your thoughts.)

_____

_____

_____

_____

_____

Perception (The faulty beliefs about your environment as a result of your faulty beliefs about yourself and your environments)

_____

_____

_____

_____

_____

_____

_____

Behaviors (What you choose to do)

_____
_____
_____
_____
_____
_____

Finally, identify the outcome and how it reinforces the self-talk.

_____
_____
_____
_____
_____
_____

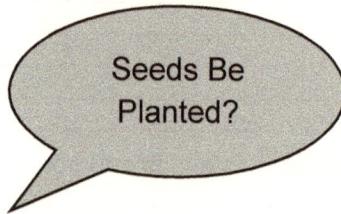

Seeds Be Planted?

1.) Who/What planted the seeds that led to your self-talk?

_____
_____
_____
_____
_____

2.) How did you allow them to take root in your mind?

_____
_____
_____
_____
_____

3.) Are the seeds that were planted seeds of fruit bearing trees, which will bring you good life and sustain you or are they seeds of weeds which will rob you and kill good things in your life?

_____

_____

_____

_____

_____

Further Thoughts

_____

_____

_____

_____

_____

_____

_____

_____

_____

_____

_____

_____

_____

_____

_____

_____

_____

_____

_____

_____

_____

_____

_____

_____

Chapter VIII What Goes in Must Come Out

Mathew 15:18-20 Updated American Standard Version (UASV)

¹⁸ But the things that proceed out of the mouth come from the heart, and those defile the man. ¹⁹ For out of the heart come evil thoughts, murder, adultery, sexual immorality,³⁹ theft, false witness, slander. ²⁰ These are the things which defile the man; but to eat with unwashed hands does not defile the man."

15:18–20. Jesus then revealed that it is not the mouth of a person that is the source of defilement, but the heart. The heart represents the invisible, "inner person." The inner person includes the mind and will—those components that determine moral character. The heart (not any external influence) is the source of all evil character, not the physical or spiritual "dirt" on a person's hands. The "renewing of your mind" (Rom. 12:2) is critical for every believer. Christ detailed here the principle that a person is as he thinks in his heart. Entry into the heart is through the eye and the ear, not the mouth.

Jesus listed seven defiling sins that begin in a person's heart. Some of these manifest themselves through avenues other than one's mouth (e.g., murder, theft), but Jesus was not inconsistent here. Although the debate began over eating and washing, Jesus now began to broaden the discussion to encompass the whole-person expression of the evil in one's heart. The mouth happened to be one of the most prominent tools for good and for evil (Jas. 3:1–12). Jesus' list of sins was not meant to be comprehensive, but he gave a series of examples.

Jesus mentioned **adultery**, a sexual sin that defiles a marriage vow. **Sexual immorality** is a broader category that includes all Kinds of sexual sin. **Slander** includes all abusive speech, whether against God or other people.⁴⁰

---

³⁹ **Sexual Immorality**: (Heb. *zanah*; Gr. *porneia*) A general term for immoral sexual acts of any kind: such as adultery, prostitution, sexual relations between people not married to each other, homosexuality, and bestiality.–Num. 25:1; Deut. 22:21; Matt. 5:32; 1 Cor. 5:1.

⁴⁰ Stuart K. Weber, *Matthew*, vol. 1, Holman New Testament Commentary (Nashville, TN: Broadman & Holman Publishers, 2000), 228–229.

Proverbs 4:23 Updated American Standard Version (UASV)

²³ Keep your heart with all vigilance,
   for from it flow the springs of life.

4:23. This verse contains the crucial concept of this section. **Above all else**, literally, "with all vigilance," keep **guard** over your **heart**. The heart in the Old Testament includes more than just the emotions; it can refer to the whole personality, the inner life of a person. And as such, it is the **wellspring of life**. As Jesus explained, the heart is the source of words and actions (Luke 6:45), so it is the key to controlling behavior. This verse may be the background for Christ's statement in John 7:38 about rivers of water flowing from one's innermost being. Solomon has been teaching on life, and the heart is the source from which life flows to all other parts of a person's being.⁴¹

---

2 Corinthians 10:3-5 Updated American Standard Version (UASV)

³ For though we walk in the flesh, we do not war according to the flesh, ⁴ for the weapons of our warfare are not of the flesh⁴² but powerful to God for destroying strongholds.⁴³ ⁵ We are destroying speculations and every lofty thing raised up against the knowledge of God, and we are taking every thought captive to the obedience of Christ,

---

10:3–5. Paul responded by reminding the Corinthians that his ministry was successful warfare. He had previously described his gospel ministry as a parade of victory in war, and he used similar military analogies elsewhere as well. His apostolic effort was a war he was sure to win.

Paul admitted that he and his company **live[d] in the world**, but insisted that they did not **wage war as the world does**. They did not employ the intimidation, coercion, and violence normally associated with worldly authorities. Instead of employing **the weapons of the world**, Paul relied on **divine power**. These **weapons** appeared weak by worldly standards, but they were actually very powerful. The preaching of the cross brought great displays of God's power in the lives of believers everywhere, including Corinth.

Consequently, Paul was certain that he was on a course **to demolish** the **strongholds** or fortifications of **arguments and every pretension**

---

⁴¹ Anders, Max. Holman Old Testament Commentary - Proverbs (p. 40). B&H Publishing. Kindle Edition.

⁴² That is *merely human*

⁴³ That is *tearing down false arguments*

that anyone set up **against the knowledge of God**. As Paul traveled the world proclaiming the gospel of Christ, he encountered pretentious disbelief supported by clever arguments and powerful personalities. But through the "weakness" of preaching Christ, Paul went about taking **captive every thought to make it obedient to Christ**.[44]

Philippians 4:8-9 Updated American Standard Version (UASV)

8 Finally, brothers, whatever is true, whatever is honorable, whatever is just, whatever is pure, whatever is lovely, whatever is of good report; if there be any virtue, and if there be any praise, think on[45] these things. **9** The things you have learned and received and heard and seen in me, practice these things, and the God of peace will be with you.

4:8. Continuing his strong imperative style, Paul suggested what should occupy our minds rather than anxiety and worry. Paul understood the influence of one's thoughts on one's life. Right thinking is the first step toward righteous living. What is right thinking? It is thinking devoted to life's higher goods and virtues. Thus Paul picked up a practice from secular writers of his day and listed a catalog of virtues that should occupy the mind. Such virtues are not limited to the Christian community but are recognized even by pagan cultures.

True is that which corresponds to reality. Anxiety comes when false ideas and unreal circumstances occupy the mind instead of truth. Ultimately, thinking on the truth is thinking on Jesus, who is the truth (John 14:6; Eph. 4:21). **Noble** refers to lofty, majestic, awesome things, things that lift the mind above the world's dirt and scandal. **Right** refers to that which is fair to all parties involved, that which fulfills all obligations and debts. Thinking right thoughts steers one away from quarrels and dissensions to think of the needs and rights of the other party. **Pure** casts its net of meaning over all of life from sexual acts to noble thoughts to moral and ritual readiness for worship. Thinking on the pure leads one away from sin and shame and toward God and worship. **Lovely** is a rare word referring to things that attract, please, and win other people's admiration and affection. Such thoughts bring people together in peace rather than separating them in fighting and feuding. **Admirable** is something worthy of praise or approval, that which deserves a good reputation. Pondering ways to protect one's moral and spiritual image in the community leads away from worries about

---

[44] Richard L. Pratt Jr, *I & II Corinthians*, vol. 7, Holman New Testament Commentary (Nashville, TN: Broadman & Holman Publishers, 2000), 416–417.

[45] Or "dwell on these things; *ponder these things*"

circumstances and possessions that project a different image to the community and which thinking cannot change.

The catalog of virtues Paul sums up in two words: **excellent** and **praiseworthy**. The first encompasses what is best in every area of life, the philosophical good for which every person should strive. Here it is especially the ethical best a person can achieve. The second term refers to that which deserves human praise. The catalog of virtues thus reflects the best life a person can live and the best reputation a person can thereby achieve in the community.

Finally, in this verse, Paul gets to his point: think on these things. That, joined with prayer will relieve all anxieties and lead one to praise God and live life the way he desires.

4:9. Is such noble thinking possible. Paul says, "Yes, it is. Look at my example." This is not braggadocio or pride. It is the state every Christian should live in, a state of being an example for all who observe you. The example includes Paul's teaching, the tradition he received from the apostles and passed on, his reputation for Christian living, and the Christian lifestyle they saw him practice. If they obey Paul, God will bless them with his peace (see v. 7; John 14:27; 16:33).[46]

Sow a thought, reap a deed. Sow a deed, reap a habit. Sow a habit, reap a character. Sow a character, reap a destiny.-Ralph Waldo Emerson

A Quick Look:

Losing sight of who you want to be is a "slow fade."

What is your path in life and do you like where it takes you?

It is tiny decisions that can lead to you going way off course.

Desensitization.

The side of you that you feed will win.

Are you walking the path alone, susceptible to easy attack, or are you walking with those who will keep you on the right path?

How do you define what is right and wrong?

---

[46] Max Anders, *Galatians-Colossians*, vol. 8, Holman New Testament Commentary (Nashville, TN: Broadman & Holman Publishers, 1999), 262–263.

Supplemental Assignments:

What does God say is right and wrong living. Look at the specific topics of homosexuality, sex, marriage, substance abuse, abortion.

> Set The Mood Music:
>
> Casting Crowns- Slow Fade

The Slow Fade

As a child I can remember singing the song, "Oh be careful little eyes what you see…" and I thought it meant that I needed to be careful of what I did to avoid punishment. I feared if I looked at something that I knew was bad, Jesus would get mad at me and I would be in trouble. As I grew up, I learned what this really meant. It became clear to me over time that this is not about consequence or punishment. It is about the idea that what I put into my mind will come into my heart, taking root and leading to my thoughts, and my thoughts control what I do. Jesus is not this punishing figure ready to rub my mistakes in my face. He created rules of right and wrong because He didn't want to lose us to the outcomes of sinful living. He understood that a person cannot live a split life; one of light and darkness. It has to be either one or the other. Casting Crowns song *Slow Fade* will help you understand just how this can happen in your life without you realizing it.

The lyrics of the song are as follows:

Be careful little eyes what you see
It's the second glance that ties your hands as darkness pulls the strings
Be careful little feet where you go
For it's the little feet behind you that are sure to follow
It's a slow fade when you give yourself away
It's a slow fade when black and white have turned to grey
Thoughts invade, choices are made, a price will be paid
When you give yourself away
People never crumble in a day
It's a slow fade, it's a slow fade
Be careful little ears what you hear
When flattery leads to compromise, the end is always near
Be careful little lips what you say
For empty words and promises lead broken hearts astray
The journey from your mind to your hands is shorter than you're thinking

Be careful if you think you can stand
You just might be sinking
Daddies never crumble in a day
Families never crumble in a day

The Bible refers to the path of righteousness, or right living, as a thin path. Imagine walking at a park; the path that everyone uses loses its' grass, and you can see how often it is traveled because of how wide and worn the path becomes. The path that is not traveled by many is very small and is almost unnoticeable, but the path where many walk becomes like a highway.

What path are you on and is it taking you to places you want to go? Explain.

_____

_____

_____

_____

_____

_____

The things you look at, the things you say, and the things you hear, all help to determine if you stay on the path you want to be on, or if you take a turn to another destination. Just as the song says, it is often a slow fade from the life you want to live to this other life. Often we don't realize we are heading in a different direction until it is too late. (Hint: this is why it is so important to have good friends because they will see it before we do and if they are true friends, they will help you get back on the right path.)

John Locke was a theorist of psychology long ago, and he had the idea that as a baby you are born as a blank slate, having no knowledge of the good or the bad in your world. Your environment, or the things you see and hear, will plant seeds in your mind that can take root and grow and become your thoughts and beliefs. Now imagine that at your birth, you were created to walk a certain path, a path unlike any other, and it was laid out before your feet; a destiny created just for you, full of hope and joy. The things you see, hear, and do, have the power to keep you on that path, or they have the power, if you let them, to slowly veer you off course. Think of a weed in a garden. The garden was created to have roses that would bloom these magnificent flowers bringing beauty, joy, and life into the world. A weed starts off very small in a garden, but if a weed is left to take root and to grow, soon it will kill off the roses and you no longer have a garden of life and beauty like you had intended, but you now have a garden of weeds that produce nothing and take everything. Those seemingly unimportant decisions, if left unchecked in your life, will decide if you remain on the path you were created for, traveling toward the purpose of your birth, or if you stray from that path and find yourself somewhere you were never intended to go. The path you were created for will allow you to produce life giving hope to you and all of those around you, whereas the path on which you may find yourself will cause you to take from all of those you love, and lose who you are and who you were created to be.

Which do you see in your life? Are you producing hope, life, and love for all of those around you including yourself, or are you taking from others, leaving destruction and pain, or nothingness?

_____
_____
_____
_____
_____
_____

All the things you see, hear, the places you go, and the choices you make, are like seeds in your mind that will take root and grow bigger and bigger until they take up all of your thoughts. What have you allowed to take root in your mind?

_____
_____
_____
_____
_____
_____

Do you like all the things you see above? If not, what would you change?

_____
_____
_____
_____
_____
_____
_____
_____
_____
_____
_____

The things you have seen, heard, the places you have gone, and the choices you have made, can never be taken back. You have walked down

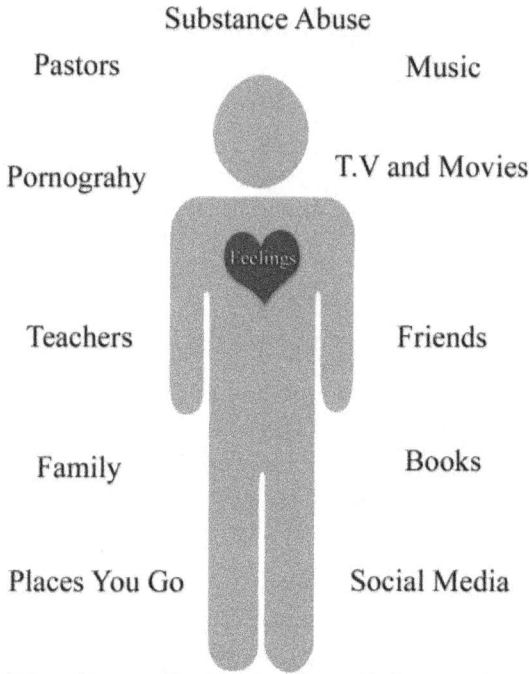

Substance Abuse

Pastors   Music

Pornograhy   T.V and Movies

Feelings

Teachers   Friends

Family   Books

Places You Go   Social Media

Your environment effects your thoughs, or self talk. Your self talk leads to your beliefs about yourself and your situation which in turn leads to your perception of the world around you. Your perception controls how you feel and respond to your world.

your path and taken detour after detour to the point that you no longer see the path you were supposed to be on. You cannot walk backward and you can never go back in time to undo what has been done, but you can find a way to get back to where you are supposed to be. Then you can put in place safeguards to prevent you from ever going off path again, traveling again toward the purpose of your birth. Picture the military when they go into war, or a place they anticipate a battle. They bring armored vehicles, weapons, and their fellow soldiers. They are never traveling alone, and they all know where they are supposed to go; they know the path on which they are supposed to be to get to them to their destination, and they work together to keep one another safe on the journey. This is what going on the right path is supposed to look like. This is the importance of having true friends who are going where you want to go in life.

The world is your battleground where the Enemy literally bombards you and sends fiery arrows at you, seeking to pull you from the path where God has placed your feet to achieve the purpose for which you are born. The world tells you that everything is okay and right to do, as long as it makes you feel good. You didn't intend to get pregnant? That's okay, just get an abortion and you don't have to be accountable for your actions that put your child there in the first place. You don't want to feel sad? We have a drug for that, or better yet a pill for that. You feel lonely? Get on this website and hook up with this stranger; use one another to feel good about yourselves, and we can get you an anti-depressant to deal with regret later. You want sex and don't want to have to leave your house? Just log onto this website, and we will bring sex to you. The three leading money-making industries in this world are drugs, human trafficking, and pornography. You want it, the world has it, and if people aren't willing, then they will force them to offer it to you. This is the reality in which we live. If your version of right and wrong is based on the world's moral compass, then do whatever you want because somewhere in the world there are always people who will tell you it is fine. You must pay attention to what is planted in your mind. The things you hear, see, and the things you do, the places you go will plant a seed in your mind that the Enemy uses as a Trojan horse to gain access inside your armor causing you to doubt

What do you put in your mind? What do you watch? Do you watch pornography? Do you lust after people? Do you go to places where there are drugs, sex, hostility, assault, a lack of empathy for people?

_____

_____

_____

_____

_____

There is a word I want to teach you; *desensitization*. Webster's tells us that to be desensitized is to make (someone) less likely to feel shocked or distress at scenes of cruelty, violence, suffering, sex, and drug use and paraphernalia, by repeated exposure to such images. If you are accustomed or use to certain behaviors, then when you see it you won't think of it as wrong. The more comfortable with something you become, the more casual it is and the more likely you will be able to do it as well. The warning, be careful little eyes what you see, ears to hear, and feet to go, is not to get you into trouble, but to protect you. When we get desensitized we miss the full story and start to lose our humanity; we stop caring about others. We allow ourselves to do things we know is wrong, and the things that use to shock us, become second nature.

Have you been desensitized by what you have allowed into your heart? If so, explain.

_____

_____

_____

_____

_____

_____

_____

_____

_____

_____

What is the path you are supposed to be on, the one created for you?

_____

_____

_____

_____

_____

_____

Look at the path you are supposed to be on. Are your friends going with you on that path, or are you a soldier walking with comrades who are taking you to a different destination than the one to which you are supposed to be traveling? Are you with the wrong company? If those around you are following the world's definition of right and wrong, then it is not the path you are supposed to be on, for it leads away from the God who loves you and the purpose He has for you. Finally be aware and always watchful for signs you have gone off course. True friends will let you know, but there will be signs in your mind and in your heart that will show you. If you are uncertain, pray to the One who created the path for you, and ask Him to show

In short, what you see, hear, and the places you go plant thoughts in your mind, your thoughts control your perception, and your perception controls how you see and respond to the world around you.

you where you are supposed to be. He may not answer in the way you want Him to, but He will answer.

Your emotions and actions are a product of your thoughts, and your thoughts are influenced by your environment. Your environment has an important role in your thinking. You cannot always control your environment, but the little control you have must be exercised to control the influence of the environment in your life. Music, television, and your environment, all of these things can plant thoughts in your mind. On average a person has 40,000 thoughts per day, and from those thoughts, you choose how you will see your world. Then you decide how to respond to it. In short, what you see, hear, and the places you go, plant thoughts in your mind. Your thoughts control your perception, and your perception controls how you see and respond to the world around you. Remember it is a slow fade and a series of small, seemingly unimportant decisions that will keep you on track or take you on a detour to a place you never imagined you would be.

Think on those little decisions, those thoughts that brought you here. What are the tiny decisions you made that took you off course?

_____
_____
_____
_____
_____
_____
_____
_____
_____
_____
_____

We're talking about the battle in your mind, right? So imagine for a moment that there are two sides to you. On one side, you have the part of you that genuinely wants to do the right thing. You want to be respectful, honest, kind, humble and so on. Then you have this other part of yourself, where you lose your temper and you do things you later regret. We all have two sides to us that we are constantly fighting. The Bible says that we are at war with our flesh and our sinful natures, and must strive to rise above what we want to do, and do what is right instead. You are not alone in this fight; we are all in this just like you. This is a concept that may help you understand. If you see two guys fighting in a boxing match, which one will you bet on? I would bet on the one who is stronger, mentally and physically, because it is likely he who will win. This is the same for the two sides of you. Your two sides are at war regularly to control who you are going to be; either side A who wants to do the right thing, or side B who wants to just have fun no matter the cost.

You get on average 40,000 thoughts per day, and you get to choose what those thoughts are based on. If you are spending your thoughts on things that are wrong, then which side of you are you feeding? You are feeding side B, the side of you that wants to do the wrong thing because it feels good. The side of you that wants to try drugs go to the party and have sex with that hot guy or girl. If you fix your thoughts, spend time watching, talking about, or hearing about things that glorify that life, then you are feeding that part of you. If you were to put both sides of you in a ring to fight, who will win? The side of you that was fed the most will always be victorious. You cannot expect the side of you that wants, to be honest, healthy, and right to win if you never feed it.

If you want to truly change what comes out of you, then you must change what goes into your mind and your heart. You cannot expect to feed your mind and heart images of hate, anger, sex, parties, and drugs and magically expect something different to come out. That is what crazy looks like. If you want something different for your life, then you must look at putting something different in. By changing what you put in your mind, you will change the choices you make, and that can change your entire life.

You need these things to safeguard you to stay on that path: know what is the path of right and wrong living, monitor what goes into your heart through your eyes, ears, and choices, and be considerate of whose company you are in. If you can do these things, you can be successful in staying on the path God created for you and resisting the attacks of the Enemy. What is the path you are supposed to be on? This does not mean you need to know your purpose; God will show you when you seek Him, but know what is right and wrong based on God's word. Don't base right and wrong on what the world tells you. Who has influence this world? The enemy, this is his playground. Who is more powerful than the enemy, our God is, and so look to Him for direction on right and wrong living.

What are the three things you must do in order to safeguard your heart?

_____

_____

_____

_____

_____

_____

What is your code of Right and Wrong?

_____

_____

_____

_____

_____

_____

_____

_____

_____

Four Pillars Assignment on this Chapter's Topic

Self-Talk (40,000 individual thoughts summarized)

_____

_____

_____

_____

_____

Faulty Beliefs (Beliefs about yourself and your situation as a result of your thoughts.)

_____

_____

_____

_____

_____

_____

Perception (The faulty beliefs about your environment as a result of your faulty beliefs about yourself and your environments)

_____

_____

_____

_____

_____

_____

Behaviors (What you choose to do)

_____

_____
_____
_____
_____
_____
_____
_____

Finally, identify the outcome and how it reinforces the self-talk.

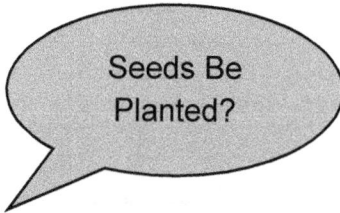

_____

_____
_____
_____
_____
_____
_____
_____

Seeds Be Planted?

1.) Who/What planted the seeds that led to your self-talk?

_____

_____
_____
_____
_____
_____

2.) How did you allow them to take root in your mind?

_____

_____
_____
_____
_____
_____

3.) Are the seeds that were planted seeds of fruit bearing trees which will bring you good life and sustain you or are they seeds of weeds which will rob you and kill good things in your life?

_____

_____

_____

_____

_____

_____

_____

_____

_____

_____

Further Thoughts

_____

_____

_____

_____

_____

_____

_____

_____

_____

_____

_____

_____

_____

_____

_____

_____

_____

_____

_____

_____

_____

_____

Section III The Enemy's Attacks And Faulty Beliefs

1 Peter 5:8-9 Updated American Standard Version (UASV)

⁸ Be sober-minded;⁴⁷ be watchful. Your adversary the devil prowls around like a roaring lion, seeking someone to devour. ⁹ Resist him and be firm in the faith, knowing that the same sufferings are being experienced by your brothers in the world.

5:8. C. S. Lewis once suggested that the two mistakes Christians make in talking about Satan are that we either joke about him or we ignore him. According to this verse, neither of these is an option. In essence, this verse says, "Wake up! Pay attention! We are involved in a spiritual battle. You need to know the enemy and his characteristics. You need to understand that we are in a life-and-death battle."

Biblically, Satan or **the devil** (*diabolos*, the slanderer) is described as the prince of this world. His residence is on this earth, and he moves from place to place. Because this earth is the devil's territory, believers are constantly under attack. Additionally, the Bible speaks of the devil as a personal spiritual being in active rebellion against God. He leads many demons like himself. Peter envisions the devil as a cunning and evil personal being who has the ability to attack Christians and to disrupt the life and unity of the church.

The biblical writers take the existence of Satan and evil spirits for granted and portray them as opposing God's purposes and the welfare of his people. Satan and his henchmen are bent on destroying life and introducing every sort of evil. They use deceit to attack believers and to blind unbelievers to the gospel. The commander-in-chief of these opposing forces is Satan himself. He is the master of ingenious strategies, and his tactics must not be allowed to catch us unaware. One scholar adds to our understanding:

> A survey of the results of demonic influence in the New Testament will indicate certain characteristics which a (self-controlled) and (alert) Christian may suspect to be caused, at least in part, by the devil or demons: bizarre or violently

---

⁴⁷ **Sober Minded**: (Gr. *nepho*) This denotes being sound in mind, to be in control of one's thought processes and thus not be in danger of irrational thinking, 'to be sober-minded, to be well composed in mind.'–1 Thessalonians 5:6, 8; 2 Timothy 4:5; 1 Peter 1:13; 4:7; 5:8

irrational evil behavior, especially in opposition to the gospel or Christians; malicious slander and falsehood in speech; increasing bondage to self-destructive behavior; stubborn advocacy of false doctrine; the sudden and unexplained onslaughts of emotions (such as fear, hatred, depression, violent anger).

(Still) caution is appropriate here, for there is much evil in the world which is not directly from Satan or demons but simply from sin remaining in our own hearts or in the lives of unbelievers around us (Grudem, 197).

5:9. The Christian response to satanic opposition is not panic or fear but firm resistance. **Resist** means "to withstand," or "to stand up against." It is a term of defense and victory. Theologically, Jesus Christ's death and resurrection won the decisive victory in the war against the powers of darkness. This, however, does not mean that the battle is over. Because of the cross, believers have the assurance that these evil powers have been disarmed. Believers share in Christ's authority over them. This does not mean that Christians have an automatic immunity to the influence of Satan and his demonic powers; otherwise, Peter's counsel regarding resisting him would make no sense.

To **resist** the devil effectively, we must draw on the power of Christ and not yield to Satan in our lives. Furthermore, to resist the devil, the believer must be **standing firm in the faith.** We should draw strength from what we believe.

First Peter overflows with reminders of the firmness of the faith of believers. We have been **chosen** by God the Father (1:2), given a **new birth** into a living hope (1:3), and provided with an **inheritance** that can never perish (1:4) because we are **shielded** by God's power (1:5). Furthermore, we have been called **out of darkness** into God's wonderful light (2:9). God himself is building up individual believers into a **spiritual house** (2:5). He views his followers as a holy and **royal priesthood**, a holy nation and **a people belonging to** [him] (2:5, 9).

This is the kind of faith in which the believer must stand firm. Regardless of personal suffering, we must join many other Christians suffering in other parts of the world in standing firm together in a united and active resistance to the assaults of the devil. Followers of Jesus Christ need to trust the God who provides them with this faith.[48]

---

[48] David Walls and Max Anders, *I & II Peter, I, II & III John, Jude*, vol. 11, Holman New Testament Commentary (Nashville, TN: Broadman & Holman Publishers, 1999), 93–94.

John 10:9-10 Updated American Standard Version (UASV)

⁹ I am the door. If anyone enters by me, he will be saved and will go in and out and find pasture. ¹⁰ The thief does not come unless it is to steal and kill and destroy. I came that they may have life and have it abundantly.

10:9–10. In addition to guarding the sheep, the Good Shepherd provides for them—unlike thieves who **steal and kill and destroy.** Throwing aside the metaphor to reveal spiritual truth, Jesus told the sheep that he had come to give life so they might live it **to the full.** False shepherds intend to injure the sheep, but that is never the behavior of the true shepherd.

We need to watch carefully the flow between metaphor and spiritual reality here. In verse 9 Jesus is clearly talking about people as spiritual sheep, while verse 10 falls back into the metaphor at the beginning and then talks about spiritual life. The word **life** in verses 10 and 11 translates the Greek word *zoe*, which we have already discussed at some length. As we move into verse 11, we see the contrast built around this spiritual eternal life. The sheep may have it only because the Good Shepherd gives his own life to make this possible.[49]

---

2 Corinthians 11:12-15 Updated American Standard Version (UASV)

¹² But what I am doing I will continue to do, so that I may cut off opportunity from those who desire an opportunity to be regarded just as we are in the matter about which they are boasting. ¹³ For such men are false apostles, deceitful workers, disguising themselves as apostles of Christ. ¹⁴ And no wonder, for even Satan disguises himself as an angel of light. ¹⁵ Therefore it is not a great thing if his servants also disguise themselves as servants of righteousness, whose end will be according to their deeds.

11:12. Paul intended to **keep on** boasting about his work in Corinth in order to discredit his opponents, who sought to be **equal with** him **in the things they boast[ed] about.** Paul had already made it clear that he did not think these men were his superiors. Now he declared his intent to **cut the ground from under** them in the confrontation soon to come.

11:13–14. Why was he so determined? Paul explained that these so-called super-apostles were actually **false apostles.** They were **deceitful** and only **masquerading as apostles of Christ.** Of course, those who

---

49 Kenneth O. Gangel, *John*, vol. 4, Holman New Testament Commentary (Nashville, TN: Broadman & Holman Publishers, 2000), 197.

followed these **false apostles** would have insisted that Paul was wrong. So he countered their anticipated objection by noting that the false apostles' deceit was **no wonder**. After all, even **Satan himself masquerades as an angel of light**.

11:15. Paul accused the false apostles of being **servants** of Satan and of imitating his tactics. They **masquerade[d] as servants of righteousness** (cf. Rev. 2:9; 3:9). The work of these false apostles led many into unrighteousness, as opposed to Paul's apostolic ministry of righteousness (see 2 Cor. 3:9).

Paul asserted that these false apostles would ultimately receive **what their actions deserve[d]**. Although this statement carried serious overtones of final judgment, Paul also had in mind that these opponents would be exposed before the church and removed from their positions when he arrived. God would judge them.[50]

---

1 John 5:18-21 Updated American Standard Version (UASV)

[18] We know that the one who is born of God does not keep on sinning,[51] but the one who was born of God is keeping him, and the evil one is not touching him. [19] We know that we are of God, and that **the whole world lies in the power of the evil one**. [20] And we know that the Son of God has come and has given us understanding,[52] so that we may know him who is true; and we are in him who is true, in his Son Jesus Christ. This is the true God and eternal life.

5:18–21. John brings his first epistle to a close by summarizing three final affirmations, each introduced with the phrase, "we know":

1. A person **born of God does not continue to sin** and is kept away from Satan's harm. Jesus keeps him safe. The believer is secure in the grace of God, and Satan cannot take his salvation from him.

2. **We are children of God**, not under Satan's control as the world is. This reinforces the distinction between the satanically-controlled world system and the Christ-controlled body of believers who have been delivered from its power.

---

[50] Richard L. Pratt Jr, *I & II Corinthians*, vol. 7, Holman New Testament Commentary (Nashville, TN: Broadman & Holman Publishers, 2000), 423.

[51] The Greek literally reads, "not he is sinning" (ἁμαρτάνει, present active indicative). The UASV and ESV correctly renders this "does not keep on sinning," as the present tense often carries with it a durative or progressive sense. The Greek here brings out that there is a difference between committing a sin and willfully living in sin.

[52] Or *insight; mental perception; intellectual capacity*

3. The **Son of God has come** into this world to give us **understanding** which leads to salvation. This strikes a one-two blow against the false teachers, the antichrists who claimed to have special inner knowledge of God and salvation apart from Jesus. God can be known in only one way—through Jesus. Truth can be known in only one way—through Jesus.

Verse 20 presents a small problem with its last sentence. Does it make an affirmation about Jesus or about the Father? Bible students argue both ways. The Bible as a whole teaches both points. God is the only true God, and life in him is the only eternal life. Jesus is also equated with God and has provided eternal life through his death on the cross.

Anything which stands in opposition to the one true God is idolatry. "Keep yourselves from it," Scripture commands. "Worship only the true God and Jesus, whom we have heard and seen and touched and proclaimed to you."[53]

2 Corinthians 11:3 Updated American Standard Version (UASV)

[3] But I am afraid that, as the serpent deceived Eve by his craftiness, your minds will be led astray from a sincerity and pure devotion to Christ.

11:3. As determined as he was to fulfill this promise, Paul was also **afraid** that the Corinthians might be **led astray from ... sincere and pure devotion to Christ**. Prior to Christ's return, the church is betrothed to him, but the possibility of infidelity and annulment still exist. Paul's responsibility was to help the church remain **sincere and pure** in its **devotion** so the marriage would eventually be consummated.

Once again, Paul drew from the prophecies of Hosea, who spoke of Israel's apostasy as sexual infidelity (Hos. 2:2–13). This analogy was appropriate in the days of Hosea because many Israelites expressed their apostasy by joining fertility rituals. In a similar way, the Corinthians were tempted by the immoral practices of Corinthian culture.[54]

---

[53] David Walls and Max Anders, *I & II Peter, I, II & III John, Jude*, vol. 11, Holman New Testament Commentary (Nashville, TN: Broadman & Holman Publishers, 1999), 226.

[54] Richard L. Pratt Jr, *I & II Corinthians*, vol. 7, Holman New Testament Commentary (Nashville, TN: Broadman & Holman Publishers, 2000), 420–421.

Chapter IX Doubts and Insecurities

Proverbs 3:5-8 Updated American Standard Version (UASV)

⁵ Trust in Jehovah with all your heart,
　and do not lean on your own understanding.
⁶ In all your ways acknowledge him,
　and he will make straight your paths.
⁷ Be not wise in your own eyes;
　fear Jehovah, and turn away from evil.
⁸ It will be healing to your flesh
　and refreshment to your bones.

3:5–8 These verses contain key words and phrases in sapiential thought. First of all, the phrase **trust in the Lord** (16:20; 22:17–19; 28:25; 29:25), and its close associate **fear the Lord**, is the fundamental definition of wisdom in Proverbs. Trust usually implies some threat or evil looming on the horizon. To trust in the Lord **with all your heart** refers to the total surrender of self. The admonition is the theological foundation upon which all the proverbs rest.

When the sage calls on the reader to **acknowledge him** (v. 6), he speaks on the level of attitude; the disciple desires to do God's will. When the disciple learns to trust completely in Yahweh, then the promise is that **he will make straight your paths**. This does not mean that Yahweh promises a life free from difficulties. Rather it means that one's life has clear direction and purpose. Abraham set off on a journey not knowing where he was going, only that God would lead him. In other words, God promised to make his paths straight.

The next imperative in the instruction is **Do not be wise in your own eyes** (v. 7). This is a stock phrase in wisdom's dictionary used some nine times in Proverbs. The sage often portrays the fool as someone who is "wise in his own eyes" (cf. 26:5, 12, 16). Those who are wise in their own eyes are those ruled by conceit, who depend on their own intellectual finesse to make it in the world (cf. Jer 9:23–24). Here the phrase is antithetic to "fear the Lord." To be wise in one's own eyes is a demonstration of pride. To fear the Lord demonstrates humility.

For those who do fear the Lord, the rewards are significant. It will result in **health to your body and nourishment to your bones** (v. 8). "Nourishment" (שִׁקּוּי, šiqqûy) can literally be translated "medicine." A healthy life flows out of one's relationship to the Creator. Such trust brings healing to the flesh and medicine for the body. This reference to the body is to the physical body and to physical health, yet it includes more than that. It incorporates the whole of a person's being.

The wisdom of Proverbs does not divide individuals or life into parts. There is no dichotomy between mind and body, physical and spiritual, or sacred and secular. Such a dichotomy is artificial. From the perspective of Proverbs, the physical, mental, emotional, moral, and spiritual are parts of the whole. When one is affected, the others are affected as well. Proverbial wisdom is about health, health that incorporates the whole person.[55]

Mark 11:23-24 Updated American Standard Version (UASV)

[23] Truly, I say to you, whoever says to this mountain, 'Be taken up and thrown into the sea,' and does not doubt in his heart, but believes that what he says will come to pass, it will be done for him. [24] Therefore I say to you, all the things you pray and ask for, have faith that you have received them, and you will have them.[56]

11:23–24. Barclay notes that this saying is in Matthew and Luke, although in different contexts (Barclay, *Mark*, p. 275). This is probably because Jesus taught on prayer more than once. Jesus was using hyperbole as he did in 10:25. He did not intend for Christians to try to move literal mountains. But he did expect us to believe that our prayers can overcome great difficulties. We must have faith when we pray. But our faith is not in the strength of our prayers, nor in the size of our faith.[57]

A Quick Look:

Do you believe you are capable of the purpose for which you were created?

Faulty Beliefs are based on three things.

The Enemy's strategy to attack you.

What is your self-worth?

---

[55] Dave Bland, *Proverbs, Ecclesiastes & Song of Songs*, The College Press NIV Commentary (Joplin, MO: College Press Pub. Co., 2002), 69–71.

[56] Christian Publishing House Blog Articles

Does God Step in and Solve Our Every Problem Because We are Faithful?

http://tiny.cc/90tviy

Why Does God Reject Some Prayers

http://tiny.cc/11tviy

[57] Rodney L. Cooper, *Mark*, vol. 2, Holman New Testament Commentary (Nashville, TN: Broadman & Holman Publishers, 2000), 188.

Anger-Secondary Emotion meaning there is always a primary emotion.

Ashes to Gold- what can God do with assertiveness and honesty?

"I feel" statements.

Four questions to have healthy assertiveness.

Supplemental Assignments:

Define *Self-Worth, Self-Esteem, Self-Image*. If you don't know the definitions, then Google it! Then Process with Support Person.

How can conflict be used to heal an impossible situation?

Document your self-talk every day, three times a day, for one week and see what you feed your brain.

"I'm not good enough."

What did you believe you could do when you were younger? Do you remember that time in your life when the impossible was possible for you; when you ran around the backyard with a towel-cape flapping in the wind as you soared through the sky? Do you remember what it felt like to think something up and then do it without a moment of hesitation to question if you could? 2 Timothy 1:7 says *For God gave us a spirit not of fear, but of power and love and self-control.* You were born to be bold, but something happened in between then, and now, something caught hold of you and told you no, and worst of all, you listened to it and started to believe it. Are you bold now? Do you believe that you can do or be anything you want? When did it stop? Do you remember?

What was it like to believe in the impossible and how did it change for you? Describe below.

_____

_____

_____

_____

_____

_____

_____

_____

_____

_____

_____

_____

Faulty beliefs are thoughts that have been planted in your mind which have taken root and have spread to where all of your other thoughts are based on these beliefs. <u>Faulty Beliefs are based on our fears and insecurities, our assumptions, and the justification of our actions.</u> This chapter is about your doubts and your insecurities. I want to hit rewind for a moment and take you back to when you were younger and you believed as I described above. Now walk me through what brought you here, to this moment in time where you no longer believe like you use

to. The you that you are now is a person who gets a good idea, but you dismiss it because no one would ever believe you, it will never work, and you think that it is just fairy tale talk. At the end of the day, you discredit yourself and sell yourself short. What happened to take you off course? Faulty beliefs are difficult because it may be a lie, but it is a lie that you see as truth, which makes it hard to identify. Our beliefs are always the most difficult to change.

What are the lies you believe that hold you back? In other words, what are the things you say to yourself about the things you want to achieve and are afraid to pursue and work for?

_____

_____

_____

_____

_____

_____

_____

_____

_____

_____

_____

If you think about it logically, in a warfare frame-of-mind, then doubt is a very effective tactic of the Enemy. He does not put the shackles, or doubts on you to prevent you from the destiny for which you were created. He just convinces you to put the shackles on voluntarily, and then to believe that you deserve them or need to keep them on. The easiest way to prevent a building from being built, is to convince the builder that he is not able to build it. Then you don't have to destroy the building, you simply stopped its' creation. This is the same idea behind your doubts and insecurities. If you don't believe you are good enough, smart enough, strong enough, good-looking enough, or fast enough to try, then you will never try in the first place and the wonderful thing that you were destined to bring to those around you, will never happen. The Enemy has now effectively prevented you from fulfilling the purpose of your life, because he convinced you to believe you were never good enough to have a purpose in the first place. Whatever purpose you were made for, has now been postponed or canceled by you because you have put on the shackles of doubt and insecurity. You have held yourself back from reaching your full potential because you were afraid and believed lies.

What are your doubts and insecurities? Be honest, no one is looking at this paper but you. Give me a picture of your self-talk, the things you tell yourself every day.

_____

_____

_____

_____

_____

_____

_____

_____

_____

_____

_____

Describe what you believe to be your worth (how much you are worth and what you are capable of).

_____

_____

_____

_____

_____

_____

_____

_____

_____

_____

_____

Look over what you have written on these pages. Look at the words you speak over yourself. If this is what you have written on a piece of paper, then imagine what you actually say in your mind when you are at a fork in the road deciding to go for it and take off the shackles to do something to achieve, or to sit it out for fear that you would fail. Forty-thousand thoughts per day on average for each person; what do you say over yourself? Your thoughts fuel your beliefs and strengthen them. What beliefs do your thoughts strengthen?

_____

_____
_____
_____
_____
_____
_____
_____
_____
_____
_____
_____

Truly, I say to you, whoever says to this mountain, 'Be taken up and thrown into the sea,' and does not doubt in his heart, but believes that what he says will come to pass, it will be done for him. (Mark 11:23) Doubts and insecurities come from a belief that you were not created for a purpose. When something is created, it is created for some use. I don't build a boat unless I intend to sell it to make money so I can eat and have a home, or so I can go play on the lake with it. That boat has a purpose and a reason for being built. Do you believe you have a purpose? We will explore this question later in this workbook, but in order for you to overcome and be released of your shackles and come out of your prison, you need to first identify your shackles. This verse is not about saying that if you want to fly, you simply have to believe in your heart that you can, and you will. It is not about how much faith you have and if you read your Bible enough you will have super-faith. No there are no faith push-ups that you can do, but it is about praying for guidance from God and His showing us that we are walking in the direction He will have us go, pursuing His will, and not being afraid that He has given you this purpose. If there are mountains in your way, you can pray and He will move them.

Faith does not give you power over the world around you, but that when you are walking in accordance to His will, nothing can stop you. You can walk boldly and fearlessly in the direction that He is leading you because you put your faith in the Creator and the King of the Universe to protect you. You trust him to clear the road for you so that you can pass through, even when the mountains in your way seem impossible.

Process the doubts and insecurities you have and where they come from. Peel back the onion and use the tool of insight as we discussed before, to explore when the seed of, "I'm not....whatever," got planted in your mind and how you have allowed it to take root to the point it controls your life.

_____
_____
_____
_____
_____
_____
_____
_____
_____
_____
_____
_____
_____
_____
_____
_____
_____
_____
_____

Finally, what are the things in your life that your doubts and insecurities have prevented you from having, doing, or seeking? How have they impacted your relationships? Fear makes us afraid to share our feelings; we close up and push people away. It is fear that allows us to express anger instead of the sadness that really is behind it. Fear keeps us quiet from telling someone we love them because we fear their rejection. Fear causes us to push others away, even though what we truly want is to be closer to them. 1 John 4:18 says that there is no fear in love, but perfect love drives out fear... Insecurities make us assume that we would never be good enough for that job, never be good enough for that guy, not pretty enough to be a singer, or whatever it is in your life. Fear makes us not want to rebuild a relationship that has been damaged because we are afraid of trusting, or afraid of facing the hard work it will take to heal what has been done. Fear makes us give up and run away, sometimes physically and sometimes figuratively. Fear drives so many of our actions and it is a strong shackle that prevents us from reaching the life we want.

What has fear and insecurity done in your life?

_____

_____

_____

_____

_____

_____

_____

_____

_____

_____

_____

_____

_____

_____

_____

_____

_____

_____

Anger is one of the strongest masks of our true emotions, especially when it comes to fear and our insecurities. We use anger to cover up how we truly feel. In therapy-talk, we refer to anger as a secondary emotion. When you have a number two, or a second, then it means you always have a number one, or a first. The same is true for emotions. Where there is a secondary emotion, anger, there is always a primary or first emotion that came before it. Look at your anger and explore with your support person what you are covering up with your anger. This will help you to conquer your anger and possibly the aggression you show. Aggression pushes people away. I don't typically want to stick around if someone is trying to throw things at me or yell at me. But so often, when a person is yelling or becoming aggressive, what they really want is people to be close and try to figure out what is happening behind the anger; to find out what is really bothering them. The problem with anger is this, it makes it unsafe, either physically or emotionally, for others to handle too much of it to find out what is behind it. Is this the situation for you? Take a few minutes to explore a few questions.

> When you have a number two, and I don't mean poop!

What emotions are you covering up with anger?

_____
_____
_____
_____
_____
_____
_____
_____
_____

What does it look like when your anger shows? Do you express it outwardly with aggression and hostility, or do you express it internally by bottling it up, self-harming, or plotting behind the scenes to get back at people?

_____
_____
_____
_____
_____
_____
_____
_____
_____

When you act-out in your anger, what is the outcome in your relationships? What happens?

_____
_____
_____
_____
_____
_____
_____
_____
_____
_____

Does it make you closer or does it tear your relationships apart? Process how.

_____

_____
_____
_____
_____
_____
_____
_____

I want to introduce an idea to you. What if I were to tell you that one of God's greatest miracles in our lives is when he uses conflict to heal a relationship; making it better than it ever could have been. When an affair that would normally tear a marriage apart, actually causes cleansing in the marriage and creates in the relationship a new level of honesty and love that was stronger than it ever could have been before. Sounds crazy right? Process with your therapist, or support person on how God can turn ashes into gold when we can learn how to be assertive and honest in a relationship. For assertiveness and conflict to bring healing, there must be some ground-rules laid first to be followed.

Assertiveness is the act of expressing your thoughts, feelings, or frustrations in a meaningful way with the motivation to bring healing and resolution to your relationship or situation. That's the kicker in healthy assertiveness; the motivation to bring resolution and healing. If your goal in being assertive is not to seek resolution and healthy, then all you are doing is stirring up more drama and adding fuel to the fire. Check yourself here and recognize the power behind your emotions. This may not be the time to be assertive because just thinking about your frustrations makes your blood boil. If you were to go right now to discuss the problem, your emotional topper might best be described as the eruption of Mt. St. Helens. You need to know that you will be able to talk and not rant process and not condemn, and most importantly be able to step into the shoes of the other person to look at the situation from their perspective. If you cannot control your tone or allow yourself to look at their viewpoint, then you won't find healing at the end of the conversation; only more damage.

This is where empathy and assertiveness meet. There are a lot of so-called assertive people in this world, but simply shouting out your thoughts, so everyone hears is not assertiveness. That just makes you a very loud person. A truly assertive person answers these questions before discussing anything, and if the answer to even one questions is no, then they choose to speak at a different time when all of the answers are yes.

175

Questions to Confirm Healthy Motivation for Assertiveness

Is my motivation in discussing this topic to help the other person, to allow there to be healing to our relationship, and to resolve a concern? If the answer is no, then continuing on will only cause more drama and pain to one or both of us.

Can I discuss this topic calmly with an even tone and without condemnation or accusation or judgment? A good suggestion here is to use "I feel" statements so that in your sentence you are stating that your reaction was their fault. An example of an "I feel" statement is, "I feel scared that you are going to relapse to old behaviors when you begin talking about going out with friends of your past." This sentence does not put the blame on them for talking about their past friends, but it does express how you feel when they do, and it keeps the focus on where it should be, what happened and not who is to blame.

Am I able to have empathy for the other person, choosing to look from their perspective instead of my own?

Is this a good time or place to have this discussion? Are they able to focus on what I have to say? Is it private where I won't be confronting them in front of others?

Four Pillars Assignment on this Chapter's Topic

Self-Talk (40,000 individual thoughts summarized)

_____

_____

_____

_____

_____

_____

_____

Faulty Beliefs (Beliefs about yourself and your situation as a result of your thoughts.)

_____

_____

_____

_____

_____

_____

Perception (The faulty beliefs about your environment as a result of your faulty beliefs about yourself and your environments)

_____

_____

_____

_____

_____

Behaviors (What you choose to do)

_____

_____

_____

_____

_____

Finally, identify the outcome and how it reinforces the self-talk.

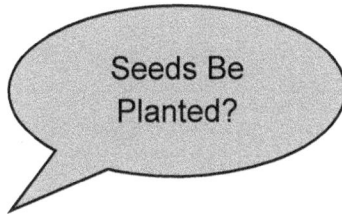

_____

_____

_____

_____

_____

_____

Seeds Be Planted?

1.) Who/What planted the seeds that led to your self-talk?

_____

_____

_____

_____

_____

_____

_____

2.) How did you allow them to take root in your mind?

_____
_____
_____
_____
_____
_____
_____
_____
_____
_____

3.) Are the seeds that were planted seeds of fruit bearing trees which will bring you good life and sustain you or are they seeds of weeds which will rob you and kill good things in your life?

_____
_____
_____
_____
_____

Further Thoughts

_____
_____
_____
_____
_____
_____
_____
_____
_____
_____
_____
_____
_____
_____
_____

Chapter X Pride, Entitlement, and Justification

Webster's Dictionary

Pride: *a high or unearned opinion of one's own dignity, importance, merit, or superiority, in the mind or shown in the way they act.*

Entitlement: *the belief that one is inherently, or born deserving of privileges or special treatment.*

Justification: *the action of showing something to be right or reasonable, often when you know it to be wrong or unethical.*

Humility: *a modest opinion of one's own importance. To display a sense of being humble or modest in behavior, attitude, or spirit; not arrogant or boastful.*

Accountability: *the act of being answerable to your actions or decisions whether they be wrong or right.*

Earned: *A person to obtain something for labor or services rendered by way of hard work.*

A Quick Look:

Do you need grace?

What is good about Mistakes?

Teaches us what is wrong and how we can improve.

Reminds us that we need God.

Personality and Character

Justification, Entitlement, and Pride

Supplemental Assignments:

Get feedback from ten of the closest people to you about if you express pride, entitlement, or justification and process the outcome on your relationship.

What do you Deserve?

Do you need grace? Grace is the free and undeserved, favor of God, as shown in his saving us from the penalty of our sins by sending his son to die on the cross. It is shown in his continued blessing in our lives even though we sin against him daily. What does this mean? It means that grace is when God looks at us, knowing every thought we have ever had, even before we have had it, every act we would commit, every choice we would make, and every word we would speak before it ever left our lips, and He still chose to send His son to die for us. This is grace and the gift of Christ that we sing about every Christmas, but you cannot take this gift at its' full depth if you do not recognize that we are all in need of grace. We all need grace desperately because we are far from perfect. We have all thought things in our minds about others, imagined things in our hearts, and sometimes made mistakes by carrying them out in our choices. We have all lied, said things to hurt one another, have been selfish and consumed by our own needs and wants, willing to sacrifice another's feelings or well-being to get it.

We have, and will forever make mistakes. Most people think of mistakes as terrible things, but I would suggest to you that mistakes are necessary in life to build us into the person we are meant to be. This does not mean for you to go out and make as many mistakes as you can. That would lead to a lot of struggle and pain in life. But what I do mean is that we have to accept that none of us are able to go through life without making some, and if we can embrace this fact, choose to be wise about the mistakes we do make, and finally choose to let the mistake teach us a few things, then a mistake can sometimes be the best thing that ever happened to us.

Mistakes have the power to teach us how to be better versions of ourselves by showing us our imperfections and the areas of our character that we need to work on. They also have an amazing ability to remind us that we are not able to go through life alone and that we need God. In the last chapter, I introduced an idea to you. I suggested to you that one of God's greatest miracles in our lives is when he uses conflict to heal a relationship making it better than it ever could have been. It is a miracle when you watch mistakes build something more beautiful than it ever could have been if the mistake had not been made. It is like a builder starting a project; after getting started, he realizes that the measurements were off and he has to start all over, but in starting over he takes the opportunity to make a few changes to the plans that he couldn't have made had he continued on with the project. After completing the building, he looks at it and is so grateful for the wrong measurements, even though at the time he was freaking out about the wasted money.

Thomas Edison, the inventor of the lightbulb, said this, "I have not failed. I've just found 10,000 ways that won't work". Mistakes in life can sometimes be stepping-stones to get us to where we were supposed to be. In order for mistakes to have the ability to do this, we must first be aware of how we view mistakes.

How do you view mistakes? Do you think of them as terrible things that signify to you that you are not supposed to do something; even suggest to you that you cannot do something? Do you see them as failures? What do you say to yourself when you have made a mistake?

_____
_____
_____
_____
_____
_____
_____
_____
_____

A faulty belief often stated during a mistake is the thought that mistakes have the power to define us. This is where I would suggest to you that a person is comprised of the following: they are born with their personality and they decide their character. A person's personality is their natural tendency to relate to the world around them. Are you naturally a bubbly person who is very energetic and socially outgoing, or are you naturally more reserved and enjoy watching the social interactions, commenting at times on the conversation, but enjoy listening to the conversation rather than commenting? This is how you were born and your mom and dad were learning your personality when you were in the womb. They could tell if you were a super chill baby or if you were super active, doing somersaults in the womb all day. Your character is a different story. Your character is made up of your beliefs and your values; these are things you decide upon and choose to incorporate into who you are as a person. It is the choice of your character that will determine your actions. What determines your beliefs and your values—your thoughts do.

We know these things for sure—your environment is experienced by your five senses. Your experiences go into your mind and then we choose what parts of our environment we will fix our thoughts on. The things we fix our thoughts on determine which side or our character we will feed; the side that you want to win is who you should be feeding. From our character, comes our behaviors. This explains that we may not be able to control all aspects of our environment, although there are aspects of our environment that we can control, but we can control what we choose to focus on and therefore which beliefs we are feeding. No part of this tells us anything about our mistakes indicating to us who we are or what type of person we are. Mistakes are simply choices we have made that did not give us the outcome at the moment that we wanted. They offer us information, though; they tell us what is not working.

One of the best ways to think of a mistake is a baby trying to walk. When a baby first starts trying to walk, they start off small; pulling themselves up on things and trying to walk while holding on. They hold your finger as you walk with them, helping them get their balance. The first time you let go, they may not even take a step before they fall. Does the baby stop trying simply because they couldn't walk on the first try—of course not, or else none of us would be walking? They get back up and keep trying until they get it. Mistakes serve a function; they teach us what is not working and that we should try a different approach.

The hard part of making mistakes is being wise about which ones will be worth making and which ones are not. I personally would rather learn from the mistakes of others so that I'm not repeating something we all know is wrong. Look around you, what are the mistakes you see made or are being made, and how is it working out? Do you think it will work out differently for you?

Think of mistakes that you have made that were not worth making.

_____

_____

_____

_____

_____

_____

_____

_____

Think of the mistakes you made that you had seen others make before you and process how it worked out for both them and you.

_____

_____

_____

_____

_____

_____

_____

_____

What are examples of choices that may be worth making even if it does not work out?

_____

_____

_____

_____

_____

_____

_____

What are examples of mistakes that are not worth making?

_____

_____

_____

_____

_____

_____

_____

_____

A key to mistakes is choosing when they are worth the risk. This is when it is good to get in the practice of looking at the pros and the cons of your choices. If you look around yourself and see mistakes being made with terrible outcomes, then it will not be a very wise thing to try to do the same thing and expect those outcomes to be different. Albert Einstein defined that as insanity. But if you look at a choice, and the outcome has a chance of being wonderful or life-changing, then isn't

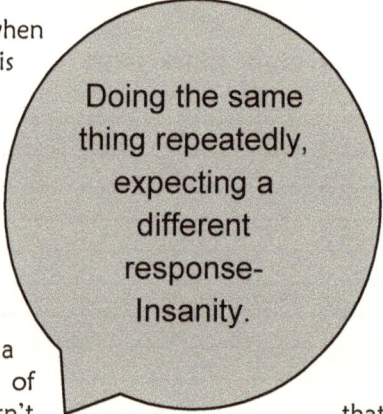

> Doing the same thing repeatedly, expecting a different response- Insanity.

that worth trying for. Let's look at life for a moment. If everyone around you is having sex and partying and their outcomes are STDs, pregnancy and/or abortions, failed relationships, legal problems, and problems in their family, is that worth repeating? Do you think that if you do these things you are magically going to have a different outcome simply because you are you? This is the definition of crazy; doing something even though you see before you what will happen, and trying it anyway. Wouldn't it be wiser to try to work this workbook instead? What is the risk? You have nothing to lose in attempting to change your life, but you have everything to gain. Make wise choices when it comes to mistakes.

Be careful because a lot of faulty thinking can happen surrounding your mistakes and the mistakes of others. Faulty beliefs like pride, justification, and entitlement are often found in these situations.

"It didn't work out for them, but they didn't do it right, and I can do it better."
"I'm smart enough to get away with it."
"It may be wrong for them, but it's not wrong for me."
"I'm different."
"That's a stupid rule, nothing bad will happen if I do it."
"I'm the exception to the rule."
"I can do it on my own; I don't need help."

Mistakes can help us better ourselves and change our approach to be more effective, and they can also remind us that we are not supposed to be doing it alone. If a baby is trying to learn how to walk, it takes so much longer, and the baby gets hurt more often when they fall if they are trying to learn alone. When mom and dad are not there to catch them when they fall, they fall harder and sometimes further each time. We are not supposed to be doing life alone, and mistakes are there to remind us that we need to have others with us as well to remind us that we cannot do anything without God. Life is so much more difficult when you go through it without God. He gave us the map (the Bible), so we don't get lost. Imagine going on a road trip without your GPS. He is the GPS who keeps us on track and helps us bypass all of the traffic and construction zones. When you go through life without Him, you may get there eventually, but you will find yourself lost, with a flat tire, and stuck in a construction zone for a while before you do.

Mistakes are there to remind us to look up and ask for help. If you go through life with faulty beliefs that tell you that you can do it alone, if you try to do the same thing the other person did and expect a different response, and that you're going to do it your own way, then you will miss the blessing found in wise risks because you were caught up in the ones we all knew to be mistakes. You will end up believing that your mistakes define who you are and seeing mistakes as something that will destroy you, instead of something that has the power to build a better you.

This faulty belief is the opposite of those discussed in chapter 9. Doubts and insecurities tell us that we are not good enough for love or forgiveness and for the plans God has for us. Pride, Entitlement, and Justification are the basis for faulty beliefs that tell us that we are more than good enough and that we don't need grace or change in our lives. By believing that you are more than good enough or that you deserve God's favor, you keep yourself away from God because you cannot recognize the importance of His son and the sacrifice for us. You think that Christ's sacrifice to take away sin is for others because you are 'not as bad as that guy.' This faulty belief also keeps you, hostage, to not recognizing your faults. When you don't recognize your faults, you don't seek forgiveness, and if you never seek forgiveness, then you are never trying to change? If you are always right and all of the feedback and constructive criticism others have given you are lies, then you won't try to work on rebuilding the damages your actions have caused in your relationships. You won't ever apologize for the pain you have caused.

Justification leads you always to be the one who was right, which means that everyone else will always be wrong. This can be damaging to a relationship because it puts you above everyone else and will allow you to always treat others as below you, but no one can talk to you about what you may have done that was wrong. If they come to you and express a problem with what you do or how you treat others, you have an excuse to justify and make your behavior 'okay.' This leads to stagnation, or you never changing, your relationships never changing, and other's needs never being met. People don't typically stick around for too much of that, just F.Y.I. This will also lead to an escalation of your behaviors because you refuse to recognize that what you did was wrong, so you continue to do it.

Entitlement is a dangerous faulty belief because it causes you to take others and what they do for you, for granted. You fail to appreciate the sacrifice of God, the sacrifice of Christ, or the sacrifice of others in your life.

Faulty beliefs of entitlement are as follows:

You see others for what they can offer you and what they owe you, instead of recognizing that they are a blessing to you and choose to love you and give to you even though they don't have to.

You believe that the world owes you and you don't have to work to earn what you want.

For many of you, this is how you view your family. You see them as people who don't have a choice, but they have to love you and provide for you.

I got what I wanted, so who cares about the rest.

Entitled Faulty Belief vs Thankfulness

Perspective:

When I look at the world, I
ask two questions:
What can you give me and
what do I have to do to get it
out of you?

Perspective:

When I look at the world, I
ask two questions:
What can I do to give back to
the world for all of the things
I have been blessed with?

Entitlement leads to people who are unwilling to work for what they have, often seeking to find ways to get what they want without having to work for it; manipulation. Entitlement leads to damage in relationships because it leads to one person receiving without appreciation and the other giving despite feelings of being taken advantage of. Entitlement causes us to use others to get what we want which will eventually lead to an inability to empathize with others and an inability to hold ourselves accountable to our actions because we fail to see how our actions affected others.

Pride is another shackle that keeps us from admitting to things, keeps us from doing what is needed, and keeps us from asking for help when we need it. Pride makes you forget about others and keeps you blinded to your own perspective. It makes you not look to God. Pride is thinking that you can do it and don't need help. Pride will keep you from learning how to make better choices, and it will keep you stuck to your habits and ways and never progress forward. When you make a mistake, you will be too prideful to admit to having made a mistake; sometimes doing the wrong thing over and over again because you won't listen to the advice of others. I wonder, are you like that with this book, so focused on not listening to the feedback of others to realize that what they bring you is life-giving?

Process Questions:

Do you need grace? If so, what does the grace of God mean to you?

_____

_____

_____

_____

187

_____
_____
_____
_____
_____
_____
_____
_____

Do you struggle with Justification? If so, what is your struggle, how have you damaged things with justification and how has it been a shackle in your life? What is your self-talk?

_____
_____
_____
_____
_____
_____
_____
_____
_____
_____
_____
_____

Do you struggle with entitlement? What are the things you believe you should get without having to earn it? What do you expect from others and take for granted? What is your self-talk?

_____
_____
_____
_____
_____
_____
_____
_____
_____
_____
_____
_____

Do you struggle with pride and how has your pride held you back? What is your self-talk?

_____

_____

_____

_____

_____

_____

_____

_____

_____

_____

_____

_____

_____

_____

How can you start showing accountability?

_____

_____

_____

_____

_____

_____

_____

_____

_____

_____

How can you start showing appreciation and to whom do you need to be appreciative?

_____

_____

_____

_____

_____

_____

_____

_____

How can you start being humble and what does humility mean to you?

_____

_____

_____

_____

_____

_____

_____

_____

Four Pillars Assignment on this Chapter's Topic

Self-Talk (40,000 individual thoughts summarized)

_____

_____

_____

_____

_____

_____

_____

_____

Faulty Beliefs (Beliefs about yourself and your situation as a result of your thoughts.)

_____

_____

_____

_____

_____

_____

Perception (The faulty beliefs about your environment as a result of your faulty beliefs about yourself and your environments)

_____

_____

_____

_____

_____

_____

Behaviors (What you choose to do)

_____
_____
_____
_____
_____
_____
_____
_____

Finally, identify the outcome and how it reinforces the self-talk.

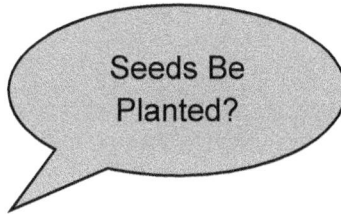

_____
_____
_____
_____
_____
_____

Seeds Be
Planted?

1.) Who/What planted the seeds that led to your self-talk?

_____
_____
_____
_____
_____
_____

2.) How did you allow them to take root in your mind?

_____
_____
_____
_____
_____

3.) Are the seeds that were planted seeds of fruit bearing trees which will bring you good life and sustain you or are they seeds of weeds which will rob you and kill good things in your life?

_____

_____

_____

_____

_____

_____

_____

_____

Further Thoughts

_____

_____

_____

_____

_____

_____

_____

_____

_____

_____

_____

_____

_____

_____

_____

_____

_____

_____

_____

_____

_____

_____

_____

_____

_____

_____

_____

_____

_____

Chapter XI Sin, Guilt, and Remorse

1 Timothy 6:12 Updated American Standard Version (UASV)

[12] Fight the good fight of **the faith**; take hold of the eternal life to which you were called, and confessed the good confession in the presence of many witnesses.

6:12. Timothy was to chase after personal behaviors, attitudes, and habits which would reflect his companionship with Christ. He was also **to fight the good fight of the faith.** As a leader he was to defend truth.

There will always be attacks upon God's truth: professing Christians who propagate false teachings and those who encourage compromise. But the inspired beliefs must be fought for and upheld. This is not a skirmish but a sustained contest which the believer must see through to the end. This requires endurance and patience.

Paul told Timothy to **take hold of the eternal life to which you were called when you made your good confession in the presence of many witnesses.**

The eternal life which believers enter is not simply a future hope; it is also a present reality. We take hold of this eternal life when we live in the power and values of God's eternal kingdom. We will not experience the fullness of Christ's dominion until the future when he reigns over all the earth. But the eternal kind of life is still accessible at the present time. We touch upon it when we order our daily lives in harmony with God and his Spirit.

This new kind of life is what every believer is called to. It is not reserved for the elite. It is available to all who make the good confession—that Jesus Christ is God's Son, delivered to death for our sins and raised from the dead to secure eternal life for all who trust him.

True faith cannot be hidden. Timothy gave public witness that he believed and trusted in Jesus Christ. He had followed in the right way. Now Paul encouraged him to continue on with strength and clarity of purpose.[58]

---

[58] Knute Larson, *I & II Thessalonians, I & II Timothy, Titus, Philemon*, vol. 9, Holman New Testament Commentary (Nashville, TN: Broadman & Holman Publishers, 2000), 247.

Jude 3 Updated American Standard Version (UASV)

³ Beloved, while I was making every effort to write you about our common salvation, I found it necessary to write to you appealing that you contend earnestly for **the faith** that was once for all delivered to the holy ones.

3–4. Jude's preference was to write a pleasant and encouraging letter on the subject of their common **salvation.** Circumstances pressed upon him, however, so that he wrote a brief but intense and potent warning against false teachers in the church. He jumped right to the point, urging them **to contend for the faith.** Why? Because false teachers, godless people, had **secretly slipped in among** them.

He described **the faith** as having been **once for all entrusted to the saints.** "The faith" is seen also in Galatians 1:23 and 1 Timothy 4:1. This refers to the body of information believed by the early church. It is the gospel, the message of truth that brings salvation to the person who believes it. "Faith" refers to a body of objective truth, not the subjective experience of believing something.[59]

A Quick Look:

Religion vs. the Faith, What's the Difference?

Judgement

I'm not good enough.

Supplemental Assignments:

What makes you so bad that you doubt you can come before God? Process with your support person or therapist and look at the sins of David and Paul in the Bible.

---

[59] David Walls and Max Anders, *I & II Peter, I, II & III John, Jude*, vol. 11, Holman New Testament Commentary (Nashville, TN: Broadman & Holman Publishers, 1999), 261.

Religion vs. the Faith

Religion: This is a form of worship that is made up of a system of religious attitudes, beliefs, and practices. These may be brought about by a religious denomination as a whole, an independent church, or personally.

The Faith: This is a group of Christians, regardless of size, which holds to the total Christian truth as revealed in God's Word, the Bible. "Faith" here refers to complete body of objective Christian truth, not the personal experience of believing them.

Christians may have God's written Word and go to their churches regularly but also lack an accurate knowledge of what lies between Genesis 1:1 and Revelation 22:21. Sadly, many pastors, ministers, and priests do not have an accurate knowledge of God's Word, which means that they have not taught their flock properly. Yes, many in the church have a great zeal for the Word of God, but at the same time, they are unable to defend foundational doctrines of the Christian faith, or to defend the Word of God as inspired, fully inerrant, and authoritative. This means that some Christians, who believe they have been taught properly, are going to hear the following words from Jesus Christ, "'I never knew you; depart from me, you workers of lawlessness.'" (Matthew 7:23) We want you, the reader to understand, what human imperfection really means and how God makes allowances for your sinful state so that you can still have a good standing before him.

Defining Sin and Sinners

Sin: (Heb. *chattath*; Gr. *hamartia*) Any spoken word (Job 2:10; Ps 39:1), wrong action (Lev. 20:20; 2 Cor. 12:21) or failing to act when one should have (Num. 9:13; Jam. 4:17), in mind and heart (Prov. 21:4; Rom. 3:9-18; 2 Pet 2:12-15) that is contrary to God's personality, ways, will and purposes, standards, as set out in the Scriptures. It is also a major sin to lack faith in God, doubting in mind and heart, even subtly in our actions, that he has the ability to carry out his will and purposes. (Heb. 3:12-13, 18-19). It is commonly referred to as missing the mark of perfection.

- **Error**: (Heb., *'āwōn*; Gr. *anomia, paranomia*) This aspect of sin refers to committing a perverseness, wrongness, lawlessness, law-breaking, which can also include the rejection of the sovereignty of God. It is focuses on the liability or guilt of one's wicked, wrongful act. This error may be deliberate or accidental; either willful deviation of what is right or unknowingly making a mistake. (Lev. 4:13-35; 5:1-6, 14-19; Num. 15:22-29; Ps 19:12, 13) Of course, if it is intentional; then, the consequence is far more serious. (Num. 15:30-31) Error is in opposition to the truth, and those willfully sinning corrupt the truth, a course that only brings forth flagrant sin. (Isa 5:18-23) We can be hardened by the deceitfulness of sin.–Ex 9:27, 34-35; Heb. 3:13-15.

- **Transgression**: (Heb. 'avar; Gr. parabasis) Sin can take the form of a "transgression." This is an overstepping, namely, to exceed a moral limit or boundary. Biblically speaking, this would be crossing the line and saying, feeling, thinking or doing something that is contrary to God's personality, standards, ways, will and purposes, as set out in the Scriptures. It is breaking God's moral law.–Num. 14:41; Deut. 17:2, 3; Josh. 7:11, 15; 1 Sam 15:24; Isa 24:5; Jer. 34:18; Rom. 2:23; 4:15; 5:14; Gal. 3:19; 1 Tim. 2:14; Heb. 2:2; 9:15+.

- **Trespass**: (Gr. paraptōma) This is a sin that can come in the way of some desire (lusting), some thinking (entertaining a wrongdoing) or some action (carrying out one's desires or thoughts that he or she has been entertaining) that is beyond or overstepping God's righteous standards, as set out in the Scriptures. It is falling or making a false step as opposed to standing or walking upright in harmony with the righteous requirements of God.–Matt. 6:14; Mark 11:25; Rom. 4:25; 5:15-20; 11:11; 2 Cor. 5:19; Gal. 6:1; Eph. 1:7; 2:1, 5; Col 2:13.

- **Sinner**: (Gr. hamartōlos) In the Scriptures "sinners" is generally used in a more specific way, that is, referring to those willfully living in sin, practicing sin, or have a reputation of sinning.–Matt. 9:10; Mark 2:15; Luke 5:30; 7:37-39; John 9:16; Rom. 3:7; Gal. 2:15; 1 Tim. 1:15; Heb. 7:26; Jam. 4:8; 1 Pet 4:18; Jude 1:15.

- **Sensuality, Debauchery, Promiscuity, Licentiousness, Lewdness**: (Gr. aselgeia) This is behavior that is completely lacking in moral restraint, indulgence in sensual pleasure, driven by aggressive and selfish desires, unchecked by morality, especially in sexual matters.–Mark 7:22; Rom. 13:13; 2 Cor. 12:21; Gal. 5:19; Eph. 4:19; 1 Pet. 4:3; 2 Pet. 2:2, 7, 18; Jude 4+.

- **Sexual Immorality**: (Heb. zanah; Gr. porneia) A general term for immoral sexual acts of any kind: such as adultery, prostitution, sexual relations between people not married to each other, homosexuality, and bestiality.–Num. 25:1; Deut. 22:21; Matt. 5:32; 1 Cor. 5:1.

- **Shameful Behavior**: (zimmā(h)) This is wickedness, shameful behavior or conduct that is lewd, shameless regarding sexual behavior. (Lev. 18:17; 19:29; 20:14; Judges 20:6; Job 31:11; Jer. 13:27; Eze. 16:27) It can also refer to the evil thought process that one goes through in plotting their wickedness. (Ps 26:10; 119:150;

Pro. 10:23; 21:27; 24:9; Isa 32:7; Hos 6:9+) Finally, it can be the plans that results from thinking person's evil desires.–Job 17:11.

Sin, Hardened by Deceitfulness of: (Gr. *sklērynthē apatē hamartias*) The sense of *sklērynthē* is stubborn or to be hardened. One is being stubborn and obstinate when it comes to the truth. The sense of *apatē* is deception. A person causes another to believe something that is not true by misleading or deceptive views. The sense of *hamartias* is sin, failure or falling short. *Hamartia* is anything that is not in harmony with or contrary to God's personality, standards, ways, and will. This can be in word, deed, or failing to do what should be done, or in mind or heart attitude.–Heb. 3:13.[60]

Understanding Our Human Imperfection

Why does human imperfection exist, to begin with? As was noted earlier, Adam and Eve rebelled in the Garden of Eden. Romans 5:12, tells us that "through one man sin entered into the world, and death through sin, and so death spread to all men, because all sinned." Paul said earlier in that same letter, "For all have sinned and fall short of the glory of God." All humans born from Adam and Eve are living in imperfection, less than perfect. In the letter to the reader, we learned that all humans are born with two things. The bad news first is all humans are mentally bent toward evil. (Gen. 6:5; 8:21; Jer. 17:9) However, all babies are born with a measure of the conscience (moral compass) that God had given Adam and Eve. If that conscience is fed bad things, it will become calloused and unfeeling, and bad behaviors will seem normal. If that conscience is fed good things, it will be strengthened, to warn you of what are good and what is bad. The world that surrounds us is filled with wickedness, which caters to the imperfect, sinful human nature. (2 Cor. 4:4; 1 John 5:9; Rev. 12:9) Nevertheless, if we possess a mind that is immersed in God's Word, i.e., the mind of Christ, we can win the war against the desires of the flesh and the wicked world that caters to those desires.

Sin vs. Sinners

Ezra writes in the 2 Chronicles 6:36, "When they sin against you (for **there is no man who does not sin**) and you are angry with them and deliver them to an enemy, so that their enemies take them captive to a land far off or near." Paul tells us in Romans 3:23, "for **all have sinned** and fall short of the glory of God." He goes on to write at Romans 5:12,

---

[60] GLOSSARY OF BIBLE TERMS from the Updated American Standard Version (UASV)

"through one man **sin entered into the world**, and death through sin, and so death **spread to all men,** because **all sinned.**" Therefore, everyone human that has ever lived, has descended from Adam and Eve, and, therefore, are sinners by nature. However, the Scriptures use the term "sinners" in another sense as well, describing those who living in ongoing sin or who are known as sinners by their lifestyle. (Lu 7:37-39) God had commanded King Saul to destroy the Amalekites, referring to them as "**sinners.**" The psalmist prayed, "Do not sweep my soul away with **sinners.**" Such sinners, he refers to as "men of bloodshed" and "shameful behavior," that is, lewd, shamelessness regarding sexual conduct. (Ps. 26:9-10) The Jewish religious leaders condemned Jesus for spending time with "tax collectors and sinners." In those days, tax collectors were viewed as disgraceful and dishonest men, on par with the sinners. (Matt. 9:10-11) Of course, Jesus used those occasions to share the good news of the kingdom. God does not look at all sins as being equal. The Bible talks very openly about how sin separates us from God. The Bible is very clear about committing a sin as compared to living in sin; the latter is referred to as a lawless one.–1 John 3:4.

The Gravity of Our Sinfulness

One Bible study website writes, "Nothing can justify sin. **Sin is sin,** and for that matter, we have to accept it as a failure on our part to resist it."[61] We will start with the fact that not all Bible scholars are equal. The Bible clearly differentiates the difference in the gravity level of sin, and some are far more severe than others are. Genesis 13:13 refers to the homosexuality of Sodom and states, "the men of Sodom were wicked and **sinners exceedingly.**" We can see here how God's author qualified the gravity level of the sin, the seriousness level of the sin. God himself said of the sin being carried out in Sodom and Gomorrah, "the outcry against Sodom and Gomorrah is great and **their sin is very grave.**"[62] (Gen. 18:20) When the Israelites' were making a golden calf, "Moses said to the people, 'You yourselves have committed **a great sin** ...'" (Ex 32:30-31) Later, the northern kingdom of Israel "made their sons and their daughters pass through the fire [child sacrifice], and practiced divination and looked for omens, and sold themselves to do evil ..." The author of Second Kings tells that they committed "**a great sin.**" (2 Ki 17:16-17, 21) Sin that is more serious, combined with a heart that lacks remorse, makes one disgusting in God's eyes. (Isa 1:4, 10; 3:9; Lam. 1:8; 4:6) Having an unrepentant heart, as one goes about committing serious

---

[61] How to deal with sin | Bible Study, http://www.amredeemed.com/bible-study/deal-sin/ (accessed February 02, 2017).

[62] Lit *heavy*

sins, his prayer becomes sin. (Ps 109:7, 8, 14) Sin is an insult to God personally. He is not complacent when it comes to sin; as its seriousness increases, his outrage and wrath are justifiably increased. (Rom 1:18; Deut. 29:22-28; Job 42:7; Ps. 21:8, 9) Therefore, **sin is not sin** in the way some Bible scholars try to play down sins that are more serious. We need to understand that our actions have consequences, especially if we are uncaring about and wrongs that we may commit. Therefore, in closing this section, sin separates us from God. We are sinners by nature and cannot go without sinning. Even though we will do our very best to 'not commit a sin;[63] but if we do sin, we have an advocate with the Father, Jesus Christ the righteous one; [2] and he is the propitiation [covers over][64] our sins ...' (1 John 2:1-2)

The level of God's displeasure with us is dependent on the gravity of the sin, our remorse over committing the sin, if we are continuously committing this sin, and what steps we are taking not to commit this sin in the future. All genuine Christians can go without committing any grave sins ever (sexual sins, physical harm to another, stealing, and the like), even though we are imperfect. All genuine Christians can go without living in sin, which is, unrepentantly doing a particular sin regularly. Yet, we cannot go without sinning in word and deed while we are living in imperfection at this time. For those individual bumps in the road, we have the ransom sacrifice of Jesus Christ that will restore and maintain our righteous standing before the Father.

Human Imperfection and ignorance

God makes it all too clear in the Bible that he takes into account that we are imperfect. The Psalmist says that God is compassionate and gracious, slow to anger and abounding in lovingkindness. He will not always find fault, nor will he keep his anger forever. He does not deal with us according to our sins, nor repaid us according to our errors. (Ps. 103:8-10) The apostle Paul had persecuted Christians and even supported having Stephen stoned to death when with the Jewish Pharisees. Nevertheless, he says of God, "I was shown mercy because I acted ignorantly in unbelief." (1 Tim. 1:13; see Lu 12:47-48) Yes, God makes allowances for our ignorance that may have led to our unknowingly sinning. However, this ignorance cannot be willful. If we have willfully

---

[63] Gr hamartete, a verb in the aorist subjunctive. According to *A Grammar of New Testament Greek*, by James H. Moulton, Vol. I, 1908, p. 109, "the Aorist has a 'punctiliar' action, that is, it regards action as a *point*: it represents the point of entrance . . . or that of completion . . . or it looks at a whole action simply as having occurred, without distinguishing any steps in its progress."

[64] Or *an atoning sacrifice; a means of appeasement*

rejected the truth that has been offered to us, there is no excuse. (2 Thess. 2:9-12; Pro. 1:22-33; Hos. 4:6-8) Then, there are those that may be misled from the truth for a time because of ignorance. However, in time, and through the help of some they return.–James 5:19-20.

God's divine power has given us everything we need to live a truly religious life through our knowledge of the one who called us to share in his own glory and goodness. In this way, he has given us the very great and precious gifts he promised, so that by means of these gifts you may escape from the destructive lust that is in the world, and may come to share the divine nature. For this very reason do your best to add goodness to your faith; to your goodness add knowledge; to your knowledge add self-control; to your self-control add endurance; to your endurance add godliness; to your godliness add Christian affection; and to your Christian affection add love. These are the qualities you need, and if you have them in abundance, they will make you active and effective in your knowledge of our Lord Jesus Christ. But if you do not have them, you are so shortsighted that you cannot see and have forgotten that you have been purified from your past sins.– 2 Peter 1:3-9 (GNT)

Repentance for Sins

It is our failure to meet the standards, set out in God's Word, which makes it necessary to repent. (1 John 5:17) Repentance reunites us back to God. If we have just found Christ; then, it is our entire life of actions, which has had us at odds with God's will and purposes, but rather in harmony with the world of humankind that is separate from God. (1 Pet. 4:3; 1 John 2:15-17; 5:19) In this case, we would be repenting for our entire life course up unto that point. Then, again, as a Christian maybe we have developed a bad habit, which now stains our relationship with God. On the other hand, it might be just a single **wrongdoing** (insulted another), or even a **wrong tendency** (excessive complaining), **feeling** (Same-sex attraction), or **attitude** (dislike for authority). (Ps. 141:3, 4; Pro. 6:16-19; Jam 2:9; 4:13-17; 1 John 2:1) Therefore, the steps to be taken to overcome our sin and work on behalf of our repentant heart will be different. As we saw in the above, the extent to which we have sinned may be major or minor.

What Genuine Repentance Involves

Genuine repentance includes both mind and heart. No progress can be made if we do not acknowledge the wrongness of our thoughts, words, or actions. Before that can ever happen, we would first have to accept the rightness of God's will and standards. Unawareness or a lack of memory of his will and standards is an obstacle to repentance. (2 Ki 22:10-11, 18-19; Jonah 1:1-2; 4:11; Rom 10:2-3) This is why God has given us the Bible, which has called all of humanity to repentance. (Jer. 7:13; 25:4-6; Mark 1:14-15; 6:12; Lu 24:27) For two thousand years now, the Christian congregation has been repeating the words of Paul. "**God** has overlooked the times when people did not know him, but now he **commands all of them everywhere to turn away from their evil ways [repent]**. For he has fixed a day in which he will judge the whole world with justice by means of a man he has chosen. He has given proof of this to everyone by raising that man from death!" (Acts 17:29-31) God's Word enables us to understand the rightness of His ways and the wrong that we do in this imperfect condition. (Luke 16:30, 31; 1 Cor. 14:24-25; Heb. 4:12-13) We must be able to accept that we have sinned against the Creator.–Ps 51:3-4; Jer. 3:25.

The world's sorrow, brought about by disappointment, discontent, defeat, punishment for misconduct, and shame, often accompanied produces resentment, anger, jealousy; and it does not lead to anything beneficial, no improvement, and no true hope. Those who have not accepted Christ and come to know the truth, have sadness over their wrongdoing because they have reaped unpleasant consequences. They do not mourn the wrongness of their thoughts, words, or actions, nor the criticism that it might bring others, like family and friends. (Isa. 65:13-15; Jer. 6:13-15, 22-26; Rev. 18:9-11, 15, 17-19) These ones simply regret the fact that they were caught and the punishment that they received, not over the wrong that they have committed. (Gen. 4:5-14) In this way, they are no different from Satan the Devil, who rebelled and caused sickness, old age and death to be our norm among humans. (1 John 3:12) These unbelievers regret their loss, be it financial, shame, embarrassment, or physical, not the thinking, feelings, and actions that contributed to the loss in the first place. We, though, true, genuine Christians, hurt emotionally after even a very small wrong that we may have committed, we weep bitterly after we have committed a serious wrong, which is genuine heartfelt repentance, leading to our being restored to a favorable position with God.

Feelings of Guilt—How Should We View Them?

Guilt is an awareness of having done wrong, accompanied by feelings of shame and regret, which leads to our accepting the responsibility for doing wrong. If we have hurt someone that we care about or if we have fallen short somehow, we are hit with a feeling of guilt; sadness comes over our heart and mind. We also feel guilt when we fail to live up to God's standard as it is set out in His Word. For those who have a personality that is more competitive, outgoing, ambitious, impatient and/or aggressive, a perfectionist, you may very well feel guilty when you are not guilty. How is that? Because you are a perfectionist, setting standards that are unrealistic, you fall short quite often, which triggers feelings of guilt. (Eccl. 7:16) Then, again, there are times that you may browbeat yourself for some minor mistake that produces feelings of shame and that is just excessive guilt. Nevertheless, guilt serves a great purpose.

When we feel guilty about some wrong we have committed, it can comfort us to know that we have good moral standards and that our Christian conscience is working well. (Rom. 2:15) In fact, one who feels no guilt is a **sociopath**, [who] is incapable of feelings such as empathy, regret, and remorse. She does not experience emotional pain herself; thus, she cannot understand the expression of those feelings in others. Sociopaths don't have feelings or emotions, nor do sociopaths cry genuinely."[65] We are all born with a conscience, which is a moral compass that helps us to determine what is right and what is wrong. This conscience can become unfeeling if it is repeatedly ignored. When we start watching some movies that are inappropriate, our conscience will scream at us. However, if ignored, it will become callused and not bother our moral standards, and us, so the level of depravity that we can watch will go up will be altered. Ignoring your conscience can be very dangerous.–Titus 1:15-16.

Therefore, guilt can help us maintain our moral standards and avoid any objectionable actions. In the same way, that a physical pain will let us know that we have some health problem, the emotional guilt or shame will let us know that we have moral or spiritual problem, which needs to be address, not ignored. Once we realize this area of falling short, we can take steps not to repeat the behavior again, to avoid hurting family, friends, schoolmates, others, or ourselves.–Matthew 7:12.

When we express our guilt to another, it is beneficial to us as well as our victim. Note King David's words, "For when I kept silent, my bones wasted away through my groaning all day long. You are a hiding place for me; you preserve me from trouble; you surround me with shouts of deliverance." (Psalm 32:3, 7, ESV) The victim will feel relief as well because they will now realize that your love for them is real enough for you to feel guilty over the pain you have caused.–2 Samuel 11:2-15.

---

[65] Do Sociopaths Cry or Even Have Feelings? – Healthy Place, http://www.healthyplace.com/personality-disorders/sociopath/do-sociopaths-cry-or (accessed February 03, 2017).

J. Wilbur Chapman, noted Methodist evangelist of the nineteenth century, told of **a distinguished minister** in Australia who preached regularly on sin. One of the church officers came to him after one sermon to talk with him. He said to the pastor, "We do not want you to talk so plainly as you do about sin. If our boys and girls hear you talking so much about sin, they will more easily become sinners. Call it whatever you will, but do not speak so plainly about sin."

The minister arose from his desk, walked to a utility closet, and brought back a small bottle of strychnine that was marked "Rat Poison." He said, "I see what you want me to do. You want me to change the label. Suppose I take off this 'Poison' label and replace it with some milder label, such as 'Essence of Peppermint.' The milder you make the label, the more dangerous you make the poison."

This is one of the values of Psalm 32. Without changing the labels and minimizing the effect of sin, this psalm speaks directly to the devastating power of unconfessed sin in the life of a believer. As seen in the life of David, sin committed against God led to sorrow and loss of vitality in his life. But as also witnessed in David's life, when he confessed his sin, there was a resurgence of great joy as well as a passion for living to the glory of God. From this magnificent piece of inspired literature, we conclude that confessing our sin is a vital part of vibrant, victorious Christian living.

This psalm reflects the time when David was king over Israel. He sent his troops into battle against the Ammonites while he remained behind. During this time he fell into adulterous sin with Bathsheba (2 Sam. 11:1–5). To make matters worse, he tried to cover up his sin by having her husband, Uriah the Hittite, killed (2 Sam. 11:6–17). For the next year David lived with his guilty conscience in deep agony of spirit. He became emotionally distraught, physically ill, and mentally disturbed.

Nathan the prophet visited the king (2 Sam. 12:1–15) and told him a story of two men, one rich and one poor. One had many flocks, the other just one little lamb. Without warning, the rich man with many flocks took the poor man's one little lamb. When David heard this, he erupted, "As surely as the LORD lives, the man who did this deserves to die!" To this Nathan said, "You are the man!" Exposed, David confessed, "I have sinned against the LORD." When Nathan heard this, he said, "The LORD has taken away your sin. You are not going to die."

This psalm records the joy that David found through the confession of his sin to God. This psalm "of David" was written after his confrontation with Nathan the prophet. It is a maskil, meaning that it was intended to instruct and teach. Specifically, this psalm was written by

David to teach the people of God to confess their sins to the Lord.[66]

Sensible View of Guilt

It is right, of course, that you feel guilty over your past wrongdoing. If we are moved emotionally and seek no excuses for our behaviors, our repentance is real. You do not want to continue to look down on yourself as a sinner, that is, one living in sin willfully. You're always making yourself feel guilty over the past that you have already been forgiven for is unloving to yourself, and will only produce problems or difficulties instead of helping you to grow spiritually. The same applies to us; we do not want to make others feel guilt and shame for things they have been forgiven for as well, which will do more harm than good. We need to praise others for the good that they have done, the progress that they have made, and evidence that we believe they will succeed. We need to be joyous about our own progress as well, knowing that we will continue to grow in the faith. Solomon writes, "Foolish people don't care if they sin, but good people want to be forgiven." (Pro. 14:9, GNT) Yes, a guilty conscience should move us to apologize to the person we hurt and God, or to confess our sins to God and inform the pastor if our sins were serious, seeking help to work on whatever brought us to err. However, our life with family, friend, neighbor and God should be about love, not guilt.

God Makes Allowances

However, we as imperfect humans can be accredited a righteous standing before God, being accepted back into the family of God. **He makes allowances** for our imperfection.

Psalm 103:9-12 Updated American Standard Version (UASV)

[9] He will not always find fault,
  nor will he keep his anger forever.
[10] He does not deal with us according to our sins,
  nor repaid us according to our iniquities.
[11] For as high as the heavens are above the earth,
  So great is his lovingkindness toward those who fear him.
[12] As far as the east is from the west,
  so far does he remove our transgressions from us.

---

[66] Anders, Max; Lawson, Steven. Holman Old Testament Commentary - Psalms: 11 (pp. 170-171). B&H Publishing. Kindle Edition.

103:8–9. God's sovereign rule over the psalmist's life is marked by **compassionate and gracious** dealings. Even in the face of his sin, God is **slow to anger**, withholding swift discipline. The Lord may be justly angry because of David's sin, but he **will not always accuse** him. God will soon forgive and restore him.

103:10–12. God's abounding mercy withholds his judgment. He **does not treat us as our sins deserve.** Nor does God **repay us according to our iniquities** [errors]. Christ's atonement has satisfied God's wrath, and, therefore, believers will never be condemned for their sins. As high **as the heavens are above the earth**—an immeasurable distance—is precisely how **great** God's **love** is **for those who fear him.** Infinite and vast is God's eternal love for his own. **As far as the east is from the west**—another immeasurable distance—is how **far God has removed our transgressions from us** (Isa. 1:18; 38:17; 43:25).[67]

Isaiah 38:17 Updated American Standard Version (UASV)

[17] Look, it was for my welfare
  that I had great bitterness;
but in love you have delivered my soul
  from the pit of destruction,
for you have cast all my sins
  behind your back.

Now Hezekiah affirms that all the credit goes to God who has "kept back, withheld" him from falling into the pit and dying. Even more importantly, God has forgiven Hezekiah by metaphorically putting all his sins behind his back so they are not seen any more (cf. Ps 103:12; Mic 7:19).[68]

Micah 7:18-19 Updated American Standard Version (UASV)

[18] Who is a God like you, **pardoning <u>error</u>**
  and **passing over <u>transgression</u>**
  for the remnant of his inheritance?
He does not retain his anger forever,
  because he delights in lovingkindness.
[19] He will again have compassion on us;

---

[67] Anders, Max; Lawson, Steven. Holman Old Testament Commentary - Psalms 76-150 (Kindle Locations 3872-3879). B&H Publishing. Kindle Edition.

[68] Gary V. Smith, *Isaiah 1–39*, ed. E. Ray Clendenen, The New American Commentary (Nashville: B & H Publishing Group, 2007), 650.

he will tread our iniquities underfoot.
You will cast all our sins
    into the depths of the sea.

7:18 The type of rhetorical question beginning this verse is used in order to express a "forcible denial." So the reply is "No one." The question is a way of affirming God's incomparability.[77] Here he is incomparable particularly in his forgiving love and grace. Mays points out that this book, "which begins with a portrayal of YHWH's advent in wrath, concludes with praise of his mercy." To emphasize the point, three different Hebrew words for sin are used and four verbs that indicate forgiveness ("pardons ... forgives ... tread ... hurl"). More literal renderings of the verbs would yield "takes away ... passes over (cf. Exod 12:12–13; 1 Cor 5:7) ... subdue ... hurl." "Sin" is the same Hebrew root that occurs in "iniquities" (v. 19) and should have been translated "iniquity" here for consistency within the same unit. The Hebrew term connotes what is twisted, crooked, or perverse. For "transgression" see comments on 1:5. Waltke notes: "The crucial vocabulary of Micah 7:18 is used in connection with the Suffering Servant of Yahweh in Isaiah 53: $n\bar{a}\dot{s}\bar{a}$' (to bear; v. 12), '$\bar{a}w\bar{o}n$ (iniquity; vv. 6, 11), $pe\check{s}a$' (transgression; vv. 8, 12)—all in connection with Yahweh's pleasure ($\dot{h}\bar{a}p\bar{e}\dot{s}$; v. 10)."

The people he thus forgives are the "remnant of his inheritance." Rather than staying angry forever (see Pss 30:5; 103:8–18) the Lord instead delights to show "mercy" (more lit. "faithful covenant love," Hb. $\dot{h}esed$; see comments on 6:8 and note). Samuel Davies nicely captures the sentiments of this verse in his hymn, "Great God of Wonders":

Great God of wonders! all Thy ways
Are matchless, God-like and divine;
But the fair glories of Thy grace
More God-like and unrivaled shine.
In wonder lost, with trembling joy,
We take the pardon of our God:
Pardon for crimes of deepest dye,
A pardon bought with Jesus' blood.
O may this strange, this matchless grace,
This God-like miracle of love,
Fill the whole earth with grateful praise,
And all th'angelic choirs above.
Who is a pard'ning God like Thee?
Or who has grace so rich and free?

7:19 The Hebrew for "compassion" suggests a tender, maternal love such as a mother would have for her child. The Hebrew for "tread underfoot" also could be rendered "subdue." Sin is pictured as an enemy that God conquers and liberates us from. "God overcomes sin and sets his people free." Fausset adds, "When God takes away the guilt of sin, that it may not condemn us, He takes away also the power of sin, that it may not rule us."[82]

Finally, just as the Lord hurled Pharaoh's chariots and his army into the sea and they sank to the depths like a stone (Exod 15:4–5), so he will hurl all "our" sins into the depths of the sea. This, of course, speaks of the complete forgiveness of sin and the removal of its guilt forever (see Jer 50:20). "God not only puts our sins out of sight [Isa 38:17]; he also puts them out of reach (Mic 7:19; Ps 103:12), out of mind (Jer 31:34), and out of existence (Isa 43:25; 44:22; Ps 51:1, 9; Acts 3:19)." Most Hebrew manuscripts of the MT actually read "*their* iniquities (better, 'sins')" instead of "*our* iniquities." However, "our" is supported by some Hebrew manuscripts and the versions (LXX, Syr., and Vg.), as well as by perhaps the context. A few commentators prefer to retain "their" and refer it to the nations of vv. 16–17. Then the forgiveness spoken of here would include both Jews and Gentiles. Of course, this is ultimately true anyway, whether or not the text explicitly states it here. In a more practical vein, Boice writes, "A stanza from a hymn by Martin Luther aptly summarizes the entire last chapter of Micah's prophecy. If we have understood and responded to the prophecy, we should be able to join in his sentiments.

> Though great our sins and sore our wounds
> and deep and dark our fall,
> His helping mercy hath no bounds,
> his love surpassing all.
> Our trusty living Shepherd he,
> Who shall at last set Israel free
> from all their sin and sorrow."[69]

It is your thinking, that is, your observation (view) of an event, which will affect your feelings and your behavior. All three stages are equally important: (1) think, (2) feel, and (3) behavior. The objective is to implement practical ways of controlling the behavior while you work on altering your irrational thinking. Behaviors are important because not all behaviors are equal in severity. If you were simply trying to overcome habitual lying, the behavior would be seen as minor in comparison to an alcoholic that is drinking and driving, or a heroin addict, even worse, someone molesting another. These would be seriously egregious behaviors. In this case, **it is not** best to let these behaviors go unchecked

---

[69] Kenneth L. Barker, *Micah, Nahum, Habakkuk, Zephaniah*, vol. 20, The New American Commentary (Nashville: Broadman & Holman Publishers, 1999), 133–135.

until the thinking is under control. You will need to learn coping mechanism that can keep such behavior in check until the thinking has been altered for the better. Paul pummeled his body to get control over his vessel, not literally of course. It means he took harsh and controlled measures. Cognitive Behavioral Therapy is vital too, and the Bible is likely the originator of this treatment, namely, changing the thinking, which changes the inner person. Yes, belief in Jesus is necessary but faith is not blind belief. The key word in the Gospel of John is the verb "believe" (Greek: pisteuo), which appears **98 times**. It requires more of us than mere belief. In other words, the things you do are proof that your faith is genuine.

Remember: change is hard. In order for gold to be purified, it has to go through the fire. This process is going to be tough, but just imagine the you that will be on the other side. Your purpose awaits you if you are but brave enough and determined enough to seek it.

Process Questions:

If all sin is not equal, what is the difference in the various types of sin? Process how this applies to you.

_____
_____
_____
_____
_____
_____
_____
_____
_____
_____

What choices in your life would be described as sinful? Identify the truth of what right living looks like compared to sinful living?

_____
_____
_____
_____
_____
_____
_____
_____
_____
_____

Feeling remorse and repentant of our actions is important but the motivation for your remorse is just as important. When you say, "I'm sorry" for the mistakes you have made, have you been sorry for the effect it has had on others and the physical or emotional pain it has caused, or have you been remorseful and "sorry" due to the consequences of having been caught? What is the significance of this?

_____

_____

_____

_____

_____

_____

_____

_____

_____

_____

_____

How suppressed or immune are you to your conscious? Have you been quieting your conscious and if so, how has this effected your ability to heal or repair the damages of mistakes in your past?

_____

_____

_____

_____

What has been your experience of confessing and accepting responsibility for your wrongdoing and has it brought you joy and relief? Process what your experience has been and identify what you believe the reason to be.

_____

_____

_____

_____

_____

_____

_____

_____

_____

Identify your self-talk regarding guilt, sin, and confession? Process your understanding and thoughts regarding these principles.

_____

_____

_____

_____

_____

_____

_____

_____

Recognize the ways in which you have sinned and process what you need to do to address these areas of your life?

_____

_____

_____

_____

_____

_____

_____

_____

Four Pillars Assignment on this Chapter's Topic

Self-Talk (40,000 individual thoughts summarized)

_____

_____

_____

_____

_____

_____

Faulty Beliefs (Beliefs about yourself and your situation as a result of your thoughts.)

_____

_____

_____

_____

_____

Perception (The faulty beliefs about your environment as a result of your faulty beliefs about yourself and your environments)

_____

_____
_____
_____
_____
_____

Behaviors (What you choose to do)

_____

_____
_____
_____
_____
_____

Finally, identify the outcome and how it reinforces the self-talk.

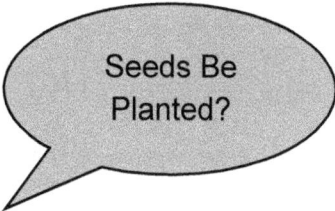

_____

_____
_____
_____
_____
_____
_____
_____
_____

Seeds Be Planted?

1.) Who/What planted the seeds that led to your self-talk?

_____

_____
_____
_____
_____
_____

2.) How did you allow them to take root in your mind?

_____
_____
_____
_____
_____
_____

3.) Are the seeds that were planted seeds of fruit bearing trees which will bring you good life and sustain you or are they seeds of weeds which will rob you and kill good things in your life?

_____
_____
_____
_____
_____
_____
_____
_____
_____
_____
_____
_____
_____

Further Thoughts

_____
_____
_____
_____
_____
_____
_____
_____
_____
_____
_____
_____
_____
_____

Chapter XII Your Past Does Not Equal Your Destiny

Isaiah 43:18-19 Updated American Standard Version (UASV)

¹⁸ "Remember not the former things,
nor consider the things of old.
¹⁹ Look, I am doing a new thing;
now it springs forth, do you not perceive it?
I will make a way in the wilderness
and rivers in the desert.

> On the basis of God's new word of promise and hope and on the strength of his consistent character, the prophet drew the consequences. The God of the exodus had something new for them. They must forget the past and its problems. They must surrender thoughts that Yahweh was only the god of the good old days. They must look forward to God's new thing. Be ready to be surprised by God! God had a new exodus through a new wilderness across new streams that were ready for his people so the people he formed might sing a new hymn to God.[70]

2 Corinthians 5:17-19 Updated American Standard Version (UASV)

¹⁷ Therefore if anyone is in Christ, he is a new creation;[71] the old things have passed away; behold, new things have come. ¹⁸ And all these things are from God, who has reconciled us to himself through Christ, and who has given us the ministry of reconciliation, ¹⁹ namely, that God was in Christ reconciling the world to himself, not counting their trespasses[72] against them, and entrusting to us the message of reconciliation.

> **5:17.** Paul asserted that every person who is **in Christ**—who is joined to him in his death and resurrection—has become **a new creation.** Paul drew from Old Testament prophetic language, describing

---

[70] Anders, Max; Butler, Trent. Holman Old Testament Commentary - Isaiah (p. 238). B&H Publishing. Kindle Edition.

[71] Or *creature*; Gr *ktisis*

[72] **Trespass**: (Gr. *paraptōma*) This is a sin that can come in the way of some desire (lusting), some thinking (entertaining a wrongdoing) or some action (carrying out one's desires or thoughts that he or she has been entertaining) that is beyond or overstepping God's righteous standards, as set out in the Scriptures. It is falling or making a false step as opposed to standing or walking upright in harmony with the righteous requirements of God.–Matt. 6:14; Mark 11:25; Rom. 4:25; 5:15-20; 11:11; 2 Cor. 5:19; Gal. 6:1; Eph. 1:7; 2:1, 5; Col 2:13.

the new world that God would bring at the end of the age (Isa. 66:22). This language also appears in the New Testament (2 Pet. 3:13). "New creation" describes those who follow Christ because they have begun the transformation that will eventually lead to their full enjoyment of salvation in the new heavens and new earth. Christ's death and resurrection introduced a foretaste of that new world to come.

Paul's ministry was compelled by the display of Christ's love on the cross. Paul had been united to Christ in his death and resurrection, and thus had been inwardly renewed and regenerated. The apostle truly was a new creation. In this changed state, he began to look at people differently. Prior to coming to Christ, Paul would not have thought about the Corinthians much. He certainly would not have worked and sacrificed for the Gentiles in that church. But now the shadow of Christ's cross fell across his view every time he looked at other people. He saw believers as new creations in Christ and unbelievers as people in need of Christ. This perspective shaped his ministry.

5:18a. Paul remarked that **all this** (the changes he had just described) was **from God**. Throughout his writings Paul consistently attested that every dimension of salvation results from divine grace. He had in mind here especially the radical transformation of his outlook on other human beings that showed his transformation into a new creation. This dramatic change was a work of God in his heart.

5:18b. Paul explained the change that God had wrought in his life in terms of **reconciliation**. He repeated the Greek terms for "reconcile" and "reconciliation" (*katallasso/katallage*) five times throughout 5:18b–20, emphasizing his point. Reconciliation is the establishment of harmony and peace between enemies. Enemies are said to be reconciled when their hostility ceases and mutual love binds them together. Paul's explanation of God's re-creative activity in his life centered on this doctrine.

Paul spoke of divine reconciliation in two ways in this context. First, he stated that God had **reconciled** Paul and his company **to himself through Christ**. By his own testimony Paul had been an opponent to the ways of God. He had even persecuted the body of Christ. Yet, God established peace between himself and Paul **through** Christ. This act of divine love and grace transformed the apostle.

Second, Paul said that God **gave** him and his company **the ministry of reconciliation**. Why had his personal reconciliation changed his outlook on other human beings? It was because God had a special destiny for Paul—**the ministry of reconciliation**. A ministry (*diakonia*) is a service to others on God's behalf. God had called Paul to be an instrument of **reconciliation;** his life was devoted to making peace between God and humanity through the preaching of the gospel.

5:19. Paul continued to focus on his ministry of reconciliation by defining what he meant. First, he explained that God was reconciling the world to himself in Christ by **not counting men's sins against them.** In Paul's view, human beings had become enemies of God because they transgressed divine law (Rom. 5:10; Phil. 3:18). Men and women without Christ are hostile to the things of God and subject to his judgment (Rom. 2:16; 8:7). Reconciliation requires that God forgive people of their sins to remove this hostility.

Paul spoke of God reconciling **the world to himself** because he knew the ultimate end of God's purpose was worldwide. This passage has been used to support the false doctrine of universalism—the belief that every person will be saved from judgment. Although Paul spoke categorically of **the world,** he described this worldwide reconciliation as taking place **in Christ.** For Paul, the expression "in Christ" referred to the union that believers have with Christ in his death and resurrection as they place their faith in him. So we must understand his categorical terminology here and in similar passages in light of his clear teaching that salvation comes only to those who trust in Christ for salvation (Rom. 11:19–20; 2 Thess. 2:10–12).

Paul also wrote that **the world** would be condemned. This cannot refer to those who trust in Christ for salvation. The reconciliation of **the world** is the goal of the gospel in the sense that salvation will extend beyond the nation of Israel to all the nations of the earth. In accordance with the prophetic word of the Old Testament, the ultimate end of the gospel ministry was the reconciliation of those who are united **in Christ** from all nations of the earth.

The apostle also explained his own role in this worldwide plan. God had **committed to** Paul and his company **the message of reconciliation.** This phrase may also be translated as "the message about reconciliation," which is exactly what Paul explained this message to be. Paul went about as an apostle of Christ, proclaiming that God had provided the way of salvation through Christ. He saw himself called by God to the task of bringing to fruition God's plan to reconcile the world in Christ.[73]

---

[73] Richard L. Pratt Jr, *I & II Corinthians*, vol. 7, Holman New Testament Commentary (Nashville, TN: Broadman & Holman Publishers, 2000), 357–359.

Does your past control you?

Are you a defective creation?

More on Guilt vs Shame.

Supplemental Assignments:

Read the The Apostle: A Life of Paul by John Pollock

Read the New Testament starting in the book of Acts to understand Paul's story

Look up your favorite "famous" person, research their biographies, and look at how they have overcome mistakes and tragedy in their life.

Your Past is in the Past...Leave it There.

What is your past? Is it so scary that you cannot imagine it? In writing this tonight, I am overcome with thoughts of so many of my patients from years back; memories of their past and how they believed it controlled them. I don't know your walk of life, but theirs was no fairy tale; a young girl abused starting as a baby by her father and mother, starved and shown she was an object to be used and then locked away in a closet; left alone to starve. She had a terrible start and believed that because of her start, her life was destined to be more of the same. Others had made so many mistakes that they were known not as the person they could be, the person I was so blessed to have met in my sessions, but known only by their mistakes. The hardest part about our past is not in accepting that it happened, but it is in leaving it in the past and not allowing it to control your future.

Our past carries with it so much shame that we sometimes feel like when others look at us, that they see the line of mistakes standing behind us. For some of you, the line of your mistakes is found in the scars on your arms. You can probably look at them right now and they trigger memories of each moment you were overcome by shame, or are now overcome by shame at the choice to pick up the razor in the first place. Whatever your reminder is, you see it and feel it follow you every day and think that because your past controlled you in that moment, you are destined to be under its' control for the rest of your life. "It" being your anger, addictions, sex, aggression, hostility, arguments, broken relationships. You tell

Shame says I am wrong, Guilt tells me that what I did was wrong.

yourself, "I told you so," every time "it" controls you again.

Our past can control who we believe we are, what we are capable of, and it can become a pit that we find ourselves falling deeper and deeper into as more and more mistakes pile up against us. Most of the time, our past is not what is really controlling us, but it is our shame that is controlling us. Shame tells us that we are what is wrong whereas guilt tells us what we did was wrong. Are you trapped by shame, unable to get past what was done to you or what you have done? Is it to the point where you allow the past to define who you are? I'm a sex offender, a liar, a prostitute, a drug addict... Has it become so much a part of you that you fear that you can never be rid of it? Do you believe that the problem is the choice, or do you think the problem is you; you're just damaged?

Hopefully, you learned a lot in the last chapter and processed with your support person a great deal because the reason you repeat the same mistake is because you are trying to fix the behavior. You think that you can fix this if you just change the behavior. When I tell you that you need to give it to God, that sounds like churchy-talk, but it really has to start with Him first. First off, do you think God makes mistakes? The God of the universe, the one who created and knows every star in the sky by name and could tell you the exact number of the hairs on your head? That same God made a mistake when he made you? He made everything else so perfectly, but you were just too much for Him, is that what you're telling me? You were made exactly as you were supposed to be made. So when you think to yourself that something is wrong with you, then you are literally telling God, "Hey dude, I need to make an exchange cuz this here is a faulty product...um, let's get me a return...". No, God made you exactly as you were meant to be made, so this means that you are off the hook, there is nothing wrong with you. Therapy done, right.

You and me, there is nothing different between the two of us except for our experiences. I make mistakes all the time, and so do you. You know what-I'm going to probably wake up tomorrow and do something stupid and maybe so will you. Or you may be better than me, who knows. The point is, God knows our stories, and He knows our choices before we even make them. The past is unchangeable, but it does not have to dictate your future because it shows nothing about you other than what we all know, that you are not perfect; you're just like me and all the rest of the people on this planet, imperfect.

Feeling guilt and remorse over what we did is a good thing. It is like pain; when we touch something hot, pain tells us that is not good and will hurt us. When we lie, and we damage a relationship with someone, it is painful to have, to be honest about our mistake and work to heal the relationship. This is a good thing because it teaches you that lying hurts, and hopefully the pain will remind you not to do it again. You need guilt to show you that what you did was wrong so that you can make it right. Guilt helps you grow and change and become better, so you don't make the same mistake again or if you do, you do it differently and are still progressing and learning. Shame keeps you stuck going over and over the same track in your mind, not allowing you to grow but forcing you to stay chained to your past and causes damage in all of the relationships you have. Shame will tell a man who cheated on his wife that he caused too much damage. He cannot ever fix it, so he pushes his wife away even when she is willing to work through it. He truly wants to rebuild the relationship but doesn't for fear that his mistake has made that future impossible. Guilt will allow him to come to his wife and apologize, willing to work with her and process how to heal the relationship. Shame will tell him that he might as well give up because he cannot overcome this. Guilt makes you stronger after a mistake shame breaks you down.

Paul in the Bible has the best story of this which I explained earlier in this workbook. If there was anyone whose past was going to define his future, it would have been him. His past name was Saul, and he was a murderer and torturer of Christians shortly after the crucifixion of Christ. He was forever changed when he went to find Christians who were residing in a city named Damascus and was suddenly blinded. He went from being the hunter and murderer of Christians to joining them and helping them preach the Good News all over the Mediterranean. If you look at the New Testament, most of it was written by him. Talk about a turn of events; from the murderer of Christians to joining them and preaching love and forgiveness. Read his letters to know more about him. Start in Acts and keep on going. Most of what you read will have been from him.

Check out Paul's story.

Process Questions:

How is shame used as a tool for the enemy to attack you?

_____

_____

_____

_____

_____

_____

_____

How have you struggled with Shame?

_____

_____

_____

_____

_____

_____

What would it look like to have guilt and allow mistakes or conflict to strengthen your relationship instead of break it down?

_____

_____

_____

_____

_____

_____

_____

_____

_____

_____

_____

What are your past experiences with conflict or mistakes and its' impact on relationships?

_____

_____

_____

_____

_____

_____

_____

_____

_____

_____

_____

_____

What are the faulty beliefs/self-talk you have regarding shame and mistakes and how can you challenge them in the future?

_____
_____
_____
_____
_____
_____
_____
_____
_____
_____
_____
_____
_____
_____
_____

Four Pillars Assignment on this Chapter's Topic

Self-Talk (40,000 individual thoughts summarized)

_____
_____
_____
_____
_____
_____
_____
_____
_____

Faulty Beliefs (Beliefs about yourself and your situation as a result of your thoughts.)

_____
_____
_____
_____
_____
_____
_____
_____
_____

Perception (The faulty beliefs about your environment as a result of your faulty beliefs about yourself and your environments)

_____

_____
_____
_____
_____
_____
_____

Behaviors (What you choose to do)

_____

_____
_____
_____
_____
_____

Finally, identify the outcome and how it reinforces the self-talk.

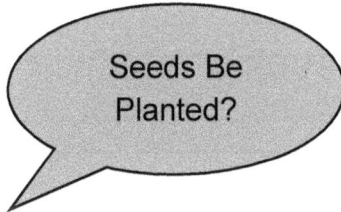

_____

_____
_____
_____
_____

Seeds Be Planted?

1.) Who/What planted the seeds that led to your self-talk?

_____

_____
_____
_____
_____
_____
_____

2.) How did you allow them to take root in your mind?

_____

_____

_____

_____

_____

3.) Are the seeds that were planted seeds of fruit bearing trees which will bring you good life and sustain you or are they seeds of weeds which will rob you and kill good things in your life?

_____

_____

_____

_____

_____

Further Thoughts

_____

_____

_____

_____

_____

_____

_____

_____

_____

_____

_____

_____

_____

_____

_____

_____

_____

_____

Chapter XIII Sex and Love

1 Corinthians 13:4-7 Updated American Standard Version (UASV)

⁴ Love is long suffering and kind; Love is not jealous, it does not brag; it is not puffed up,⁷⁴ ⁵ does not behave indecently;⁷⁵ is not seeking its own interests, is not provoked, does not keep a record of wrong, ⁶ does not rejoice over unrighteousness, but rejoices with the truth; ⁷ bears all things, believes all things, hopes all things, endures all things.

13:4. Paul's deep concern for the unity of the church at Corinth caused him to address several aspects of Christian love. The first quality Paul listed was **love is patient**. Patience is a quality of love that the New Testament frequently mentions by this or closely related terminology. It signifies forbearance, slowness to repay for offenses. God is patient because he does not immediately punish those who offend him. God's patience slows down the judgment process and opens the way for reprieve from punishment altogether. Believers should behave similarly because of their love for one another.

One must be careful to distinguish patience from indifference. Patience bears with an offense, but indifference ignores it altogether. When an offense takes place that is harmful or destructive to oneself or to others, it must not be entirely overlooked. Paul, for instance, loved the Corinthians. He patiently bore with them and worked with them slowly and carefully to edify them and honor Christ.

Love ... is kind. The term *kindness* (*chrestotes*) appears many times in Paul's epistles. It is connected with patience again in Galatians 5:22, apparently because these concepts are similar. Paul's distinction between patience and kindness was probably similar to that of English speakers. Patience has a more temporal focus, while kindness refers to the manner in which a person treats others.

Kindness takes many forms. In general, it is soft and gentle. Occasionally, however, kindness must take the form of a careful rebuke designed to bring about a good result. Paul demonstrated this as he dealt kindly, but firmly, with the Corinthians. Jesus' own life demonstrated such kindness (Luke 13:15–17).

Love ... does not envy. One may admire another for something

---

⁷⁴ I.e., self-important or made proud

⁷⁵ Or *is not rude*

that person is or has, and he may desire many of the same good things for himself. Jealousy and envy begin when admiration and desire turn to resentment of others for what they have. They are the attitudinal roots of many terrible actions in the world. The Bible illustrates this time and again. To envy is not to display the love of Christ, who gave up all for the sake of others (Phil. 2:3–8).

Love ... does not boast. Paul's word for "boast" (*perpereuomai*) appears only here in the New Testament, and infrequently in the rest of hellenistic literature. The meaning seems to be "bragging without foundation," and may also encompass sinful acts that Paul elsewhere called *kauchaomai*. The NIV also translates *kauchaomai* as "boast," but *kauchaomai* does not always carry a negative connotation.

At the same time, loving other people does not mean failing to acknowledge the good God has done in oneself and in others. Paul was not beyond complimenting the Corinthians. He even asserted his own standing on occasion. Love does not mean lying about human accomplishments. Rather, it means not exalting ourselves over others as if our accomplishments were based on our own merit and ability.

Love ... is not proud. To be proud is to be overly self-confident or insubordinate to God and others. The Scriptures of the Old and New Testaments condemn pride as the source of much destruction and pain in the world. When one cares about other people, he does not find himself full of self-importance or arrogance toward others.

Unfortunately, many Christians avoid pride so studiously that they deprecate themselves. Whether in ourselves or others, the image of God must be held in high regard. Pride reproaches other images of God. Self-hatred reproaches oneself as the image of God.

13:5. Love ... is not rude. Paul at least expressed the need to follow customary decorum. The definitions of "rude" vary from culture to culture. At the heart of rudeness is a disregard for the social customs that others have adopted. When one does not concern himself with the likes and dislikes of others, he shows a disrespect for them. Proper regard, on the other hand, indicates love for other people.

Nevertheless, love does not always require a person to go along with the crowd. When the customs of a culture contradict the higher ideals of the Christian faith, it is not unloving to break these social mores. In fact, it may actually show Christlike love to break with such cultural norms. For instance, every loving Christian bears the responsibility to break the customs that perpetuate racial discrimination.

Love ... is not self-seeking. Paul probably had in mind here the practice of always putting oneself in first place without due consideration of others. Many situations in life call upon Christians to choose between benefit to themselves and to others. The loving person puts the benefit of others over his or her own good. Paul exemplified this practice when he refused to receive money for his work as an apostle (9:6–15). Jesus' humiliation was the greatest expression of putting others' benefit above one's own (Phil. 2:4–8).

It is also important to realize that this practice does not mean ignoring one's own legitimate needs. Jesus himself withdrew from the crowds for his own benefit, sometimes just to get away and other times to pray (Luke 5:16; 22:41).

Love ... is not easily angered. The NIV probably catches the sense of Paul's expression even though the text says nothing explicit about the ease with which one becomes angry. Those who love others do not normally become irritated and angry whenever others do wrong, but rather are slow to anger. They are patient.

Still, there are times when anger is appropriate. Paul himself became angry when he saw the idols of Athens (Acts 17:16). Luke described him with the same word Paul used here (*paroxunomai*). Even Jesus became angry when he saw people's hardness of heart (Mark 3:5) and the money changers in the temple (John 2:14–17). We must never allow an avoidance of anger to become indifference to the suffering of others or to the honor of God.

Love ... keeps no record of wrongs. People who love others do not keep meticulous records of offenses. They offer forgiveness time and again. Both Jesus (Luke 23:34) and Stephen (Acts 7:60) demonstrated this type of love by forgiving the people who put them to death.

But Paul did not speak absolutely here. With no record of offenses, one cannot help others with many of their problems. Paul received reports on the wrongdoings in the Corinthian church. Someone had to keep a record in order to give him these reports. Yet, the purpose of the records was restorative, not vengeful or begrudging.

13:6. Love ... does not delight in evil but rejoices with the truth. Paul juxtaposed **evil** and **truth** in this description of **love**. This contrast suggests that the term *truth* means something like "living according to the truth." In other words, those who truly love do not enjoy seeing their loved ones stumble into evil. They rejoice when their loved ones try to live according to the truth of the gospel. Sin destroys people's lives, so to rejoice in their sin is to rejoice in their destruction.

13:7. Love ... always protects. Major English Bible versions translate the term *protects* (*stego*) very differently from one another. The word can mean "to endure" or "to cover, protect." If Paul had in mind the concept of endurance, he meant that love bears with many offenses and does not stop loving even under the strain of difficulties imposed by others, even going so far as to love enemies (Luke 6:27). If he had in mind the concept of covering, then he may have meant that love will not seek to expose the sins of others. Love handles the sins of others in ways that will not bring exposure or shame.

It is evident that Paul limited such endurance or protection. For example, he instructed Timothy that "those who sin are to be rebuked publicly" (1 Tim. 5:20). Likewise, he called public attention to the strife between Euodia and Syntyche (Phil. 4:2). He commanded the Corinthians to stop tolerating the man who had his father's wife (1 Cor. 5:1–13). Wisdom is required to know when and how to protect or to expose, and love always tends to protect.

Love ... always trusts. Perhaps this characteristic of love is best expressed in contemporary English idiom as: "Love gives the benefit of the doubt." Suspicion and doubt toward others do not indicate affection or love. On the contrary, when someone loves with Christlike love, he entrusts himself to the person he loves time and again. Still, love does not demand that a person trust even when the basis for trust has been destroyed. Love does not give the "benefit" when there is no "doubt." In these circumstances trust is folly. Yet, the general practice of those who love is to trust the good intentions of others as much as possible.

Love ... always hopes. Loving someone requires maintaining a measure of optimism on that person's behalf. Hope is an attitude that good will eventually come to those who may now be failing. Failure invades every Christian's life, and it often causes others to give up on the one who fails. Yet, Christians who love continue to hope for the best. This optimism encourages others to keep moving forward. This hope is based not on the Christian, but on Christ. The hope of each Christian is that Christ will preserve him to glory. When a brother falls, it is Christ who picks him up and makes him stand (Rom. 14:4). Christ is the one who promised to finish the work he began. Optimism can also become foolishness and wishful thinking. For example, Paul did not believe that the incestuous man at Corinth would repent without undergoing church discipline.

Love ... always perseveres. Loving someone is easy when the other person does not challenge one's affections by offending or failing. Love's quality becomes evident when it must endure trials. The New Testament encourages Christians to persevere in their Christian walks (1 John 5:2–5). Here Paul had in mind particularly the need to persevere in love for others. Christians should look to the length and perseverance of Christ's love as the standard for their own.[76]

Ephesians 5:31-32 Updated American Standard Version (UASV)

[31] For this reason a man shall leave his father and mother and shall be joined to his wife, and the two shall become one flesh. [32] This mystery[77] is great; but I am speaking with reference to Christ and the congregation.[78]

5:28–32. After having presented the work of Christ for the church, Paul now comes back to the reality of husband-wife relationships. He repeats the fact that husbands are to love their wives as their own bodies. Even though the husband lives in an imperfect body, he loves it, nourishes it, and cherishes it. So he is to do the same for his wife, even though she is imperfect.

Paul repeats Genesis 2:24, establishing that a husband and wife are to become one flesh, and closes by restating that the relationship between the wife and a husband is like the relationship between Christ and the church.[79]

1 John 4:16-18 Updated American Standard Version (UASV)

[16] We have come to know and have believed the love which God has for us. **God is love, and the one who remains in love remains in God, and God remains in him**. [17] By this, love is perfected with us, so that we may have confidence[80] in the day of judgment; because as he is, so also are we in this world. [18] There is no fear in love; but **perfect love casts out fear**, because fear has to do with punishment,[81] and the one who fears is not perfected in love.

4:14–16. John's readers probably never saw Jesus in the flesh. False teachers, however, claimed to have made heavenly journeys during which they saw God in heaven. This is impossible. God cannot be seen. How do

---

[76] Richard L. Pratt Jr, *I & II Corinthians*, vol. 7, Holman New Testament Commentary (Nashville, TN: Broadman & Holman Publishers, 2000), 229–233.

[77] I.e., *secret plan*

[78] Gr *ekklesia* ("assembly")

[79] Max Anders, *Galatians-Colossians*, vol. 8, Holman New Testament Commentary (Nashville, TN: Broadman & Holman Publishers, 1999), 175.

[80] Gr., *parresia*; Lit., "freedom of speech" "outspokenness"

[81] Gr., Kolasin (Lit., lopping off cutting off), the punishment is the fear of being cut off, i.e., not remaining in God's love on judgment day.

you deny the claims of these teachers and still say, **we have seen?** How, if your readers have never seen Jesus, can they testify that God sent his Son to be our Savior? First, John and his fellow apostles saw Jesus in the flesh, but the majority of those who saw Jesus did not join in the testimony. They cried for his crucifixion.

Second, such testimony is based on more than eyewitness. It comes through eyes of faith. Only after the resurrection did this testimony become real for the apostles. They testified to the church. Then the church accepted and repeated their testimony. We do the same.

Third, you do not have to see the earthly Jesus to testify about what God has done through him. You need only hear and believe in the testimony to him from Scripture and from faithful followers. Such testimony is both verbal testimony and God's love exercised through our lives. The impact God has made in other Christians—this is what **we have seen.** Based on the manifestation of Jesus in the lives of Christians, those who have witnessed it can testify that the Father sent Jesus to be the Savior of the world. That is, God sent Jesus to the cross to pay for our sins so we do not have to suffer the wages sin pays, namely, death.

Testimony about Jesus tells more than what Jesus did—save from sin. It also tells who he is—the Son of God. Again, all this goes against false teachers. They apparently claimed Jesus could not be human, thus could not die on the cross. On the other hand, Scripture claims that anyone who acknowledges this Savior they have seen is a true Christian, living in union with God.

This section concludes by repeating an affirmation made earlier—that God is love and that the person who **lives in love lives in God, and God in him.** This is the test of true Christianity in the letters of John. We must recognize the basic character of God, rooted in love. We must experience that love in our own relationship with God. Others must experience this God kind of love in their relationships with us. That's why God sent Jesus to die on the cross for our sins.

4:17–18. The judgment seat of Christ received brief mention in 2:28 and now reappears briefly to assure us we can face Christ on that day with confidence. Such confidence comes because we live in love toward God and one another. The person who does not live in love toward his brother may experience shame (2:28). However, if we live in love toward our brothers, we will have confidence when we face Jesus because in this world we are like him. No one who was like Jesus in this world can fear approaching Jesus' judgment seat. Fear expects punishment. One who loves expects to receive love.

Why? Because mature love has no fear. A Christian who fears the judgment seat of Christ shows that God's love has not yet reached maturity (been made perfect) in him. A person who lives in love toward God has nothing to fear on the day of judgment.

4:19–21. God first loved us and made a relationship with him possible. The text drives home its refutation of the antichrists and false prophets. We cannot claim we love God and then show that we hate our brothers. This only proves one thing: we are liars.

It is difficult to prove whether or not we love God based on our actions toward him because we cannot see him. Love for God is reflected in love for his children, our brothers and sisters, whom we can see. Therefore, God gave us this verifiable command: Whoever loves God must also love his brother. Jesus stated the principle in other words: whatever you did not do for one of the least of these you did not do for me (Matt. 25:40).[82]

Proverbs 5:15-19 Updated American Standard Version (UASV)

¹⁵ Drink water from your own cistern,
  flowing water from your own well.
¹⁶ Should your springs be scattered abroad,
  streams of water in the streets?
¹⁷ Let them be for you alone,
  and not for strangers with you.
¹⁸ Let your fountain be blessed,
  and rejoice in the wife of your youth,
¹⁹ a loving doe, a graceful mountain goat.
Let her breasts satisfy you at all times;
  be intoxicated always in her love.
²⁰ Why should you be intoxicated, my son, with a strange woman
  and embrace the bosom of a foreigner?

5:15. Water is precious, particularly in the arid climate of Palestine. Here Solomon makes an extended comparison between the water that supports physical life and the sexual intimacy that brings such zest to life. He speaks primarily of water in verses 15-16. A man who has his **own well** or **cistern** (storage chamber for rain water) would certainly want to drink from that personal supply rather than carrying water from a public stream.

5:16. Some have translated this verse as an exhortation, "Let your

[82] David Walls and Max Anders, *I & II Peter, I, II & III John, Jude*, vol. 11, Holman New Testament Commentary (Nashville, TN: Broadman & Holman Publishers, 1999), 210–212.

springs overflow in the streets." This would describe the way that good marriages produce a flow of blessings to everyone around. But the context supports the idea that verse 16 is a question, expecting a negative answer. If a person has a well, it would be ridiculous to let the water spill over and drain down the street.

5:17. This verse answers the question of verse 16. Your water sources should be for the exclusive use of your household, not open for foreigners to consume. In the same way, physical intimacy should be strictly for one's own spouse, not wasted on strangers. This verse forbids any form of marital infidelity.

5:18. Marital love is pictured as enjoying a **fountain** in Song of Songs 4:12,15, and this verse develops the same concept. God will bless physical intimacy between a husband and the **wife of your youth** but not in any other relationship.

5:19-20. No one can deny the excitement of physical attraction. Proverbs calls on the man to channel that excitement toward his wife. He should appreciate her beauty as if she were **a graceful deer** and be satisfied with her body and her love. He should love her "alone" (v. 17) and **always**. The word translated **captivated** is sometimes used to describe the effects of intoxication, to stagger or to be exhilarated (Prov. 20:1; Isa. 28:7). So God intends a man to be exhilarated with the affection of his own wife, not some other man's wife.[83]

Set The Mood Music:

Start Over- Flame ft. NF

Je'kob- Love is All

A Quick Look:

What does the world tell us about sex?

Why does the Bible encourage us to have only one partner and to save sex for marriage?

How does the Enemy corrupt what was made to be beautiful?

---

[83] Anders, Max. Holman Old Testament Commentary - Proverbs (pp. 49-50). B&H Publishing. Kindle Edition.

Supplemental Assignment:

Read Redeeming Love by Francine Rivers

The Dirt on Breaking Up by Hayley Dimarco

Dateable by Hayley Dimarco and Justin Lookadoo

Boy Meets Girl: Say Hello to Courtship by Joshua Harris

Quick Facts According to Equality Now.org:

Trafficking women and children for sexual exploitation is the fastest growing criminal enterprise in the world.

At least 20.9 million adults and children are bought and sold worldwide into commercial sexual servitude, forced labor, and bonded labor.

About 2 million children are exploited every year in the global commercial sex trade.

Almost 6 in every 10 identified trafficking survivors were trafficked for sexual exploitation. Women and girls make up 98% of victims in sexual exploitation.

The growing demand for those that are willing to purchase sex is what fuels the growth of human trafficking. If people weren't willing to pay for it, then people wouldn't be willing to sell it.

The Internet pornography industry generates $13 billion per year in the U.S. alone ($100 billion worldwide)—bigger business than professional football, basketball, and baseball combined. (According to msmagazine.com)

According to the World Health Organization, every year in the world there are an estimated 40-50 million abortions. This corresponds to the approximately 125,000 abortions per day. In the USA, where nearly half of pregnancies are unintended, and 4 out of 10 are terminated by abortion, there are over 3,000 abortions per day.

Then Jesus called for the children and said to the disciples, "Let the children come to me. Don't stop them! For the Kingdom of God belongs to those who are like these children."

Sex: The Worlds' Definition vs. God's

Let us begin by discussing what the world says sex is and how the world shows us every day what is acceptable sexual behavior in our society, and what is not.

What does the world tell you about sex?

_____

_____
_____
_____
_____
_____
_____
_____

What the World Says Sex is.

Either by the news, television shows, or music, there is an ever present message being communicated in our society about what sex is, and how we should act in regards to it. *Friends with Benefits, No Strings Attached, The 40 Year-Old Virgin,* and *The Affair,* are just a handful of shows and movies I could think of in about 30 seconds that have very clear messages about what society says sex is. Without even having to watch these shows, you can guess simply from the title what their message is.

Sex is most often treated as though it is an activity used to simply pass the time. It is the way to get to know someone to see if they are a good fit. It is a way to meet people. It is an occupation or job. It is a form of currency, traded for favors or money. It is a sign of how popular, or how "pimping," you are. It is a funny story to show how manly you are. It is a way to show how independent you are and free-thinking. It is just a way to make yourself feel better and has nothing to do with your emotions. Sex can be just a "booty-call" between friends.

Research disproves all of this of course; the same part of the brain that is connected to sexual arousal is hard-wired with your emotions. Therefore you cannot physically have sex without impacting your emotional state in reference to the person with whom you are being intimate. This means that you can claim all you want that, "it was just sex," but at the end of the day, even though you may never admit to it, your body is hard-wired to have feelings about that person on some level. Based on society's rules and expressions about sex, love and sex are words used interchangeably like when people say making love. Sex is also referred to as the 'F' word, a term to describe an activity between two people simply as a means to pleasure their physical selves, attempting to have no emotional connection. Sex can go to the highest bidder, and some individuals are treated as though they are only good for sex. If you have not done it, or know about it, then you are lame according to the standards communicated in music and television. Sex then becomes something cheap, often cheaper than a dinner at a restaurant; to be shared with the guy you meet at the party who you think is hot when you are drunk or high. Then you wake up the next morning and don't even know his name. He won't remember you; you won't remember him.

There are many different definitions of love. Love is defined very clearly in the Bible through the life of Christ and His sacrifice for us. Love is described between a man and a woman to be representative of the relationship Christ has with us, the church. The Bible described Christ as the groom and the church as the bride. (By the way, we are the church, since we are his temple and when we are saved by Christ, He resides in our hearts.) Just as Christ served others and did not come here to be served, so too are a husband and wife supposed to treat one another, willing to sacrifice himself in the pursuit of each other. Whoever wants to become great among you must be your servant, and whoever wants to be first must be your slave, just as the Son of Man did not come to be served, but to serve and to give his life as a ransom for many. Mathew 20:25-28 says that greater love has no one than this that he lay down his life for his friends. John 15:13 says that love is defined as an unstoppable force capable of withstanding anything this world has to throw at it. Love is not about self-serving but is found in the sacrificing of what we want, so that we can give to the person we love. When you both are doing that, both putting the other person ahead of yourself, you create a freeing and safe space for love to grow. Is this the type of love that you see every day, or is the world showing you love that is about me-me-me and self-serving? As a society, we hear it sung about in music, that love is sex and sex is love, but the type of sex that is shown in the media is casual and cheap, all about getting your physical need met and not showing love. Sex then becomes no different from what you see two dogs doing in the front yard. Something others point and laugh at, and no longer something sacred and special.

This is what the Enemy wants it to become, and his campaign in our world to make sex cheap is widely successful. Just turn on the T.V., and you can see it. When God wants something to be sacred and beautiful for us, something meant to be treasured; the Enemy wants to corrupt this gift and make it something to be shared by all so that we lose sight of what it is meant to be. God understands the impact of sex on our emotions; He created us after all and designed us to respond to sex in this way. The Enemy understands how dangerous sex can be if it is perverted. Sex is meant to be the physical display of love between a man and a woman who are pleasing one another and showing, in the most intimate moment, that they accept and care about one another on every possible level. Is that what you see when you look at the world's depiction of sex? Is that what you think of when they refer to sex as the 'F' word?

The world likes to focus on what they call passion, but the world's version of passion is perverted. It is the adrenaline flooded passion, fueled by not knowing the individual with whom you are being intimate; the risk-taking behavior in that sexual moment. There is an entirely different type of passion when you are with someone that you care about so deeply that you would sacrifice your life, all of your belongings, for and would be with no matter what happened. The love shared between two people who have seen one another at their best and their worst. The love between those who still accept one another, and still love one another even after pain, mistakes, or loss; now that is a beautiful thing. It is this type of love that the Bible talks about; this special love that withstands time, affairs, bankruptcy, lies, manipulation, pain, child-loss, weight-gain, disfigurement. It is the type of love we sing songs about.

Check out *Come to Me* by Goo Goo Dolls

What Happens When Sex is Cheap

Sex is used for so many things in our society, to bargain with, as a currency, an income, a coping skill, a past-time, a hobby, self-pleasure, or for the expression of love. The confusion in our world about sex and love is a shackle that is so strong; it sometimes seems impossible to break. It is one of the most effective and cunning lies of the Enemy to use against us. Sex introduced in the wrong way, by the wrong person, and at the wrong time, defined to be something it is not, is a scary thing that can ruin lives. I have seen it. I won't get into that because it is a topic many don't want to know about, but killers, rapists, and child molesters have been put on a path toward these behaviors often because of this lie. Some of what seemed to me as the most impossible situations were like these in my career. It seemed the Enemy at times had won, because sex feels good and when you have had it defined as an ugly thing to be used as a tool to hurt others, it ruins lives and tears families apart which is exactly what the Enemy wants.

What is the emotional impact of listening to the Enemy's lies; that sex is cheap instead of sacred? There is a book called *Redeeming Love* written by Francine Rivers, and in the book is a fictional telling of the Bible story, Hosea. Hosea was a man told by God to marry a prostitute. This is the story of their journey together. In it are the best descriptions of what happens when we are raised to believe that sex is cheap. Angel, the prostitute in the story, says I cannot sing, "singing has to come from the inside, and I don't have anything left inside." Ruth asked, "Really? How did that happen?" and she replied, "It all just drained out. We all just use each other in one way or another. To feel good. To feel bad. To feel nothing at all. The lucky ones are real good at it." Later when Hosea and Angel are speaking, Hosea says to her, "A woman is either a wall or a door, beloved." She gave a bleak laugh and looked at him. "Then I guess I am a door a thousand men have walked through." "No. You are a wall, a stone wall, four feet thick and a hundred feet high. I can't get over you, all by myself, but I keep trying."

When sex becomes a pass-time, we lose sight of how calloused and numb we can become to things like love, intimacy, and vulnerability. We start to lose our ability to feel, and when we lose that, we lose what makes us who we are, including our ability to connect with others; our most basic need. Sex is supposed to be a gift; a gift given to the most deserving person that we choose to show our full self to. The person we trust to be exposed to; the person we dare to show our good side and bad side to. The person who has proven they will be there no matter what they find when they see us for all we are. The person who will look at us and see nothing but beauty, even in the midst of our pain is who we are meant to share this gift with. If this gift is given over and over again to anyone who passes by, is it a gift anymore? Is it special anymore? This is how love and sex become corrupted. We no longer see it as a gift, and we become numb feeling like Angel felt in *Redeeming Love*; used up, gone, empty, as though we have been passed around from person to person.

Desensitization to Intimacy

The Bible teaches us that sex should be between a husband and a wife and should be shared between the two of you only. I want you to imagine this for a moment. The acts leading up to sex can be described as these invisible barriers that you pass through. As you pass through each barrier, it gets easier and easier to keep going. Imagine when you hold hands with someone for the first time. Your hands got sweaty you were so nervous. You had the jitters, afraid that they may not take your hand and may reject you. When they don't reject you, accepting you, it makes your heart beat to the point where it feels like it is going to come out of your chest.

We all remember this moment; it was the same for the first time you danced with someone, hugged them, or felt your date put their arm around your shoulders. You know the feeling that I'm describing. If you participate in this activity multiple times, just like with anything in this world, the more that it is done, the more it will lose its newness. The roller coaster isn't as exciting on the tenth time as it was the first. You will no longer see how special that moment is. It will no longer cause you to feel jitters and nervousness, or the same type of excitement that it once did. In our society some people call this, falling out of love, because the same feelings or 'spark' are no longer there, and they feel much different than they did at the start of the relationship.

We are taught in the Bible that sex is something to be shared after a commitment in marriage; when vows have been taken. Wedding vows traditionally are as follows: I take you to be my husband or wife. To love, honor, cherish, and protect you, forsaking all others, and holding only to you from this day forward, for better, for worse, for richer, for poorer, in sickness and in health, until death do us part. Nowhere in these vows do you see the words "but" or "except" do you? It doesn't say, "I promise to love, honor, cherish, and protect you, forsaking all others, and holding only to you, except if this happens. These vows say "until death do us part" and "for better or worse." This is a vow, not just a promise. A promise is a commitment that something will happen, but a vow between two people is not supposed to be able to be broken. In the Bible, it describes that when two individuals make this vow to one another, they go from being two separate beings to one being, together never able to be separated. You may get a divorce, but you are literally splitting yourself when you do.

Why is it so important then to wait until marriage to share the gift of sexual intimacy with someone? Because in this oath that the two of you make, there is an understanding that you will work together to overcome everything. This is not a passing relationship that is meant to fade when faced with adversity. This relationship is described in the Bible as a "great mystery." This relationship is supposed to represent the way that Christ loves the Church; the way He loves us. That no matter what we do to Him, we curse His name, turn away from Him and run to listen to His Enemy when we sin, we deny Him; we crucify Him, and yet He still loves us. His love is unstoppable, incomprehensible; you simply cannot understand it. This is the love that is meant to be found in our marriages. That is why the vows say, for better or worse, till death do we part. There is nothing that can separate us from the love of God, and our marriages are supposed to be the same. The love found in a marriage is a covenant, an unbreakable promise that no matter what happens, you will persevere and look to God to heal your wounds and create in your marriage something more beautiful than you could have ever imagined.

Trust me this is worth waiting for, and it is worth being picky over. If this promise is meant to be a forever, unbreakable agreement between the two of you, then it would be a wise thing to be very considerate about the person you say it to. If they are drug addicts, abusers, addicted to pornography, or if they are promiscuous, do you think it would be wise to say that you will put up with that for the rest of your life? Do you want your children with that life, and if not, they why are you wasting your time in a relationship with behaviors that you don't want? This should all show you that there is a major difference between sex and love according to our world, but in God's definition, sex is the illustration of your love shared with one person.

Sex and love are two different things. Love is a choice that is made every day, combined at times with feelings of passion, but sex is a behavior supposed to illustrate your love. Behaviors can be used for anything, just like holding hands can be a sign of affection, sympathy, or to keep your child close by while you cross the road, but sex is a behavior used in our world for any number of different things. Love is a choice, and it is one we make every day. Sometimes it is the hardest and scariest choice in the world. Sex is supposed to be the way you show love in the most intimate setting.

What is Infatuation?

I think in our world, that newness is often mistaken for love or attraction, but I caution you to not fall into this lie. Newness is not love or attraction; it is simply someone new who you do not know yet; it is infatuation. After a while of being with the same person, that newness falls away, and you are back in the same boat you were in with the last person before, no longer feeling the awe of new experiences. This is why love is not a fleeting thing like an emotion that comes and goes, but it is a choice. If sex is just a behavior with the sole motivation to simply pleasure yourself, then you will become bored after you have tried all there is to try. The only way then to have that same feeling is to have partner after partner, and you will eventually not be fulfilled because you are missing the purpose of sex, the emotional component of love.

When you have so many moments of sexual behaviors with others, they are no longer new behaviors to you. You and your lover are not on even playing field. You may have more experience compared to them or vice versa, and this can bring fear and insecurity into your relationship before you are even married. You could have an STD which you will give to your husband or wife when you are intimate, not to mention that your children could have it passed to them during birth. They may have children from past sexual encounters that will be brought into your marriage automatically, and you will not get the newness of this journey together. There is a reason the Bible says to cling to the love of your youth, because God is trying to protect your marriage by building a bond between the two of you that is strong because it is all new for the two of you together, not separate. It is much more difficult to start off a journey when you are at two different starting lines compared to if the two of you are starting this journey at the same point in life.

You both experience sex for the first time, no fear, no intimidation, learning all the nuances of this together, playing and enjoying one another. When you have your first baby, it is a new experience for the both of you to share which makes you stronger together. Everything is the two of you, not you or them separate, and this makes you stronger together. All those opportunities for the enemy to have a foothold to plant seeds of doubt, anger or fear into your relationship are automatically prevented because you are both together for every first. God is not trying to prevent you from the pleasures of sex, but rather saving it for you so that the first time you have sex you will have all the excitement and jitters, and nervousness that makes the first time such an experience and you won't have to experience fear of judgement or being compared because if both of you are experiencing it for the first time, then there is no comparison. For the first time, you will stand before your spouse completely vulnerable, emotionally and physically, and not be afraid.

The difference in the relationship is on the one hand, you enter the bedroom for the first time with your husband or wife a virgin, and they enter having been sexually active for 5 years already. They have a son or daughter already. You start off your marriage with them having experienced sex, childbirth, intimacy not only in having sex, but also the intimacy of having a baby with another person, a highly intimate experience. You now you have all of the responsibilities of their experiences. You now have the stress of raising a child and dealing with being a step-parent navigating the social interactions with your husband or wife's ex all the time. That sounds like loads of fun. You start off your marriage already with foot-holds for the Enemy to whisper thoughts of insecurity, fear, resentment, stress, and anger. This is what God wants to protect you from.

What do you do then if you have already passed through every barrier there is to pass and have done everything there is to do? Don't fear; God can restore anything and just because that is your past, that does not have to be your present or future. I will warn you, though, now that you have experienced sex, it will be much more difficult to withstand temptation because unlike someone who has never experienced these things, you know what you are missing and it will be much easier for the enemy to tell you, "Ehh you have already done it, the damage is already done". The truth is that just because you didn't wait for your husband or wife, does not mean you can't start. God can overcome any insecurity, fear, or doubt if you give it to Him and ask Him for help.

At the beginning of this chapter, I shared a scripture out of Proverbs. I want you to quickly go back and look at that. Often times we know what the rules are for healthy living, but we fail to ask ourselves the why behind the rule. Imagine that you see me walking down the street. I have a bottle of water in my hand, and as I walk down the sidewalk, I offer a drink to every stranger I pass no matter who they are. Then I approach you, and I offer you a drink telling you how special this water is and that it is something only I share with you. How would you respond to me? What would you do if you were my friend and you saw me take a drink after these strangers do? Would you drink from the community water bottle or would you think I was gross for sharing it with everyone?

Most responses in our society would be out of disgust that I just shared saliva with all of these perfect strangers. Let me ask you this, what is the difference between this and a one-night stand? We like to glorify sexual encounters in music and in movies as romantic and exhilarating but if you think that sharing a bottle of water, sharing the saliva and backwash with all of those people is gross, then think of what is spread in a one-night-stand. You just spread the cooties of the five people before this night that you had been with and got the cooties from the five they had been with before you. That sounds like a really special night (sarcasm). Food for thought.

Read this and consider what passion is.

To my dear daughter,

As you grow, many boys will enter your years. They will speak words of love and passion, of wanting you-all of you. Their sex will be lacking. Believe me, dear girl, I know what crazy hot lovemaking is made of. Until the boy can assure you of the following, it is not a true passion.

If he can patiently wait for over three years. From pregnant to nursing to pregnant to nursing, with your hormones fierce, and desire for sex often dead. "Please, just let me sleep. I am so tired." will be your common response. Until he can love you still, choose you still, it is not a true passion.

If he can call you beautiful when even your feet are swollen from baby belly. Call you sexy when your legs run thick with varicose veins

242

from the same. Call you perfect after your belly hangs loose with skin and your eyes are deep with bags. Until he can still call you these things, it is not a true passion.

You may throw things at him, yell words of hate and shame as you feel the hormones of post baby blues run deep. Until he can love you even deeper, piercings through the pain into your heart, it is not a true passion.

He will go to work where there are other women, pretty women. Pretty women with no children and varicose free, high heeled legs. I know the way they toss their pretty little hair to and fro.

He will come home to you; your hair pulled back into the frizziest of buns, a baby on your hip, spit-up down your arm. Until he can come home to you-you with no makeup- and express there is nothing as wonderful as seeing your face, it is not a true passion.

You are touched by his love and whisper tonight you will return the favor. Tonight there is a crying baby and a feverish toddler who just joined you in bed. Until he can laugh, fully laugh about this, it is not a true passion.

Can a man like this exist? Yes, dear girl, and you call him your dad. He has shown me what true love is.

The hormones have faded. I am not pregnant. I am not nursing. My own passion has returned. Can I truly say "returned?" I really had no idea what passion was. So intense, so raw, I cannot put it fully into words.

I am not in love with just another man. I am in love with the father of my babies. The one who called me beautiful through my nights of ugly called me strong through days of weakness called me valuable through days of uncertainty. The one who waited patiently for me. Who washed sheets of vomit as I bathed a fever infested child.

This is love dear girl. This is passion. It is being one with he who is going to be there for you, till death do you part, regardless. It is something mystical and unexplainable. It is something crazy. It is crazy hot sex.

Wait, dear girl. Wait for him. there is nothing so beautiful as finding your heart in his, the one who will wait for you even in marriage.

Love,

MOM (foreverymom.com)

What type of an effect has the confusion between sex and love had on your life?

_____

_____

_____

_____

_____

_____

_____

Do you have sex to feel love? Do you equate the two? Remember: sex is a behavior, so if you have had it, what is your purpose in having it?

_____

_____

_____

_____

_____

_____

_____

It was created as an act of love and love is a choice to be about the other person, not about you or your wants and needs. Is that what it was for you? If not, explain.

_____

_____

_____

_____

_____

_____

_____

What type of lies has been told to you regarding sex and love?

_____

_____

_____

_____

_____

_____

_____

What shackles has sex put around your life?

_____
_____
_____
_____
_____
_____
_____

What is sex supposed to be?

_____
_____
_____
_____
_____
_____
_____
_____
_____
_____

What is Love?

_____
_____
_____
_____
_____
_____

Why does the Bible teach us to wait and save sex for marriage?

_____
_____
_____
_____
_____
_____

What is the difference between sex, love, and infatuation?

_____
_____
_____
_____
_____
_____

What is love supposed to look like in a marriage?

_____
_____
_____
_____
_____

What are the areas a relationship can be attacked by the enemy, in a relationship where you are starting at different points in life?

_____
_____
_____
_____
_____

God's Definition of Sex	The World's Definition of Sex

God's Definition of Sex	The World's Definition of Sex

Four Pillars Assignment on this Chapter's Topic

Self-Talk (40,000 individual thoughts summarized)

_____
_____
_____
_____
_____
_____
_____

Faulty Beliefs (Beliefs about yourself and your situation as a result of your thoughts.)

_____
_____
_____
_____
_____
_____

Perception (The faulty beliefs about your environment as a result of your faulty beliefs about yourself and your environments)

_____
_____
_____
_____
_____
_____
_____
_____

Behaviors (What you choose to do)

_____
_____
_____
_____
_____
_____

Finally, identify the outcome and how it reinforces the self-talk.

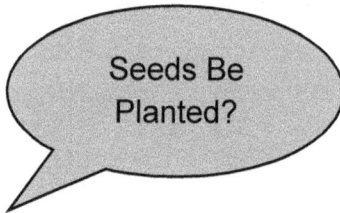

_____
_____
_____
_____
_____
_____

Seeds Be Planted?

1.) Who/What planted the seeds that led to your self-talk?

_____
_____
_____
_____
_____
_____
_____

2.) How did you allow them to take root in your mind?

_____

_____

_____

_____

_____

_____

_____

3.) Are the seeds that were planted seeds of fruit bearing trees, which will bring you good life and sustain you or are they seeds of weeds which will rob you and kill good things in your life?

_____

_____

_____

_____

_____

_____

_____

_____

_____

_____

_____

_____

_____

_____

_____

_____

Further Thoughts

_____

_____

_____

_____

_____

_____

Section III Truth & Your Weapons Against the Enemy

Psalm 139:1-18 New Living Translation (NLT)

¹ O Lord, you have examined my heart
　and know everything about me.
² You know when I sit down or stand up.
　You know my thoughts even when I'm far away.
³ You see me when I travel
　and when I rest at home.
　You know everything I do.
⁴ You know what I am going to say
　even before I say it, Lord.
⁵ You go before me and follow me.
　You place your hand of blessing on my head.
⁶ Such knowledge is too wonderful for me,
　too great for me to understand!

⁷ I can never escape from your Spirit!
　I can never get away from your presence!
⁸ If I go up to heaven, you are there;
　if I go down to the grave, you are there.
⁹ If I ride the wings of the morning,
　if I dwell by the farthest oceans,
¹⁰ even there your hand will guide me,
　and your strength will support me.
¹¹ I could ask the darkness to hide me
　and the light around me to become night—
¹²　but even in darkness I cannot hide from you.
To you the night shines as bright as day.
　Darkness and light are the same to you.

¹³ You made all the delicate, inner parts of my body
　and knit me together in my mother's womb.
¹⁴ Thank you for making me so wonderfully complex!
　Your workmanship is marvelous—how well I know it.
¹⁵ You watched me as I was being formed in utter seclusion,
　as I was woven together in the dark of the womb.
¹⁶ You saw me before I was born.
　Every day of my life was recorded in your book.
Every moment was laid out
　before a single day had passed.

¹⁷ How precious are your thoughts about me, O God.
They cannot be numbered!
¹⁸ I can't even count them;
they outnumber the grains of sand!
And when I wake up,
you are still with me!

139:1. Nothing in his life, David realized, was hidden from God's all-seeing gaze. He declared, **O LORD, you have searched me**, using a word meaning "to explore, spy out, to dig deeply into, to explore a country." God knew the very depths of his being, what no one else saw. **You know** (*yadah*, "to know intimately, experientially") **me** thoroughly (i.e., his character, being, his very heart).

139:2. **You know when I sit and when I rise**. These two activities are intended to represent when David rests and rises to work during his day's activities and everything in between. He pondered how God knew his **thoughts from afar**. Others saw his actions, but God saw into his heart.

139:3–4. God does **discern**—that is, "to sift through something, to winnow as grain, to sort out the good from the bad"—his life. He sees through his **going out** to labor and his **lying down** to sleep. God saw David's morning departure to work, his evening retiring at home, and, implied, all the other events of the day. God was deeply **familiar** with all his **ways**. He even knew what he was going to say before he said it. David could only conclude, **You know it completely**.

139:5. God surrounded David like a city being besieged with no way of escape. There was no way for him to escape his all-knowing thoughts. God had **laid** his **hand upon** him so that he was always near. Under this kind of close scrutiny, God saw the entirety of his life up close, inside out.

139:6. David's response to all this is, **Such knowledge is too wonderful** and too high. God's omniscience is both convicting and comforting. For David, it was humbling, beyond his human capacity to grasp.

139:7. Further, David understood that God is all-present, and he could never escape the divine presence. **Where can I go from your Spirit? or Where can I flee from your presence?** These two rhetorical questions imply a negative answer. There is nowhere God is not present. God's "Spirit," a reference to the Holy Spirit, is omnipresent.

139:8–10. **If I go up to the heavens**, David declared, God is **there**. Heaven above is God's eternal dwelling place. Or **if I make my bed in the depths** of hell, the other extreme, God is there. David would never be more face-to-face with God than after he died. **If I rise on the wings of the dawn** and fly to the east, or **if I settle on the far side of the sea**

(i.e., the Mediterranean Sea), God is there. North, south, east, and west are represented here. No matter where he goes in life or after death, **your hand will guide me** into the divine will and **your right hand will hold me fast**. God is always in touch with his life, which is never beyond the divine reach.

139:11–12. If David says, **The darkness will hide me**, even then, God sees in the dark and is present there. This **darkness** refers to the dark nights of the soul (i.e., dark trials). **Even the darkness will not be dark to you**. Dark times are light to God. He is present in them, knowing perfectly all that is transpiring and what his eternal purposes are.

139:13. Moreover, David knows that God is all-powerful. This is proven in that the Lord has made him skillfully in his mother's womb. God created his **inmost being** (i.e., his kidneys, symbolic of his vital organs, his heart, liver, lungs, even his innermost emotions and moral sensitivities). God knit him like a skilled artisan would weave a beautiful tapestry. This work of creation was done in his mother's womb, beginning nine months before he was born.

139:14. David could only **praise** God for this display of wonderful omnipotence. He understood he was **fearfully and wonderfully made**, producing awe and astonishment within him toward God who created him so perfectly.

139:15. **My frame** (i.e., bones and skeleton) **was not hidden from** God but in full view to divine eyes. God **made** David **in the secret place**, a euphemism for the womb, that unseen place concealed from human eyes. There he was **woven together** like a multicolored piece of cloth or fine needlepoint. All these threads picture his veins, arteries, muscles, and tendons.

139:16. God **saw** his **unformed** body before he was made. **All his days** were sovereignly **ordained** for David before he came into the world. The span of his life was **written** by God in his divine **book** containing his eternal decree. The precise length of his life was determined by God before he was born. There could be no changing the number of his days (Job 14:5).

139:17–18. These divine truths were **precious** to David, **vast** and beyond his human comprehension. If he tried to list these truths about God, **they would outnumber the grains of sand** on the beaches of the world, far past his ability to understand. When he awakens, his thoughts are still dominated with God. He cannot remove such towering thoughts about God from his mind.[84]

---

[84] Anders, Max; Lawson, Steven. Holman Old Testament Commentary - Psalms 76-150 (Kindle Locations 8134-8185). B&H Publishing. Kindle Edition.

Set The Mood Music:

Derek Minor- Until I'm God ft. BJ the Chicago
Kid

Chapter XIV Created with Love

Psalms 143:7-8 Updated American Standard Version (UASV)

[7] Answer me quickly, O Jehovah!
My spirit fails!
Do not hide your face from me,
Or I will become like those who go down to the pit.
[8] Let me hear in the morning of your loyal love,
for I trust you.
Teach me the way in which I should walk,
for to you I lift up my soul.

> **143:7.** David prays, **answer me quickly**, showing an urgency to have this matter resolved. He cannot continue to live this way. Living in spiritual lukewarmness and disobedience is destroying him. Emotionally drained, his **spirit fails** within him. His zest for living is gone. **Do not hide your face from me**, he prays. God seems so far away and distant. **I will be like those who go down to the pit**, devoid of passion for living any more, he declares.
>
> **143:8.** This time of spiritual decline in David's life is as dark as the night. He longs for a new **morning** to dawn in his spiritual life. He longs for the warm sunrise of God's **unfailing** love to rise upon his soul and to radiate God's presence in his life. Turning to God with a repentant heart, he puts his **trust** in the Lord. David asks that God **show** him the steps that lead back to walking in close fellowship with him. He requests that God teach him how to get his life back on spiritual track. Sin has led David astray. Only God can show him the way to come back.[85]

Romans 5:5-8 Updated American Standard Version (UASV)

[5] and hope does not disappoint, because the love of God has been poured out within our hearts through the Holy Spirit who was given to us.

[6] For while we were still helpless, at the right time Christ died for the ungodly. [7] For one will scarcely die for a righteous man; though perhaps for a good man one would dare even to die. [8] **But God shows his love for us in that while we were still sinners, Christ died for us.**

---

[85] Anders, Max; Lawson, Steven. Holman Old Testament Commentary - Psalms 76-150 (Kindle Locations 8531-8539). B&H Publishing. Kindle Edition.

5:5–8. "Hope deferred makes the heart sick," Proverbs 13:12 tells us, "but a longing fulfilled is a tree of life." Some things we **hope** for in life do not come to pass. When that happens, disappointment sets in. Disappointment produces discouragement; discouragement, unproven character; unproven character, despair. How does the Christian know that he will not one day be sick of heart? How does the believer know that one day she will not have suffered in vain? First the answer, then the two proofs, says Paul.

The answer is that we are the recipients of God's love for us ("the love of God;" subjective genitive; not "our love for God," an objective genitive), and hope that is based on God's love does not disappoint. Why? Two proofs: one subjective, the other objective.

The subjective reason is that **God has poured out his love into our hearts by the Holy Spirit, whom he has given us.** Significantly, this first mention of the Holy Spirit in Romans in relation to the life of the believer comes in the context of justification by faith. This means at least three things (Stott, p. 142): first, if you have been justified by faith, you have received the Holy Spirit. Second, the giving of the Holy Spirit is connected with the act of justification, meaning that all who are justified have experienced the Holy Spirit's presence. Third, the Holy Spirit bears witness to the believer's spirit that God loves him or her.

This last point, the subjective reason by which the believer knows that **hope does not disappoint**, is said a different way by Paul in Romans 8:16: "The Spirit himself testifies with our spirit that we are God's children." No child who is loved by its father has any doubt that the father is trustworthy; any doubt that the hope directed toward the father will not one day be a "tree of life." And the Spirit tells us—in our heart—that we are children of God.

Objectively, Paul goes on, God has already proved his love for us, in that **while we were still sinners, Christ died for us.** It is unnatural to think that one person would volunteer to die for another, even if that person was good or righteous. But who would die for an enemy? At the time when **we were still powerless** to help ourselves—strapped to the executioner's block, guilty as charged, about to die—Jesus Christ stepped forward and took the place of us, his enemies! In a godless culture, "What's Love Got to Do With It?" is a valid question. But in God's world, in Paul's day and in ours, love has everything to do with it. The Holy Spirit tells us continually of God's love for us (**poured out** is perfect tense of *ekchunno*; past action with continuing results), and points our thinking back to the space-time reality of that love—[86]

---

[86] Kenneth Boa and William Kruidenier, *Romans*, vol. 6, Holman New Testament Commentary (Nashville, TN: Broadman & Holman Publishers, 2000), 162–163.

1 John 3:1 Updated American Standard Version (UASV)

3 See what sort of love the Father has given us, so that we should be called children of God; and such we are. That is why the world does not know us, because it did not know him.

3:1. The apostle breaks out in spontaneous wonder at the love of God in making us his children. A further wonder grasps him: **that is what we are.** The world does not **know us,** because it does not **know** our father. To "know" in this context has the sense of "accept." It appears in John 1:10–11: "He was in the world, and … the world did not *recognize* him. He came to that which was his own, but his own did not receive him" (italics added). The failure to recognize him was based on the fact that they did not accept him. If the world rejects God, it is no surprise that it would reject us, God's children.[87]

Romans 8: 35-39 Updated American Standard Version (UASV)

35 **Who will separate us from the love of Christ**? Will tribulation, or distress, or persecution, or famine, or nakedness, or danger, or sword? **36** As it is written,

"On account of you we are being put to death the whole day long; we are considered as sheep to be slaughtered."

37 But in all these things we are more than conquerors through the one having loved us. **38** For I am convinced that neither death, nor life, nor angels, nor rulers, nor things present, nor things to come, nor powers, **39** nor height, nor depth, nor any other created thing, will be able to separate us from the love of God that is in Christ Jesus our Lord.

8:35–39. *Question 5:* **Who shall separate us from the love of Christ?** In this final section, Paul asks his final question in the first verse of the section and answers it in the last:

Q.: What can separate the believer from God's love? (v. 35)

A.: Nothing can separate the believer from God's love. (v. 39)

Paul (knowingly? unknowingly?) takes on the prophet's mantle in verse 36 as he quotes from Psalm 44:22 to demonstrate that there will always be opposition to God's people and the work of God in the world.

---

[87] David Walls and Max Anders, *I & II Peter, I, II & III John, Jude*, vol. 11, Holman New Testament Commentary (Nashville, TN: Broadman & Holman Publishers, 1999), 189–190.

The world is cursed; it is an antagonistic environment; it is under the control of the evil one (1 John 5:19). There will be many natural and supernatural attempts made to convince the believer that he or she has been separated from the love of God. (Paul knows that nothing can separate us from the love of God, but he also knows that it can *appear* that we have been separated from the love of God. He wants to dispel both notions.)

Paul himself will become like a **sheep to be slaughtered** within a few short years under the brutal hand of the Roman emperor Nero. He could have included "Roman emperors" in the list in verses 38–39, but that would probably seem trivial to Paul—like a gnat bite or a speed bump on the high-way to heaven. Let us not consider **trouble or hardship or persecution or famine or nakedness or danger or sword…. No, in all these things we are more than conquerors through him who loved us**. Rather, let us consider the giant spectrums of impediments to our remaining in God's loving care:

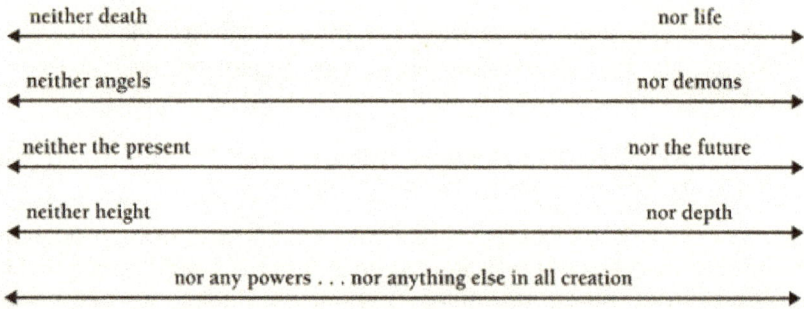

neither death	nor life
←————————————————————————————→	

neither angels	nor demons
←————————————————————————————→	

neither the present	nor the future
←————————————————————————————→	

neither height	nor depth
←————————————————————————————→	

nor any powers . . . nor anything else in all creation
←————————————————————————————→

Paul was a man of unshakeable confidence in the love of God. He feared neither the tangible hardships of life (see his experiences in 2 Cor. 6:3–10; 11:16–33) nor the intangible fears that creep into the consciousness of any normal person. Am I suffering for a reason? What if I wake up on the other side of death and discover I have been fooled? What if I do not wake up on the other side of death? Where will the love of God be then? All normal saints have considered these questions, and Paul is just bold enough and confident enough to get them out on the table and answer them. He wanted the Romans to deal with them, and wanted third-millennium believers to deal with them as well. His answer then, and his answer now, is that **[nothing] will be able to separate us from the love of God that is in Christ Jesus our Lord**.[88]

---

88 Kenneth Boa and William Kruidenier, *Romans*, vol. 6, Holman New Testament Commentary (Nashville, TN: Broadman & Holman Publishers, 2000), 263–264.

Psalm 147:2-5 Updated American Standard Version (UASV)

² Jehovah builds up Jerusalem;
    he gathers the outcasts of Israel.
³ He heals the brokenhearted
    and binds up their wounds.
⁴ He counts the number of the stars;
    he gives to all of them their names.
⁵ Great is our Jehovah, and abundant in power;
    his understanding is infinite.

147:2–3. God should be praised because he builds up Jerusalem. This psalm was probably written on the occasion of the dedication of the reconstructed walls of Jerusalem (Neh. 12) under Nehemiah. Returned to their promised land, these exiles of Israel had strong reason to praise God. They were brokenhearted because they had been in Babylonian captivity and had suffered much. But God healed their despair and bound up the wounds of their devastated souls.

147:4–5. The billions of stars are all named by God and kept up with by him. Everything is in its rightful place in the universe. He counts and names the vast starry host above and calls them each by name. To name something is to assume the care of that thing, as a parent does in naming a baby. God is mighty in strength to order the starry hosts and planets above. His understanding of each of the stars has no limit. He knows their exact location and size.[89]

A Quick Look:

The truth about every creation; that we all have a purpose in our life.

A review of the possible excuses and doubts you may have.

Supplemental Assignments:

Research project: Identify individuals in the world who have been born despite being recommended for abortion or the circumstance from which they were born and how they have overcome.

---

[89] Anders, Max; Lawson, Steven. Holman Old Testament Commentary - Psalms 76-150 (Kindle Locations 8846-8854). B&H Publishing. Kindle Edition.

259

We just finished a section reviewing all of the lies spoken over us by the Enemy, by others in this world, and the lies we speak over ourselves in our minds that we have repeated so often that we no longer doubt their truthfulness. One of the biggest lies we tell ourselves is that we don't matter. I don't know where this idea was planted in your life, by your biological parents, by your peers, by your mistakes, or your significant other, but it is a lie. It is a lie that shackles you down to the ground when you were made to soar like the eagles. *But those who hope in the Lord will renew their strength. They will soar on wings like eagles; they will run and not grow weary, they will walk and not be faint.* Isaiah 40:31

> One of the biggest lies we tell ourselves is that we don't matter.

You were not put on this world to be a prisoner to the fears and lies that shackle you. You were created for a purpose, and that purpose was literally woven into every fiber of your being, and you will never be satisfied in your life until you seek the Lord and find your purpose in Him. *For I know the plans I have for you," declares the Lord, "They are plans for good and not disaster, to give you a future and a hope.* Jeremiah 29:11 This promise was spoken from the Lord to his people during a time of great struggle. They had just lost a war to another nation and were being exiled from their homes, persecuted because they believed in God. People were being hurt, killed, and mistreated and this promise was spoken over them. Just because your situation may look dire and hopeless, this does not mean it is the end of your story. Sometimes the hardest part of the journey is just before the best parts.

Imagine that there is this path laid out before your feet for the destiny you were created to have, and then there is this other path which you have taken that has led you along places and people that have planted seeds of fear, doubt, pain, and death in your heart. You have

> You have a purpose woven into your life and a path laid out for your feet.

heard it and spoken these thoughts in your mind for so long that you have believed them to be true and now you voluntarily walk up to this wall and put shackles of fear and doubt on your own arms. The whole time, your Creator is looking on, begging you to take off the shackles, to stop believing in the lies of the Enemy and believe in His truth; that He made you for good and not for bad, to be a conqueror of evil and with the strength through Him to withstand everything when you are protected by His love.

Scripture tells us that the Lord loves you so much that He can quite literally number every hair on your head. *Indeed, the very hairs of your head are all numbered. Don't be afraid; you are with more than many sparrows.* I fear that people don't understand that God loves them, and I want to highlight to you what the above scripture in Psalm 138 states to you; that He knows every thought you have, every desire of your heart, and every choice you are going to make even as He is weaving his plans into your being, and He is still choosing to not only create you for this purpose, regardless of if you choose to fulfill it and follow Him, but He still chose to have His son die for you. You are loved, unconditionally. You are not just good enough, but you are more than perfect for the purpose He has in mind for you, and you were created for it, the only one in the world with your destiny.

You may have questions like, if God knew what kind of life I would have, why on earth would He have created me? I was born into an abusive home, I was born into a country riddled with war, I was born and seven years later fell from a tree and was paralyzed. I don't pretend to know the plans of God. I have heard terrible stories of the life some children were born into. Some children are created who never get the opportunity even to leave the womb. I don't pretend to understand the purpose. You aren't going to get a step-by-step description of God's intent because it is far too complex for any mind to comprehend. This is what I know, we live in a broken world. We live in a world where evil has power, but this is not the end. This life is not the full story, where our soul will reside in eternity is the full story, and that is the most important part to God; having you back by His side is the goal.

I know life is hard, and I know bad things happen to good people. Some people have babies who don't want them, and some who desperately want babies cannot have them. It's not fair. There is darkness in our world that we cannot control. I wish I could, but in this world the only thing we can control is ourselves, and if we allow the Enemy to win by letting the bad separate us from God, then the battle is lost in that moment. Choose to run into Love's arms, and let Him heal our broken hearts and bind our wounds. Trust me I wish every baby had a mommy who loved them, a daddy who stayed, a home, a car, and their mom and dad never had to work, and we could all enjoy life together. I wish everyone had that, but we don't. It is not how the world is.

Our world is broken because a long time ago a man named Adam and a woman named Eve had life the way it was meant to be, free from sin, but they betrayed their Creator by choosing to listen to the first lies of the enemy. They were told to try to be like God, and they did the very thing the Enemy did when he fell from heaven. They tried to eat the forbidden fruit to have the knowledge of God. They were tricked, but they opened the door for Satan to have power in this world and they let lies and sin enter our world. Now that it is here, we will have things happen in our world that is not right. People will sin; it is our reality now, but just you wait for Christ is going to return and when he does, all sin will be banished. You cannot believe that just because the bad happened to you or in your life that it means you are bad or not created for something better.

Why is there death and pain in our world? —ask your pastor for more.

You have to choose to believe that God has a plan to bring you out of the pit that you started in, a plan to deliver you from the hardship you now face, and trust in Him to show you the way. If you do not, that pit that you are in right now will start to claim you and control you. You will find yourself remaining in it, instead of overcoming it and then you will continue the trend in your life for your own children. You have to recognize the lies you tell yourself like you did in Section III (identify the shackles on your life), then every day you have to choose to start believing the Truth, that you were made with love and a purpose for your good, no matter what this world has to throw at you. Finally, after you do both of those things, you have to refuse to voluntarily return to prison. It feels weird not going with what your habit was. If your habit was to say that you were worthless, it will be hard to do the opposite.

Please remember; we look for what we want to see to prove to ourselves that what we believe is right. If you believe you are worthless, you will seek evidence to prove this, but if you believe you have worth and are priceless, you will look for proof of that. Also keep in mind that everything He does is for you. He created all of the wonderful things of our world, and it wasn't enough until He made you. Scripture says He delights to bless us. He is actively looking for ways to bless our life, but He cannot do it if we are not open to Him. No matter how much you are loved, if you don't accept that love, it won't matter how hard others try to bless you if you are unwilling to receive it.

One question this makes me ask is about all of the children called accidents, or those of you born to parents who tell you that you were not wanted; for all of those children who have been given up for adoption who feel unwanted; what was their purpose. I think about this; sometimes in life, we do things that bring outcomes that we may not have been expecting. This can be the truth for pregnancy. In life sometimes people do not realize that what they do will bring life changing and life creating outcomes and they treat sex as though it is just an activity meant for pleasure and pleasure only. When the reality that they have been playing with something that is life changing sinks in, people often get scared.

Having a baby can be an amazing experience and it is meant to be wonderful, but it also brings with it an amazing amount of fear especially when it is your first time. Fear, as we have discussed, is not of God. God is love, and true love casts out all fear, so our Enemy uses our fears to whisper concerns and worries on our hearts. Sometimes people listen to them. Stress and fear are never a good combination; they make people say and do things that they never would do under the best of circumstances. Please, don't misunderstand a person's words of fear and stress to be the truth. We often make our worst mistakes when we are listening to fear and doubt in our lives. If you are a child that was created in the midst of fear and doubt, don't let the actions of another that was influenced by their fears be the basis of your beliefs about yourself.

No matter what the circumstance of your birth; you are loved and treasured, and you just like any other child on this planet, even the ones that never get to experience life, we are all loved by the one true Father who delighted in our creation and loved us so much that he sacrificed His own Son for us. So many children base their self-worth on how they are valued by others. If that is the case, then base your worth on how you are valued by God, because to Him you are priceless. This is the truth; all other statements are lies that you have to challenge and if you can understand that you are a priceless creation, then all other things; your self-worth, self-esteem, and self-image will improve for out of all three of these things comes how you treat others.

We are our own worst critic and if we don't value ourselves if we don't like ourselves, and if we see ourselves' as worthless and damaged, then can you imagine how we will allow others to treat us and how we will then treat others? Self-image is how you view yourself, or the labels you use to describe who you are. Self-esteem his how much you like yourself. Self-worth is how much you value yourself. If you don't find that you have much value, will you demand that others treat you with respect? If you allow others to disrespect and mistreat you, then how do you think you will treat others? What is inside always comes out, including how we view and feel about ourselves.

Check out These Promises of Love:

John 3:16 Updated American Standard Version (UASV)

[16] For God so loved the world that he gave his only-begotten Son, in order that everyone trusting[90] in him will not be destroyed but have eternal life.

Romans 5:8 Updated American Standard Version (UASV)

[8] But God shows his love for us in that while we were still sinners, Christ died for us.

Ephesians 2:4-5 Updated American Standard Version (UASV)

[4] But God, being rich in mercy, because of his great love with which he loved us, [5] even when we were dead in our trespasses, made us alive together with Christ[91] (by grace you have been saved),

1 John 4:9-11 Updated American Standard Version (UASV)

[9] In this the love of God was made manifest among us, that God sent his only begotten Son into the world, so that we might live through him. [10] In this is love, not that we loved God, but that he loved us and sent his Son to be the propitiation for our sins. [11] Beloved ones, if God so loved us, we also ought to love one another.

Zephaniah 3:17 Updated American Standard Version (UASV)[92]

[17] Jehovah your God is in your midst,
  a mighty one who will save;
he will exult over you with great joy;
  he will quiet you in his love;
he will rejoice over you with shouts of joy.

---

[90] **Believe, faith, Trust in:** (Gr. *pisteuo*) If *pisteuo* is followed by the Greek preposition *eis*, ("into, in, among," accusative case), it is generally rendered "trusting in" or "trust in." (John 3:16, 36; 12:36; 14:1) The grammatical construction of the Greek verb *pisteuo* "believe" followed by the Greek preposition *eis* "into" in the accusative gives us the sense of having faith into Jesus, putting faith in, trusting in Jesus.–Matt. 21:25, 32; 27:42; John 1:7, 12; 2:23–24; 3:15–16, 36; 6:47; 11:25; 12:36; 14:1; 20:31; Acts 16:31; Rom. 4:3.

[91] Two early mss read *in Christ*

[92] Just as was the case in 537 B.C.E., some 2554-years ago in the restored ancient Jerusalem, God's servants today enjoy a great spiritual prosperity by way books such as this, which bring about spiritual and personal growth. Just a word of caution, though, not all Christian books about life and about God are created equal.

1 Peter 5:6-7 Updated American Standard Version (UASV)

⁶ Humble yourselves, therefore, under the mighty hand of God, that he may exalt you at the proper time, ⁷ casting all your anxieties on him, because he cares for you.

Job 34:19 Updated American Standard Version (UASV)

¹⁹ who shows no partiality to princes,
 nor regards the rich more than the poor,
 for they are all the work of his hands?

Psalm 86:15 Updated American Standard Version (UASV)

⁵ For you, O Jehovah, are good, and ready to forgive,
 and abundant in lovingkindness to all who call upon you.

1 John 3:1 Updated American Standard Version (UASV)

3 See what sort of love the Father has given us, so that we should be called children of God; and such we are.

John 13:34-35 Updated American Standard Version (UASV)

³⁴ A new commandment I give to you, that you love one another, even as I have loved you, that you also love one another. ³⁵ By this all men will know that you are my disciples, if you have love for one another."

Process Questions:

What do you believe your worth to be?

_____
_____
_____
_____
_____
_____
_____
_____

What does God say your worth is?

_____
_____
_____
_____
_____
_____

How much are you loved, what is God willing to sacrifice for you to win your love?

_____

_____

_____

_____

_____

_____

_____

What type of Love does God have for you?

_____

_____

_____

_____

_____

_____

What type of care went into your creation?

_____

_____

_____

What are the Lies you speak about this and what is the Truth?

_____

_____

_____

_____

_____

_____

_____

Define what Self-Worth, Self-Esteem, and Self-Image are.

_____

_____

_____

_____
_____
_____
_____

Describe what your Self-Esteem is.

_____
_____
_____
_____
_____
_____

Describe what your Self-Image is.

_____
_____
_____
_____

How do you allow others to treat you?

_____
_____
_____
_____
_____
_____

How do you treat others?

_____
_____
_____
_____
_____
_____
_____
_____

Four Pillars Assignment on this Chapter's Topic

Self-Talk (40,000 individual thoughts summarized)

_____
_____
_____
_____
_____
_____
_____

Faulty Beliefs (Beliefs about yourself and your situation as a result of your thoughts.)

_____
_____
_____
_____
_____
_____

Perception (The faulty beliefs about your environment as a result of your faulty beliefs about yourself and your environments)

_____
_____
_____
_____
_____
_____

Behaviors (What you choose to do)

_____
_____
_____
_____
_____

Finally, identify the outcome and how it reinforces the self-talk.

_____
_____
_____
_____

1.) Who/What planted the seeds that led to your self-talk?

_____
_____
_____
_____
_____
_____
_____

2.) How did you allow them to take root in your mind?

_____
_____
_____
_____
_____
_____

3.) Are the seeds that were planted seeds of fruit bearing trees which will bring you good life and sustain you or are they seeds of weeds which will rob you and kill good things in your life?

_____
_____
_____
_____
_____
_____
_____
_____
_____
_____
_____

Further Thoughts

Chapter XV Plans for Your Future

Jeremiah 29:11 Updated American Standard Version (UASV)

11 "'For I know the thoughts that I am thinking toward you,' declares Jehovah, 'thoughts of peace, and not of calamity, to give you a future and a hope.

These words apply to God's people, the Israelites, some 2554 years ago, in 537 B.C.E., where He "assured the prophet [Jeremiah] and the people that he had not forgotten the reason for Israel and Judah's existence. He would provide for their present needs, both temporal and spiritual. At some time in the future, they would be ready for deliverance and further blessings. When this occurred, he would be available for them."[93] These words by extension still apply to us as well. The apostle Paul gave a principle to the Christian in the first century, to use in interpreting the Old Testament. He wrote, "For whatever was written in former days was written for our instruction, that through endurance and through the encouragement of the Scriptures we might have hope." (Rom. 15:4) The objective is to determine what the Old Testament author meant by his words, as his original audience would have understood them, and then apply them correctly to the present-day audience. The thing to do is stay with the same pattern of meaning.

God was telling Jeremiah to tell his people about "'thoughts of peace, and not of calamity, to give you a future and a hope.'" (Jer. 29:11) Jeremiah wrote in about 580 B.C.E. but the words would not apply until 537 B.C.E. (before Christ years went down, not up), decades later. The Israelites were going to be freed from Babylonian captivity, being able to return to their homeland in peace and pure worship. The future that the Father has thought out for us is one of eternal life with peace, prosperity and happiness through his Son, our King, namely, Jesus Christ. This future is our as long as we stay submitted to God's universal sovereignty.

Proverbs 3:5-8 Updated American Standard Version (UASV)

5 Trust in Jehovah with all your heart,
 and do not lean on your own understanding.
6 In all your ways acknowledge him,
 and he will make straight your paths.
7 Be not wise in your own eyes;
 fear Jehovah, and turn away from evil.

---

[93] Anders, Max; Wood, Fred M.; McLaren, Ross H.. Holman Old Testament Commentary - Jeremiah, Lamentations (p. 241). B&H Publishing. Kindle Edition."

[8] It will be healing to your flesh
and refreshment to your bones.

3:5–8 These verses contain key words and phrases in sapiential thought. First of all, the phrase **trust in the Lord** (16:20; 22:17–19; 28:25; 29:25), and its close associate **fear the Lord**, is the fundamental definition of wisdom in Proverbs. Trust usually implies some threat or evil looming on the horizon. To trust in the Lord **with all your heart** refers to the total surrender of self. The admonition is the theological foundation upon which all the proverbs rest.

When the sage calls on the reader to **acknowledge him** (v. 6), he speaks on the level of attitude; the disciple desires to do God's will. When the disciple learns to trust completely in Yahweh, then the promise is that **he will make straight your paths**. This does not mean that Yahweh promises a life free from difficulties. Rather it means that one's life has clear direction and purpose. Abraham set off on a journey not knowing where he was going, only that God would lead him. In other words, God promised to make his paths straight.

The next imperative in the instruction is **Do not be wise in your own eyes** (v. 7). This is a stock phrase in wisdom's dictionary used some nine times in Proverbs. The sage often portrays the fool as someone who is "wise in his own eyes" (cf. 26:5, 12, 16). Those who are wise in their own eyes are those ruled by conceit, who depend on their own intellectual finesse to make it in the world (cf. Jer 9:23–24). Here the phrase is antithetic to "fear the Lord." To be wise in one's own eyes is a demonstration of pride. To fear the Lord demonstrates humility.

For those who do fear the Lord, the rewards are significant. It will result in **health to your body and nourishment to your bones** (v. 8). "Nourishment" (שִׁקּוּי, šiqqûy) can literally be translated "medicine." A healthy life flows out of one's relationship to the Creator. Such trust brings healing to the flesh and medicine for the body. This reference to the body is to the physical body and to physical health, yet it includes more than that. It incorporates the whole of a person's being.

The wisdom of Proverbs does not divide individuals or life into parts. There is no dichotomy between mind and body, physical and spiritual, or sacred and secular. Such a dichotomy is artificial. From the perspective of Proverbs, the physical, mental, emotional, moral, and spiritual are parts of the whole. When one is affected, the others are affected as well. Proverbial wisdom is about health, health that incorporates the whole person.[94]

Romans 8:28 Updated American Standard Version (UASV)

[28] And we know that all things work together for good for those who love God, for those who are called according to his purpose.

8:28. The purposes of God are the most important reality in the spiritual life. The purpose (*prothesin*) of God's will is what controls everything (Eph. 1:11) in light of eternity (Eph. 3:11). God **called** us to a holy life on the basis of his purpose and grace, and it is that purpose to which we have been **called** that verse 28 invites our submission (God's calling here is not the calling of the many in Matt. 22:14, but the effectual calling to salvation of Rom. 11:29; 1 Cor 1:9; Eph. 4:4; 1 Thess. 2:12; 2 Tim. 1:9; and 1 Pet. 2:9).

Our new life in the Spirit is based on God's good purposes for our lives, and that includes suffering. The suffering (v. 17) and groaning (v. 23) that Paul has been discussing is what is in view in verse 28. When we find ourselves in trying circumstances in life, we can **know that in all things God works for the good of those who love him, who have been called according to his purpose**. Read literally, it is easy to see why some consider this the greatest verse in Scripture. It tells us that nothing happens outside of God's plan for our good.

An important grammatical question clarifies the role of God in accomplishing his purposes. "All things" can be taken either as the subject (as in KJV; "all things work together"), or as the object (NIV [adverbial], "in all things God works"; NASB [direct object], "God causes all things to work"). As the subject, "all things" are in control, and while they end happily, they do so seemingly in and of themselves. When God is the subject, he causes (*sunergei*, from *sunergeo*, to work with) all things to work together for good. In other words, there is no doubting the outcome's ultimate good. Lest we translate according to our theological preferences, it must be noted that (a) there is not a compelling grammatical reason to translate one way or the other (see the commentaries for minor possible reasons), and (b) the meaning is not radically altered with either translation.

It should probably be agreed with Moo that the plainest rendering of the text is that of the KJV ("all things work together for good"), but that

---

[94] Dave Bland, *Proverbs, Ecclesiastes & Song of Songs*, The College Press NIV Commentary (Joplin, MO: College Press Pub. Co., 2002), 69–71.

"it does not finally matter all that much" between the choices mentioned above (Moo, p. 528). The reason is that **God** and **his purpose** are the controlling elements of the verse. Paul is clearly subordinating **all things** to the **purpose** of God, regardless of how the verse is written.[95]

Isaiah 58:11 Updated American Standard Version (UASV)

[11] And Jehovah will guide you continually
and satisfy your desire in scorched places
and strengthen your bones;
and you shall be like a watered garden,
and like a spring of water,
whose waters do not fail.

Verse 11 explains how God will guide his people (cf. 57:18) at all times (just as he did in the past during the wilderness journey in Deut 32:12; Ps 23:3) and will satisfy their souls in "dry places" (just as he did in their wilderness journey). He will strengthen their bones, and they will be like a well-watered metaphorical garden or a spring that never stops.[217] These are pictures of life, vitality, and blessings. This picture implies not only the blessing of God on his people, but the ability of his people to impart blessings to others who come to this garden or spring.[96]

Jeremiah 1:5 Updated American Standard Version (UASV)

[5] "Before I formed you in the womb I knew you,
and before you were born I consecrated you;
I appointed you a prophet to the nations."

According to Jeremiah 1:5, God had been at work in the life of Jeremiah before he was born—indeed, before he was even conceived. A series of four verbs points to God's work before Jeremiah's birth: God **formed** him, **knew** him, set him **apart**, and **appointed** him. The biblical teaching is consistent and constant: God is involved in the forming and shaping of the preborn in the womb. Job testified to this truth (Job 10:8–12). But nowhere is it stated more eloquently than by David in Psalm 139:14–16. God personally weaves the preborn child together in the secret place of the womb. He causes the development of the bodily frame.

But more than just forming the preborn, God said to Jeremiah, **I**

---

[95] Kenneth Boa and William Kruidenier, *Romans*, vol. 6, Holman New Testament Commentary (Nashville, TN: Broadman & Holman Publishers, 2000), 259–260.

[96] Gary Smith, *Isaiah 40-66*, vol. 15B, The New American Commentary (Nashville, TN: Broadman & Holman Publishers, 2009), 582.

knew you. A careful reading of verse 5 indicates the knowing actually came before the forming: **Before I formed you in the womb I knew you**. God took an interest in and had an intimate knowledge of Jeremiah even before the first cells and sinews began to develop. There is more. For Jeremiah, before he was born, God set him apart. God put Jeremiah in a special category. He was consecrated or sanctified to God's service. And then, still before he was born, God appointed Jeremiah to a particular service—to be a prophet for him, to be a prophet to the nations.

In verse 5, the Hebrew word translated "formed" is the same one used in Genesis 2:7. The root idea is to be straitened or distressed. From this comes the meaning of "to form, fashion, make." Another derivation is "to devise, meditate." The nouns maker, creator, and potter come from the participle form of this verb. As a composer constructing the instrument on which the music will be played, God created Jeremiah to be a spokesman for him.

The word translated "knew" has a broad usage. It indicates more than factual knowledge, meaning experiential knowledge as well as sexual intimacy. It is consistently used for physical intercourse. In this present context, the verb indicates a relationship. God chose Jeremiah and set him apart before he was born to share a special affinity with his Creator.

The expression "to the nations" poses no problem for the person who knows the political climate of that time. Jeremiah's call coincided with the death of Ashurbanipal, king of Assyria, and the beginning of Assyria's decline as the dominant power in the Middle East. Babylon, under Nabopolassar, was entering the struggle for world domination. Egypt was watching with hopeful eye the decadence of the Assyrian Empire. Jeremiah was called that year to be a prophet. How could one with the broad insight he would develop be anything less than a prophet "to the nations"?[97]

Psalm 32:8-9 Updated American Standard Version (UASV)

[8] I will instruct you and teach you in the way that you should go;
  I will counsel you with my eye upon you.
[9] Be not like a horse or a mule, without understanding,
  which must be curbed with bit and bridle,
  or else it will not come near you.

---

[97] Anders, Max; Wood, Fred M.; McLaren, Ross H.. Holman Old Testament Commentary - Jeremiah, Lamentations (pp. 14-15). B&H Publishing. Kindle Edition.

32:8–9. David also counseled others: **I will instruct you and teach you in the way you should go**. On the basis of David's own painful experience, he instructed others: **I will counsel you and watch over you. Do not be like the horse or the mule, which have no understanding**. The Lord exhorted the people not to be like the obstinate horse or stubborn mule that refuses to go where its rider leads. Instead, the godly should respond promptly to God on their own accord. David was like a wild horse that rushed into sin, but when it came to confessing his sin, he held back like a stubborn mule.

The warning is clear for the person who will not humble himself before God's sovereign rule. If we do not submit to the Lord, we will be controlled by bit and bridle. If the people of God act as disobedient children, he will use severe means to get their attention and gain control (cp. Prov. 26:3). Persistent disobedience by the godly will lead to the chastening hand of God (Heb. 12:5–11).[98]

1 Corinthians 2:9 Updated American Standard Version (UASV)

⁹ But just as it is written,

"Things which eye has not seen and ear has not heard,
    and have not entered into the heart of man,
all that God has prepared for those who love him."

¹⁰ For to us God revealed them through the Spirit; for the Spirit searches all things, even the depths of God.

2:9–10a. Paul here contrasted the belief that the rulers of this world understood wisdom with the reality that they did not understand. To draw out this contrast, he alluded to Isaiah 64:4, and added elements from Isaiah 52:15; 65:17 and Jeremiah 3:16. He pointed out how the prophets occasionally indicated that God's wise plan remained hidden from all but those who loved him. The ordinary ways of understanding (**eye, ear, mind**) cannot perceive the mysteries of God. The rulers of the world may be adept at these means of perception, but these senses cannot discern the wisdom of God. God must reveal wisdom in a special way.

To drive home his main point, Paul applied the prophetic word directly to the Corinthians. Although the world cannot perceive the wisdom of God, **God has revealed it**. It has come in a supernatural way directly from God. Moreover, this word came not to the world but **to**

---

[98] Anders, Max; Lawson, Steven. Holman Old Testament Commentary - Psalms: 11 (p. 174). B&H Publishing. Kindle Edition.

us—to Paul and other followers of Christ.

Many in Corinth relied on pretentious human reason in their struggles within the church, so Paul reminded them that they did not perceive the gospel of Christ by human ingenuity. It was foolish for the Corinthian believers to turn to human insight when they had discovered the ways of Christ through divine revelation **by his Spirit**. Paul affirmed as before that the wisdom of God comes through the ministry of the Holy Spirit in the church (1:4–5; 2:4).[99]

Purpose

I feel that many people are confused when we talk about purpose because, in our society, purpose must mean your job or what you will do with your life. So much is focused on it from the moment we are born. When a baby is born people start to wonder, is she going to be the next president, is he going to be a doctor, or are you going to be an astronaut. We tease as parents when Halloween comes, and children want to dress up to be a chef, a policeman, a princess and so forth. People start believing that your interests will guide your occupation and we as a society tend to put the two together as one; our purpose with our job. Let me ask you, does God focus on what job you will have and how you will pay your bills? I don't believe He does. Not that He does not care about the things that we care about, but I don't know that God focuses so much on our job as much as He focuses on what our gifts will be. Let us look at the facts. We know there is a battle waging for the souls of the people of this world. Some of those souls have been saved, and some are still lost. The Enemy is seeking to get back at God in the best way he can; by taking those who God loves most away from Him and having them volunteer to imprison themselves to sin and away from God's love. God is seeking to rescue his beloved, you, from the lies of the Enemy if you will let Him. How does He do that.

Behold, I stand at the door and knock; if anyone hears My voice and opens the door, I will come into him and will dine with him, and he with Me. Revelation 3:20 In the story of the prodigal son we are told of a young man who spent his inheritance on wasted efforts to please himself. He runs out of money, having wasted it all on parties, women, and alcohol and decides to finally return home to a father who has been looking and longing for him. In this story, we see God in the father of this

---

[99] Richard L. Pratt Jr, *I & II Corinthians*, vol. 7, Holman New Testament Commentary (Nashville, TN: Broadman & Holman Publishers, 2000), 35.

young man. He is constantly looking out the window for the day we decide to come home. This is our God, running out of the house the second He catches a glimpse of you. This is our God who is anxiously waiting to hear you say you love Him so He can finally embrace you the way He has been dying to. He is longing to have you back. So how does He work to find you and bring you home? He pursues you. He waits patiently for you. He stands there, ever ready to accept you and wrap a blanket around your shoulders, excited to celebrate your return. He whispers to your heart that He loves you and sometimes He has created other's purposes to be symbols of His love for you. He introduces you to people in your life that will show you His love in hopes that you will listen and turn back to Him. Maybe the person who gave you this workbook was just one of those people. Maybe my purpose in writing this workbook was just for you to read it and be encouraged to turn your eyes to God the Father.

1 Corinthians 12:27 says that *all of you together are Christ's body, and each of you is a part of it.* You are His hands and I am His feet. We are called to be *as sheep among wolves. Be as wary as snakes and harmless as doves. But beware! For you will be handed over to the courts and beaten in the synagogues and courtyards of kings because you are my followers. This will be your opportunity to tell them about me—yes to witness to the world* Mathew 10:16-18. This means the Enemy will target you because you are going against his plans in your work for God. In battle, the Enemy attacks you when you choose the side that is against him. When you follow your purpose and serve God, the Enemy will begin to attack you to prevent you from spoiling his plans.

Sometimes trouble in your life will be the result of the imperfect world we live in, troubles that the Enemy will seek to take advantage of. Other times, like in Job's story, the Enemy will create trouble in your life to prevent you from reaching the purpose that you were created for. Therefore, trouble in your life does not have to be something that destroys you, but that it can be something that molds you into gold. God does not want you to have to go through troubles and trials in life, but it is a result of the world we live in which is broken. Don't think for a second that while God is trying to help you get closer to Him when life gets bad, that the Enemy is not seeking to plant seeds of anger and resentment in you toward God because of the troubles you face, in an effort to distance you from Him. Peter who was crucified upside down after being beaten and tortured for sharing with others about the love of Christ said this, *These trials are only to test our faith, to show that it is strong and pure. It is being tested as fire tests and purifies gold—and your faith is far more precious to God than mere gold. So if your faith remains* strong after being tried by fiery trials it will bring you much praise and glory and honor on the day when Jesus Christ is revealed to the whole world. You love him even though you have never seen him. Though you do not see him, you trust him, and even now you are happy with a glorious inexpressible joy. 1 Peter 1:7-8 The promise from God is this that we are to remember that the temptations that come into your life are no different from what others experience. And God is faithful. He will keep the temptation from becoming so strong that you can't stand up against it. When you are tempted, he will show you a way out so that you will not give in to it 1 Corinthians 10:13. God is always in control, even over the Enemy. He will return one day to finish the war with Satan, but He waits to give all of us a chance; a chance to understand the choice we have to make and then to choose who we will follow, God or Satan. That is what we wait for before our Father returns.

This is a battle, and the prize is to not only become saved ourselves but then to turn around and show the face of God to others so that when they look at us they see God only, and they too will choose to be saved. In each of us is a gift that will allow us to do that in a unique way that no other can do. For some of us, the way we overcome the evil in this world is our gift; our story to share with others who experience the same evil as we did; a story only they and you will understand. For others, it is the passion to serve. For some, it is their ability to share the love of God through music. We all have our special talents that can be used to serve the Enemy or to serve God and bring more of our brothers and sisters home with us. When others look at you, do they see the love of God? I aspire to this, but I know that personally, I do not always show the love of God. His love is pure and is fearless and bold. It does not worry about injustice but rejoices when the truth wins out.

We talked about the people of the Bible and their stories. Paul is my favorite above them all. Paul openly admits he was not talented with public speaking 2 Corinthians 11:6, but he is very educated on scripture, and because of his education and knowledge with Scripture, he was the perfect person to show those of the Jewish faith that Christ was the Messiah, come to save them from their shackles and sin because he could prove it with his knowledge of the scriptures. Paul did not start off this way. He had studied the scriptures but not for the intent to bring others to Christ, but he came to Jerusalem and heard of Christ's death and set out to help the Pharisees and Jewish leaders to hunt down Christians and imprison them to shut them up. He sought to use his tools against Christ, and it was not until he was quite literally blinded did he stop and start serving Christ because his soul was shown the truth when his eyes could not see it.

He is the perfect image of one who made all the wrong choices and only possessed two things to allow him to achieve his purpose; his knowledge and his determination. He was not a great speaker, not a world leader, not a religious teacher, he was a Roman citizen, a murderer, and he fumbled his words, yet he was chosen to be the tool of God to have the Good News spread throughout all of Europe and Asia. Most of the New Testament was written by him and not the twelve who walked with Jesus.

No matter if you flip burgers at McDonalds or if you become a world renowned surgeon, you were created with special talents and a perspective when you look at the world that is unique to you. It is your special ability to laugh and make others laugh with you that is your purpose. It is your story of how you have overcome hardships and struggles that will encourage another person that is your purpose. It is your empathy and your ability to feel what another feels and let them know they are not alone that is your purpose because someday you will meet someone who needed you right at that moment and you will change their life. These are parts of you that are not going to decide what you do to make a living, but they will decide who you are and how you act while you are working to make a living. You will interact with everyone in that place, wherever it is doing whatever it is that you choose, and it is the way you interact with others that is your purpose. The encouraging words you use, the laughter you bring, the hug at just the perfect moment, that God saw long before you did it and knew how much it would mean to the person you met. You may never know the type of impact you will make on others in your life, but someday you will see the plan that God had when He placed you in that McDonalds or in that law firm. What you do to make a paycheck is not your purpose, but how you impact the lives of those around you is.

Do you understand what I am stressing to you? Can you hear me? God chose to use Paul, someone with the worst reputation and no special talent to change the world. If Paul can do it, then you most certainly can. I have no doubt, my brother or sister. There is nothing you did or could ever do to separate you from His love or from the purpose for which He created you. Look at your talents, your life experiences, and your story and use how you have overcome even the direst and ugly sin and situation to bring yourself closer to God and to bring others with you. That is your miracle, that is your destiny. I cannot wait to hear how you rock the world so don't make me guess!!! Share with me!

Process Questions:

Were you born with a purpose?

_____

_____
_____
_____
_____
_____
_____
_____

What does it mean to have a purpose?

_____

_____
_____
_____
_____
_____
_____
_____

Compare and Contrast your job and your purpose.

_____

_____
_____
_____
_____
_____
_____
_____

Why did we discuss the story of the Prodigal Son?

_____

_____
_____
_____
_____
_____
_____
_____

Did Paul think that he was going to end up writing most of the New Testament? What was Paul's story of finding his purpose?

_____

_____

_____

_____

_____

_____

_____

_____

What does all of this have to do with you?

_____

_____

_____

_____

_____

_____

_____

_____

Four Pillars Assignment on this Chapter's Topic

Self-Talk (40,000 individual thoughts summarized)

_____

_____

_____

_____

_____

_____

Faulty Beliefs (Beliefs about yourself and your situation as a result of your thoughts.)

_____

_____

_____

_____

_____

_____

Perception (The faulty beliefs about your environment as a result of your faulty beliefs about yourself and your environments)

_____
_____
_____
_____
_____
_____
_____

Behaviors (What you choose to do)

_____
_____
_____
_____
_____
_____
_____

Finally, identify the outcome and how it reinforces the self-talk.

_____
_____
_____
_____
_____
_____
_____

Seeds Be Planted?

1.) Who/What planted the seeds that led to your self-talk?

_____
_____
_____
_____
_____
_____

2.) How did you allow them to take root in your mind?

_____
_____
_____
_____
_____
_____

3.) Are the seeds that were planted seeds of fruit bearing trees which will bring you good life and sustain you or are they seeds of weeds which will rob you and kill good things in your life?

_____
_____
_____
_____
_____
_____
_____
_____

Further Thoughts

_____
_____
_____
_____
_____
_____
_____
_____
_____
_____
_____

Chapter XVI The Armor of God

Bring It All Together

When you know how the Enemy attacks you, you have chosen sides in the war, and you understand what the Truth is, you must now put all of this knowledge together by putting on the armor of God to protect yourself from further attacks. That is when the defensive approach gives way to the offensive; and your God sounds the order to, "Advance!" and spread the Good News.

A Quick Look:

Belt of Truth: The world's version of right and wrong vs. God's.

Breastplate of Righteousness: Not only knowing the Truth but acting in the Truth.

Shoes of Peace: Standing firm when doing the right thing causes you to face adversity.

God's promises when we do not give in to the pressure to give in and go against our beliefs.

Faith is your shield that will allow you to battle the doubts the Enemy attempts to plant in your mind.

Helmet of Salvation- Is your mind with God or is is with the Enemy, have you been saved or are you still lost?

The offensive weapon: the Sword of the Word of God. The Enemy knows the scripture likely better than a preacher, and he will manipulate it to suit his needs.

Supplemental Assignments:

Discuss what your code of right and wrong is and in what ways has your version of right and wrong has been influenced by others or the media.

Challenge: Spend one month listening to nothing but positive and uplifting Christian music on you MP3 player or the radio and write down your observation of the impact it has on your thinking and how you view the world.

Process what your experiences have taught you about right and wrong and how the places you have been in life and your experiences have impacted your morals and values so far.

Discuss your character traits and the difference between personality and character. What character traits do you value in others as well as yourself.

Putting on Your Armor

Ephesians 6:12-17 Updated American Standard Version (UASV)

¹² For our wrestling[100] is not against flesh and blood, but against the rulers, against the powers, against the world-rulers of this darkness, against the wicked spirit forces in the heavenly places.

¹³ Therefore, take up the whole armor[101] of God, so that you will be able to resist in the evil day, and having done everything, to stand firm. ¹⁴ Stand firm, therefore, with your loins girded[102] about with truth, and having put on the breastplate of righteousness, ¹⁵ and with your feet shod with the preparation of the gospel of peace; ¹⁶ in all things, taking up the shield of faith with which you will be able to extinguish all the flaming arrows of the evil one. ¹⁷ And take the helmet of salvation, and the sword of the Spirit, which is the word of God.

¹⁸ Through all prayer and petition praying at all times in the Spirit, and with this in view, keep awake with all perseverance and making supplication for all the holy ones.

6:12. The reason this spiritual armor is needed is that **our struggle is not against flesh and blood**. The picture of warfare here implies that we do not face a physical army. We face a spiritual army. Therefore our weapons must be spiritual. **Against the rulers, against the authorities, against the powers of this dark world and against the spiritual forces of evil in the heavenly realms** seems to suggest a hierarchy of evil spirit-beings who do the bidding of Satan in opposing the will of God on earth.

6:13. When we have obeyed all the instructions implicit in the **full armor of God**, we can resist Satan's attempts to deceive and destroy us.

---

[100] Or struggle

[101] **Armor:** (Heb. *keli*; Gr. *panoplia*) The weapons and armor worn by soldiers used in fighting, which makes up the whole of his offensive and defensive equipment. This would include a helmet to protect the head, the girdle, and a leather belt worn around the waist or hips to protect the loins, the breastplate to protect vital organs, especially the heart. It also included a coat of mail, i.e., scale body armor for protection during battle, greaves, namely shin guards, and the shield, usually carried on the left arm or in the left hand.–1 Sam. 7:5-6; 31:9; Eph. 6:13-17.

[102] (an idiom, literally 'to gird up the loins') to cause oneself to be in a state of readiness–'to get ready, to prepare oneself.'

288

The day of evil is anytime during this era in history until Jesus returns. All days are evil in their potential and become evil in reality when Satan or his demons decide to use that day to attack you.

The clear implication here is that, if the Christian has all his armor on, he has the ability to **stand firm** against Satan. At times the spiritual warfare in which we find ourselves may be frightening. However, the only thing we have to fear, if our armor is in place, is fear itself. "The one who is in you [Jesus], is greater than the one [Satan] who is in the world" (1 John 4:4). "Submit yourselves, then, to God. Resist the devil, and he will flee from you" (Jas. 4:7). "Be self-controlled and alert. Your enemy the devil prowls around like a roaring lion looking for someone to devour. Resist him, standing firm in the faith" (1 Pet. 5:8–9). Scripture is utterly consistent. If we have our armor in place, if we are firm in our faith, we may resist the devil. If we do, he will flee from us.

6:14. After instructions to put on the full armor of God and the promise of the power of God in victory over the devil, Paul specifically describes the various pieces of armor. **The belt of truth** pictures the large leather belt the Roman soldier wore. It held other weapons and kept his outer garments in place. To put on the belt of truth can be understood as accepting the truth of the Bible and choosing to follow it with integrity.

The breastplate of righteousness pictures the metal armor in the shape of a human torso common to the Roman uniform. To put on the breastplate can be understood as choosing not to harbor and nurture known sin. It is striving to be like Christ and live according to his ways of righteousness.

6:15. Feet fitted with the readiness pictures the hobnailed shoes which kept the soldiers footing sure in battle. To put on these shoes could be understood as believing the promises of God in the gospel and counting on them to be true for you. Faith in these promises yields peace in the Christian's life.

6:16. The shield of faith pictures the small, round shield the Roman soldier used to deflect blows from the sword, arrow, or spear of the enemy. To take up this shield can be understood as rejecting temptations to doubt, sin or quit, telling yourself the truth and choosing on the basis of the truth to do the right thing.

6:17. The helmet of salvation pictures the Roman soldier's metal protective headgear. It does not refer to our salvation in Christ. First Thessalonians speaks of the helmet of the "*hope* of salvation," which is probably a parallel idea. That being the case, taking the helmet of salvation could be understood as resting our hope in the future and living in this world according to the value system of the next.

The sword of the Spirit pictures the soldier's weapon sheathed to his belt and used both for offensive and defensive purposes. Taking the sword of the Spirit—defined for us as the Word of God—can be understood as using Scripture specifically in life's situations to fend off attacks of the enemy and put him to flight. We see the example of Jesus using the Scripture this way in Matthew 4:1–11.

6:18. Finally, while preparing for and doing battle, we are to be on the alert and **always keep on praying**. We petition God for our own needs in the battle, and we pray for the spiritual victory of other saints.[103]

The first time I read this, I remember thinking to myself, 'what the heck does this mean'...'how do I put on the belt of Truth. Then I did some research, and it started to make sense. Just how those we fight are not physical, so too are our tools with which we fight them and protect ourselves. Let us break this down a bit. The *sturdy belt of Truth*, think on what you know now to be the truth. Our world is full of many types of people. God created all of us. Therefore all of us have the capability for greatness because our God would not create something to be anything but amazing. However, we all have a choice of what we believe. We have the choice to follow the One who created us or to follow His enemy, the one who speaks lies and is attempting to make us appear more like him so that we will deny our God and believe ourselves to be better off without Him. If we choose to listen to the lies of the enemy and turn from our God, then we have already started to resemble the enemy who believed that he was above God. The Truth helps us to remember that we are not above God and cannot do anything in this world without Him for He created everything with which we would attempt to do it.

The Lord tells us things that are right and wrong for a reason, to protect us, but the enemy will whisper like he did in the Garden of Eden; that we are above God and should rebel against Him, and make our own choice. The world tells us that whatever makes us feel good is right. We have learned that this is not the truth. The truth is that true happiness does not come from receiving, but from giving because we find happiness in making others happy, who then, in turn, want to make us happy. See how this works? The world says to use others to make yourself happy. What does that leave us with—used up people who feel taken advantage of and who eventually leave us, or try to use us in return. Either way, you look at it, you see people trying to use people for their own gain. Life

[103] Max Anders, *Galatians-Colossians*, vol. 8, Holman New Testament Commentary (Nashville, TN: Broadman & Holman Publishers, 1999), 190–191.

and relationships built on that leave one another feeling empty, and unfulfilled when it is all said and done. The belt of Truth is what we referred to in earlier chapters. This is your code on right and wrong according to God's word and not the world's. By following God's directions, you can stay on the course, God set before your feet and not get pulled by the temptations of the Enemy. You know the Truth even when everyone else in your life or the world around you is telling you that it is not.

The breastplate of righteousness; in order to understand this, you must first understand that righteousness means being morally right according to God's moral code. So this starts with the belt of truth, knowing what is right according to God, and then is followed by the breastplate of righteousness, doing what is morally right according to God's code. Does this mean you have to be perfect, O Lord I hope not because I fail at this regularly, but it does mean that you strive to do what is right. When you are attempting to walk in line with what God describes to be right, then you are going to be protected. This is an act of doing what is right, right for yourself, and to stand up for what is right for others, putting action to your words. Practice what you preach so-to-speak. Knowing what is right is not enough. It is private and in your mind. You can sit there seeing things happening around you that you know to be wrong, but unless you act and do what is right in that moment, you will encourage others to do the same thing you are— nothing. But if you do what is right, others will see this and be encouraged by your choice and will join you, and you will have maintained your Integrity. Edmund Burke has a quote about this; The only thing necessary for the triumph of evil is for good men to do nothing. The breastplate of righteousness protects your heart from the regret and shame you could feel if you do not do the right thing.

Next, is putting on the shoes of peace from the Good News. Our feet determine where we go. It is our feet that do the walking. Therefore it is our feet that take us place to place. It is also the feet of a soldier that must be planted firmly in the ground they are protecting as not to allow enemy forces to push past them. Do you plant your feet in the Lord? Do you trust in the Lord and lean not on your own abilities but on the Lord's abilities and power. You alone cannot defeat evil, but you with God can do the impossible. Trusting in God will give you peace because you never have to worry about being good enough, strong enough, or smart enough to do what needs to be done. If God has called you to do it, it will not matter if you feel like you have the right credentials for the job. As long as you have God with you, you can feel at peace because through you, He will act and in your weakness, He will be strong.

Remembering God's promises will also give you peace when you face adversity. In life, there will often be times where you will be standing alone to do the right thing. Others may tell you that you are backwards, that you are not modern or even call you names and attack you verbally or physically because of your stand for what is right. The Peace of God will allow you to remember His promises in times when doing the right thing means you have to face adversity. Jesus encourages us when he says that the world will not treat us any differently than it treated Him, so He knows how it feels to be abandoned and left alone facing everyone else on your own. He understands the temptation to give in to avoid pain and insult. He is not asking us to do anything that He did not already do, and He does promise us that all of the adversity we may face will be rewarded in heaven.

Right now, the world tells you it is okay to sleep around and "have fun," it is okay to party and become so drunk or high you cannot control yourself or even remember what you do. The world tells you it is okay to treat those that love you with disrespect, acting as though they know nothing, to dismiss the words of your elders, and to act entitled for the things you have instead of appreciating the sacrifice of others on your behalf. The world tells you to buy this, do this, or look like this to be lovable. In the end, God is the only one saying, "I made you just the way I intended, you don't have to change a thing because when you accept Me, I will clean house and restore you to the glory for which I made you." Stand fast in the promise of God and in the teachings of the Lord, for He will reward you when you oppose the enemy, and His promises are never forgotten.

Faith is your shield against the Enemy's attacks. Faith is the act of believing in what cannot be seen or proven. The enemy's attacks are going to be doubts with which he will seek to plant in your mind making you doubt not only the will of God in your life but His promises to you. Eventually, if you allow any doubt to be planted, that doubt will grow until you forget to think of God at all and start to doubt in His existence entirely. Faith is what will prevent the doubts of the Enemy from taking hold because it will keep you focused on what you know to be true in your heart; that your Father loves you and created you to be an eagle soaring high, not in-prisoned; a slave to your sins.

In battle games, you get extra points for headshots right? Why is that? Because the brain controls everything in the body; everything from your environment goes through your mind before it goes anywhere else. Therefore the Enemy will attack you in your mind, where all of your thoughts are found which control your actions and feelings. Salvation will determine which side of the field you are on. In battle, if you are not wearing a helmet, you are an easy shot, but if you are saved by God, and your mind is protected by Him, then you are on His side in the battle, and your soul is safeguarded by God. The Holy Spirit protects you wherever you go. Scripture tells us that until we are saved by Christ, we are still blinded and cannot fully hear the word of God in our lives. Imagine being a soldier on the field and the commander is giving orders telling you where you need to go to be safe and what you need to do to get out alive, but you cannot hear him. You see his lips moving but cannot tell what he is saying. If you have not been saved, this is what life is like, a deafening to the word of God, but when you are saved, suddenly you can hear everything, and you see the path you need to be on. You can see the difference between life before and how life is meant to be, and best of all, you know the direction to go to navigate out of the battle.

Finally, the offensive weapon, the sword, is the Word of God and you only find this when you go to the Bible. When we spread the word of God, we are speaking truth in a world of lies which directly contradicts what the Enemy has been speaking. We are undoing what the Enemy has done. If you stay silent, you are not fighting back, merely protecting yourself, but when you pray over others and speak the truth over them, you are protecting not only yourself but those around you from the attacks of the Enemy. This is your only offensive weapon, and Jesus struts His stuff when He used it against the enemy when the enemy tried to tempt Jesus in the dessert. Read Mathew 4:1-11. Every time the Enemy quoted scripture, Jesus responded with, "it is written" and quoted scripture right back to him. It was a duel in the dessert between Satan and Jesus, and Jesus kicked butt. You cannot kick the Enemy's butt if you do not have your weapon.

> Oh yes, the Enemy knows scripture quite well and will use it against you.

This is the total picture, all brought together, to show you how you will be able to defend yourself from the Enemy and his attacks; the picture of how you can fight back in your life to release the hold of his shackles on your mind. This whole workbook has taken you to this point where you have to ask yourself, are you wearing the armor of God and maintaining your armor. Do you surround yourself with those who will help you or hurt you? Do you put things into your mind that will be a foothold for Satan to plant seeds of doubt or sin? Or do you plant positivity in your mind with the things you watch and the things you hear? A soldier who leaves his company is an exposed soldier. A soldier who is not wearing armor in battle is open for easy attack. This may be a battle of the unseen, but the same principles that prove to be true in physical battle are also true for spiritual battle.

Process Questions:

What are the six pieces of armor in God's Amor and explain each piece in your own words.

_____
_____
_____
_____
_____
_____
_____
_____
_____
_____
_____
_____
_____
_____
_____
_____
_____
_____

What happens to a soldier who leaves his Company?

_____
_____
_____
_____
_____
_____

Apply this to your life? What does this look like in your experiences?

_____
_____
_____
_____
_____
_____
_____
_____

What does the world tell you is the Truth?

_____
_____
_____
_____
_____
_____
_____
_____
_____
_____
_____
_____

What do you know to be the Truth according to the Bible? (Go to your support person to ask for guidance on scripture if needed.)

_____
_____
_____
_____
_____
_____
_____
_____
_____
_____
_____

List some examples of wearing the Breastplate of Righteousness in your life and putting action to your words to do the right thing.

_____
_____
_____
_____
_____
_____
_____
_____
_____
_____
_____
_____

Four Pillars Assignment on this Chapter's Topic

Self-Talk (40,000 individual thoughts summarized)

_____

_____
_____
_____
_____
_____
_____

Faulty Beliefs (Beliefs about yourself and your situation as a result of your thoughts.)

_____

_____
_____
_____
_____
_____
_____

Perception (The faulty beliefs about your environment as a result of your faulty beliefs about yourself and your environments)

_____

_____
_____
_____
_____
_____
_____
_____

Behaviors (What you choose to do)

_____

_____
_____
_____
_____
_____
_____

Finally, identify the outcome and how it reinforces the self-talk.

_____
_____
_____
_____
_____

Seeds Be
Planted?

1.) Who/What planted the seeds that led to your self-talk?

_____
_____
_____
_____
_____

2.) How did you allow them to take root in your mind?

_____
_____
_____
_____
_____

3.) Are the seeds that were planted seeds of fruit bearing trees, which will bring you good life and sustain you or are they seeds of weeds which will rob you and kill good things in your life?

_____
_____
_____
_____
_____
_____
_____
_____

Further Thoughts

Chapter XVII Breaking the Shackles

Putting It All Together

A Quick Look:

A step-by-step look at how to navigate change.

Graph to identify the truth for every lie so that you have a new thought already prepared to challenge the lies you use to believe.

Surveys to get feedback from accountability partners you trust.

Supplemental Assignments:

Remember that though journal and document your thoughts throughout the day at breakfast, lunch, and dinner. Do this for a week and bring it to your meeting with your support person or therapist.

Complete the steps identified in this chapter for yourself and process what you have with your support person.

Take a day and ask those who you trust to give you an honest answer, even if it is not going to be what you want to hear if you have been operating on lies in your life and identify what they are. Be willing and open to accepting honest feedback, even when it may be hard.

Finding Freedom

Step 1. You first have to decide that you want to change.

Step 2. Once you decide you want to change, you must identify what you are unhappy about in your life that is under your control.

Step 3. You must understand what thoughts (specifically your self-talk) are leading to the problem.

Step 4. You must decide, are these thoughts faulty thoughts or are they based on reality?

Step 5. Decide to change the faulty thoughts with the truth. If you do not know the truth, you must seek the truth in the only place it exists, with God.

Step 6. Start to believe the truth over the lie, even when it is hard to believe. You probably won't believe the truth at first, but the more you say it to yourself, the more you will come to believe it. Your lies became your beliefs in the same way.

Step 7. Watch as the Truth starts to set you free and your behaviors and reactions to others will change as you start to see the truth, as oppose to responding to lies and doubts.

(That's how you find freedom. Staying free is the hard part, but we address that in the next chapter)

Step One is a seemingly easy step, but as we discussed in earlier chapters, there are times when people become so accustomed to living in mud, that they forget there is any other way to live. That is a dangerous place to be, living in a life that is harmful to you and others but becoming so used to it that it feels right. If things happen in your life that causes no reaction to you, but others respond with emotion and are astonished that you are not fazed by it, then this should be a warning to you that you are no longer sensitive to your environment. We should feel safe in relationships to talk about our feelings. We should feel valued and worthy of love and acceptance. We should be able to relax with no fear of where food, shelter, or love will come from. You should be able to trust those around you to protect you and care for you both emotionally and physically. This ability to trust and feel safe should be for all parties equally in the relationship. If you do not feel these things, then something needs to be addressed. Don't fail to change, because you have gotten so used to life as you know it that you cut yourself off from something better. That's like getting the keys to your shackles and then passing them on to someone else saying, "no thanks, I'll stay right here."

Step Two is a tricky one, so I want to bring your attention to a specific part of the sentence, "that you can control." You cannot control anything in this world but yourself. You cannot control if you are in foster care or if you were adopted and do not know your biological parents. You cannot control what your family does and what they believe any more than they can control you, but you can control you and how you view your world. The world is a series of relationships and how we respond to our environment is a relationship as well, a 50/50 relationship. This should be good news because even though there are a lot of things that have possibly happened to you that you wish you could control, you can control yourself which is half of everything. If you can change how you respond to everything, then you can have an impact on what that other people do and how your environment responds to you. See how this cycle works? You cannot control the bullies at school, but you can control your responses to them, which means you control how you feel about and see them.

Our world at times is filled with people who will speak terrible lies over you, telling you that you are only good for how you can please others, that you are stupid, ugly, worthless, never should have been born,

301

are damaged, mean, a jerk, or however you want to fill in the blank. You can choose to believe the lies others speak over you, allow their seeds of doubt, and hate to take root in your mind. On the other hand, you can choose to believe the truth the Creator of the universe said when He was creating you. That you are worth the life of his perfect son. That you were created for good and not for evil. That it does not matter if your mother and father meant to have you or not, God meant for you to be here and so here you are. You cannot control others or any part of the world, but you hold so much power because you are one person who holds fifty percent. Don't give your fifty percent away by letting them control your responses.

This also means that, since we have fifty percent ownership, in certain situations, you hold fifty percent responsibility for what happened. Don't misunderstand me, you have no ownership of another's actions, but if a relationship is bad, it takes two to create a relationship, so it is a good thing to take a look at your actions to see if you are helping or hurting. If you are hurting, then you have to fix what you can control. You cannot fix a relationship by telling the other person what to do; you have to fix your part.

The Power and Impact of our Words

When our words become biting like arrows, our defenses go up. When defenses are up, both people are so worried about how they will attack and defend, that no one is heard. How do you get this interaction to stop and allow both individuals to feel safe enough to drop the walls, stop shooting jabs at one another, and listen so that the problem can be solved. Imagine if every fight were visibly seen like this.

Step Three is where the insight comes in. This step does not say, stop doing this or that, but rather to understand what your thoughts are that are leading you to your feelings and behaviors. This is when you

302

need to sit down and do a Four Pillars tool to start understanding your self-talk and how the thoughts planted in your mind have led you down this path. Keep a log if you are having a hard time recognizing your thoughts. It is amazing how journaling once a day and then looking back at it can show you so much about yourself. I use to keep a journal when I was a teen. My husband and I were cleaning out our spare bedroom closet one day, and I found it. Oh, my goodness, how I laughed when I read it because my way of thinking back then was so different compared to now. It was like a different person entirely. If you are struggling to recognize your self-talk, keep a journal for a week, a month, or however long you need to and then go back and read what you wrote from the beginning. This will show you your thoughts. Start by checking in with yourself three times a day. Record a summary of your thoughts on the day at breakfast, lunch, and dinner. Process what you see after one week with your support person.

Step Four is understanding if your thoughts are faulty or not. Remember how to recognize faulty thinking; is it based on fear, insecurity, justification, or assumption. If it is based on any of these, then it is a lie you are believing instead of the truth. Then you must go immediately to **Step Five** and start recognizing the truth instead. If you need to make a chart to help you, do it. List the lies on the left and the truth on the right and look at what happens. Your mind will be blown by how the two look side-by-side and you will laugh to yourself as I did. If you are having a hard time finding the truth and still wanting to believe the lies, then you need to get some perspective. Speak to someone you trust to give you a clear picture of the situation. Go to someone who knows the Truth and will direct you to Him and His word so you can learn what the Truth is. This is why I caution you so much on surrounding yourself with people who are traveling to the same places in life as you, not physically but spiritually. If you go to someone who often has faulty beliefs, then they will struggle just like you and cannot give you a new perspective. They will just reiterate more of what you are trying to get away from. But if you go to someone who has a clear perspective, then they can help you get back on the path of walking in the truth.

Step Six is tough. You must start to tell yourself the truth, even when you want to continue to believe the lies. For those of you who have been living based on lies for years, this will be more difficult because believing for the first time that you have worth and deserve respect, when you have been believing that you are worthless and it's okay to be abused, will feel weird. This will feel like you are

> Whatever you have to do, don't give up because the best is yet to come.

peddling your bike backward and you are going to struggle to do it. Just as it took time for those thoughts of worthlessness to become a belief, it will take time for thoughts of worth to become belief. Give it time, give yourself reminders, leave sticky notes all over the place to trigger you to remember, but whatever you have to do, don't give up and eventually, this will become your new norm and then the best part will start to happen.

Step Seven, you will get to look back at the old thoughts of worthlessness, hopelessness, and defeat, see the actions of anger, hostility, abuse and laugh as you hardly recognize the person you use to be. You will now be living a life with thoughts based on God's Truth, and His truth is powerful at changing a person from the inside out. You will laugh and cry because you look back at that person you once were and see how God literally entered your heart and mind and restored you to this new being full of glory and beauty; the very being He intended you to be from the very beginning. Change is not outside-in trying to suppress your "bad" behaviors or thoughts, but inside-out, letting Truth enter your mind and reminding yourself to believe it every day. He will change everything else by changing what you believe inside. Challenge me and test it. I promise, if you genuinely do it and are dedicated to it, you will not fail; He will not fail you.

Process Questions:

What does it mean if you no longer allow your environment and people in your environment to control you?

_____
_____
_____
_____
_____
_____
_____

How much control do you have in your relationships with others and your environment?

_____
_____
_____

How do you sometimes give your control away?

_____
_____
_____

_____
_____
_____
_____

If you have partial control in your relationships and environment, then it means you also have the same amount of what?

_____
_____
_____

Why is it important to surround yourself with others who are traveling in the same direction as you in life (spiritually)?

_____
_____
_____
_____
_____
_____
_____

Change comes from where to where?

_____
_____
_____

What happens if the Truth is hard to believe? What do you do when you struggle to challenge the lies?

_____
_____
_____
_____
_____
_____
_____

Compare and contrast the truth compared with the faulty beliefs you have been living life with.

_____
_____
_____
_____
_____
_____

_____
_____
_____
_____
_____
_____
_____
_____
_____

Below is a chart of two columns. In the column on the left, list the lies (faulty beliefs) you have believed. In the column on the right, list what the truth is in contrast to the lie you have listed.

Lies	Truth

Four Pillars Assignment on this Chapter's Topic

Self-Talk (40,000 individual thoughts summarized)

_____
_____
_____
_____
_____
_____
_____

Faulty Beliefs (Beliefs about yourself and your situation as a result of your thoughts.)

_____
_____
_____
_____
_____
_____

Perception (The faulty beliefs about your environment as a result of your faulty beliefs about yourself and your environments)

Behaviors (What you choose to do)

_____
_____
_____
_____
_____
_____

Finally, identify the outcome and how it reinforces the self-talk.

_____
_____
_____
_____
_____
_____
_____
_____
_____
_____
_____

Seeds Be Planted?

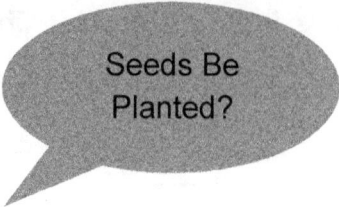

1.) Who/What planted the seeds that led to your self-talk?

_____
_____
_____
_____
_____
_____

2.) How did you allow them to take root in your mind?

_____
_____
_____
_____
_____
_____

3.) Are the seeds that were planted seeds of fruit bearing trees, which will bring you good life and sustain you or are they seeds of weeds which will rob you and kill good things in your life?

_____
_____
_____
_____
_____
_____
_____

Getting feedback from others is important as it can give us an outside perspective on our accomplishments and our struggles. When we are attempting to better ourselves, having an individual who will be honest about what they see is important. We can call these individuals accountability partners. Take the survey listed below to three individuals you can trust to give you honest feedback, even if that feedback is not what you want to hear. Ask them to complete this survey to the best of their abilities and return it to you when they have completed it. Process the results with your support person.

I, _____, am currently working through struggles in my life using *Waging War: A Christian's Cognitive Behavioral Therapy Workbook*. I am asking you, as a person I trust, to give me feedback on areas of my life that have been held back by shackles of fear, insecurities, and my justifications. Please answer the following questions as honestly as you can. I am open and am accepting of any feedback you may have to offer.

Thank You.

In what ways do you see me lie to myself about my life, my situation, or myself?

_____
_____
_____
_____
_____
_____
_____
_____

How do these lies hold me back from achieving my full potential?

_____
_____
_____
_____
_____

What do you see is my potential if I can overcome these lies?

_____
_____
_____
_____

What steps do you believe I need to take to change how things have been so far in my life, and open up the possibility of achieving my goals?

_____
_____
_____
_____
_____
_____

Thank you for believing in me.

I, _____, am currently working through struggles in my life using *Waging War: A Christian's Cognitive Behavioral Therapy Workbook*. I am asking you, as a person I trust, to give me feedback on areas of my life that have been held back by shackles of fear, insecurities, and my justifications. Please answer the following questions as honestly as you can. I am open and an accepting of any feedback you may have to offer.

Thank You.

In what ways do you see me lie to myself about my life, my situation, or myself?

_____
_____
_____
_____
_____
_____
_____
_____
_____
_____
_____

How do these lies hold me back from achieving my potential?

_____
_____
_____
_____
_____
_____

What do you see is my potential if I can overcome these lies?

_____
_____
_____
_____
_____
_____
_____
_____

What steps do you believe I need to take to change how things have been so far in my life, and open up the possibility of achieving my potential?

_____
_____
_____
_____
_____
_____

Thank you for believing in me.

I, _____, am currently working through struggles in my life using *Waging War: A Christian's Cognitive Behavioral Therapy Workbook*. I am asking you, as a person I trust, to give me feedback on areas of my life that have been held back by shackles of fear, insecurities, and my justifications. Please answer the following questions as honestly as you can. I am open and an accepting of any feedback you may have to offer.

Thank You.

In what ways do you see me lie to myself about my life, my situation, or myself?

_____
_____
_____
_____
_____
_____
_____
_____
_____
_____

How do these lies hold me back from achieving my potential?

_____
_____
_____
_____
_____
_____
_____

What do you see is my potential if I can overcome these lies?

_____

_____
_____
_____

What steps do you believe I need to take to change how things have been so far in my life, and open up the possibility of achieving my potential?

_____

_____
_____
_____
_____
_____

Thank you for believing in me.

Further Thoughts

_____

_____
_____
_____
_____
_____
_____
_____
_____
_____
_____
_____
_____
_____
_____
_____
_____
_____
_____
_____
_____

Section V Maintaining your Freedom

The hardest part about becoming free is staying free.

Galatians 5:1 Updated American Standard Version (UASV)

5 For freedom Christ has set us free; stand firm therefore, and do not submit again to a yoke of slavery.

> **5:1.** Christ died to set us free from slavery to the law. Our responsibility is to stand firm and not to fall back into law and sin.[104]

Galatians 5:13-15 Updated American Standard Version (UASV)

¹³ **For you were called to freedom**, brothers; only **do not** turn your freedom into an opportunity for the flesh, but **through love serve one another.** ¹⁴ For the whole law is fulfilled in one word: "You shall love your neighbor as yourself." ¹⁵ But if you bite and devour one another, watch out that you are not consumed by one another.

> **5:13–14.** In verse 1, Paul states that Christian freedom is the right and privilege of every believer. Then he points out six negative consequences of falling back into slavery. Now he warns them not to use this freedom as a license to sin. Rather than liberty being used for selfishness, the true objective of their newfound freedom is love. Quoting Leviticus 19:18, Paul summarizes the law as **"love your neighbor as yourself."** Always remember that we are slaves commissioned to love one another (Matt. 22:39).
>
> **5:15.** As a result of the legalists, this church was divided. They were **biting and devouring each other**. Their church and community of faith were on the verge of destruction. Legalism treats people harshly and often leads to divisions.[105]

Mathew 12:33-35 Updated American Standard Version (UASV)

³³ "Either make the tree good and its fruit good, or make the tree bad and its fruit bad, for the tree is known by its fruit. ³⁴ Offspring of vipers, how can you speak good things when you are wicked? For out of

---

[104] Max Anders, *Galatians-Colossians*, vol. 8, Holman New Testament Commentary (Nashville, TN: Broadman & Holman Publishers, 1999), 62.

[105] Max Anders, *Galatians-Colossians*, vol. 8, Holman New Testament Commentary (Nashville, TN: Broadman & Holman Publishers, 1999), 63.

the abundance of the heart the mouth speaks. **35** The good man brings out of his good treasure what is good; and the wicked man out of his wicked treasure brings out wicked things.

12:33–35. Finally, Jesus concluded his confrontation of the hypocrites by pointing out that their own words were their worst enemy. Those words would testify against them in the eternal courtroom of heaven. There is a major lesson here for us. Words are important. They come out of the heart. They expose the heart and therefore are a clue to final justification or judgment.

Jesus used the same argument as in 7:16–20—that no tree can produce any fruit other than its own kind of fruit, and that any tree can be identified as good or bad by examining its fruit. Specifically, the Pharisees' fruit was their words. Because Jesus had just demonstrated the deep evil in their words against the Holy Spirit, the natural implication was that these men were evil to the core. A good heart cannot produce evil words.

In verse 35, Jesus was referring to the inner, unseen person—equivalent; to the **heart** in 12:34. The **good** or **evil** illustration restated what Jesus had already said in different words—the outside is only reflective of the inside.

12:36–37. Again Jesus emphasized the seriousness of what he was about to say, introducing it with **I tell you.**

Not only do a person's words demonstrate his inner character in the present day, but they will be either his defense or his incrimination in **the day of judgment.** Words are so easy to produce that we can forget how powerful they are. They have great potential for building up as well as tearing down. They can be used to advance God's kingdom, or to attack it, sometimes subtly, in ways even the speaker does not realize. Words must be used with care. **Careless** words are like loaded guns that are handled recklessly. Just as the handler of a gun would have to explain any damage done by his weapon, so every person with a tongue (cf. Jas. 3:2–12) will be held responsible for how he or she has used it.

The Pharisees had responded to Jesus' exorcism carelessly. Their only interest was in keeping their status and power over the people, and their speech attempted to protect their selfish interests. They spoke out of total disregard for the truth, so their words would return to condemn them on the day of judgment. Judgment would come not only because what they said was false but also because their words led many of their followers astray. We see similar abuse of words among misleading preachers today.[106]

Mathew 12:43-45 Updated American Standard Version (UASV)

[43] "Now when the unclean spirit has gone out of a man, it passes through waterless places seeking rest, and does not find it. [44] Then it says, 'I will return to my house from which I came'; and when it comes, it finds it unoccupied, swept, and put in order. [45] Then it goes and takes along with it seven other spirits more wicked than itself, and they go in and live there; and the last state of that man becomes worse than the first. In this way, it will also be with this wicked generation."

12:43–45. This is a difficult analogy to interpret. Jesus' parable seemed to emphasize that Israel had a limited window of time in which to respond to him. His limited time on earth paralleled the period during which the man in the parable was free of demons (perhaps Jesus was holding off the forces of evil during this time). This period would be long enough for Israel, particularly their leaders, to repent and believe in him. But if they persisted in their conscious disbelief until this "limited-time" offer expired, their **final condition** would become **worse than the first**. They would be even more hardened by their rejection of the obvious, and they would be held even more accountable because they had abundant opportunity to repent.

Jesus was not saying that there was literally a demon that had been cast out of Israel, nor that there would be more literal demons controlling Israel after they had finally rejected him. What Jesus meant to carry over from the parable is that Israel was in danger of an even worse condition than before he came, if it did not take advantage of the window of opportunity presented by his coming.

What we learn here about demons and demon possession is secondary in importance to Jesus' message in the parable. The demon's wandering **through arid places seeking rest** served as the demon's motivation for returning to the man. This heightened Israel's awareness that they were in imminent danger. Israel's former condition was their desperate need of the Messiah. If they persisted in their unbelief, they would have no Messiah and they would be held responsible for rejecting him.

The condition of the man (the demon's "house")—being **unoccupied, swept clean and put in order**—parallels the short period

---

[106] Stuart K. Weber, *Matthew*, vol. 1, Holman New Testament Commentary (Nashville, TN: Broadman & Holman Publishers, 2000), 178–179.

of time during which Israel's options were open. Even those who continued to "sit on the fence" were rejecting Jesus: **He who is not with me is against me** (12:30). An active affirmative decision for the Messiah was what was required—nothing less. If the demon had returned to the man and found him occupied by Christ, there would have been no room for the demon.

The seven other spirits likely parallel the deeper state of disbelief and the greater judgment incurred after the window of opportunity has closed.

Jesus closed his confrontation with the Pharisees as he began, declaring **this ... generation** to be **wicked** (12:45 cf. 12:39) because they refused God's gracious gift, the Messiah and his salvation. Jesus' mention of **this ... generation** is the clue that convinces us that the story about the demons is an analogy describing Israel (or at least the rebellious portion represented by the Pharisees).[107]

---

[107] Stuart K. Weber, *Matthew*, vol. 1, Holman New Testament Commentary (Nashville, TN: Broadman & Holman Publishers, 2000), 180–181.

Chapter XVIII Sixty-Six Days of Awkward

Sometimes, change feels awkward and healthy living can feel weird.

A Quick Look:

It takes 66 days to create a habit.

The challenges facing you when it comes to teaching others a new behavior to anticipate from you.

Possible fears you may have and urges to give up.

Supplemental Assignments:

Discuss your fears regarding change.

Identify the possible challenges you face when it comes to returning to your environment and avoiding relapsing back to your old habits.

The "Weirdness" of Change

Ever hear the saying, 'old habits die hard'? That is what this chapter is all about. Hopefully, by the time you reach this chapter, you have worked with your therapist, your support person, or on your own, to decide the areas in your life that you want to change and you no longer feel shame, but recognize the motivating power of guilt. You have worked through recognizing the lies you struggle with that the Enemy uses against you, and the Truth of God to combat those lies so that you are now at a point in your life where you are applying the tools you have learned to see change happen. If you have been at this for any amount of time (some of my patients had been trying to do this for years) you have really learned the tough lesson, that change does not happen from the outside-in, but from the inside-out. In other words, you have to challenge the lies you act on with the truth of the situation so that from there your actions and feelings will change; first, control your thoughts in order to control your emotions and behaviors.

By this time, you have surely learned that change can be hard, scary, and awkward. Change is hard because of the reputation you have created and that often times, our actions are more than just simple choices we make that can be undone, but they are a group of choices regularly made which have created a lifestyle. The best example of how a choice can create a lifestyle is drugs. You don't typically start off doing drugs when you are flying solo, but most often people are introduced to drugs by a friend or at a party. Maybe eventually you reach a point where you are getting high by yourself, but we never start off with stuff like this all alone. After all, you don't just wake up one day knowing how to shoot-up, someone has to teach you.

Doing drugs opens you up to so much more; the other people who are okay or find it to be acceptable, the other behaviors that often comes with drugs such as drinking and having sex with strangers, and parties. This will eventually lead to sneaking out at night and then stealing to maintain your habit because drugs aren't free and if you are not paying in money, you are eventually going to be paying in other ways. Next thing you know, that one yes to the question to do drugs takes you down this road where none of the so-called 'good kids' will hang out with you because you are one of 'those' kids. You get caught at school or by the police with drug paraphernalia and just like that; you have a legal label to go along with your reputation. Actions have far more consequences than simply legal, grounding from parents, or assigned consequences, but you have to deal with the reputation you have created.

Let's stay with the example of drugs and say that you decide, after completing this workbook, that you no longer want to sneak out, go to parties, do drugs, or have sex with random people and want to start instead going to class and actually stay there, start studying and trying to get into college, and say no to the party scene. Do you think that tomorrow when you find yourself back at school with all of those people you use to party with or who knew you were one of 'those' people, that they are going to magically know that your mind has changed and you have decided to do something different? They will have to see it to believe it. Your friends are still going to come up to you and invite you to cut class with them. They will still walk up to your locker, just like they use to, and try to buy some weed from you or sell it to you. They will still offer it to you because, in their mind, you are the same person you were yesterday. The old hangouts will still be there. The dealers will still be there; the same stressors will be there, your environment will not have changed unless you decide to change it.

You have spent the last, however, many years, teaching people to expect one thing from you....fill in the blank, and now you are wanting them to expect something else. You have to teach them to expect something different from you. You have also been creating a habit for yourself. Growing up my dad use to smoke cigarettes. He started smoking when he was 16 years old, in the late 60's, and he smoked well into his forties. This was a very established habit for him. Smoke breaks at work, going into the gas station, any time he went to take a drink, he would still stick his fingers out like he had a cigarette in his hand. He had a habit of always lighting up when someone called him on the phone. I remember he would only buy t-shirts that had a breast pocket so that he could keep his pack of cigarettes there. When he would answer the phone, even years after quitting, he would start patting his shirt pocket looking for his pack of cigarettes.

A habit is not just a biological habit for the nicotine, but a social habit, and a physical habit that he had to break to stay off cigarettes. He has not smoked a cigarette since he was in his forties and he is in his sixties now. He no longer reaches for his shirt pocket when someone calls, but he will tell me anytime we are driving down the road that he can smell the person smoking a cigarette two cars up from us. Habits are hard to break. Change is not an easy thing to do, and at first, you will have to fight to not fall back into it. You have removed something from your life, not just a behavior, but the people you use to hang out with, the situations in which you use to do it. All of it will have to be filled somehow with an alternative or else that behavior or something worse will flood back in. A great step is choosing not to act out aggressively when you get mad, but you have to decide what you will do instead the next time you are upset. You cannot go forever without friendship, or you will quickly find your old friends who use to encourage you to get into trouble. Depriving yourself of your needs will simply make you so desperate you won't care who you spend time with. You have to decide other places to go that help you to feel better, or you will find yourself going back to the same old places.

If you remove or change something in your life, you must fill the void that is left behind. There was a reason you did drugs. There was a reason you snuck out. There was a reason you would refuse to talk to people about how you felt. There was a reason you would become aggressive and hostile with people. There was a reason you slept around. You have addressed a major part of it in addressing the thinking that led to those behaviors and then changing that behavior, but those things were how you coped with the faulty thoughts. You need new outlets because when those thoughts come back, and they will come back, sometimes ten times stronger than you ever experienced before, you will need something different to do to deal with them while you are trying to fight them with the truth.

Those parties you use to go to to distract yourself will need to be replaced by something else. At the end of the day, those parties, the sex, the drugs, they were all just ineffective coping skills you were using to deal with the faulty beliefs you had. When you conquer those faulty beliefs with truth, you no longer have to do those things, but while you are getting better practiced at conquering those attacks, you need someone to go to, somewhere to go, and something to do that is safe and helpful so that you can challenge the lies with the truth, pray, and win the battle over your mind. Your 'go-to" was what you did in the past; you need to have a new 'go-to' that you can jump to just like your old habits. At first, it will feel weird. It will feel weird not going into school and standing by the same lockers you and your friends use to. It will feel weird not to cut the third period. It will feel weird not to call that person to come pick you up when you sneak out of the house because you and your mom started fighting. It is going to feel weird, like my dad patting his empty shirt pocket, but over time and with practice, this new behavior and this new habit of believing the truth will start to feel like the new normal.

I know that you have been living your life like this for a long time and I understand that your thoughts about yourself have often been terrible. It feels weird, after all, this time believing that you are worthless, to suddenly start believing that you have purpose, you were created to live and be loved, and that the God of the universe loves you. I can't promise you that it will be easy. I promise you that it will be hard. I promise you that sometimes you will make mistakes and fall back into old habits. I promise you that you will get frustrated and want to give up. I promise you that others who love you will get scared and when you make a mistake, they will fear that you are falling back into the old life. But I also promise you this; God will never forsake you or give up on you. He will never leave your side no matter how many times you fall; He will be there encouraging you and cheering you on every time. And I promise you this above all else, if you never give up you will see change that lasts. If you keep your eyes on Jesus, you will see your life get changed in ways you never imagined possible, experiencing a peace, unlike anything you have ever imagined.

Always be full of joy in the Lord. I say it again REJOICE! Let everyone see that you are considerate in all you do. Remember, the Lord is coming soon. Don't worry about anything; instead, pray about everything. Tell God what you need and thank him for all he has done. If you do this, you will experience God's peace, which is far more wonderful than the human mind can understand. His peace will guard your hearts and minds as you live in Christ Jesus. Philippians 4:4-7 He promises that He will guard your heart and your mind as you live in Him. He promises that His peace will comfort you as long as you seek Him and thank Him for all He does. It is amazing the power of thankfulness. It is two days out from thanksgiving when I am writing this. You should try it. Just focus on the things you have that you are thankful for and don't think on anything else and watch what happens in your life. He promises that if you seek Him and thank Him for all He has done, that He will have your back. Test Him on it. See what happens.

It takes sixty-six days on average to form a habit. Try to challenge your faulty thinking every day with the truth for sixty-six days and see what happens in your life. For sixty-six days, don't spend time with those that encourage all of the drama and trouble in your life, but spend time with those that experience peace from God. See what happens. Spend time with a different clique in your high school. Actually, go to all of your classes and pay attention. You will be amazed at what God does in your life if you can just start by giving Him sixty-six days to try to do life differently.

Process Questions:

What will happen if I just take away all of the 'bad' choices and don't have something positive to replace them with?

_____
_____
_____
_____
_____
_____

What is the hardest part of change and why?

_____
_____
_____
_____
_____
_____

Why is it going to be awkward trying to live your life differently?

_____
_____
_____
_____
_____
_____
_____
_____
_____

Why do you have to teach people to expect something different and what does this mean to you?

_____

_____

_____

_____

_____

_____

_____

How long does it take to form a habit?

_____

_____

_____

How have your actions created a lifestyle for you and what does that lifestyle look like?

_____

_____

_____

_____

_____

_____

_____

So when it comes to change, what are the behaviors you have to change and what are the things in your lifestyle that have encouraged that behavior? (think location, common triggers, think people, think the entire picture of your lifestyle.)

_____

_____

_____

_____

_____

_____

_____

_____

_____

_____

_____

_____

Four pillars assignment processing your efforts to change.

Self-Talk (40,000 individual thoughts summarized)

_____
_____
_____
_____
_____
_____
_____
_____
_____

Faulty Beliefs (Beliefs about yourself and your situation as a result of your thoughts.)

_____
_____
_____
_____
_____
_____
_____
_____

Perception (The faulty beliefs about your environment as a result of your faulty beliefs about yourself and your environments)

_____
_____
_____
_____
_____
_____

Behaviors (What you choose to do)

_____
_____
_____
_____
_____
_____

Finally, identify the outcome and how it reinforces the self-talk.

_____
_____
_____
_____
_____
_____
_____
_____

Seeds Be Planted?

1.) Who/What planted the seeds that led to your self-talk?

_____
_____
_____
_____
_____
_____

2.) How did you allow them to take root in your mind?

_____
_____
_____
_____
_____
_____

3.) Are the seeds that were planted seeds of fruit bearing trees which will bring you good life and sustain you or are they seeds of weeds which will rob you and kill good things in your life?

_____
_____
_____
_____
_____
_____

Further Thoughts

Chapter XIX Accountability and Trust

Change is Scary...for Everyone.

A Quick Look:

Keys to Rebuilding Trust:

It is 50/50. You both have to be willing to work at it.

Recognize the sacrifice of the other.

Make it safe, to be honest and transparent. This is all a two-way street.

Hold each other accountable.

Open communication.

It was not destroyed overnight. Therefore it cannot be rebuilt overnight.

Supplemental Assignments:

Discuss what it means to be validated and to validate other's feelings and experiences, even if their pain is a result of our actions. Process how this applies in your life.

Natural Consequences: outcomes from the environment or situation that occur as a direct result of our choices. Assigned Consequences: outcomes of a choice that are put upon us by others, like a punishment, to teach us not to continue with our choices.

Take a moment and write yourself a letter imagining you are the other person with whom you need to rebuild trust, looking at what you imagine to be their fears and concerns.

Change—for You and Them

Change is not only scary and difficult for you, but for all of those who love and care about you. Change and trust often go hand-in-hand. The reason there is a need for change is often because what was happening before was causing harm emotionally or physically to others and would eventually lead to problems in the future. Our actions have far-reaching consequences;

think of it as a ripple effect. You toss a stone in the water, and the immediate splash may be gone, but the ripples continue, sometimes up to a few minutes after the stone has long ago sunk to the bottom of the lake. Your actions don't just bring with them a consequence, maybe natural or assigned, but your actions also have a lasting impact on all of those whom it touches. As a side-note, natural consequences are the outcomes from the environment or situation that occur as a direct result of our choices. Example: if I touch an oven when it is hot, I will get burned. Assigned consequences are outcomes of a choice that are put upon us by others, as a punishment, to teach us not to continue with our behaviors. Example: I reach to touch the hot oven, and my mother yells loudly for me to stop. If I continue to reach for it, she may put me in time out or smack my hand away. See the difference? Another example just to make sure we are crystal clear; you punch the wall your hand hurts—natural consequence. You punch the wall and have your X-box taken away until you fix it—assigned consequence.

Fighting your peers, for example, seems to be a simple act at the moment. The two of you get upset, you go outside, and you throw a few punches. A circle forms of friends and his friends, all yelling and screaming for one of you to win. Punches are thrown, and blood is spilled. Eventually, there will be a presumed winner and loser, even if the fight gets broken up. Before when the fight was over it was over, and people quickly forgot about it. Today with social media, the fight is not over with the last punch, but it is recorded on phones, posted on social media, shared and liked for all to see and comment on. The supposed 'loser' is made fun of not only in the moments leaving the fight but for months on end having to deal with being the butt of every joke.

Your actions of choosing to fight have caused not only physical harm, but also emotional harm in the moment of the fight and for months after. This is not even considering the consequences to the peer's parents who see their son or daughter whom they love, walk through the door with a bloody lip, and then have to see them hurt emotionally from being targeted and laughed at by everyone on Facebook. Our actions have far reaching consequences to not only ourselves and our families, but the families of those we interact with. Trust is like this. All of those who are connected to you, in particular, your family, have had trust broken with you as a result of the choices you have made. Trust can be the easiest thing and sometimes the most difficult thing to understand, so let's dive in.

First, trust is a two-way street just like relationships; it is 50/50 meaning you are responsible for fifty percent of how the relationship is and the other person is responsible for fifty percent. Just like you cannot kill a relationship all by yourself, you cannot rebuild it all by yourself. In rebuilding trust, both people and groups involved have to make a sacrifice. You who are rebuilding trust have to sacrifice some of your privacy and have to work to be more open and patient, while the other individual or group, such as your family, have to sacrifice their peace of mind and allow you to have a chance. They have to give you trust even though your past has shown them that they should not. This is a sacrifice for both of you. It is hard and scary, and you both will have to be understanding of a few things in order to be successful.

To rebuild trust, you both have to <u>recognize the sacrifice of the other</u> and act in a manner of respecting and <u>making it safe</u> to sacrifice in order to rebuild trust. You must <u>hold one another accountable</u> to rebuilding trust, which will require that you have <u>open communication</u>. Finally, you must understand that <u>trust was not broken overnight. Therefore it cannot be rebuilt overnight</u>. It takes time, and you must be patient to allow it to be rebuilt

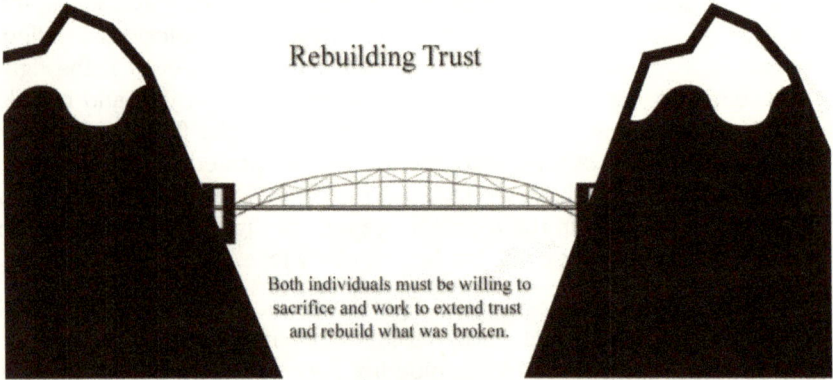

Rebuilding Trust

Both individuals must be willing to sacrifice and work to extend trust and rebuild what was broken.

Why is rebuilding trust a sacrifice? Think of trust as a bridge that connects two cliffs together. It is scary going over that cliff to extend out to the other side. Let us assume that you are the one who has made mistakes to cause there to be damage in your trust. Trust being broken does not happen overnight, but it happens by mistake after mistake after mistake being made, often after you have apologized and then repeated the same action. You sneak out after telling your parents it won't happen again. Your parents give you freedoms with your phone, trusting that you are being safe with it and responsible with social media and the internet at your fingertips, and you use it to talk to strangers, take pics and send them out publicly, or sneak out and meet with people you meet online. A single act like this is not going to ruin everything, although choices like this will damage things very quickly, but all of those choices combined time and time again, will. Each incident is one part of your bridge being removed, and if you remove too many supports, your bridge falls down the cliff, leaving you disconnected and hurt.

I want to caution you at this moment. Often the individual in the relationship who has made the 'big mistake' is blamed for ruining everything, but I encourage you to remember, relationships are 50/50 which means that the 'big mistake' may have been the last support holding up the bridge causing it to collapse, but it was the combination of choices made by both people in the relationship that made it possible for that one choice to cause so much damage. What does this mean? This means that you may have made the 'big mistake' but the responsibility for trust being broken is a shared burden that you and the other individual must both carry, and if you both do not recognize your equal fault, this will not work effectively. Suck up your pride for a moment, and both of you, admit to what has brought you here to this point in your relationship. You may need to pause here with your support person or counselor to work through this part; it's a tough one.

Family Therapy Objective

The same concept goes for rebuilding trust. In order to rebuild trust, it does not happen overnight. One act of following through, doing what you say you will, or following the rules will not all of a sudden rebuild an entire bridge. It has to be consistent choices that will rebuild the supports for your bridge so that after a time, you have a brand new bridge and you are connected again with your parents, able to trust one another. This is hard for people to remember because it is uncomfortable being on the side of having to rebuild trust. Feeling like you are being tested, monitored, and on guard gets exhausting. You will have moments where you say it is too hard and feel like you might as well give up. Your parents are going to make mistakes and feel like one mistake you make just means that you are going back down that road again and all hope is lost. That is fear talking, and at that moment, it is so vitally important that you both work together to recognize fear when it is talking. You must hold one another accountable to this, and help one another in moments when fear is pulling you back. Thoughts you may have of, 'this is too hard' or, 'I may as well give up' or, 'it's not working, they will never trust me again' is your fear controlling you, and they are faulty beliefs that are trying to come shackle you all over again. Do not give up because it is uncomfortable or you fear that it will never happen. You worked to build trust at one point in your relationship, so you can do it again.

The sacrifice you have to make is your effort to assure your family that you are being honest and true when in the past you have not been. Understand, they are afraid of losing you and when we are afraid of losing what we love most, we tend to hold on really tight. Think of something that you love or that is really important to you—you're a teenager so think of your phone hahaha. Imagine someone trying to take your phone from you; you hold on really tight to it and try to put it somewhere safe that you know no one will take it. This is what your parents are going to want to do with you. They love you. Trust me, as a mom, the strongest urge you have as a parent is to protect your child, even from themselves, and you want sometimes to put your baby in a bubble to keep anything from ever hurting them or worse, to keep them from hurting themselves. Holding tighter only makes your children want to push you away even harder so be understanding of your parent's or loved ones' fear of losing you and the urge they are fighting to put you in a bubble to protect you. Recognize their sacrifice to let you go in the open where they know you can choose to do things that will bring you harm.

Side Note for Parents: Holding on even tighter to your children will only cause them to push harder against you.

You have to sacrifice your comfort and privacy a little bit in order to be open to letting them see that it is safe. Let them check up on you, and better yet, instead of making them check up on you, be proactive and check in yourself to show them it is okay. When they extend trust to let you go to the movies with your friends, even though they know you use to skip the movie and go do other things, text them a pic of you sitting in the movie theatre waiting for the movie to start, just to reassure them that you are doing what you said you would. Don't make them go through your Facebook to make sure you are not talking to strangers who could be dangerous. Share it with them by sitting down and asking, "Hey Mom, do you need to go through my FB today?" Offer it to them; be willing to be open to show that nothing is hidden. If you are willing to do that, not forcing them to snoop to make sure you are being true, those supports will be built so fast, and trust will be rebuilt much more quickly. I cannot stress to you enough; relationships are 50/50, just like trust.

This is where the open communication is the most important. If your parents or guardians are worried that you may be going back to the 'old' behaviors, they need to talk to you about it. In fact, I will go even further in saying, it is their responsibility as a parent to hold you accountable and talk to you about it. If there are places you use to go that lead to bad choices, it is their job, their 50 percent as a parent, to talk to you about this and set boundaries for you. A parent's job is to set boundaries with you and provide structure. If they are not doing that, then they are not doing their job, and they are in fact allowing you to make unhealthy choices by their choice not to act. It is a sign of love that they work to help shape you into the best man or woman you can be, and if they allow you to get anything or do anything you want, they are not doing their job. I know this is not what you want, you want to be told yes to everything, but if they do, they are doing the easy thing and not the loving thing. Love sometimes means doing what you need, instead of what you want.

With that in mind, do you make it safe for them to come to you? What is your reaction like when they express fear to you? If you get defensive, yell, walk away, freak out, or slam your door, they will fear that their questioning you pushed you over the edge. This is not healthy or fair. You have to be accountable to yourself, and at the end of the day, your actions are your own, not the fault of anyone else but you. If you choose to go off the deep end because someone was fearful that you were making bad choices, then that is on you. Trust cannot be built if one or both of you are afraid, to be honest; honest with one another as well as honest with ourselves. You know the things that use to lead to your bad choices. Your responsibility is to communicate those to your parents. Who are the people that encourage you to do things you should not? Where are your 'stashes' and your hang-out spots? How did you use to sneak out of the house? Give up all of your secrets and show all your angles to your family. First, so that they can begin trusting you again, and second so that they can start holding you better accountable.

The goal is to get you to the change you are wanting, and one thing we know about humans is that we are social beings, we cannot do it alone. Open communication means giving up all your tricks, all your negative influences and dealers, telling your family the warning signs of your actions and making it safe to let them question you and express their feelings. You need to be safe to express your feelings and so do they. You both have to come together to talk about what is going on with you. Your parents are going to be working on how to set boundaries with you; you need to be willing to acknowledge these boundaries and your place in the household as the child or adolescent who has to answer to them, whether you like it or not.

Remember, rebuilding trust is 50/50 so you both are at fault equally, and both have to work equally as hard to rebuild. Your parents have to be able to hold you accountable, and you need to be willing to play ball.

You need to have open communication with them about everything, giving up all of your tricks, and they need to be able to come to you with concerns and fears. You both have to make it safe, to be honest and transparent, not hiding anything from one another. Finally remember, it was not destroyed overnight therefore, it cannot be rebuilt overnight; consistency and time is the key to trust.

Process Questions:

What is your 50 percent responsibility for the trust being damaged in your relationships?

_____
_____
_____
_____
_____
_____
_____

What is their fifty percent responsibility for the trust being damaged in your relationships?

_____
_____
_____
_____
_____
_____
_____

What sacrifice do you have to make in order to be successful in rebuilding trust?

_____
_____
_____
_____
_____
_____
_____
_____

What sacrifice do they have to make in order to be successful in rebuilding trust?

_____
_____
_____
_____
_____
_____

What do they need to hold you accountable to? (What behaviors are the ones you want instead and the behaviors you do want to change? What are the places, people, and things you should stay away from to be successful in your efforts for change?) Be thorough and work with your support person.

_____
_____
_____
_____
_____
_____

What do you need to hold those in your relationship accountable to? What were the choices that they made that helped lead you both down this path of damaged trust and how can you help them to change so you both don't find yourselves here again?

_____
_____
_____
_____
_____
_____
_____
_____
_____
_____
_____
_____
_____

What are the secrets you need to give up? What do you need to be honest about? (Ask them what they need to be honest about with you.)

_____

_____
_____
_____
_____
_____
_____
_____
_____
_____
_____

What are the possible faulty beliefs or fears that will come during this process that will make you want to give up. Recognize them ahead of time so you can be prepared to fight them when they come. Remember, trust cannot be built overnight. What are the things your family could do that will make you want to give up. What are the things you could do that will trigger their fears? Think with insight and work with your support person.

_____

_____
_____
_____
_____
_____
_____
_____
_____
_____
_____
_____
_____
_____
_____
_____
_____

The 3, 6, 9 Plan to Prevent Relapse

Trust takes time to build. When you are rebuilding trust, the first three months will be the most strenuous because you are starting things over. This is a very delicate time where you will be reintegrating back into your community and your temptation to return to old habits will be very high, possibly at its' highest. Develop a plan of checks for accountability for the first three months of your process toward change with your family. Identify specific rules you will have with them, a scheduled time where you will all process your progress and feelings together, and a plan for how you will respond to frustrations and fears.

At three to six months, if you have been able to maintain trust, more freedoms should be allowed to you so that you can continue to display for your family that you are still trustworthy, even when temptations are more available. This will be scary because some of the fears may return for both you and your guardians, but maintaining open communication will allow you to work together as a team to address them. Remember, we are all human, and therefore, we make mistakes. One mistake is not a relapse. Relapse is if you make a mistake and use that one mistake as justification to continue making more mistakes. If you make a mistake, the greatest display of honesty will be in communicating it to your family and asking for help to prevent it from happening again. Parents, your challenge will be in making it safe for them to be honest, even when they have made a mistake. Your response to their mistake will let them know if it is safe, to be honest with you about the next one. This is your 50 percent, and it is an important part.

When you reach six to nine months, you will be at your most lenient of restrictions. It will also mean that you and your family have progressed to this point where you are able to trust one another. Congratulations on your efforts toward change. Remember, if you are not able to show trust in one section, then you will need to stay in that section before progressing to the next stage. If you fall behind the schedule, work with your support person to set SMART goals to get you back on track. Use the table below to help you. God Bless! You are in my prayers always!

Restriction or Expectation Topic	0-3 Months	3-6 Months	6-9 Months
Example: Spending Time with Friends	I, your parent or guardian, need to have notice of plans to have friends over. I need to have met your friends and their parents prior to your spending time together one-to-one. They will be allowed to come to our home after these requirements have been met. You will not be allowed to go out to their home or to events without my attendance during this time.	I, your parent or guardian, will need to know the Who, What, Where, and When's of the event you want to attend. I will need to have met the friend, their family, and they will have had to spend time with our family so that we can judge their character and make a family decision whether to allow you to go to their home alone or not. You will not be allowed to go to events on your own at this time, but will only be permitted to go to events with parental supervision of myself or the friends parents.	I, your parent or guardian, will permit you to go to an event with a friend or to a friend's home without adult supervision (depending on age) but I have expectations on communication and check-ins that will be discussed on a different topic line. I still need to know the who, what, where, when's of the event or sleepover. The friends have to be the same friends whom you have had over to the home and who have interacted with the family. I also have to know their parents and have contact info.

Restriction or Expectation	0-3 Months	3-6 Months	6-9 Months
Restriction or Expectation	0-3 Months	3-6 Months	6-9 Months
Restriction or Expectation	0-3 Months	3-6 Months	6-9 Months

Restriction or Expectation	0-3 Months	3-6 Months	6-9 Months

Restriction or Expectation	0-3 Months	3-6 Months	6-9 Months

Four Pillars Assignment on this Chapter's Topic

Self-Talk (40,000 individual thoughts summarized)

_____
_____
_____
_____
_____
_____
_____
_____
_____

Faulty Beliefs (Beliefs about yourself and your situation as a result of your thoughts.)

_____
_____
_____
_____
_____
_____
_____

Perception (The faulty beliefs about your environment as a result of your faulty beliefs about yourself and your environments)

_____
_____
_____
_____
_____
_____
_____
_____

Behaviors (What you choose to do)

_____
_____
_____
_____
_____
_____

Finally, identify the outcome and how it reinforces the self-talk.

_____
_____
_____
_____
_____
_____
_____
_____
_____

Seeds Be
Planted?

1.) Who/What planted the seeds that led to your self-talk?

_____
_____
_____
_____
_____
_____
_____
_____
_____

2.) How did you allow them to take root in your mind?

_____
_____
_____
_____
_____
_____
_____
_____
_____
_____

3.) Are the seeds that were planted seeds of fruit bearing trees which will bring you good life and sustain you or are they seeds of weeds which will rob you and kill good things in your life?

_____

_____

_____

_____

_____

_____

_____

Further Thoughts

_____

_____

_____

_____

_____

_____

_____

_____

_____

_____

_____

_____

_____

_____

_____

_____

_____

_____

_____

_____

_____

_____

_____

_____

_____

_____

_____

Chapter XX Boundaries

How to be handling the relationships of the old you.

Casting Crowns *Jesus Friend of Sinners*.

Luke 5:29-32 Updated American Standard Version (UASV)

²⁹ Then Levi spread a big reception feast for him in his house, and there was a large crowd of tax collectors and others who were reclining at the table with them. ³⁰ And the Pharisees and their scribes began grumbling at his disciples, saying, "Why do you eat and drink with tax collectors and sinners?"[108] ³¹ And Jesus answered and said them, "Those who are well have no need of a physician, but those who are sick. ³² I have not come to call the righteous but sinners to repentance."

> **5:29–30.** Following meant more than just wandering the countryside listening to Jesus teach and preach. Following meant using your influence and skills for Jesus. Levi left the tax table to invite people to the supper table. Following Jesus meant telling others what Jesus had done for him. The others were friends Levi had known for a long time—not new acquaintances formed for convenience and prosperity.
>
> **5:31–32.** In typical Jewish teacher fashion, Jesus cited a proverb to emphasize his message. Wellness did not drive people to the doctor. Illness did. Jesus was the spiritual doctor. He came with a message of repentance. That message seemed misdirected. It did not save Israel and the Middle East, where political confusion reigned. It saved those religious leaders considered unworthy of God's attention. Power began to reveal true positions in life. Who was sick? The tax collector's friends, people willing to work for the Roman government and thus against Israel? Or religious leaders who knew more about God than God did? The title Righteous One given them by humans was the only title they would ever receive. Jesus picked out the lowest social positions as the positions through which he would work.[109]

A Quick Look:

Building long-lasting relationships is much like laying the foundation for a building. It takes time and preparation as well as curing time to

---

[108] **Sinner:** (*hamartōlos*) In the Scriptures "sinners" is generally used in a more specific way, that is, referring to those willfully living in sin, practicing sin, or have a reputation of sinning.–Matt. 9:10; Mark 2:15; Luke 5:30; 7:37-39; John 9:16; Rom. 3:7; Gal. 2:15; 1 Tim. 1:15; Heb. 7:26; Jam. 4:8; 1 Pet 4:18; Jude 1:15.

[109] Trent C. Butler, *Luke*, vol. 3, Holman New Testament Commentary (Nashville, TN: Broadman & Holman Publishers, 2000), 79.

allow the relationship to grow so that it can withstand the burdens of life when necessary.

You have to know what type of man or woman you want to be in order to be selective of the type of people you will call your friends.

How to have healthy boundaries with friends of your past.

Just because you disagree does not mean you have to be against one another.

More time—more influence.

Supplemental Assignments:

Look at the boundaries of others in your life. Discuss what the example has been for you in your life thus far.

Come up with ways to express to those you care about that you still care about them, they are just going down a different road than the one you choose to be on anymore.

Process with your support person what their reaction to your moving on will communicate to you about their friendship.

Friends: Past and Present

When you meet someone for the first time, do you tell them all of your secrets right away? No, of course not. You would get looked at like a crazy person, and the person would walk off going, "Oh my gosh, T.M.I." No, we wait until we get to know others before we tell them things to see if we can trust them. We don't test them so much as we get to know them to see if they will be accepting of what we have to say. We like to see if we are going to be accepted for what we do. You know people in your life that would be okay with you dropping the "F" bomb left and right, and you also know people who would be offended. You know what they will accept because you see what their reactions are to yours as well as to others' behavior. These reactions are called social cues, and they are powerful, as evidenced by everyone getting into an elevator and facing the same way. It is not like there is a sign on the door telling you which way to face, but everyone faces the same direction. If there is any deviance from this, people start to get uncomfortable and they will likely say something to you or will give you a funny look that makes you want to turn the 'right' way. The people you spend most of your time with are naturally going to be those who accept what you do, how you live, and what you say; people who look, live and act in similar ways as

346

you. It is just natural and often not something we sit there and think about.

It is normal not to think about it. You just kind of naturally associate with others based on what you have in common. This is not usually a problem, but when it comes to healthy vs. unhealthy living, it quickly can be. If you grow up in a setting, in which you are given a healthy example to follow, then you have nothing really to worry about, but this is not the experience for all of us. Sometimes we are caught up in the wrong crowd, we lose our way, or we are born into families that do not set us up for success in life. Unfortunately, not all of us are given the best examples, and if we are, sometimes we fail to follow the example provided. This leaves us with a few alternatives; superficial, surface level, short-lived relationships in which we have attempted to have emotional or physical intimacy by jumping right to sex or sharing personal information very quickly, or very deep, long-term relationships with members of our community that are on a road leading to things in our life that we want.

Let us gauge for a moment which boat you are in; superficial and shallow relationships or deep relationships that will challenge us to become a better version of ourselves and strong enough to withstand life's circumstances? I want to apologize in advance for how I can be received. I hate wasting time. It is above all other things, my pet-peeve, so my effort is not to offend you or make you angry, but to get to the point. There is no point in beating around the bush. Let us just be honest with one another. There are several levels of relationships, and there is a place for relationships that are just surface level, you make nice, "Hey how is your day going?" "Oh it is good" kind of relationships, but those never last. Those relationships never come to comfort you in loss, or stand by your side when you are the only one doing the right thing. The lasting relationships are the ones that have solid foundations.

To build a solid foundation, it takes <u>time and preparation</u>. Before you can even lay concrete for a building, you must clear the land. Then you have to get it all leveled which is tedious, and finally, you must lay rebar as support for your framework. After that, you have to mix your concrete, and if it is not mixed with just the right amount of water, it will be weak and crack under pressure. The weather has to be a certain temperature and moisture level in the air to be able to lay the concrete or else it is going to make your foundation weak. After you lay it, you have to leave it and let it sit. They call it curing time, and this allows it to get solid and ready for the weight it will have to support. Relationships are no different than this. Relationships that have had the proper preparation will stand the test of anything life has to throw at it, but relationships that have been rushed and formed without preparation and curing time will crack under pressure.

While I am describing to you how a relationship is built, I want you to think on how you start yours. Are your relationships lasting through time? This will tell you how strong your foundations are. When drama strikes, does your relationship sway with the struggles of life, or does it stand firm and withstand the pressure. Just like the foundations of a building, if there are cracks or uneven places, these are warning signs that someone didn't do their job right when preparing for the foundation to be laid.

How do you build strong relationships? Before you can have healthy relationships with others, you have to know who you are and what direction in life you want to go. What is your code of right and wrong as we discussed earlier in this workbook? This in important because if you do not know what type of man or woman you want to be, you will be accepting of anyone who comes to you in life, allowing them to influence you in any direction. This is dangerous because they can take you down a different road than you had wanted to go dow. Step one; <u>know yourself and what type of woman or man you want to be.</u>

Next is <u>where you go</u> to find people to interact with; this will heavily determine what type of people you will find. If I go to a party, I will find people that believe partying is right. If I go to class, then I will find others who value that because they invest their time in it. If I go to work, then I will find others who value work. Now obviously there is a wide range of people found at locations like this, but you have to use judgment to determine what type of person they are. An individual's motivation will be displayed by their actions, and this will show you their character. It is their character that will help you determine if they are on the road you want to be on, or if they are on the road leading to a different life than the one you want to lead. Observe others and remember, a person can say a lot of things, but <u>it is what they do that shows their true priority</u> and focus. Remember what we talked about earlier regarding the power of our interactions with others and their interactions with us. Where you go determines who you meet and who you meet determines what you get introduced to. Make sure you are going places you want to go, and the people found there will have the impact on you that you want.

This is where it will take <u>time,</u> and you must start small. <u>Trust begins with the small things, and if they show that you can trust them with the little things, then you can expand what you trust them with in the future</u>. Don't give a perfect stranger your

Trust starts small.

address and invite them over. Meet up at a well-known coffee shop or restaurant. You meet them at school, have your mom take them with you when the family goes to the mall to get to know them, meet their parents, go on group dates. Do all of this before you ever trust a person one-on-one.

Think of it like barriers. See the image below and picture that the person starts on the outside of all of the boundaries. After they show they are safe and trustworthy, they graduate to the next boundary, and you decide how close they get. It is boundaries for others that you have to have; not allowing a person to see the most intimate part of you physically or emotionally until they have earned that privilege. You are a treasure and the most loved creation of God, so cherished that He felt you were worth the sacrifice to have His son die for you. Do not give yourself away as though you were cheap and worthless.

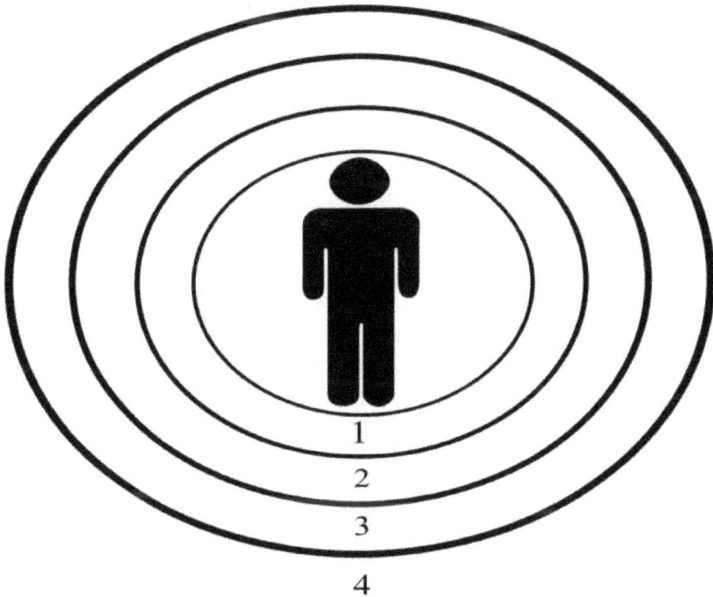

You and the person you choose to be your significant other will be in your circle.

Boundary Level 1: Those closest to you outside of your significant other; lifelong friends.

Boundary Levl 2: Friends

Boundarty Level 3: Co-workers or Acqaintances

Boundary Level 4: Strangers or the coffee barista.

If another individual does not realize how priceless and invaluable you are, then they have not earned the privilege to get to know more of you. Share yourself with those that will treasure you, see your gifts and your value as well as see your faults, and they choose to value your gifts and help you improve on your faults. Being able to be open and vulnerable with another is a wonderful gift, but it is a gift that is kept safe and special when it is not shared with everyone. Imagine when you get a gift. Do you want the phone that 15 people before you have had and dropped or scratched? No, you would much prefer the brand new one that you can unwrap and take out of the plastic. You peel off all of the coverings and another person, but you have never touched it. This is your phone and none others'. It is the same with intimacy with another person. It is not as special when it has been shared with others. It comes with baggage and regrets and memories when it has been shared, compared to it being brand new.

The opening scripture illustrates this perfectly, and that scripture applies to you in every way. First I want to ask you, who were Jesus' best buddies? The twelve disciples were His best buds who went everywhere and did everything with Him. Even among the twelve, He had some who were mentioned in scripture more than the others. Jesus' surrounded himself with those who believed in Him. He knew their faults and their strengths and often addressed both with them, but just because Jesus had certain beliefs did He reject all others who didn't agree with Him? No, He dined with them and met with those who were considered the lowest of the lows. He met with the tax collectors, people who worked for Rome, the enemy of the Jewish people. He ate dinner with them and associated with the poor and those who were sick and ill of heart, the tax collectors, the prostitutes, the lepers, and the slaves. He was the friend of the rejected, the isolated, and the embarrassment of society.

Just because you disagree with others does not mean you have to reject them, but it does determine the degree to which you allow them to influence you. Remember more time—more influence. Jesus associated with all people and loved and greatly cared about those who disagreed with him, but his closest friends, people that were with him constantly, his homies, were the twelve disciples who were on the same path as he. You have to have boundaries for yourself so that you can love and care for all people and you can associate with all people, but you must ensure that your closest circle are those that are on the same path as you or else you will be taken off course.

If you stand for nothing, you will fall for everything. You must decide what you stand for in this life and then choose to stand with others who will stand for those things with you. Standing for something and believing in something does not mean you stand against others. A person's choices are not who they are, it is their behavior at that particular moment, and it gives you insight to who they are right then and there, but it does not have to be who they are forever. Like you, your previous behaviors indicated who you were choosing to be at that moment, but it does not have to define you forever. You can always change what you do and who you want to be today and tomorrow.

The friends that you had before you changed do you now have to stop being their friends? I don't believe that you should, but I do believe that some changes need to be made in regard to where they are in your circle. They use to be who you spent all of your time with, but if we know that those with whom we spend the most time have the strongest influence on us, should they remain in that circle? No, they should not or else you will be back to the same person you were. You must change who is in your inner circle and choose people to go there who will better represent the type of person you want to be. The people in your inner circle must be on the same road, aspiring to the same principles of right and wrong as you so that you can challenge one another and hold each other accountable, encouraging one another. This does not mean that the friends of your past cannot be your friends, but you need to be spending less time with them and be more selective of the location in which you spend time together.

Identify where and how much time you would spend with them before. It needs to decrease, and the location that you hang out needs to change. If they are into drugs and parties, then you need to have stronger boundaries with them choosing to not spend any time with them where there are not adults who will prevent this behavior from happening. I would suggest to you that the only place you interact with them is in classes you share and even then, you should still surround yourself with other friends who will encourage you to stay on track. Those past friends can still invite you to parties in class or slip you drugs if they are sneaky enough. It is a matter of being safe, safe from your past and all that would pull you back to it. You have to ask yourself, who is more important in your life, your friends who were encouraging the things that brought strife and struggle to your life, or your family and other friends, even if you haven't met them yet, who will bring a future to you filled with success, a career, travel to see the world, love, and happiness.

More Time = More Influence

Those you spend the most time with will resemble you and your future. They will show you where you are going to go in life and will help determine your story. Have boundaries for this is the hardest thing to do because the friends of your past will expect the same person they once knew, but you will be different, and you can still be friends with them, but like Jesus, they will not be your closest friends any longer. Just as an observation, when Jesus went to spend time with tax collectors or prostitutes, he never went alone, his closest friends, his twelve homies, were always with him. They protected him from false accusations, they kept people from wondering what was going on, and they helped keep him strong to always walk on the right path in the midst of those who were on different paths.

Process Questions:

Draw your boundaries and list where all of your friends and family were located along the boundaries before you changed.

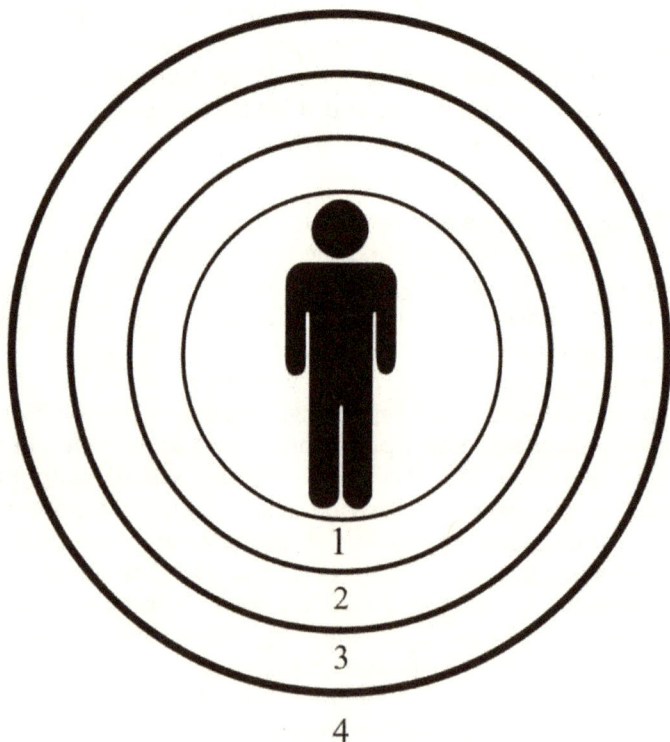

Draw your boundaries and list where all of your friends and family are located now.

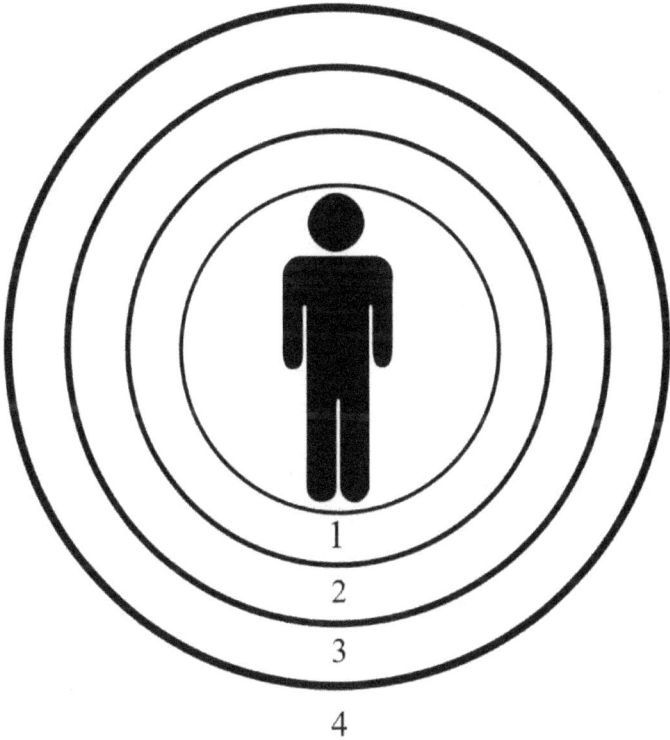

1
2
3
4

What type of people use to be in your inner circle? What were their behaviors and values?

_____

_____
_____
_____
_____
_____
_____
_____
_____
_____
_____

What should the qualities and behaviors of those in your inner circle be if you will be successful in maintaining your freedom?

_____
_____
_____
_____
_____
_____
_____

What did the scripture of Jesus meeting with his twelve disciples at the home of Levi the tax collector mean to you and teach us?

_____
_____
_____
_____
_____
_____
_____
_____
_____
_____
_____

What does it mean to have boundaries? Explain the impact of having boundaries on making friends and handling past relationships that use to lead to negative things in your life.

_____
_____
_____
_____
_____
_____
_____
_____
_____
_____
_____
_____
_____

Chapter XXI Wrapping Up

Congrats!

You Survived. Now go Enjoy a life of Freedom!

A Quick Review of the High-Points

The End Has Come

You are officially at the end. If you have been participating in our day-treatment program, Awaken360, then you are about to say goodbye to all of us and return to your former school. Words cannot express how proud of you I am. In saying goodbye, I want to take a moment to highlight the things that I feel are the most important to remember. If you leave remembering nothing else other than this, then I will feel as though even in some small way, I did my job. First, do not every forget how loved you are. I know how this world can be. It can be an amazing place offering some of the most beautiful adventures possible, but it can also bring you pain and suffering. I want you to experience the beauty that this world has to offer, able to see all of the wonderful things God created hoping that you would enjoy it. I also understand reality, and just as we are able to feel and experience happiness, we are able to experience pain and sadness.

I urge you to remember that despite the trials and struggles that may come your way, Jeremiah 29:11 reminds us that God always has a plan. He may not reveal it to you until one day when you are in heaven, but He always has a plan, and if you look to Him with humility and surrender, He will protect your heart no matter what you are experiencing. I want you to remember the power you hold over your mind. You will have many paths to walk through this life, but no matter where you find yourself, you can overcome anything by controlling your mind and therefore your reaction to it. Troubles in this life do not have to cause you to lose hope. Troubles can strengthen you and teach you how to overcome anything in your life by preparing you for the greatness that lies ahead. Luke, do not underestimate the power of the Dark Side lol. Just kidding, but seriously, do not forget that just like good exists in God, evil does exist in Satan and he is seeking ways to bring you down to his level so that he can have one more dig on God. Do not let him win in your life, but be victorious over him.

Remember to control your mind and never give your power away by saying that someone made you feel or act the way you do. Rise up and overcome adversities by not letting it bring you down and persevering despite it. Remember the lies that will be used in your mind to overcome you. Sometimes our greatest adversity is not found outside of us in our environment, but rather inside our minds where we battle daily to keep on going. Do not let the Enemy control your mind by planting seeds of doubt and insecurity. Remember who created you and who loves you. Remember that you are a prince or princess of the one true King over all other kings. You have a heritage of greatness in you if you can but focus on it and put all other doubts to the side.

Remember that the past does not hold you back unless you allow it to. The past is in the past, and your future is today in the next step you take. You can change anything you want to change about your life if you can learn to control your mind. Remember the type of man or woman you want to be and take inventory of the things in your life right now. Determine if they are helping you become the man or woman you want to be or if they are turning you into someone you don't recognize. If your so-called friends freak out because you don't want to party anymore, then sorry to say, they weren't very good friends in the first place because a true friend would support you pursuing what will make your life better. Remember that trust is not broken overnight, nor can it be earned overnight and DO NOT GIVE UP! I say again DO NOT GIVE UP when it gets hard. Rules will be strict, and there will be a lot of structure, but you have to restart, and trust is earned in small steps, but hold onto hope because when you are successful with the small steps, those steps to earning trust start to get a whole lot bigger.

Remember the difference between love and lust. Lust is a one-night-stand where you don't even remember their name. Love is a choice you make, sometimes even when it hurts and you really don't want to. Sex can be anything you make of it, but if you want it to mean something special, then stop sharing it with strangers, or people you hardly know as a pass-time activity for when you are bored. You are too valuable. I want your relationships to be protected, and I want you to be loved the way you deserve to be loved; the way He intended for you to be loved. Bottom-line, if you can remember how much God loves you and you can start to believe the Truth instead of the lies that this world will feed you, then you are started in the right direction. As you go out and start putting what you have learned into practice, remember always to communicate what is going on in your head. No one can help you if you don't talk about the thoughts you are having, the struggles you are facing, and the questions or doubts you may have. You have to talk about it with someone that you trust to give you the best advice and guidance. Your teenage friends should not be in this category because they likely have similar questions and cannot guide you in the right directions. Don't try that "they don't understand me" bit about adults. We may no longer be teenagers, but we were at one time in similar shoes as you. Talk, process, pray, and share but most of all, enjoy all of the wonderful things this world has to offer! I will be praying for you and ahead of you before you had even started this workbook. I'm praying for you right now as I'm writing this line.

You are so loved, and there is always someone out there who cares, even if you haven't met them yet. They are there, just around the next corner! God Bless you and may His hand be ever on your life guiding you back to Him.

Now Go Get to Work! :)

Four Pillars Sheets

Self-Talk (individual thoughts summarized regarding a single topic)

_____
_____
_____
_____
_____
_____
_____

Faulty Beliefs (Beliefs about yourself and your situation as a result of your thoughts.)

_____
_____
_____
_____
_____
_____
_____

Perception (The faulty beliefs about your environment as a result of your faulty beliefs about yourself and your environments)

_____
_____
_____
_____
_____
_____
_____

Behaviors (What you choose to do)

_____

_____
_____
_____
_____
_____

Finally, identify the outcome and how it reinforces the self-talk.

_____

_____
_____
_____
_____

Four Pillars Sheets

Self-Talk (40,000 individual thoughts summarized)

_____

_____
_____
_____
_____
_____
_____

Faulty Beliefs (Beliefs about yourself and your situation as a result of your thoughts.)

_____

_____
_____
_____
_____
_____

Perception (The faulty beliefs about your environment as a result of your faulty beliefs about yourself and your environments)

_____

_____
_____
_____
_____
_____

Behaviors (What you choose to do)

_____

_____
_____
_____
_____
_____

Finally, identify the outcome and how it reinforces the self-talk.

_____

_____
_____
_____

Four Pillars Assignment on this Chapter's Topic

Self-Talk (40,000 individual thoughts summarized)

_____

_____
_____
_____
_____
_____
_____

Faulty Beliefs (Beliefs about yourself and your situation as a result of your thoughts.)

_____

_____
_____
_____
_____

Perception (The faulty beliefs about your environment as a result of your faulty beliefs about yourself and your environments)

_____

_____
_____
_____
_____
_____
_____

Behaviors (What you choose to do)

_____
_____
_____
_____
_____
_____

Finally, identify the outcome and how it reinforces the self-talk.

_____
_____
_____
_____
_____
_____

Seeds Be
Planted?

1.) Who/What planted the seeds that led to your self-talk?

_____
_____
_____
_____
_____
_____
_____
_____

2.) How did you allow them to take root in your mind?

_____
_____
_____
_____
_____
_____
_____
_____

3.) Are the seeds that were planted seeds of fruit bearing trees, which will bring you good life and sustain you or are they seeds of weeds, which will rob you and kill good things in your life?

_____

_____
_____
_____
_____
_____
_____
_____
_____
_____

Bibliography

Akin, Daniel L. *The New American Commentary: 1, 2, 3 John*. Nashville, TN: Broadman & Holman , 2001.

Anders, Max. *Holman New Testament Commentary: vol. 8, Galatians, Ephesians, Philippians, Colossians*. Nashville, TN: Broadman & Holman Publishers, 1999.

—. *Holman Old Testament Commentary - Proverbs* . Nashville: B&H Publishing, 2005.

Anders, Max, and Doug McIntosh. *Holman Old Testament Commentary - Deuteronomy*. Nashville: B&H Publishing, 2009.

Anders, Max, and Steven Lawson. *Holman Old Testament Commentary - Psalms: 11*. Grand Rapids: B&H Publishing, 2004.

Anders, Max, and Trent Butler. *Holman Old Testament Commentary: Isaiah*. Nashiville, TN: B&H Publishing, 2002.

Andrews, Stephen J, and Robert D Bergen. *Holman Old Testament Commentary: 1-2 Samuel*. Nashville: Broadman & Holman, 2009.

Benner, David G., and Peter C Hill. *Baker Encyclopedia of Psychology and Counseling (Second Edition)*. Grand Rapids: Baker Books, 1985, 1999.

Blomberg, Craig. *The New American Commentary: Matthew*. Nashville, TN: Broadman & Holman Publishers, 1992.

Boa, Kenneth, and William Kruidenier. *Holman New Testament Commentary: Romans*. Nashville: Broadman & Holman, 2000.

Borchert, Gerald L. *The New American Commentary: John 1-11* . Nashville, TN: Broadman & Holman Publishers, 2001.

Borchert, Gerald L. *The New American Commentary vol. 25B, John 12–21*. Nashville: Broadman & Holman Publishers, 2002.

Brand, Chad, Charles Draper, and England Archie. *Holman Illustrated Bible Dictionary: Revised, Updated and Expanded*. Nashville, TN: Holman, 2003.

Bromiley, Geoffrey W. *The International Standard Bible Encyclopedia (Vol. 1-4)*. Grand Rapids, MI: William B. Eerdmans Publishing Co., 1986.

Brooks, James A. *The New American Commentary: Mark (Volume 23)*. Nashville: Broadman & Holman Publishers, 1992.

Butler, Trent C. *Holman New Testament Commentary: Luke.* Nashville, TN: Broadman & Holman Publishers, 2000.

Cooper, Rodney. *Holman New Testament Commentary: Mark.* Nashville: Broadman & Holman Publishers, 2000.

Easley, Kendell H. *Holman New Testament Commentary, vol. 12, Revelation.* (Nashville, TN: Broadman & Holman Publishers, 1998.

Elwell, Walter A. *Baker Encyclopedia of the Bible.* Grand Rapids: Baker Book House, 1988.

Gangel, Kenneth O. *Holman New Testament Commentary: Acts.* Nashville, TN: Broadman & Holman Publishers, 1998.

Gangel, Kenneth O. *Holman New Testament Commentary, vol. 4, John .* Nashville, TN: Broadman & Holman Publishers, 2000.

Garrett, Duane A. *The New American Commentary: Vol. 14 (Proverbs, Ecclesiastes, Song of Songs).* Nashville: Broadman & Holman Publishers, 1993.

George, Timothy. *The New American Commentary: Galatians .* Nashville, TN: Broadman & Holman Publishers, 2001.

Larson, Knute. *Holman New Testament Commentary, vol. 9, I & II Thessalonians, I & II Timothy, Titus, Philemon.* Nashville, TN: Broadman & Holman Publishers, 2000.

Lea, Thomas D. *Holman New Testament Commentary: Vol. 10, Hebrews, James.* Nashville, TN: Broadman & Holman Publishers, 1999.

Lea, Thomas D., and Hayne P. Griffin. *The New American Commentary, vol. 34, 1, 2 Timothy, Titus.* Nashville: Broadman & Holman Publishers, 1992.

Martin, D Michael. *The New American Commentary 33 1, 2 Thessalonians .* Nashville, TN: Broadman & Holman, 2001, c1995 .

Mathews, K. A. *The New American Commentary vol. 1A, Genesis 1-11:26 .* Nashville: Broadman & Holman Publishers, 2001.

Matthews, K. A. *The New American Commentary Vol. 1B, Genesis 11:27-50:26.* Nashville: Broadman and Holman Publishers, 2001.

Mounce, Robert H. *The New American Commentary: Vol. 27 Romans.* Nashville, TN: Broadman & Holman Publishers, 2001.

Polhill, John B. *The New American Commentary 26: Acts*. Nashville: Broadman & Holman Publishers, 2001.

Pratt Jr, Richard L. *Holman New Testament Commentary: I & II Corinthians, vol. 7*. Nashville: Broadman & Holman Publishers, 2000.

Richardson, Kurt. *The New American Commentary Vol. 36 James*. Nashville: Broadman & Holman Publishers, 1997.

Schreiner, Thomas R. *The New American Commentary: 1, 2 Peter, Jude*. Nashville: Broadman & Holman, 2003.

Smith, Gary. *The New American Commentary: Isaiah 1-39, Vol. 15a*. Nashville, TN: B & H Publishing Group, 2007.

—. *The New American Commentary: Isaiah 40-66, Vol. 15b*. Nashville, TN: B&H Publishing, 2009.

Stein, Robert H. *The New American Commentary: Luke*. Nashville, TN: Broadman & Holman , 2001, c1992.

Walls, David, and Max Anders. *Holman New Testament Commentary: I & II Peter, I, II & III John, Jude*. Nashville: Broadman & Holman Publishers, 1996.

Weber, Stuart K. *Holman New Testament Commentary, vol. 1, Matthew*. Nashville, TN: Broadman & Holman Publishers, 2000.

Wight, Russell. *Interview with the Devil: What Satan Would Say (If He Ever Told the Truth)*. Uhrichsville: Barbour Books, 2012.

www.ingramcontent.com/pod-product-compliance
Lightning Source LLC
Chambersburg PA
CBHW021500090426
42739CB00007B/399